INTO

ABOUT THE AUTHOR

Ørjan Karlsson grew up in Bodø, a town north of the Arctic Circle. He holds a master's degree in sociology and received officer training in the army. He has participated in international missions for the EU, UN, and NATO, and has worked for the Norwegian Ministry of Defence and the Directorate for Civil Protection.

Ørjan has written a large number of thrillers, sci-fi novels and crime novels for adults, including an acclaimed thriller series featuring Major Frank Halvorsen and Lieutenant Ida Vinterdal of the Norwegian special forces. *Into Thin Air*, the first book in the Jakob Weber series, is his sixteenth novel.

Follow Ørjan on X @orjankarlsson, Instagram @orjan_nk, Bluesky @orjannk.bsky.social and facebook.com/orjan.karlsson.

ABOUT THE TRANSLATOR

Ian Giles has a PhD in Scandinavian literature from the University of Edinburgh. Past translations include novels by crime and thriller luminaries such as Arne Dahl, Carin Gerhardsen, Michael Katz Krefeld, David Lagercrantz, Camilla Läckberg and Gustaf Skördeman. His translation of Andreas Norman's *Into a Raging Blaze* was shortlisted for the 2015 CWA International Dagger.

INTO THIN AIR

ØRJAN KARLSSON
TRANSLATED BY IAN GILES

**ORENDA
BOOKS**

Orenda Books
16 Carson Road
West Dulwich
London SE21 8HU
www.orendabooks.co.uk

First published in the United Kingdom by Orenda Books, 2025
First published in Norwegian as *Det siste stykket hjem*
by Gyldendal Norsk Forlag, 2022
Copyright © Ørjan Karlsson, 2022
English translation copyright © Ian Giles, 2025

A catalogue record for this book is available from the British Library.

ISBN 978-1-916788-50-3
eISBN 978-1-916788-51-0

This book has been translated with financial support from NORLA

Typeset in Garamond by typesetter.org.uk
Printed and bound by Clays Ltd, Elcograf S.p.A

MIX
Paper | Supporting
responsible forestry
FSC® C018072

For sales and distribution, please contact *info@orendabooks.co.uk*
or visit *www.orendabooks.co.uk*.

For Eilif

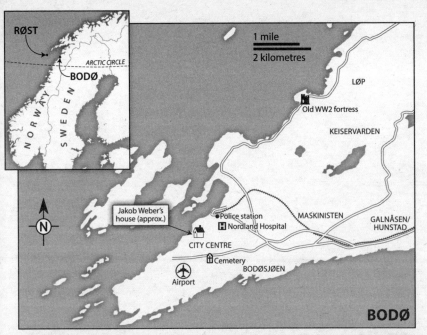

RØST

ARCTIC CIRCLE

NORWAY
SWEDEN

BODØ

1 mile
2 kilometres

LØP

Old WW2 fortress

KEISERVARDEN

Jakob Weber's
house (approx.)

●Police station
H Nordland Hospital

MASKINISTEN

GALNÅSEN/
HUNSTAD

N

CITY CENTRE

✠ Cemetery

BODØSJØEN

✈
Airport

BODØ

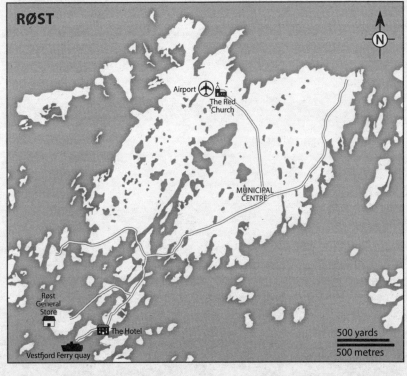

RØST

N

Airport ✈ ♦
The Red
Church

MUNICIPAL
CENTRE

Røst
General
Store

🏨 The Hotel

⛴
Vestfjord Ferry quay

500 yards
500 metres

He exited the E6 motorway half an hour north of Gothenburg. He passed a service station surrounded by a fence crowned with small Swedish, Norwegian and Danish flags. He pulled over a little further down the road, got out the road atlas and opened it at the page he had marked earlier.

He had never been here before. Not like this.

After making sure that it was the right place, he drove on down a narrow road, the asphalt ragged at the edges. It wasn't long before the coast opened up before him, the lights of Denmark just visible in the dusk descending on Kattegat. Shining pearls of light. Each point a house.

A home.

A family.

Sweden's west coast was a popular area for second-home owners, but this lane was bordered by rocky coves, patches with brackish water and hardy yellow grass that tolerated both salt water and frost. It was boggy, verging on outright swamp, with iridescent dragonflies hovering above pitch-black pools of water.

His kind of landscape.

On the way down to the small cove, branches scraped against the sides of the vehicle. There was barely room to turn around, but he was used to this kind of thing. He was able to steer his vehicle with pinpoint accuracy without clipping sharp rocks or anything else which might scratch the paintwork. The imprints left by the tyres in the hard, dry ground would disappear within a couple of days – if the rain didn't wash them away first. Scandinavian summer weather was fickle.

It took him a couple of minutes to park so that he was facing back the way he had come. He unfastened his seat belt, killed the engine and applied the handbrake. Then he leaned back in his seat and sat there with the window rolled down until the ticking of the cooling engine had ceased and all he could hear was the lapping of waves and the faint breeze through the treetops.

He got out and removed the two twenty-litre plastic containers that were strapped to the rear of the van. He took these down to the water's edge. Then he returned to the van to retrieve the thermal binoculars. They were a heavy, solid German make; he had bought them on the black market in Warsaw.

He raised the lenses to his eyes. The passenger ferry from Gothenburg to Frederikshavn blazed in his field of vision. When viewed through the binoculars, the ferry lost its defined contours. Instead, it became a blurry rectangle made up of shades of red and orange, as if the vessel were on fire.

He returned the binoculars to their case and filled the two containers with seawater. He put them down on the ground by the van and opened the sliding door. It slipped noiselessly backward on its oiled tracks, revealing the space within. The compartment was concealed behind a partition wall that separated the driver's cab from the rest of the vehicle.

Ordinarily, this would be the living area of the camper van, with its kitchenette and small dining area allowing the family to eat together and perhaps play a game of cards in the evenings. This one, however, looked rather different.

The night before, he had dismantled the interior. He had taken the furniture apart and stowed the pieces in the roof box. Then he had rolled up the carpet. The green fabric had been hiding a floor coated in hardwearing, light-green industrial paint. The type that could withstand a high-pressure jet wash. The last thing he had done was to fit the steel bench. He had screwed the frame into the vehicle chassis using robust bolts. All told, it hadn't taken him more than an hour or so.

He heaved the containers of water into the back. Then he climbed in himself and closed the door. He switched on the battery-powered light attached to the ceiling and turned on the small black-and-white monitor fixed to the partition. The screen was connected to a video camera showing the view through the windscreen. If anyone came down the gravel track he would spot them.

He raised one of the containers and poured the water into the receptacle at the end of the steel bench. He needed some of the water from the second container to fill the tank up to the brim. Experience had shown him that he would need to refill later on.

There was a thick rubber apron hanging on a hook on the back door. He stripped down to his underpants. He folded each item of clothing and placed his garments in a clear plastic bag. Then he put on a hairnet, slipped an overshoe onto each foot and put the apron over his head, tightening the belt at his waist.

All the while, he kept an eye on the figure lying under the white sheet on the bench. He could see the ribcage calmly rising and falling.

Finally, he put on rubber gloves – plain, old yellow washing-up gloves. He took hold of a corner of the sheet with his thumb and forefinger and pulled it back to reveal the naked, bound body beneath.

He took a hair clip from the pocket of the apron. The blue topaz in the middle of the clip glittered in the light cast from the ceiling. He pulled her black hair to one side, over her left eye, securing it with the clip.

Her eyelids quivered.

It wouldn't be long before she woke up.

CHAPTER 1

JAKOB WEBER

Jakob Weber took Garm off his lead and let the dog through the gate into Bodø cemetery. The Jack Russell Terrier looked up at him quizzically, his body trembling with pent-up energy.

'Go to Mum.'

Garm raced off. He set a course between the trees and the tombstones, occasionally stopping to make sure that Jakob was following.

There was no one else in the cemetery at this early hour. The flat, almost featureless, burial site was crammed in between Olav V gate and Bodø Airport. She had joked that there would be no shortage of transport options when she left this world. Jakob turned up the collar of his jacket. The westerly wind – chilly for this time of year – rustled through the leaves on the trees lining this narrow avenue.

He preferred to visit the cemetery at this time of day. It felt as if he had Lise to himself. Her grave was in one of the new rows right by the airport boundary fence.

He crouched in front of the simple, grey granite headstone. It was inscribed with copper-gilded letters that spelled out *Lise Alvdal Weber*, followed by her dates of birth and death. An absurd calculation where the difference was always too small: forty-one years.

He removed the remains of the old flowers from the vase, before inserting a new bouquet of fresh red roses. He took a cloth from his jacket pocket and ran it across the top of the stone. Then he took a step back and looked up. On the horizon, he found the peak of Børvasstindan – that grey mountain with its flecks of white just in front of its compatriots, Breitind and Rundtind. Thirteen peaks. One disciple too many. One left over. Like him after Lise. It had been six months and it was still just as incomprehensible.

Garm brushed his muzzle against Jakob's trouser leg. He bent down and scratched the dog behind the ears. His shirt sleeve slid up, revealing his wristwatch. No wonder the dog was impatient. He'd been standing at the grave for twenty minutes, lost in thoughts that were already forgotten.

On his way back to the car, he caught sight of a passenger jet above the waters of Saltfjorden. Based on its course, he could tell the captain was planning to fly past the town before turning and landing from the east. The plane would make landfall just a few hundred metres from Lise's grave. He still had plenty of time. In fact, just enough to buy a cup of coffee before the passengers emerged in the arrivals hall.

He opened the boot of the Mitsubishi Outlander. Garm hopped in without waiting for the command and lay down on the blanket inside the cage, his gaze fixed on his master. He wanted some reassurance that he'd be getting out again soon. Jakob gave the dog a treat. Every week, he would buy a one-kilo bag of small meatballs. He let Garm have two or three after a walk or a longer stint in the car. He would hear Lise whispering to him, a smile in her voice:

'You've gone soft.'

The first thing Jakob noticed when he parked outside the terminal was the blue-and-white liveried van with the logo of the local news broadcaster, NRK Nordland, on the side. A camera crew were standing outside the revolving door into the arrivals hall. There were three of them: the camera man, the sound man and a reporter. And not just any old reporter – it was Sigrid Malmsten. She was the journalist who had won the SKUP Award the year before for a revelation about the overly cosy ties between the mayor of Bodø council and key certain businesses in town.

The aftermath of the story had seen the council down a mayor, while the police had eventually filed corruption charges against two of Bodø's top-ten richest names. Jakob assumed things were mostly back to normal by now. People with money made their own rules. They claimed – albeit never openly – that they were entitled to special treatment. After all, they created jobs for the 'common people'. Jakob had met enough of them to realise that they really did believe what they said.

'What's the story here then?' he asked as he walked up to Sigrid.

'Strictly speaking I think *I'm* supposed to ask that,' the journalist replied sharply. Only the expression in those green eyes told Jakob that the response was meant as a joke. One of the officers at the station had described Sigrid as 'a woman with facial expressions like a brick wall'. Although, upon reflection, he didn't think the officer had said 'woman'.

Sigrid brushed a blonde lock of hair off her face. She was a smidge shorter than his own decidedly average 179 centimetres, and she was fit. The shadow of a scar ran from her left ear diagonally down to her chin – the result of a climbing accident. She had told him about the incident a couple of weeks earlier when they had bumped into each other at the City Nord out-of-town shopping centre. Sigrid had asked whether he fancied a coffee. Jakob had accepted, even though he thought he'd be putting himself on the receiving end of journalistic questions. He had been pleasantly surprised. They had mostly chatted about normal stuff: the new airport; military exercises further north; the travails of local football club Bodø/Glimt. When the conversation had taken a more personal turn, Sigrid had told him about the accident and Jakob had opened up about Lise. It had been nice.

'I'm here to pick up a colleague,' Jakob said. 'What about you?'

'Celebrity alert,' Sigrid replied. 'Marte Moi, better known as "Nature Lady", has decided to showcase Lofoten to her followers. First stop is Bodø before she heads on to Røst and Værøy and then the full tour of the archipelago. You know, the Svolværgeita pinnacle, whale watching, the village at Henningsvær, trip on a fishing smack. The whole tourist caboodle.'

'And that merits a full camera crew from the local news?'

Sigrid looked askance at Jakob. 'You don't know who Nature Lady is?'

'Should I?'

'Well, that depends. Do you use Instagram or TikTok?'

'I barely even use Facebook.'

Sigrid took out her mobile phone. 'Let me show you.' She pulled up Nature Lady's Instagram profile. She dragged her finger down the screen, and dozens of photos and videos scrolled by so quickly he didn't have time to take them in, his impression being that most of the posts depicted colourful natural landscapes with the protagonist posing in the centre of shot.

'This is the last one she posted.'

Sigrid tapped on a photo showing a girl on a plane. She was around twenty-five to thirty years old, with prominent red lips, brown eyes and black hair that was fastened up with a copper-coloured slide. A braid hung over one shoulder. A line written at an angle read:

'Crossing the Arctic Circle! Stay tuned for my northern adventure!'

'She's no Lars Monsen,' Jakob commented dryly.

'No, you're not wrong. Monsen has about 140,000 Instagram followers. Nature Lady has...' Sigrid raised her phone to him.

'One point three million?!' Jakob exclaimed.

'Spot on. She's one of the best-known influencers in Scandinavia. She combines nature with food, music, fashion, wellness and anything else that happens to keep the attention of her followers. She's got a good nose for this stuff – no doubt about it.'

'Well, a nose plus a good manager,' the cameraman interjected.

'And now she just happens to be coming to Bodø and Lofoten?' Jakob asked.

'Nothing that Nature Lady does is ever by chance. Her trip's sponsored by Visit Norway.'

Sigrid's mobile emitted a soft chime. She checked the message. 'Got to run. She's on her way to the luggage belt. See you!'

She vanished through the revolving doors together with the crew, only to reappear a moment later with a thin paperback in her hand. She offered it to Jakob. 'I finished this one yesterday,' she said. 'Why don't you take it? Please, you'll be doing me a favour. It'll look like I'm fangirling if I wave it in Nature Lady's face. It's not bad, actually. Especially the first chapter.'

Jakob took the book. The cover showed Marte Moi – Nature Lady – standing on the front steps of a log cabin. Behind her, the mountains were piercing holes in the sky. The title of the book was *My Journey* and in parentheses underneath there was a subheading reading *Join in!*

'Enjoy.' Sigrid winked at him and hurried back into the arrivals hall.

Jakob slipped the book onto the back seat of the car. He liked reading, but he'd had problems concentrating for the last few months. If he plumped for a novel, his eyes would slide across the pages, unable to hook onto a single word or sentence. His colleague Armann had a sixteen-year-old daughter who would probably be familiar with Nature Lady. He'd give the book to Armann, and he could pass it on to her. Bank some decent dad points.

Inside the terminal, he bought a cup of coffee from the machine in the newsagent's. He scrutinised the passengers as they came down the stairs from the first floor. He spotted that Sigrid had already intercepted her target. The journalist almost disappeared in the crowd of eager onlookers who flocked around her and the influencer.

The spectacle left him in no doubt that Marte Moi really was a celebrity. Jakob caught quick glimpses of her as she spoke, gesticulating to the camera. The copper hair slide shone in the flashes from the mobile-phone cameras. She seemed energetic. Switched on. As if she were on duty. Nevertheless, he struggled to understand the concept. Marte Moi didn't actually do anything except post pictures of herself standing in front of natural wonders and sights that anyone could travel to.

Good God. If Lise had heard him say something like that, she would have slapped the back of his head and called him a grumpy old man. He had to be careful not to end up like the old-timers at the station who were fond of declaring that it had all been better back in their day. Just like Rolf Kvist, his now-retired partner. He had sworn by his old-school typewriter with its correction key until the head of HR had personally confiscated it from his desk. That had been three years ago.

'Jakob Weber?'

He turned around. The woman behind him already had her arm extended, a khaki wheelie suitcase on the floor at her side. He'd seen her headshot on the intranet, but she was taller than he'd been expecting. Her shoulders broader. His inner detective filtered through his impressions. Around 175 centimetres tall, Asian features. Dark, straight, shoulder-length hair. Brown eyes. A straight nose with freckles at the bridge. A hint of burgundy lipstick. Slightly crooked left canine. Running shoes, blue jeans and a white top under a black leather jacket.

Firm handshake. Police.

CHAPTER 2

NOORA YUN SANDE

He was different from how she had imagined. Kind of stooping. But his handshake was firm, and his voice deep and warm, with that musicality so typical of northern Norway.

'Jakob Weber. Welcome to Bodø.'

'Noora Sande. Thanks for picking me up.'

'Don't mention it.'

He let go of her hand. He was evidently at a loss as to how to proceed. The uncertainty surprised her. Jakob Weber was a detective held in high esteem down in Oslo. An analyst from the old school. In Kripos-speak, he was someone who 'lived and breathed the case', as they put it at the National Criminal Investigation Service. Which was generally a polite way of describing monomaniacal tendencies. A recluse. But in this respect Jakob was different. Those who had worked with him described him as sociable and affable. A leader who always went first and knew the way. Now, though, he seemed uncertain.

Noora knew that Kripos had tried to lure him south, but Jakob had declined for family reasons. Judging by the ring on his finger, Noora assumed that meant a wife and kids.

Only a handful of people knew that she hadn't really wanted to come to Bodø. She was happy at Kripos. She was on her way up. A young and promising rising star.

What would Jakob have made of her had they met at Kripos a year ago?

As far as she was concerned, the partnership with Jakob was a bonus. A blessing in disguise. Two or three years in Bodø and then she'd be packing her bags to return to Oslo. Maybe she'd have another star on her shoulder and more responsibility in the criminal-investigative section at Kripos.

Maybe.

That single word pretty much summed up her whole life.

'Been up north before?' Jakob asked as they made for a recently washed Mitsubishi Outlander.

'I did a year at college in Kabelvåg after I finished senior high.' Noora inhaled through her nostrils, filling her lungs. She had forgotten how fresh the air was here. Cool and salty. 'I took the outdoor programme. Lots of mountain climbing and surfing,' she added. 'Over forty days in a tent. Bloody freezing in winter – and absolutely fantastic.'

Jakob turned to her, and smiled. 'Then I reckon you know Lofoten better than I do. That may come in handy. We sometimes get sent out there to help the local force with their inquiries. Remind me what they call it these days at Police University College? Complementary skills?'

'Something like that.'

He opened the boot and Noora heaved her case in. A shrill bark had her reeling backward in surprise.

'Garm!' Jakob exclaimed before turning to her. The streak of uncertainty was back on his face. 'You're not afraid of dogs, are you? I sometimes have Garm with me, but he hasn't got that used to other people after...' The rest of the sentence petered into nothingness.

'Not a bit,' Noora replied. 'We had standard poodles back home. My mum did dog shows with them when I was little. I reckon I've been inside every single sports hall in Eastern Norway. I was just surprised.'

Jakob's face relaxed. 'Garm's a good boy, but he's a bit possessive about me. It'll soon pass once he gets to know you.'

He got into the driver's seat. 'Do you want to drop your bag off at your flat first, or should we just head down to the station?'

'Station,' Noora replied. 'Still not got a flat. I'll be crashing with a friend from college until I find my own place. Apparently she lives round the corner from the police station.' Noora opened the messages on her phone. '9D Nordlysbuen,' she says.

'Ah, in East,' Jakob said. 'Yes, it's only five minutes' walk from the station.'

They pulled out of the airport car park and went left at the first roundabout. On the right-hand side she could see a football pitch with floodlights in each of its four corners.

'Bodø/Glimt?'

'Spot on. Their home stadium – the Aspmyra. I was a season ticket holder for years, but work was always getting in the way. Nowadays I watch the games on TV even though I'm only down the road. I could hear the roaring from my veranda the day we beat Roma six-one.'

It wasn't more than five or six minutes after they left the airport that Jakob parked outside Bodø police station, which was a modern, three-storey brick-built building. He opened both rear windows to make sure Garm had fresh air.

Noora looked around. The building was next to a big roundabout. On the horizon, she caught sight of a blue mountain through the low sea clouds.

'That's Landegode,' said Jakob. 'If you've seen a postcard of Bodø in the midnight sun, you'll have seen *that* mountain.'

'Way too close to be Lofoten, right?'

'Spot on. Round the back of Landegode you've got Vestfjorden, which stretches out as far as the Lofotens. But on a clear day, you can see the Lofoten Wall from the top of Keiservarden.'

'Keiservarden?'

'I'm getting the feeling that you stuck to Kabelvåg that year you spent at college. We'll do a geography lesson some other day. But don't worry about it; it's easy to find your way around Bodø. The town is at the tip of a peninsula. We're mostly surrounded by the sea.'

She followed Jakob and Garm through the main entrance and into a bright and airy foyer that stretched right up to the vaulted roof of the building.

'We work in the Joint Unit for Intelligence, Prevention and Investigation. It's one hell of a mouthful, but the official abbreviation isn't much better,' Jakob added.

'JUIPI?'

'Spot on. We usually just call it "Investigation". It's a good fit with our job. And as Bodø police station is also the headquarters for the Nordland police district, we often help out the smaller offices around the district. Either by going there or with video calls.' Jakob held his keycard up to a door on the right-hand side of the foyer. Beyond it there lay a lift and a staircase. 'Our offices are on the first floor. The Crow insisted on meeting you as soon as you arrived. Just as well to get it over with.'

'And the Crow is...?'

'Our boss. Konrad Råkstad.'

'Ahh. And the nickname...'

'...is one we only use behind his back.'

'Good to know.'

On the first floor, Jakob led her into a bright and pleasant open-plan area. On the far side, there were three small offices with windows onto the main space, as well as views of a park. Towards the centre of the space, she saw a bigger office. The Crow's nest, Noora guessed.

'There are currently four detectives, including the two of us,' Jakob informed her. 'I'll introduce you to the other two later. Right now, it's probably best you say your hellos to Police Superintendent Råkstad. Then we can sort out the formalities: access cards, car and all that. I'll be waiting in our office.' Jakob nodded towards the cubicle furthest away from Råkstad's office.

'Any tips?'

'Smile, nod and keep your trap shut.'

As Noora approached Råkstad's office door, she saw that the blind on the window next to it was pulled down. She stopped. She noticed her pulse increasing as she pictured another office door somewhere else, not that long ago. She saw the contours of the man who had been waiting for her on the other side when she had opened it. Felt his hand around her neck.

'Come in!'

Noora stared in surprise at her own fist, which was now resting against the door. She didn't remember having knocked. But the tenderness in her knuckles told her she must have knocked hard.

The office was reminiscent of a showroom in a new office building. Råkstad was sitting behind a rectangular glass-and-steel desk. The shiny surfaces shone dimly in the glow from the concealed ceiling lights. Apart from a PC display, keyboard and mouse, there was nothing on the desk except a glass of water on a tray. Noora couldn't see so much as a sheet of paper anywhere.

Råkstad leaned back in his chair, studying Noora over the top of his square steel spectacles. His mop of fine blond hair was swept sideways across his brow. His eyes were slate grey, his face angular, like his glasses. He had sharp cheekbones and the bridge of his nose ran down towards his mouth like a dorsal fin. But his lips stood out – they were fulsome, almost sensual.

'Police Detective Noora Yun Sande,' he said at last. His dialect, if it could be called that, was Greater Oslo. Bokmål. Råkstad had pronounced her name in completely flat tones.

'That's right.'

'It wasn't a question, Sande,' Råkstad replied. 'Graduated third in your class at Police University College. Degree in Bioscience from the University of Oslo. A degree of snowboarding talent as a young woman, but not good enough to represent Norway.'

Råkstad raised the glass to his lips, drinking soundlessly from it. He set the glass down in the centre of the tray. Then he clasped his hands in front of him on the glass desk. His manicure wasn't much to look at, Noora thought to herself.

'I demand two things from the people who work for me,' Råkstad continued. 'Absolute honesty and absolute loyalty.'

Noora stood there, trying to conceal the discomfort she felt. She'd heard the same lecture before. She knew from experience that those who demanded absolute loyalty rarely wanted honesty in equal measure. Was Råkstad expecting her to reply? A military-style 'Yes, sir'?

She remembered Jakob's advice and kept mum.

'Let me start by welcoming you to Bodø. You come highly recommended by Kripos. That's a good start.' Råkstad paused for breath. The office became so silent that Noora could hear the whirring of the ventilation system above her. 'Let me lead by example when it comes to honesty,' Råkstad said at last. 'You were not my first choice for this job. I was set on another candidate for the role – someone with more hands-on police experience than you. But I was overruled by Chief of Police Telle. That's something I must accept, in the same way that you must accept that I have high expectations of you.' Råkstad met her gaze. She noticed a hint of yellow in his left eye. 'I shan't speculate on whether you are a quota candidate or have in some other way that I'm unaware of been given an advantage in the application process. You work for me now, and you will henceforth be measured on what you deliver. Do we understand each other?'

Noora nodded. She broke eye contact with him. It seemed like a good idea to give Råkstad the victory in this staring contest.

'What the hell happened to northern hospitality?' Noora sat down opposite Jakob.

'I'm sure he'll have welcomed you to Bodø,' Jakob said dryly.

'Sure, but he made me feel anything but welcome.'

'Don't take it personally. Like his specs and hair, the Crow's leadership philosophy comes straight from the fifties. But it's no coincidence that he's in charge of the section. His brain is at least as sharp as his tongue. Since he took over, our clearance rates have increased significantly. And, look, there was a lot of competition for the job and they picked you. That's all *I* need to know about your qualifications.'

Noora swallowed. She looked out of the window. Just like Råkstad, Jakob had no idea what had gone on behind the scenes when she had got the job. In Bodø, only Chief of Police Vigdis Telle knew – but not even she was aware of all the details.

Jesus, Noora, she thought. *Don't underestimate yourself. You're good enough for this job.*

'Ready to do the rounds?'

'Rounds?'

'Meeting your new colleagues. Napping your way through the fire-safety demonstration. Being briefed on internal procedures and plans. Access card for the building, keys for your car. Forgetting which names go with which faces as soon as you're told them. All that jazz.'

'When you put it like that, it's hard to say no.'

The administrative hoops that Noora had to jump through to officially call herself a Bodø police detective took around three hours. Most of the people Noora met were nice enough – only the head of the police security service, Ivar Kjellemo, seemed a little reserved.

'Ivar's a bit nostalgic,' Jakob explained after Kjellemo's concise security briefing.

'How so?'

'I think he wishes he'd been in the security service during the Cold War. A time when there were fewer grey areas and we knew who the enemy was. It's all a bit chaotic these days. As well as the Russians' unpredictability, he has to keep up to speed with international cybercrime, hybrid threats and suspicious Chinese acquisitions.'

'The old Cold War was better than the current one?'

'I reckon he thinks so.'

Jakob's smile transitioned to a grimace when he caught sight of the clock in the foyer.

'Good Lord. I completely forgot about Garm. He'll need a breather. Fancy coming with me?'

Noora shook her head. 'I might as well find out whether the username and password they gave me in IT actually work.'

'Good idea. See you in about half an hour.'

CHAPTER 3

ARMANN FEMRIS

'It's down towards the sea. On the other side of that hill,' said Ronald Janook, head of forensics for Nordland police district. He turned around, waving Armann to follow him along the narrow path. Ronald wore sturdy rubber boots. The white disposable coverall that forensics used at crime scenes was rolled up to his knees.

Armann looked sceptically at his own ankle-high boots and black jeans. Not exactly hiking gear. Normally, he would have changed into more suitable attire at the office, but the duty officer had called him in the car while he was en route to the station. He'd been told to head straight to the old Bremnes coastal fortress built by the Germans at Løp, north of Bodø town centre. His partner, Josefine – she went by Fine – had to drop off her daughter at nursery and wouldn't be here for another twenty or thirty minutes. Armann ran his hand through his shoulder-length black hair. His palm became moist. The morning air on this June day was both cool and damp. Typical Bodø weather.

'Afraid of ruining your dress shoes?' Ronald was already halfway up a steep and slippery slope. Armann bit his tongue. As head of forensics, Ronald sometimes came across as a Viking feudal lord, but Armann knew it was a bad idea to butt heads with him.

His soles lacked grip, so Armann had to grab hold of the branches of the birch trees along the path to avoid slipping backward. Even before he had reached the top, his shoes were mucky and the hems of his jeans were soaked.

'She was found by a hiker,' Ronald told him, without looking around. 'One of those World War Two junkies. He told me he's built an exact replica of the cannon battery in his basement.'

'He's a bachelor, I take it?'

'What do you think?' Ronald replied, laughing in his characteristic bass tone. 'Uniform have his name and number in case you want a word with him later.'

Armann nodded at Ronald's back. He would have to discuss it with Jakob when he and Fine got back to base.

During the war, Bremnes Fort had been part of the German Atlantic Wall, comprising multiple cannon positions, bunkers and underground munitions stores. Most Bodø locals were familiar with the place, and after it had been closed by the Norwegian armed forces in 1994 it had been converted into a military-history-themed hiking trail. But it was also a place where youngsters came to party, as well as – on a couple of tragic occasions in recent years – to end their lives.

Armann stopped to scrape mud off his shoes on a mossy hillock. Rainy, dark-grey skies shrouded Landegode mountain. Armann could still feel the presence of the peak through the cloud. It was a weight on his very consciousness.

'She was found in the bunker beneath cannon emplacement eleven.' Ronald's voice emanated from the trees ahead of him. Armann hurried to catch up.

'Aren't the bunkers sealed off?' he asked as soon as he spotted the white overalls again.

Ronald shrugged. 'Might be, but it's not unusual for people to break into the bunkers. A couple of years before the pandemic, I seem to remember someone organising a rave in one of the bigger ones to mark the end of high school. They brought in a generator and lights. Apparently they nearly topped themselves thanks to all the carbon monoxide.'

Cannon emplacement eleven was located in the space between the trees and the rocks. Yellow-and-white tape had already been extended around the outside of the emplacement wall. An officer was on duty by the tape, his back to it and a cigarette in his hand.

'Jesus Christ,' Ronald shouted. 'You know better than to smoke here.'

The officer hurried to stub out the cigarette on a rock at his side.

'Pick that up,' Ronald ordered in a flat voice.

The officer obeyed.

Ronald raised the cordon for Armann and pointed to a plastic bag containing gloves, hairnets and foot covers. Armann pulled these on before following Ronald, who was now standing by the steel door that led into the bunker.

Only now did Armann noticed a faint but sour smell. It made him think of kimchi – the Korean fermented pickle that used vegetables and sometimes shrimp. A jar of kimchi left open for too long in a hot room.

'The entrance to this bunker was covered in a sheet of plywood. She must have put it there after she went inside. It's probably why she was here for so long before anyone found her.'

The bunker was a circular, grey room cast from concrete. Armann had to bend his neck to avoid hitting his head against the ceiling. Two battery-powered floodlights ensured that every last detail was visible in their harsh glow.

The woman was lying by the wall close to the door. Had Armann not already known it was a woman, it would have been difficult to make out the sex. She wore jeans that were tattered at the seams. A faded T-shirt had begun to disintegrate into the gelatinous, yellowing torso. Some of the letters that had been printed on the T-shirt were still visible. Remains of skin and tufts of dark-blonde hair were still attached to parts of the skull. The lips were gone. The teeth were even, a shade of yellowish white.

Armann crouched beside the body, pulled out his torch and shone it at the lettering. He recognised the two distinctive J's at once: a band logo.

'She's wearing a Jinjer T-shirt. They're a Ukrainian rock group.'

Ronald crouched beside him. 'Who would have thought that your peculiar taste in music would ever come in useful?' he commented, without any hint of irony or sarcasm. 'That would go with the ID card we found in her pocket. Name on the card is Galyna Ivanova. I checked the missing-persons register, and apparently a Ukrainian woman called that went missing in March.'

Armann nodded. 'Galyna, her younger brother and their mother were among the first Ukrainian refugees to arrive in Bodø. They had fled Mariupol. The mother told the media they were struggling with PTSD from the war. Galyna must have had a meltdown when the civil defence force tested their air-raid siren.'

Ronald stood up. He didn't move, his face thoughtful.

'How do you think she did it?' asked Armann.

Ronald produced a sealable plastic bag containing a pill box. 'Rohypnol. It's both anti-anxiety and a soporific. It takes a lot of it for someone to die, but I'm not ruling out that she took the pills with alcohol. That would cast a different light on this.'

'But you haven't found a bottle?'

'No. But she might have drunk it outside the bunker and chucked it in the sea before she came in here.'

Armann leaned towards the corpse. Then he pulled out a pen and pointed to a gash running across the woman's partially decomposed neck. 'What's that from, would you say?'

'At first I thought it might indicate suffocation,' Ronald replied. 'But then I found this on the floor next to her.' He produced a second sealed bag, which contained a wooden cross on a string of what appeared to be twisted cloth or twine.

'As the body swelled as a result of putrefaction, the string strained across the neck until the knot burst. Hence the gash.' Ronald returned the bag back to his pocket. 'Of course, we'll be doing an autopsy, but my preliminary conclusion is suicide.'

'Have the family been notified?' Armann asked.

'No – isn't that your job?'

'One hell of a start to the day.'

'If it's any comfort, it's probably going to get worse before it gets better.'

'You've always been a ray of fucking sunshine.'

On his way back to his car, Armann called Fine, who said that she had dropped her little girl off and was en route to Løp. Armann asked her to divert to the police station and meet him there.

After their brief call, he stood by his car for a few minutes. He regretted not bumming a cigarette off that officer on duty by the cordon. It had been years since he had quit smoking, but now he would happily have taken a long drag on a ciggie to vanquish the sensation of kimchi past its best. Back inside the car, he found Jinjer online and began playing their song 'Hello Death' so loudly that the intense rock music drowned out his thoughts.

CHAPTER 4

NOORA

Once Jakob had left to take Garm for his walk, Noora returned to the investigation section's offices.

The three cubicles were empty. The light in Råkstad's office was off and the blind in the window by the door was now up. In the semi-darkness, Noora could just make out his office chair. For a moment an image entered her head of Råkstad sitting there watching her, the yellow flecks in his eyes sparkling like gold dust.

She switched on her PC and logged on. She headed straight for the police's universal interface, from which she could access all the databases and records she needed. Well, not everything. The details of her own case – the report that had led her to this office in Bodø – were held on a separate server at Kripos.

'One person's word against another,' was what the Kripos lawyer had told management. 'A clear case of sexual harassment and abuse of power,' was what the lawyer Noora's trade union had engaged on her behalf had said.

The lawyer had recommended that Noora take her case to the press and had given her the name of a tabloid hack at *VG*. Noora had refused. She hadn't wanted to become a whistleblower, with all the stresses that entailed. And she knew she would be a pariah in the police forever afterwards if she did.

'You know he'll do it again. To other women?' her lawyer had said to her. Noora had replied 'Yes' and almost added 'But there are things you don't know. Things I haven't told you.'

Despite her refusal, Noora suspected the union lawyer had told the top brass at Kripos that she was weighing up whether to contact the media, because the very next day the 'Bodø solution' had been put on the table. Noora had agreed on one condition: 'Don't tell him where I've gone.' Of course, he would find out eventually. But for the time being, her name was only searchable by officers working in Nordland police district.

It'll get better. It'll all be fine in the end.

She was in Bodø now, not Oslo. That was all that mattered.

Noora went to STRASAK – the electronic national criminal records database – and filtered her search geographically to Nordland police district.

Drunkenness, vandalism, drugs, violence, burglary, embezzlement and smuggling. A statistical cross-section of any police district in the country. But Noora noticed that there was far less gang crime here than in the big city. She skimmed the titles of the latest cases entered and spotted one recurring crime: fish smuggling.

She clicked on the most recent one. Following a tip-off from the public, three German camper vans had been raided at a campsite outside Bodø. The freezers in two of the three vehicles had contained in excess of three hundred kilos of cleaned fillets. Each. The maximum tourists were permitted to take out of the country was eighteen kilos.

The fine was set at ninety-seven thousand kroner.

Ninety-seven thousand! Noora stifled a snort of laughter.

'I see you've found the number-one mortal sin in these northerly climes.'

Noora spun around in her chair. The man who had spoken was standing in the doorway to her office. He was leaning against the frame. He looked exactly like a male fashion model: distinctive jawbone, shoulder-length black hair, blue eyes, a salt-and-pepper five o'clock shadow, charcoal jacket over a T-shirt emblazoned with a Ramones logo.

He was forty – give or take.

Only his footwear marred his otherwise well-groomed appearance: the black ankle boots were caked in mud.

'And you are?'

The man turned his head and said over his shoulder: 'She's only been here half a day and already acting as if she owns the place.'

'Then she'll fit right in,' said a woman that Noora now realised was standing by the coffee maker on the far side of the room. She wore a simple but tasteful black trouser suit with matching black trainers. Her platinum-blonde hair was cut in a short military style.

The man held out his hand to Noora. 'Armann Femris. That caffeine slave's name is Josefine Skog.'

'You can call me Fine,' said the woman. She came over to them, clutching a mug of coffee, and shook hands with Noora. 'And you must be Noora Sunde – our token southerner in the section.'

'That's right.'

'Welcome on board. And don't pay Armann any attention. He's just overcompensating after a rough start to the day.'

'How's it going with you and Jakob?' Armann interjected. 'Found the tone, the electricity, the emotion?'

'Um ... excuse me?' Noora stammered.

'No excuse necessary,' Armann grinned. 'Jakob is a dagger in a velvet sheath. A charlatan disguised as a charmer.'

'Bloody hell, Armann,' came Jakob's voice. 'You might give her a couple of minutes to get to know you before you let loose.' Jakob appeared, Garm trotting along behind him. He looked at Noora apologetically. 'Armann is a great investigator and semi-okay person. The problem is he never knows when to keep his mouth shut.'

'Semi-okay?' Armann exclaimed, extending his arms in a theatrical gesture. 'High praise from a sourpuss like you.'

'Pretty ballsy bringing Garm into the office,' Fine said.

'The Crow's car wasn't in the car park, so I thought I'd take a chance.'

'He'll know about it when he starts sneezing, what with his allergies,' Fine warned.

'Hope so,' Jakob said, and the other two laughed.

'I spoke to Ronald on my way up,' Jakob continued, his voice now more serious. 'He told me about the woman in the bunker.'

'Probably suicide,' Armann said with a nod. 'Fine and I are going to pay a visit to the family as soon as we've confirmed the woman's identity.'

'Good. Incidentally, it's almost time for us to submit our quarterly report on unsolved cases. Telle isn't one to give extensions.'

'Unlike the Crow, you mean?' said Fine in a way that Noora interpreted as heavily ironic.

Noora examined her three new colleagues. She saw how relaxed they seemed in each other's company. And she felt something settle inside her. The anxiety that had been simmering away within her seemed to be dissipating. The investigative team in Bodø might be small compared with Kripos, but a small team didn't mean insignificant cases. In rural areas, police detectives were more jacks-of-all-trades than in the cities, where every imaginable form of specialist expertise was just minutes away.

Her 'other' mobile emitted a soft chime. Noora hesitated briefly before she retrieved the small Nokia from her jacket pocket. The mobile had no apps and no internet access – it was the very opposite of a modern smartphone. On the screen the text message icon had appeared.

The good-natured ribbing outside her door continued, but she could no longer hear what they were saying. Her attention was directed at the phone. Noora didn't want to open the text. But she knew she wouldn't be able to resist.

She gave in.

You do realise I'll never let you go?

CHAPTER 5

ISELIN HANSSEN

She was one step closer to her goal. Iselin let out a howl of joy. She felt both ridiculous and elated.

She read the first line of the email yet again:

'You are hereby invited to the physical tests for admission to Police University College.'

The police academy!

She had got over the first hurdle.

What a relief. It was a more overwhelming feeling than she had expected. She wanted to call Casper and share the news right away. But she hesitated, her thoughts returning to the run a week ago.

It had been really crappy weather that day. One low-lying cloud after another dumping its contents, turning the landscape grey and reducing visibility. Nevertheless, she had gone for a run. Iselin knew that as long as she kept moving she wouldn't get cold. But after the run – in the almost-empty car park by the Maskinisten hiking trail – she had sought shelter under an oak and stretched her calves.

At first she hadn't noticed the blue Volvo parked a few metres away. There were generally plenty of hikers around there – people would drive in after work for a quick walk before dinner. But not on days like this.

Only when she had turned her back to the trunk to stretch her hamstrings did she notice the two men in the back seat of the car. They were facing each other, caressing each other's faces. Exchanging rushed kisses that became long and tender embraces.

The rainwater pouring down the window had distorted the scene within. It reminded Iselin of an old black-and-white movie. Then the figure closest to her had turned his head and his characteristic profile had been unmistakable: receding hairline, straight nose and prominent chin. Otto Jahrberg. Casper's dad.

Iselin remembered how she had been rooted to the spot, unable to tear herself away from what she was seeing. There was something deeply personal – almost desperate – about what was unfolding in the back seat of that car. Two grown men hiding like teenagers on their first date.

Who was Otto Jahrberg with?

Iselin hadn't made a conscious decision to get closer – it had just happened. Her movement had caught the attention of the unknown figure. The man had looked up and stared straight at Iselin, who then realised that she knew exactly who he was: one of the two police officers who had come to give a talk on careers in policing a few months ago.

She had turned on her heel and run, not looking back. She hoped Otto hadn't recognised her from behind. And surely the policeman didn't remember her? She supposed he must give talks like that to hundreds of students a year. Then again, Iselin had asked him several questions. She'd been one of the most animated members of the audience.

That was why she had been so nervous about the decision from Police University College. What if the policeman had done something to prevent her from being summoned for the physicals? Only now did Iselin realise how mad that idea was. A crazy conspiracy theory.

But it didn't solve the issue with Otto Jahrberg. Iselin had seen him with someone else – a man. But was that really her problem? It was up to Otto whether he wanted to tell Casper and Julia – Casper's mother – about the relationship. Still, she knew something that Casper didn't. A secret that would turn the Jahrbergs' lives upside down if it got out.

But perhaps there was another solution? Casper hadn't been particularly enthusiastic about Iselin's plans to study in Oslo. He'd kept saying 'You do know there's a police academy in Bodø, right?'

like a stuck record. At least until yesterday. All of a sudden, Casper had suggested that if she got in then perhaps they might go to Oslo together, and get themselves a flat in Grünerløkka.

Iselin had been so stunned by this change of mood that all she had said was 'suppose so'. The doubts had crept in after Casper had gone home later that evening. Did she really want to go to Oslo with Casper? Had she only said yes because she had a guilty conscience about not telling him about his father?

Iselin knew one thing for sure: she needed to get out of here. She needed to experience something new. She needed to meet new people. There was nothing wrong with Bodø, but sometimes the town felt kind of ... claustrophobic. Just like her relationship with Casper. She was nineteen, while he was three years her senior and already acting as if they were soon to be married.

Perhaps it was time for a break? She would talk to him about it tomorrow. And when she left Bodø, she'd take the secret about Casper's dad with her.

Iselin logged off and changed into her fitness gear. She was slightly dreading her run, which would follow the same route that she had taken the day she'd come across Otto and the policeman. Thirteen kilometres from the door, up the gravel track to the northern edge of the Vågøyvannet lake. From there, she would follow the forest trails up to Keiservarden and then back. A climb from ten metres above sea level to 366. It was tough, but this kind of workout gave her a chance of getting into the academy.

Since Easter, she'd been running this trail every Wednesday after school, come rain, shine or snow. Her dad had come with her on the first few occasions, but then he'd started turning her down. He claimed he couldn't keep up with her. That was his way of giving her praise.

Iselin set off at a leisurely pace and didn't up her speed until she had overcome the steep climb up to the plateau, where the paths and trails meandered through the lush Bodø landscape. She turned off onto the path down to the lake. The ground was soft after the rain overnight. The leaves of the birch trees along the trail sprinkled her with cooling droplets of water. Iselin filled her lungs. She felt her head clear and all thoughts of Casper and their relationship fall away.

'You never regret a run,' was what her dad always said. Now she understood what he meant. Some days it was hard to get going, but the endorphins were like magic. As soon as they began to course through her body, she forgot her troubles and how worn out she was. All that mattered was the here and now.

When she reached the northern end of Vågøyvannet, there was a small area of marshy ground with a stream running through it, like a deep channel in the greenery. Iselin usually crossed the stream via a toppled tree trunk, but today the ground leading up to the darkened log was too wet and muddy for her to reach it without her shoes filling up with smelly bog water.

She took a swig from her bottle and turned around to jog back the way she had come. But she stopped when she caught sight of something green moving between the white of the birch trunks a little way ahead of her.

Iselin waved her hand to keep the gnats and midges at bay. This was a popular hiking area, so it wasn't unusual to bump into other people. But wasn't there something off about the way the person had been running? Bent forward. As if they were trying to make themselves small.

Iselin clipped her bottle back onto her belt and headed for the two white birch trees the figure had already passed.

The footprints in the soft ground were clear to see. They continued in the same direction she was heading. Iselin listened. She could hear nothing but the rush of blood in her own ears.

She began to run again, but the peace she'd felt before was gone. Her breathing was uneven: she'd managed to get out of sync. Suddenly she began to notice spots along the path where someone might be able to hide: in the shadows under a tree, behind the dense foliage in a bog, on the other side of a craggy rock.

Jesus Christ, pull yourself together!

Before long, the path grew into a full gravel track and all trace of the other runner disappeared. The landscape became more open and she could see further. When Iselin reached the top of Keiservarden some fifteen minutes later, she simply shook her head at herself.

Mind games and fantasies. This wasn't like her. But she had been sleeping badly lately. Her application to the Police University College, Otto in the car with that policeman, her relationship with Casper, leaving Bodø and Dad for three years – maybe longer. Decisions and resolutions. It was all tangled up together. It made her doubt which choices to make. But not here. Out under the vast sky, everything seemed so simple. She knew what she had to do. She had known all along.

As soon as she got home, she would call Casper. She would tell him she needed a break. Tell him that some distance would do them both good.

If nothing else, it would make Dad happy. Iselin knew he was sceptical about the relationship. Not because of Casper, but because of his dad. Otto Jahrberg. Dad wasn't one to talk about the past, but Iselin knew enough to realise that Otto and Bjørn hadn't been the best of mates in their younger days.

She ate half her chocolate and her energy bar, and stopped on top of the flat stone slab that was the summit of Keiservarden, looking down towards Bodø town centre. The slick runway at the airport glistened like a streak of silver. Iselin turned ninety degrees and looked towards Landegode, following the line of cloud on the horizon that demarcated the Lofoten Wall beyond Vestfjorden. High above Bodø with a cool westerly breeze on her face, she knew this place would always be a part of her. While she might be leaving home, she would take the landscape with her.

Wild. Beautiful. Weathered.

It was part of her personality.

A hidden strength.

Her route took her back past Kretjønna, a tarn in a small depression in the terrain that was sheltered from the wind. Iselin opted for a path running above the water's edge. It was rocky and uneven, so she had to walk the first part. She didn't want to risk a twisted ankle just before the physicals.

On the far side of the small lake, a group of hikers were settled at a picnic table, sipping coffee. One of them waved to her, and Iselin waved back before she picked up her pace as the path began to wind between young birch trees and grey, rocky mounds.

Ahead of her, two ravens took flight, letting out hoarse, irritable cries. They circled the tree they had been sitting in before making for Iselin. She heard the rush of air through their feathers as they passed over her.

Had they been scared by an animal? Or perhaps a dog walker? Dogs were meant to be kept on the lead around here, but plenty of people ignored the rules. Iselin slowed down. She didn't want to startle someone else's wandering mutt. But the path ahead remained empty, and the whisper of wind through the treetops made it difficult to hear much else.

After a few minutes, she aimed for a large rowan tree just off the path. She leaned against the smooth trunk and stretched the back of both her calves before the final leg home. It was mostly downhill from here, which meant she would use her muscles differently.

Once again her thoughts returned to Casper. They had been friends before they'd got together. Iselin missed that side of him. Her friend Casper. They'd hung out differently back then. It had been more relaxed, Iselin thought to herself. Now there was suddenly so much at stake. There were so many more expectations – often unspoken.

She would call him as soon as she got home. Get it over with. Then she'd turn off her mobile, because Casper would probably call back as soon as he got over the shock. He'd be calling, emailing, sending dozens of texts. But he'd just have to suck it up – they could talk it out once he'd calmed down.

CHAPTER 6

PEDER SKARVHEIM

He took three slices of bread from the bag. He toasted two of them for two and a half minutes, and the last one for only a minute. Just long enough for it to turn golden. Mother was very particular about that – she would send him back to the kitchen if her slice was too well done or too soft.

He smeared his mother's slice with butter, and the other two with margarine. He added marmalade to all three. Then he made two cups of tea: Prince of Wales blend for his mother, rose hip for himself.

'Peder?'

He looked up the narrow staircase to the first floor. 'Coming, Mother.'

He put the plates on the serving tray. It had been his gift to his mother on her eightieth birthday. A tray with a porcelain base. The base depicted a fishing smack heading towards the open sea, a flock of gulls hovering above the boat in the shape of the letter M. The picture reminded Peder of his father. The day when he'd gone to sea and hadn't come back.

'Peder?'

'I'll be right up!' he called back. She was always a little impatient in the mornings. She'd be in a better mood once she'd eaten.

Remembering the time he'd tripped, he climbed the stairs carefully. What a scolding his mother had given him after that. He'd spent hours cleaning jam smears and tea stains off the stairs and white walls.

Peder opened the door to his mother's bedroom. She was sitting in the chair by the window, a yellow shawl knotted over her nightgown, curlers visible in her hair beneath the thin hairnet that she always slept in.

He set the tray on the table by the window and opened the blackout curtains. The bright morning sun made the sea glitter, as if it were covered with white electric sparks. Peder checked his watch. He leaned against the window and spotted the Widerøe aircraft above the island of Vedøya. The plane, with its green-and-white livery, lowered its flaps as the pilot adjusted course north towards the runway on Røst.

'He's on time today,' he commented.

His mother didn't answer – but he could tell she was satisfied. She appreciated things working the way they were supposed to. The ferry docking and departing from the quayside on schedule. The planes landing and taking off at the appointed hour. Breakfast being brought up to her at the same time every day.

'Man's task is to create order in the world,' she used to remind him. She still had a cross and a picture of Jesus on the wall above the bed. The Son of God stood there, hands clasped, staring straight up to heaven, his face bathed in gentle light. Waiting for a sign. A signal from above.

Peder knew what waiting felt like. He had removed both the cross and the picture from his own room three weeks after his father had disappeared. He hadn't visited the cemetery since the day when the empty coffin had been lowered into the barren earth.

They lived at the end of a gravel track in Rimøya on the island of Røst. From his bedroom window, Peder had a view of the sea and the grocery store on the other side of the strait. From Mother's window, you could see Simon Michalsen's house.

Bloody Simon Michalsen.

Peder looked nervously at his mother, afraid he might have said that bit aloud. Luckily there was no reaction. She preferred to follow what was going on beyond the window.

While Peder's father had been a crofter fishing on another man's licence, Simon had inherited his own smack and quota from his father. Just a few years later, he had sold the quota on for an astronomical sum. Now he did little else except party and play music so loudly that Peder couldn't sleep. And sometimes he liked to do target practice with his saloon rifle in the middle of the night. Peder had contacted the district sheriff, or the 'head of the police station' as the role was now known, but by the time old Thorsen had finally managed to drag himself out here, it was – inevitably – all quiet at Simon's. Fortunately, at this time of year things became calmer. As soon as spring arrived, Simon went on his holidays. He would disappear in his outsized camper van and be gone for weeks – sometimes a couple of months.

'Are you full?'

'Thanks for breakfast, Peder. You're a good boy.'

The praise warmed Peder's heart. He tidied the cups and plates onto the serving tray and went back down to the kitchen, where he put the toast crusts in the food waste and washed up the crockery.

Afterwards, he fetched a can of cola from the fridge, picked up the book lying on the kitchen table and settled down on the front step in the sunshine. Mother didn't like him to drink more than a can of cola a day, and he usually kept it for the evening and the nine o'clock news on television. But today she was in such a good mood that he'd decided to treat himself to a can now too.

He opened the battered paperback and put it down on his thigh. Peder had probably read the book at least twenty times. He knew the content almost by heart. But Marte wrote so vividly about her childhood and all the trips she went on, Peder felt as if the two of them were on her travels together. That was probably why it said *Join in!* in green letters under the title. He missed travelling. But who would care for Mother if he left the island?

Peder had considered getting a smartphone just so he could follow Nature Lady on Instagram. He hadn't dared to ask his mother whether he could use some money from their joint account. Maybe that was something to ask her today.

He drained the last of the cola as he read chapter four, in which

Marte discussed with honesty how unhappy she'd been with her own body growing up. Just like him. They were so alike. It had been no surprise to Peder when he'd heard on the local news a few days ago that Marte was coming to visit Røst. It was almost as if she knew he lived there. As if she understood how much they had in common. Him and Marte.

It had been a long time since he'd felt like this.

Peder closed the book and slipped it into his pocket. He fetched the crutches and straightened up the picture of Mother in the hallway before going out.

The Blimo microcar he'd received through the technical aids centre in Bodø was parked in the barn. The vehicle that arsehole Simon called a 'wheelchair with a roof'. But Simon wasn't here now to ruin his good mood.

Peder opened the door at the back and put the crutches inside. He had expanded the space behind the seat by attaching a steel plate on a bracket, welding it to the rear axle. Now he could carry up to six sacks of firewood at once if he stacked them right. When Thorsen had by chance discovered the makeshift cargo space, the policeman had muttered something or other about 'illegal modifications to motor vehicles', but he hadn't done anything about it. Which was a fair summary of Thorsen's career as the representative of the long arm of the law on Røst, Peder reflected. Bumbling and indifferent. Running on automatic, letting the clock tick down to retirement.

He opened the barn door and got into the driver's seat. He pressed the start button. On his way across the yard, he looked up towards Mother's bedroom window.

He swerved around the knee-deep potholes by the mailbox. Yet another thing he'd promised his mother he would fix. He made up his mind to stop by the quay before he went to the shop. Perhaps the staff would know more about when Marte was due to arrive on Røst.

CHAPTER 7

JAKOB

Five years after graduating from the Norwegian Police University College, Jakob took a temporary job as the district sheriff in Beiarn, a municipality in the interior with scarcely more than one thousand souls. Beiarn was a truly beautiful area, bordering Bodø to the north and the Saltfjellet mountains to the south. During the salmon-fishing season, the population doubled, but it wasn't the picturesque landscape or fishing opportunities that had persuaded Jakob to take the job. It had been for personal reasons.

On his first day as district sheriff, he arrived unannounced at a farmhouse perched on high ground above Moldjord, the Beiarn's principal town. When he rang the bell and his father opened the door and saw his son for the first time in thirteen years, Manfred Weber seemed completely unmoved. It was different for Jakob. He still remembered the visceral reaction to seeing his father, the piercing sensation in his chest. The heart palpitations. The discomfort was entirely unexpected and almost threw him off balance.

'Manfred.'

'Jakob.'

Manfred didn't say anything else, no doubt hoping that the embarrassing silence would oblige Jakob to say more – to stammer something incoherently, just like when he'd been little.

But he didn't this time. Instead, Jakob stood there, holding Manfred's gaze even though it felt as if his ribcage was contracting, constraining his heart.

'Well, Jakob, I suppose you'd best come in.'

The reluctance in his father's voice was unmistakable. The old man didn't even want to let him across the threshold, and Jakob realised why when he met Yvonne.

In Jakob's eyes, Yvonne was young – perhaps only ten years his senior. She was slim with pale skin and eyes that were always looking for a grip without finding one. When she greeted Jakob, she withdrew her hand before he was able to properly grasp it. Then she laced her fingers together as if she were nervous that her hands might otherwise get up to something she didn't want them to.

Jakob recognised the signs – he'd seen them before. The way she made herself smaller until she was invisible in her own home. Yvonne Tollås Weber was behaving just like Jakob's mother had before she'd plucked up the courage to leave his father. Jakob felt as if he'd travelled back in time. The piercing sensation in his chest wouldn't stop and cold sweat gathered in his armpits.

Jakob offered his apologies before the cakes had even been laid on the table, pointing to his mobile and explaining that he needed to see to a case. He promised to pay them a visit another time. But he'd been rumbled – the shadow of a smile on his father's face proved it. As Jakob made for the front door, he felt a hand on his shoulder.

'You're as weak as your mother.'

He ought to have turned around and socked the old man there and then.

Jakob broke his own promise – he didn't return and slowly the feeling of guilt mounted within him. He was the local district sheriff. If he didn't stop Manfred from destroying Yvonne, who else would? But Manfred never struck with his fists clenched. He was always making one veiled threat after another, and only occasionally would he follow through with an unexpected swing, his palm open. Living with Manfred Weber was like moving into a room where the door handle was on the outside.

Jakob constantly fantasised about being called out to his father's house. For once, Manfred would have lost his temper and given Yvonne a real beating. Jakob would picture himself yanking his father's arms behind his back and pushing his face into the wall. Over and over.

But no calls about domestic disputes ever came in, and on the rare occasions he bumped into Yvonne she avoided meeting his gaze. Shame met guilt. It was unbearable.

This nagging guilt left Jakob feeling uneasy. He struggled to concentrate on his work, and at night he would only sleep in short spurts interrupted by hours of staring at the ceiling. One night, he reached the end of his tether and got up, and spent the couple of hours between one and three in a solitary wakefulness.

This eventually became a habit.

At first, he would wander around inside the former rectory he was renting, feeling the worn floorboards beneath his feet and listening to the silence. He noticed everything that he didn't hear in the daytime: the various creaks and groans of the building, the soft clicking of the old fuse box and the uneven whisper of the wind through the cracked living-room window. He felt oddly free, as if this untouched space of velvet night were governed by its own laws.

One night, he went onto the balcony completely naked. Goosebumps covered his skin as he inhaled the cold air streaming down the river valley from the expanses of snow in the mountains. He tracked a lonely pair of car headlights along the main road, imagining that it was him behind the wheel, leaving the place.

A month later his fantasy came true. CID at Bodø police station needed a junior detective. It was another temporary position, but with the possibility of an extension. Jakob noted his interest on the Tuesday, partook in a brief telephone interview with the head of CID on the Friday and then spent the weekend packing his things. He departed Beiarn as unceremoniously as he had arrived.

Jakob still remembered the relief that had flooded through him as he crossed the mountain pass and put the valley behind him. It was a relief swathed in self-loathing. He should have done something for Yvonne. At the very least, Jakob should have told her how Manfred had treated his mother. But Jakob didn't think it would have made any difference – or at least that was what he told himself.

A few years later, the chief municipal medical officer in Beiarn called to inform him that Manfred had collapsed while shovelling hay for the cows. 'He'd been dead at least an hour by the time I arrived,' the doctor said. After that call, Jakob opened a bottle of whisky. The first toast was to Yvonne. When had she realised that her husband had taken a turn? How long had she waited to call the doctor?

The next day he woke up with an awful hangover and not even a hint of regret. Manfred Weber was out of his life – for good. When he called his mother to let her know, all he heard was a faint sigh before she hung up. They didn't attend the funeral.

Jakob thought of his spell in Beiarn as a dark chapter in his life, but in the few months he'd spent there wakefulness had become a part of him. As a newly minted detective in Bodø, he continued to turn in at ten o'clock before waking of his own accord at around one in the morning. However, he now devoted those small hours to getting to grips with more complex cases.

At around three, he'd turn in for a second time. When the alarm on the clock radio went off at half past six, he felt more rested than the times when he slept straight through the night.

When he met Lise, something fell into place for Jakob – or perhaps his nocturnal self left him. He still worked a lot, but it no longer felt as if he was living his life against the current. He preferred to spend a couple of extra hours at the office at the weekend rather than leave Lise alone in bed at night.

He and Lise were accommodating of each other. She was the first and only person he told about his relationship with his father. Together, they coped with whatever life threw at them – including his mother's nascent dementia and their involuntary childlessness.

When Lise got her cancer diagnosis, they'd already applied to child-welfare services to be foster carers.

'Once you're better, we'll get back in touch with them,' Jakob reassured her. He recalled Lise squeezing his hand in response. She had already accepted what he refused to grasp.

After Lise's death, he once again sought out those wakeful hours of the night. He found his way back to a place where he could unmask, be himself, cry openly. He cursed and pounded his punch bag until plaster dust began to fall from round the hook in the ceiling.

Once he had calmed down, he would try to separate the memories from the grief – and just like everyone before him, he failed. He learned that grief colours everything that passes before it. The best he could hope for was some kind of acceptance – and perhaps that was where he was headed?

In the last month, he'd been working intensely on a cold case: the murder of an unidentified woman in Lofoten twenty-nine years earlier. Her body had been found among newly planted trees by the landowner, parts of her body having already been dug up and devoured by the foxes and crows.

What had begun as a distraction to keep the grief at bay had gradually come to engross him. The reconstructed image of the woman stared down at him from the cork board on the wall, begging him not to give up.

Brown eyes, lacklustre black hair. A straight, rather wide nose. Height 160 centimetres. While the body had been partially decomposed when it was found, there were clear signs of torture. According to the pathologist who had conducted the autopsy, she was in good shape. Did that mean she had been denied a quick death? Jakob hoped not.

The kettle clicked off. Jakob poured boiling water over the tea leaves. A fresh squall of rain struck the dormer window beyond the blackout curtains. While it never really got dark outside at this time of year, with the lights off it was as dark as the depths of December in the bedroom, study and bathroom.

Jakob blew on the tea and then took a sip, leaning back in his chair. There was a reason why this case had been left on ice for so long: there were no witnesses, no biological evidence and no crime scene. The woman had most probably been murdered elsewhere and then buried among the young trees.

The only thing that resembled a clue was the reported sighting of an unknown vehicle in the area at around the time the pathologist estimated the body had been buried. The witness – an elderly woman who had passed away several years ago – had described the vehicle as a van of some kind. It had been dark in colour, possibly navy or green. The woman thought the first letter of the registration had been a Y. Or possibly a T. It wasn't much to go on, but the observation had only been followed up on superficially.

Jakob pulled a sheet out of the case file. On it there were twenty-one columns that all began with the letter Y. As well as Nordland, Troms and Trøndelag both had areas where the letter Y appeared first in vehicle registrations. The combination for Bodø was YE.

He pulled out his mobile and snapped a picture of the document before attaching it to a text message and writing: *Hi Rolf. How's retirement treating you? Was wondering whether you fancied taking a look at something for me?*

Jakob tapped out in detail what he needed before sending the message to Rolf Kvist. His old partner would probably be over the moon at having something to do. There was a limit to how many times he could repaint the house and wash the car.

He was about to make himself another cup of tea when his phone lit up on the desk in front of him. On the display, it said 'Officer on Duty, Nordland Police'. It didn't take much policing experience to know that a call just before three o'clock in the morning was rarely good news.

CHAPTER 8

NOORA

Ellen hadn't changed much. Perhaps her waistline was a little thicker, but that laugh was still the same. Not to mention her wild dating stories.

After hugging Noora at the front door of her two-bedroom flat in the neighbourhood that Jakob had simply referred to as 'East', Ellen opened a bottle of wine and regaled her friend with details of her romantic adventures the preceding weekend. To Noora, it felt as if it had only been seven days, not seven years, since they had parted that summer's day at college in Kabelvåg.

'He was obviously pretty high on himself,' Ellen said while pouring a generous slug of wine into each of their glasses.

Noora knew she should decline. She couldn't risk showing up for her first proper day of work hungover. But Ellen wasn't one to be told no. Not eight years ago. Not now.

'...He was sitting there on a bar stool with his shirt unbuttoned down to his belly button, banging on about how much he'd made on Bitcoin lately. I couldn't stop myself staring at his chest.' Ellen gesticulated with her glass, causing a localised maelstrom. 'Don't get me wrong. These weren't pecs that you flex. I'm talking saggy man boobs that a baby thirsty for milk would have grabbed.'

'Er ... disgusting,' Noora said, trying to avoid red wine getting into her nose. 'So, what happened?' she asked.

'I went back to his place. Obviously.'

'You ... what?'

Ellen leaned back and burst into her deep laugh, rich as a full-bodied whisky. And this woman didn't even smoke or drink spirits. 'Jesus, Noora. You're just as gullible now as the day I met you. How on earth did you get into police college?'

'Immigrant quota,' Noora said, straight faced. She managed to maintain the expression for long enough that she saw a hint of uncertainty flit across Ellen's face.

'Good one!' Ellen drained her glass and then divided the remainder of the bottle between them, which meant that Noora had to take her next sip from the very top of the glass.

'How are you doing? I don't even know where you've been working since you finished your architecture degree.'

'I did what most recent architecture grads do to begin with,' Ellen said.

'Which is?'

'Bar work.'

'Expensive education for a job like that.'

'Fortunately it wasn't for long. I got a temporary job in the planning department in Fauske and then I applied for a role at Flame Architects – they're a new outfit up here in Bodø. Mostly young people. It's a kickass kind of place. The boss is heading for fifty, but luckily there's very few signs of midlife crisis.'

'Great.' Noora leaned across the table and clinked glasses with her friend. 'And how about on the man front? Apart from saggy-boobs guy?'

'Slim pickings. It's mostly wrecks and old blokes looking for round two. What about you?'

This innocent question prompted Noora to touch the pocket containing her Nokia. She hadn't checked her phone since receiving the message at the police station. 'Same,' she said quickly. 'It's a seller's market. Too many clit-teases out there.'

'Clit-teases?' Ellen snorted.

'You know, male teases. Blokes who don't keep their word.'

'Don't keep their word, huh?' Ellen tapped her nail against the wine glass, making it gently chime. 'God, we'll make a proper Nordlander of you yet, girl.'

Noora awoke in the semi-darkness. Rain was rattling against the window and grey light was seeping in around the edges of the blind. Even when it was raining, it was light at night. She had forgotten how long it had taken her to get used to the midnight sun last time she was here.

The fitness tracker lying on the bedside table said it was 03:11. Noora's head was heavy. She was glad she'd managed to persuade Ellen to save the next bottle for the weekend.

She put her hands under her head and stared at the ceiling, listening to the rain – trying to think about nothing at all. She wanted to prevent her mind from veering back to the subject she would do anything to avoid. But if she wanted to avoid it, why hadn't she left the Nokia behind in Oslo? Her other phone – the one she usually used – had a secret number and was untraceable. That should have been sufficient. Nevertheless, she'd taken the extra phone and old SIM card with her to Bodø. It was a control thing really, and a twisted logic – as long as she kept an eye on the messages she knew she was shot of him.

'It's the two of us against the world,' he used to say when they were in bed together, and it had made her feel like the heroine in a Hollywood movie. Then he would stroke her hair and whisper: 'You're mine. Never forget that.'

Her trousers were folded over the foot of the bed. Noora knew exactly which pocket the Nokia was in. She knew she shouldn't, but she couldn't help sitting up, pulling it out and reading what he had last sent.

Sorry. Forget the last message. I just feel so vulnerable when you don't reply.

Please call me...

The apparent fragility of the message scared Noora more than his threats. She wondered what would have happened if she had encountered this side of him sooner. Would she have been able to break free?

A harsh buzzing sound made her jump. It took her a couple of seconds to realise that it was her other phone ringing. The work phone. She usually kept it on silent, but the numbers of her colleagues were all set to make her phone vibrate.

The display showed Jakob Weber's name.

'Hello?'

'Sorry to wake you,' Jakob said. 'But we've just taken a call about what might be a serious incident.'

'What's up?' Noora had already put the mobile on speaker-phone and was beginning to get dressed.

'A nineteen-year-old girl – Iselin Hanssen – didn't come back from her run yesterday. Search teams with dogs have been searching for her since just before midnight. There's also a helicopter with a thermal-imaging camera deployed in the area. We can't discount that a crime may have taken place.'

'Meet you at the station?'

'I'll pick you up from your friend's. I'll be two minutes.'

CHAPTER 9

The Østerdalen valley – indeed, the whole stretch from Lillehammer to Trondheim – was a risk zone. Roadside checkpoints. Crowded laybys. A network of logging roads that weren't shown on the map, where you could easily lose your way.

Just like the year before, he pulled off at the petrol station in Kvikne, and that was where he saw her. She was sitting on the bench by the small hut with the turfed roof, eating an ice cream with her rucksack on the ground beside her. There was something indescribable about her that filled him with desire. He pictured his hand brushing her dark hair aside. It was an innocent image. Nevertheless, he began to feel a tingle extending from his fingertips to his scalp.

He pulled the cap down over his brow. He filled up with diesel, paid cash and then pulled away from the pumps. He poured himself a cup of coffee from the Thermos. Then he opened the sliding door and sat down heavily on the retractable step. He made sure the well-kept interior of the camper van was visible: the seating upholstered in royal blue; the polished tabletop; the cupboard doors covered in photographs of the wife and kids. Obviously not his. But he knew their story as well as if they were his own.

His son, Alex, lived with him in Bodø. He'd just turned seven. This summer, Alex was spending a fortnight with his Aunt Lillian. Lillian was great with kids. She was a primary-school teacher.

'Where's his mum?' is what most people asked when they surveyed the pictures on the wall. 'Isn't she with you?'

He would respond with a big gulp, gripping the steering wheel even tighter. 'Cancer,' he would almost whisper. 'She ... Theresa died nine months ago. I've come on this trip to remember all our good times together. I'm trying to put the pain behind me so that I can be the best dad I can for Alex.'

Most people relaxed after that – their gazes would become sympathetic and caring, no matter how young they were.

Out of the corner of his eye, he saw the young woman on the bench stand up and lace up her rucksack. She seemed familiar in the same way that a stranger in a dream never did.

She glanced in his direction as she passed the camper van, making for the petrol station itself. Her dark eyes were uncertain and inquiring.

He knew it was a risk to pick someone up in a place like this. That was why he had parked in a spot where the petrol station attendants couldn't see him. Nevertheless, he was still at risk of being caught on camera by a random passer-by.

That said, he was always at risk of featuring in the background of some tourist's holiday snap. At first this had worried him, but with time his unease had dissipated. His girls weren't ever investigated. They were all written off as disappearances. Personal tragedies or someone who had left it all behind to start anew somewhere else. They weren't front-page material. At best, they might get a paragraph or two in the local news.

He stood up and pushed the step back into place. Then he shut the door and did a circuit of the vehicle to check that everything was as it should be, before crouching and inserting his hand into the wheel arch. He poked gravel out of the tyre tread, waiting.

'Excuse me?' She spoke in English marked by a distinctive accent. Dutch? Perhaps German? His money was on the former.

He turned around. 'Yes?'

'Are you going north?'

He nodded. 'I certainly am. Heading for Trondheim.'

She laughed. She was pretty in a slightly awkward way. Brown eyes. Black, shoulder-length hair. She was powerful-looking, although it was hard to tell whether she was fit or plump beneath the slightly oversized anorak.

'Are you going to Trondheim too?' he asked.

'Tromsø,' she said.

He nodded and looked pensive. 'I'm not in the habit of picking up hitchhikers...' He stood up, taking a little extra time to do so, supporting himself against the side of the camper van. He grimaced as he straightened his back. He had rehearsed every single gesture in front of the mirror until they were so natural that even he believed them. 'But I can always make an exception,' he added after a soft groan. 'It's not far to Trondheim and it'd be nice to have some company for a change.'

'Great! I'm Marijeke.'

'Jan,' he replied. 'Nice to meet you. You can put your bag in here.' He opened the door at the back where the two plastic containers were lashed to the bike rack.

Marijeke deposited her rucksack. Then she pulled a string shopping bag containing a paperback out of it. On the cover there was a woman in a summery yellow dress walking away along a beach while peering over her shoulder. Marijeke took off her anorak and stuffed it into the top of the rucksack. Underneath the jacket, she was wearing just a T-shirt. He noted that she was fit rather than plump. He liked them best when they were fit. It accentuated the muscles under the skin and the way that he was able to make them quiver uncontrollably.

'Next stop Trondheim,' he said.

She smiled. There was a narrow gap between her upper front teeth. He could feel the pressure building within him, as if his body wasn't big enough to accommodate his expectations.

He knew that soon he would burst at the seams.

CHAPTER 10

JAKOB

Jakob came to a halt outside 9D Nordlysbuen to find Noora already waiting for him in the shelter of the canopy over the main door. The midnight sun was shaded by the dense cloud cover, making the night seem like dusk. Noora's skin looked pale in the grey light.

Noora got into the passenger seat and stifled a yawn.

'Sleep badly?'

She nodded. 'It's the midnight sun – it's a real headfuck.'

Jakob spotted the red-wine stain on her lips but did not pass comment. 'Try a sleep mask,' he suggested. 'The kind they give you on the plane. My brother lives in Denmark and always has to use one for the first week whenever he comes to visit.'

Noora nodded. Then immediately changed the subject. 'What do we know so far?'

Jakob drove past the police station and carried on straight through the roundabout heading north. He switched the windscreen wipers onto automatic now that it was raining less. There was just a slight drizzle, which was leaving the dark asphalt even darker.

'The missing woman is called Iselin Hanssen and she's nineteen years old,' he said. 'She's a final-year student at Bodø Senior High and she lives with her dad, Bjørn Hanssen. Iselin's mother moved to Stjørdal nine years ago. She's remarried and has two other children.' Jakob noticed that Noora had pulled out her notebook but he couldn't make out a word of what she was jotting down.

'Shorthand,' Noora said, responding to his unaired question. 'I picked up the Melin system from a Swedish professor while I was at uni.'

'Impressive.'

'Nerdy,' she replied. 'But it's handy for a detective to be able to take notes as quickly as people talk. By the way, where are we going?'

'Maskinisten,' Jakob said. 'That's the name of the local hiking spot. I suppose you might call it the gateway to the Bodø wilderness.'

Jakob came to a halt behind a Mazda estate and took the opportunity to pull his own notebook out of his inside jacket pocket. He double-checked that he had recalled all the details of the case so far.

'Bjørn Hanssen reported his daughter missing at nine o'clock. They were supposed to have dinner at home at five. He said that his daughter runs the same route every Wednesday – the trail goes from their home up to Keiservarden and back again. Bjørn was worried that she'd had an accident – maybe fallen or hurt herself.'

The Mazda turned left. Jakob put his foot down and pressed ahead.

'Sounds reasonable,' Noora said.

'That's what the officer on duty thought too, so he alerted the joint rescue coordination centre, and they organised a search. The incident manager discovered that Iselin had posted details of her standard run on Facebook on a different occasion, so the search teams concentrated on that area. The first patrol hit the ground at half past eleven.'

'And?'

'No sign of her. Not on the trail itself or five metres either side. What's more, the rain has washed away most footprints.'

'Was she running alone?'

'Yes, as far as we know. They also ran a routine search for other information in our systems. It emerged that Iselin has just been summoned for her physicals at Police University College. Beyond that, we've got nothing on her.'

'At the police college? It's almost like she's one of our own.'

'Armann and Fine reacted the same way,' Jakob said. 'The Bodø Police visit all the senior high schools every year to talk to the students about training to be a police officer. We generally send someone from the department. Iselin has almost certainly been to one of those talks.'

'All the things we can't know...' Noora said aloud.

'You're not wrong.' Jakob drummed his fingers against the steering wheel. 'Fine and Armann are talking to the dad now. He's beside himself – blames himself for waiting so long to call us. He didn't know that she'd applied to the college. In Fine's view, he's telling the truth about not knowing what's happened to Iselin.'

Noora glanced up from her notebook. The fatigue that Jakob had previously seen writ across her face was now gone. She looked concentrated. On point. 'Does Iselin have form? Any friends of note?'

Jakob nodded. 'There's one or two that stand out. Iselin's been coupled up with Casper Jahrberg since the start of her second year at senior high. He's three years older than her. Casper's father is Otto Jahrberg, who is a bit of a big shot in Bodø. The family owned a significant chunk of the mining operations at Sulitjelma until the early seventies. Otto's heavily invested in fisheries these days – our very own multimillionaire captain of industry.'

'Will that pose any problems?'

'Will what?'

'Casper's dad being an official Bodø alpha male.'

'Don't think so,' Jakob said. But he felt less certain about that than he was letting on. The recent corruption case involving Bodø council had left a bitter aftertaste in the mouths of many detectives at the station, himself included.

'Any other friends of interest?' Noora asked, flipping back and forth in her notebook.

'Her best mate, Mona Straumsnes. The two of them have tonnes of pictures of each other on their Instagrams. Their friendship goes back to their final year of primary school.'

'Girls that age often confide in each other. We should have a chat with Mona about Iselin's relationship with Casper.'

'I thought the same thing,' Jakob said. And couldn't help

reflecting upon how different Noora was as a partner compared with the now-retired Rolf Kvist. Different, but in a good way. At least so far.

A woman of about sixty was waiting for them at the start of the NATO trail, which was a four-kilometre gravel track leading from Maskinisten, through the hiking area and up to the top of Keiservarden, and which the troops from the nearby airbase used for exercises. Jakob explained to Noora that the woman had contacted the police as soon as the news about the search operation had appeared on the website of the local newspaper *Avisa Nordland*. The woman claimed to have seen a girl she thought might be Iselin at Keiservarden. Even though it was the middle of the night, she had offered to meet the police.

Jakob stopped the car and opened the door. 'Gudrun Hemnes?'

The woman nodded, nervously rubbing her palms together. She wore a yellow anorak and matching trousers. Her grey hair was protruding from beneath a thin, blue knitted hat.

'Get in and we'll drive up. This is my colleague, Noora. We're both detectives with Bodø police.'

Gudrun got in and put on her seat belt. She glanced at Noora before her gaze turned to Jakob. 'Such a dreadful business with that young girl. What can possibly have happened? What if she's lying injured somewhere in the woods? Or worse...' Gudrun gazed expectantly at Jakob, but he concentrated on the winding track.

Noora took over, turning around in her seat. 'We appreciate you coming out to see us,' she said.

'You're a southerner?'

Jakob did his best to suppress a smile.

'That's right. I'm from Oslo.'

'Oslo, huh? My grandson lives there. Went to study medicine but found himself a girl. Now they're talking about buying a small-holding in Telemark. Going organic. I don't understand—'

'Iselin Hanssen,' Noora said, firmly but gently interrupting her. 'What can you tell us about her?'

'Sorry.'

In the rear-view mirror, Jakob saw the woman bite her lip as she looked down. She was presumably trying to gather her thoughts. The older generation were always nervous when they encountered the police.

'There's a group of us ladies who often go hiking together,' Gudrun said. 'Sometimes we take a dip as well. Lake Kretjønna is one of our favourite spots. It's easiest if I show you the place when we get there.'

Once they reached Keiservarden, Jakob parked behind a small log cabin. The rocky outcrop at the summit with a rotary viewpoint sign showing the distances to mountains and other locations in Nordland county was on a gravelly plateau above them.

Gudrun was the first to climb out of the car, clearly eager to be of assistance. She walked past the viewpoint sign, heading across the outcrop for the top of the other, sherpa-built, trail that was the most common route used by hikers.

Jakob stopped and turned when he realised that Noora wasn't following. She was still standing by the car, one arm resting on the edge of the open door, seemingly taken aback by the view.

He tried to see the landscape through her eyes. The way that the island of Landegode rose out of the sea, its bluish mountain surrounded by rain-laden clouds. Here and there rays of sunlight pierced the cloud cover, making the wet rocks sparkle. The play of light made Landegode seem simultaneously close and distant – like an otherworldly mirage that might vanish as soon as he blinked.

'You coming?'

Noora jumped, and Jakob got the impression that her thoughts had been directed at something completely separate from the landscape.

She closed the door and followed him. Ahead of them, Gudrun had already reached the bottom of the first downhill section.

CHAPTER 11

NOORA

The rain had relented and in the cool air the scent of trees and grass was almost overwhelming. The night-time light was also doing something to Noora – it was as if it were shining through her, obliterating the hangover and making the messages on her phone fade from her mind. She felt in better shape than she had in a long time.

Ahead of them, Gudrun was leading the way with a swing of the arms that told Noora the woman usually exercised with walking poles.

Gudrun came to a halt by a knoll overlooking a small lake located in a hollow in the terrain.

'About here,' she said.

'About here what?' Noora asked.

'The girl who looked like Iselin was standing about here.' Gudrun pointed. 'We – the ladies and I – were sitting on the other side of the lake.' Noora estimated the distance to the far shore to be upward of three hundred metres. At that distance, facial features were blurry, which made it difficult to discern both sex and age.

'And you're absolutely sure that it was Iselin?' said Noora. 'You were a fair distance from her.'

'Absolutely positive,' Gudrun said, folding her arms.

'Are those binoculars you've got around your neck?' said Noora.

Gudrun nodded, tugging down the zipper on her anorak and pulling out the field glasses, which were a contemporary Zeiss model. Noora had been expecting compact travel binoculars of the kind anyone could pick up cheaply, but these were completely different. She wasn't an expert, but she reckoned they must have cost a pretty penny.

'A gift from the grandkids for my sixtieth,' Gudrun said proudly.

'Do you mind if I try them?' Noora said.

Gudrun's gaze shifted to Jakob, as if seeking his approval first. 'Of course.' She pulled the strap over her head and handed the binoculars to Noora.

'Where were you sitting?' Noora said.

'On the bench you can see on the knoll on the other side.' Only now did Noora notice the picnic table that effectively merged into the grey rocks it was positioned on.

She focused the binoculars and then raised the lenses to her eyes.

The picnic table leapt out at her – crystal clear – and in the strong light the rest of the scene was clearly visible. Noora could even see the scrapes and knots in the timber. A New Energy chocolate-bar wrapper had been shoved into one of the cracks between the planks making up the tabletop; Noora recognised the yellow lettering. She now understood why Gudrun was certain that she had seen Iselin.

'Impressive quality.' Noora handed the binoculars back to Gudrun, who slung them around her neck and zipped her anorak up again.

'Did you notice anything else?' asked Jakob.

Gudrun shook her head. 'I don't think so. I waved to her, and the girl waved back – you know, the way people usually do when they run into each other on a hike.'

'Did you get your binoculars out when you spotted Iselin, or did you already have them out?' said Noora.

'I already had them out,' said Gudrun. 'There's a pair of ravens nesting in a tree close to the water. They return to the same spot every year. I've been watching them for the last three years. When Iselin disappeared out of sight, it was in the direction of the bird's nest. I know because both birds took off a few moments later.'

'Was there anything else you recall seeing?' said Noora. 'Before you saw Iselin?'

Gudrun pushed her hat up and scratched her ear. 'There are always a lot of hikers and joggers up here – especially on a fine day like yesterday.'

'Is that right?' Noora said, raising her eyebrows, hoping this would encourage Gudrun to elaborate.

'Yes, generally. Maybe two or three minutes before I saw Iselin, I noticed a figure in the woods over here. I remember it because the person was wearing a green sports jacket and a hood or cap with mosquito netting covering their face. You know, the kind anglers often wear if they stand still for a long time. The netting made it impossible to tell whether it was a man or a woman.' Gudrun pointed towards the spot. 'There's a small footpath over there. It's covered in roots that get slippery when it rains. Not a lot of people know about it. I've only gone along it a couple of times. I ... I'm sorry,' she stammered. 'I can't think of anything else.'

Jakob placed his palm gently on her shoulder. 'You've been a great help. Let's get you home so you can get some sleep. It's the middle of the night – you must be exhausted.'

Gudrun stifled a yawn. 'Well, now that you mention it.'

'Jakob?' Noora beckoned him to her.

'Yes?'

She waited until Gudrun was out of earshot. 'While you run Gudrun home, I'll follow the route we think Iselin took from here down to Maskinisten.'

'You're sure?' said Jakob. 'The search teams have already trudged up and down it several times without finding her.'

Noora nodded. 'I won't be looking for her. I want to form an overview of the area. If we accept that it was Iselin Gudrun saw through her binoculars, then something must have happened to her during the final third of her run.'

'I'm with you so far,' said Jakob.

'If Iselin has been the victim of a crime, that means she encountered the perpetrator around here. When I follow the route, I won't do it like Iselin would – I'll do it like the person who wanted to hurt her. That way I can form an understanding of how best to ambush her.' *I'm good at this kind of thing*, she almost added.

'Good idea,' said Jakob. 'Do it.'

CHAPTER 12

JAKOB

NRK's Sigrid Malmsten was waiting for them in the middle of the deserted car park. The reporter didn't have her cameraman or sound engineer with her, which Jakob thought was unusual. Like a conductor without an orchestra. He stopped and opened the window.

'Found her?' Sigrid asked.

'And a good morning to you too,' Jakob said. From her position in the passenger seat, Gudrun did her best not to seem too curious. It had the opposite effect.

'If Iselin doesn't show up soon then this is going to turn into a bloody media circus,' said Sigrid. 'That's my bet. You'll maintain an open channel of communication with me, won't you?'

'Did you walk here?' Jakob said.

'My car's a bit further down the road.'

'I saw her,' Gudrun blurted out.

'Iselin?' Sigrid said. She looked as if she'd caught scent of her quarry.

'Yes, up by Lake Kretjønna.'

'I'm not so sure that—' Jakob began.

'Have you asked her not to speak to the press?'

'Not directly.'

'Or indirectly, for that matter,' Gudrun said. Jakob was now in the crossfire in his own car.

'Where do you live?' Sigrid said. 'I'll drive you home – I'm sure Jakob's got more important things on his plate.'

'Get in!' Jakob said, more tersely than he'd intended.

Sigrid looked askance at him. She hadn't been expecting an invitation like that. Or was it his tone she was reacting to? He felt as if he'd blundered.

'Get in the back,' he said, in a conciliatory tone. 'Then you and

Gudrun can talk while I drive her home. Afterwards, the two of us can talk turkey.'

Gudrun lived in a residential neighbourhood above the Camp Bodin garrison, which housed soldiers working at the Norwegian Joint Headquarters at Reitan.

In the few minutes it took them to drive there, Sigrid had to make very little effort to get most of the facts out of a rather talkative Gudrun. Only the part about the other hiker or jogger – the one in green – was omitted, probably because it didn't occur to Gudrun to mention it.

'If you remember anything else just give me a call,' Sigrid said, handing a card to Gudrun as Jakob pulled over in front of a bungalow painted blue.

'Of course,' said Gudrun enthusiastically. Jakob felt like a taxi driver – invisible and unimportant. Gudrun's expression told him that for her, the press trumped the police. The woman no doubt sensed that she was on the brink of her fifteen minutes of local fame.

Jakob let her make it halfway out of the car before he took control. 'I'd be most grateful if you didn't discuss Iselin with anyone else right now,' he said amiably. 'At this stage of the investigation, it's still unclear what information we need to hold back from the public.'

Gudrun glanced at Sigrid before focusing on Jakob, her lips about to form the word 'But...'

Jakob lowered the pitch of his voice a notch, and spoke in a leisurely manner. 'Think of Iselin's parents. They'll do anything to get their daughter back. They'll be looking for the tiniest spark of hope. Surely you wouldn't want any details to emerge that might harm the investigation?'

Gudrun took off her hat and stood clutching it before Jakob as if he were a priest. Her grey hair was damp and lifeless against her scalp. 'Of ... of course not,' she stammered.

'Thank you. I knew we were on the same page. I'll be in touch.'

Sigrid took Gudrun's now-vacant seat in the front. 'Smooth,' she said, buckling her seat belt. 'Have you ever considered a career in the media?'

'Too much stress,' he said. Out of the corner of his eye, he was able to make out a twinkle in hers, creating a fine web of crow's feet around them. It made her face open up. Jakob reflected that this was Sigrid as she was in private, among friends.

He liked her smile.

Jakob stopped behind a blue-and-white Volkswagen with the NRK logo on the boot. The car was parked a few hundred metres from the Maskinisten car park. He turned to Sigrid. 'You're right, by the way,' he said.

'About what?'

'There's going to be an almighty circus if it turns out that there's more to this than Iselin meeting with an accident. But we can't rule out the possibility that she decided to take her own life. So I hope you won't publicise what Gudrun just told you, or at least not yet, no matter how innocent it may seem.'

Sigrid didn't reply. She was making use of the same approach he deployed during interrogations – allowing the silence to continue until the suspect filled the void with their own voice.

'You've got a big network in Bodø,' Jakob said. 'In some areas it's better than ours at the police. We can help each other. I promise to keep you in the loop and let you know before we release anything to the press.'

'And in return?'

'In return, you'll let me know if anything crosses your radar that might be significant to the case.'

Sigrid nodded. 'That's fair enough. But you won't be getting the names of any sources.'

'Nor would I expect to,' Jakob said.

'Good.' Sigrid opened the car door, but didn't get out. 'Jakob, I like you. But don't you go fucking with me. I expect you to keep your word.'

He was taken by surprise on both a personal and professional level. Sigrid had never spoken to him like that before. He also got the feeling that he had disappointed her somehow – and it threw him.

'I'm a man of my word,' he said, a little defensively.

'Good. I'd prefer to come to you first.'

'What do you mean by that?'

'You're the detective, Jakob. I'm sure you'll figure it out.' Sigrid smiled, but it wasn't the same smile as before. This smile was that of a professional journalist.

He stayed in the car until Sigrid drove past him on the way back to town. She waved to him as she passed.

I'd prefer to come to you first. Did Sigrid have another source in the police? If so, that would explain why she had been waiting for him when they'd come back down from Keiservarden. Who might it be? In addition to Noora and himself, Armann and Fine knew about Gudrun. But the initial call had gone through to the officer on duty, who had doubtless told others about it. Potentially a whole bunch of people.

Jakob let it go. Sigrid was just doing her job, and NRK was hardly a sensationalist online gossip site. There was nothing to worry about.

He parked up at the end of the NATO trail and checked his phone. Noora hadn't called. That meant she was still somewhere in the woods on her way down to the car park.

Where are you? he tapped out before hitting send. Then he waited.

The clear morning light sparkled in the rain-drenched crowns of the trees on the ridge above him, but it was cool and shaded where he was. He walked a short way along the gravel track, stamping his feet to stay warm. He buried his hands in his pockets, regretting not bringing a hat. It was nearly half past five. Had Garm woken up? He took the dog for a half-hour walk every morning. Then he made breakfast for the two of them before leaving for work.

'It's important that you establish some day-to-day routines,' Lise had insisted from her sick bed. 'So that you don't lose yourself.'

He hadn't listened to her. Not really. Listening meant giving up. Accepting what he hadn't wanted to imagine.

The mornings were worst. Coffee and one plate on a table that should have been laid for two. Increasingly, he'd taken to eating breakfast on his feet, standing at the counter with his back to the table. Denial or grief. Jakob thought it was much the same thing.

Another ten minutes passed and Noora still didn't reply. The area was so close to town that there weren't any gaps in phone coverage.

'Where the fuck are you, Noora?' he muttered. Had he misunderstood her? Were they supposed to meet at the summit? But wouldn't she have called?

He deviated away from the trail and into the trees. Ahead of him, animal tracks zig-zagged up the hillside. The whole area was a maze of small footpaths. If Iselin had chosen a different route to her usual one and hurt herself, she could be more or less anywhere. But then, surely, the helicopter's thermal imaging equipment would have found her? Jakob realised that he was thinking about Iselin but picturing Noora. She definitely ought to have reached the car park by now. Had something...

There was a rustle in the foliage nearby, the sound of branches against a jacket. Jakob spun around and his right hand sought out the spot on his belt where his service weapon was absent. He hadn't used the gun since his mandatory requalification exam at the range eight months earlier. Why hadn't he brought the hefty Mag-Lite torch with him from the car? It made a perfectly adequate blunt instrument.

A figure appeared from a thicket of crooked birch trees, her black hair in marked contrast to the white bark. She jumped when she caught sight of him, but her eyes didn't widen in surprise. Instead they narrowed and became calculating. This metamorphosis only lasted a moment.

What's she experienced in her past to make her react like that? he thought in the beat before Noora said: 'I've found something. Follow me.'

CHAPTER 13

PEDER

The sea fog enveloped the island of Røst like a shield, thick and obstinate. What little sunlight made it through the cloud cover was pale and sickly. Peder woke early and slipped quietly downstairs to avoid waking his mother. He boiled water and stirred instant coffee into his mug before sitting down at the kitchen table.

He wasn't partial to instant coffee – or regular coffee for that matter – but this was the kind his father had always taken with him when he went fishing. Nescafé *Gull*. Peder needed to add two sugars before he was able to drink it. There was always a tingling sensation across his brow afterwards.

From the kitchen table, he had a view of the driveway and the green mailbox hanging lopsidedly from a fence post. Beyond the fence, on the far side of the gravel road separating the two properties from each other, he could see the light above the front door of Simon Michalsen's house. In the fog, he could quite easily imagine that the house had been abandoned and that he and his mother now had this small corner of Røst all to themselves.

Should he go down to the hotel today? Peder couldn't make up his mind. Yesterday, Aslak had been on reception. Peder didn't like Aslak. He was always sarcastic. And he always delivered his scorn through faux compliments.

'What's the top speed on your moped then, Peder? Must be north of thirty kilometres an hour?'

'Did you get a haircut? Your mother sure is good with her hands.'

Whenever Peder went to pay for his coffee at the hotel, Aslak would always take a step backward as if he feared that Peder was suffering from an infectious disease. Peder had watched how Aslak treated the other patrons and knew that he never behaved like that with anyone else. On the contrary, he made small talk and laughed. He ran his hand across his greying three-day stubble. Rocked his head back and forth. Gave them attention. But not Peder.

Yesterday, it hadn't been Aslak's usual veiled hostility that he had committed to memory, but the way the guy had reacted when Peder had asked if Marte Moi had booked a room at the hotel. Aslak's gaze had wavered, as if Peder had caught him doing something unseemly. In the end, he'd told Peder that hotel staff weren't allowed to disclose information like that to strangers.

Strangers! He was hardly a stranger. Everyone on the island knew who he was. And no one knew Marte as well as he did. He knew that Marte went for a run every morning, and that she only used almond milk in her coffee, for environmental reasons. He knew this from her book and from the many interviews she gave. But he had kept his composure. Aslak would probably just poke fun at him. It was only when he'd left the hotel that Peder realised he hadn't paid for his coffee. That had never happened before. Aslak was usually very particular about that kind of thing – especially where Peder was concerned.

His thoughts still focused on the events of the previous day, he stirred the spoon in the mug. It made a hollow sound against the ceramic finish. His father used to sit here like this, staring out of the window until the first light of dawn signalled that it was time to head out to the fishing grounds. His father had left the house in all weathers, while Peder and his mother had still been asleep upstairs.

After Aslak's peculiar behaviour at the hotel, he'd gone over to the shop. Røst was a small community with a population of only slightly more than five hundred, and that was dwindling. If someone as famous as Nature Lady came to visit then everyone would be talking about it, and the shop was where people met.

He took one of the biggest shopping trolleys and rested his crutches across the top. He supported himself on the handle as he pushed the trolley up and down the aisles. Filled it with goods he had no intention of buying. Stood in the queue for the checkout, listening to the conversations of the other customers. Pretended that he'd remembered something just before it was his turn to place his items onto the conveyor belt, made his excuses and left the queue. Then he did another lap of the shop before once again joining the back of the queue.

Everyone knew who he was. The people ahead of him in the queue turned around and greeted him with brief nods. They didn't make any attempt to start a conversation and looked away again before he could say anything. Peder could feel the silence expanding. He heard the beeping of the barcode scanner. Heard the squeak of the trolley wheels. Heard the shuffling of soles against the floor. In the end, he'd ditched the full shopping trolley by the freezers and left.

He knew full well who was the source of this ostracism. People treated him like a leper because of that scumbag Simon Michalsen. Peder was sure that their neighbour was spreading lies about him. It had begun three years earlier, after Simon had asked whether he could widen the road that ran between their two houses.

It had seemed innocent enough at first. Simon had told Peder he was afraid the edge of the gravel track might give way when he drove his hefty camper van along it. He'd assured Peder he would cover all the costs. But he needed Peder's permission to expand the road half a metre onto the Skarvheims' property, because the slope on the other side, towards Simon's house, was too steep.

Peder had discussed it with his mother. 'What have the Michalsens ever done for us?' she'd asked. before answering her own question: 'Not a damn thing. They're not even from Røst, but they do whatever they like as if they've been here for generations.'

Mother was right. She generally was. The Michalsens had moved to Røst in the late nineties and bought the neighbouring house. They had paid good money for a fishing quota that old man

Michalsen had used for ten years before he'd had his stroke and the quota had passed on to Simon. Five years ago, Simon's mother had been moved into a retirement home. They'd said it was dementia. Peder reckoned she could probably have stayed at home if Simon had wanted it. What kind of son didn't take care of his own mother?

So Peder had turned down Simon's request to widen the road, and since then the man had been spreading untruths about him. He would honk his horn every time he drove past Peder's driveway. Sometimes it woke his mother and left her scared and confused.

Peder poured the remainder of his coffee down the drain. His head slumped forward and he supported himself against the counter. He always looked forward to these weeks in the spring and early summer when Simon left the island in his camper van, but this year it had been different. The longer Simon had been gone, the more Peder had dreaded his return. It was as if he had some illness coming on, something that made him restless. Irritable. On occasion, he even contradicted his mother.

He stood on the front steps and squinted towards the barn. In the fog, the building looked like a ship run aground. Peder's mother's father had kept cows. It had been a marginal enterprise – there was insufficient pasture to graze on and the grass was salty. It was possible to transport the cattle to one of the other islands that offered better prospects, but it was time-consuming and expensive if you didn't have a boat of your own. His grandfather had thrown in the towel after five seasons and sent the cattle to slaughter. But the barn had stayed. A monolith commemorating a failed project. At any rate, that was how his mother described it, and she continued to criticise her father even after he'd succumbed to a stroke at just fifty-three.

She could be scathing, could his mother. The men of the farm were weak. A husband who had vanished at sea. Her own father with his fragile heart.

'But not you, Peder,' she would whisper, staring at him with her sky-blue eyes. 'You're not like the others. You're special. You must never forget that.'

Peder walked across the yard towards the barn. He unlocked the padlock and pushed the drawbar aside. Once inside the barn, he stood still until his eyes had adjusted to the darkness.

The microcar was standing there, right in front of him. Behind it was an assortment of equipment from the cattle days: a trough, a couple of mouldy hay bales, fence posts and rolls of rusty barbed wire. Hanging across two of the rafters in the centre of the barn was a sea-green net, falling almost to the floor. It was swaying slightly in the draught from the open door, as if there were still fish caught in it after all these years.

CHAPTER 14

ARMANN

Armann opened the car door and sank into the driver's seat. He stared back up at the Ivanovas' living-room window. A pale strip of light was escaping through a crack in the heavy curtains.

He hated this part of the job – being the one who called on the next-of-kin to tell them what they most feared. The worst thing was when they realised what he was going to say before he said it. The way grief made their faces collapse, as if there were a tsunami inside them trying to get out. A tidal wave washing away all semblance of hope. Then they would bombard him with questions he couldn't answer, leaving him feeling helpless and useless.

Armann turned on the radio. He twiddled the dial until he found Radio Rock. The host, Stein Johnsen, was introducing the next song: Wonderworld's 'Ready to Die'. Armann tapped his right foot in time with the beat as he went over the brief conversation he'd just had with Natasha Ivanova, the mother of the late Galyna Ivanova.

At first, Natasha had refused to believe him. She had insisted her daughter was in Oslo, that she'd got a job at the Espresso House on Karl Johans gate. The last conversation between mother and daughter had been nine weeks ago, which fitted the time of death estimated by Ronald Janook.

It had been when Armann described the T-shirt that Galyna had been wearing that Natasha had broken down. He'd held her shaking body and asked where her son – Galyna's brother – was. Perhaps the kid hadn't dared to come out of his room. No surprise, if so. The small family had fled Mariupol only to find death in Bodø.

The decision to tell Natasha about her daughter had been made earlier that day, albeit with some reservations. Ronald Janook had wanted to wait, because he was no longer certain that it was a suicide. There was something about the wound – the tear – on Galyna's neck that necessitated closer examination. But word that a body had been found at Bremnes Fort had already begun to spread. Officially informing the Ivanovas meant they avoided speculation that the deceased might be Iselin.

A new song began to play on the radio, even though Armann hadn't noticed the last one ending. He sat up and took a couple of deep breaths. If he didn't get his skates on, he'd be late for his next appointment. It was yet more of the same. He could feel part of himself resisting, but he pulled out of the car park and set a course for Stordalen.

Fine was waiting for him on the driveway of a narrow, blue, three-storey detached house, each storey flush with the steeply sloping terrain to form a kind of building-block staircase. She passed him a cup of coffee from her Thermos. 'How did Galyna's mum take it?'

'As you'd expect,' he said, taking a sip. The coffee was strong, and it was delicious. Its acidity had dark undertones. Possibly Java.

Fine waited for a moment in case he had anything to add. Then said:

'I can take the lead while you observe Bjørn and intervene if you think there's an answer that requires elaboration or further inquiry.'

'Alrighty, pardner,' Armann said, without quite managing to nail his cowboy accent. Fine raised an eyebrow at him before making for the front door. Armann drained the coffee and tried not to think about Natasha.

'Have you found her?' Bjørn Hanssen looked as if he hadn't slept a wink that night, which was presumably true, Armann thought. His hair was tousled and his eyes were bloodshot.

'No, not yet, but we have all available teams out looking for her,' Fine said, touching his wrist.

'Quite. Quite.' Bjørn shifted his weight from one foot to the other and his hands were in constant movement. He ran his fingers through his hair, clawed his chin through the stubble and then scratched his belly.

'Can we...' Fine nodded towards the door.

'Of course.' Bjørn abruptly turned on his heel and led them inside and upstairs to the first floor. The Hanssens' home was decorated in bright pastels. Armann spotted two pictures of Iselin – in the downstairs hallway was a typical, staged smile portrait, while another on the stairs showed her and her father grilling sausages on a campfire. Behind them two fishing rods were leaning against a tree. Iselin was probably eleven or twelve in the picture.

Armann and Fine sat down at the kitchen table. Bjørn Hanssen lingered by the cooker, as if all his restless energy made it impossible for him to sit down. Fine began by informing him what the police and search teams had done so far. She then asked him to recount when he had last seen Iselin. Bjørn's reply correlated with the one he'd given to the police in his earlier statement.

Armann became aware of a sheet of paper fixed to the fridge with magnets. At first, he thought it was Iselin's college timetable, but then he realised that it was a handwritten table of some kind. He asked Bjørn about it.

'Those are Iselin's times for her circular route at Maskinisten. She took up running and she was hooked. I ... I encouraged her.' Bjørn gulped.

Armann stood up and took a closer look at the sheet. With the exception of Easter Week, times had been added to every single week until now, all of them showing a consistent improvement. Armann took a photo of the sheet with his phone.

'Is there anything missing from Iselin's room or the rest of the house?' Fine asked.

'Like what?'

'It could be anything. Her computer, for instance. Jewellery. Clothes. Maybe a backpack.'

'Do you think my daughter's run away from home?' Bjørn took a step towards them.

'We don't think anything,' Fine said. 'We're keeping all options open.'

'Iselin and I have no secrets from one another,' Bjørn said peevishly.

'Then you know that Iselin found out that she'd been invited to take the entrance exams for the Police University College the same day she went missing,' Armann said.

'I...' Bjørn looked confused. 'Is that true?'

'You didn't even know she'd applied?'

'No.' Bjørn ran the back of his hand across his eyes, shaking his head. 'I'll go through her stuff.'

'Good,' said Fine. 'Call Armann or me if there's anything you can't find. We already know that her phone is missing. We've asked her network to trace it.'

'There's one more thing we have to ask you,' Armann said. 'And I should tell you that this is standard procedure.'

Bjørn nodded and crossed his arms. He clearly knew what was coming next.

'Can you account for your movements at the time of Iselin's disappearance?'

Bjørn's face hardened before a tremble in his lower lip made him look down. 'I can't believe you'd ask...' he said, keeping his gaze on the floor to stop himself losing control. 'I was on a job in Vestbyen. I was working on a transformer with some guys from another company.' Bjørn jotted a name and phone number down on a scrap of paper. 'Call my foreman. He'll tell you.'

'Thank you.' Armann took the scrap of paper and slipped it into his pocket.

'We'll be in touch as soon as there are any developments,' Fine said, getting to her feet and heading towards the stairs with Armann at her heels.

Bjørn Hanssen didn't escort them to the front door – he stayed

where he was, standing in the middle of the kitchen, his expression
vacant.

CHAPTER 15

JAKOB

Jakob followed Noora up the hillside. He struggled to keep up with her – she was powering ahead of him with short, rapid steps. Jakob gritted his teeth, realising he wasn't in the best shape he'd ever been in. Garm's walks were never at this tempo. It was time to get fit – for both him and Garm. Time to ditch unhealthy food and Swedish meatballs.

'Not far now,' Noora said over her shoulder. 'I found it by chance when I went down what I hoped might be a shortcut to the car park.'

'Found what by chance?'

Noora stopped beside a mossy rock. 'This.' She waited until he caught up. Then she pointed at something at head height that Jakob couldn't see at first. But then he spotted it. It was a piece of mosquito netting hanging from a dry twig. No bigger than a matchbox. Set against the dark forest, the material was practically invisible. Jakob was impressed that Noora had found it at all.

'The stranger that Gudrun caught a glimpse of up near the summit was wearing a hat or a hood with mosquito netting attached to it,' he said.

Noora nodded. 'It's a squeeze between the trees here. I wouldn't have chosen this path if I had known how impassable it was.'

'So they either calculated that the chances of meeting someone here were slim, or they were as unfamiliar with the area as you.'

'My money's on the former,' Noora said.

'Because?'

'When Gudrun told us about where she'd seen the person in green, she mentioned they were on a path that very few people know about. That tells me they know the area very well.'

'It's still not certain that there's a connection. The netting on the twig may not have come from the person Gudrun saw.'

'Agreed. But we do know that Iselin was running in this direction yesterday afternoon. It wouldn't take much wind to blow a piece of fabric like that onto the ground. *Ergo*, the netting hasn't been here long.'

Noora had a point.

'Secure the netting and mark the location. I'm going to head down to the car and call Ronald Janook – he's head of forensics. They might be able to find footprints or other useful trace evidence deeper into the woods.'

A little after nine o'clock, Jakob, Noora, Armann and Fine assembled around the whiteboard in the main office. Armann had arrived a few minutes ahead of the other detectives and was now decanting freshly brewed coffee into mugs.

'We have to work from the assumption that this is no longer a search for a missing person and that a crime has taken place.' Jakob took the cap off a marker and wrote Iselin's name at the very top of the board, in the centre. Underneath her name, he noted the time: 15:43. He tapped the marker against the board. 'This is our last confirmed sighting of Iselin Hanssen. We know the exact time because Gudrun remembered that one of her hiking buddies called her granddaughter around the same time she was looking through her binoculars and spotted Iselin and the figure wearing mosquito netting.'

Fine borrowed Jakob's marker and wrote 14:52 above Iselin's name. 'This is the time Iselin logged out of the online system after she'd found out about her invitation to the police college. The time tallies with how long it would have taken her to change into her gear and run up to Keiservarden and on to the location where she was seen by Gudrun. It also tallies with the times she had noted herself. Armann took a picture of a sheet of the times on her fridge door.'

'That means,' said Noora, 'that we can say with a high degree of certainty that the woman Gudrun saw was Iselin. We've got her observation, the digital trail on the online portal and Iselin's regular route in the area.'

'What's more,' Armann interjected, 'we don't have any sightings of Iselin between Keiservarden and her house. Although, to be honest, that doesn't necessarily mean much. Nine in ten people have got their eyes glued to their phones and don't notice a damn thing going on around them.'

'Nonetheless, I suggest,' Jakob said, 'our working hypothesis is that Iselin never made it out of the woods and onto the gravel track.'

'An assumption that is bolstered by our piece of mosquito net,' Noora said.

'Agreed. That's the wild card. But unless we find Iselin's DNA on it, it's nothing more than circumstantial evidence of the fact that our mosquito-net wearer was following her.'

'And the chances of that are slim,' Noora added, 'unless it was Iselin herself who tore that scrap of it off.'

Jakob turned to Armann. 'What have we got on Iselin's nearest and dearest so far?'

Armann opened his notebook. 'There are three people in Iselin's life who are of particular interest. We've got her father, Bjørn; her boyfriend, Casper; and her best mate, Mona. There's one thing we can say for sure right off the bat: Bjørn Hanssen has an alibi for the time of the disappearance. I've just spoken to his foreman, and he confirmed that Bjørn was on a job for a customer in the Vestbyen industrial estate. He was repairing a transformer with a couple of guys from another company, who have also vouched for him. We've also found nothing to suggest that father and daughter had anything other than a good relationship.'

'But he *was* surprised when we told him that his daughter was going through the police college admissions process,' Fine interjected.

'I'd say he was pleasantly surprised,' Armann countered.

'My point is that she didn't tell her dad everything.'

'Daughters rarely do,' Noora said.

'Thank goodness.' Armann's quip made the others laugh.

'We need to make efficient use of today,' Jakob urged the team. 'I know it's a cliché, but that doesn't make it any less true: if we don't find the missing person in the first twenty-four hours then the probability of finding them at all decreases significantly.'

Jakob thought about the case file lying in his study at home. The Lofoten murder mystery. The woman with no name – about Iselin's age. The unknown family who had never found answers, who had never had any closure, allowing them to move on. He trusted his colleagues. Fine and Armann were experienced detectives, while Noora came highly recommended from Kripos. But he still felt he needed to make sure they understood the gravity of the situation.

'Last year, one hundred and twenty-one people were reported missing in the Nordland police district, while the nationwide figure was more than eighteen hundred. Most missing people are found, but far from all of them are. Some of them probably start new lives elsewhere, while others meet with accidents in the wilderness and are never found. We also have to assume that there's a cohort of missing persons who take their own lives in ways that make them difficult to find. Then there's the final category...'

Jakob looked around. Armann, Fine and Noora had heard this before. Nevertheless, he could tell from their faces that they found the subject just as unsettling as he did. Because the final category – murders masquerading as unsolved disappearances – was probably bigger than they cared to think about.

If you added up the number of unsolved disappearances over the last twenty years, homicide detectives couldn't be blamed for speculating that there were multiple serial killers on the loose in Norway. Predators lurking among the social-democratic flock.

But was there still any hope for Iselin? The thought had turned into a question against his own will. Accompanying it was a small voice in his head whispering: *You're already too late.*

Jakob ignored the doubts, or at least he tried to, but he knew the voice would only grow louder and more insistent. Triumphant. The best thing to do was to immerse himself in the investigation – to do something practical.

'While we are waiting to hear from the scene-of-crime officers, Noora and I will have a chat with Iselin's best friend, Mona. Fine and Armann, get in touch with Casper.'

'Are we bringing them in to the station?' Fine said.

Jakob gave this some thought. 'No, not to begin with. Before we do that, we need to determine whether Casper and Mona can account for their movements around the time of Iselin's disappearance. Did they notice anything specific or unusual about Iselin's behaviour in the days before her disappearance? We also need to find out if there was anyone else close to Iselin. Old boyfriends. Online contacts. Cast the net wide. Right now, too many names is better than too few.'

The door to Råkstad's office opened and the man himself appeared in the doorway. The Crow spent a second registering who was in the room before his gaze locked on to Jakob.

'Weber, have you got a minute?' Weber. It never boded well when Råkstad used his last name. 'Preferably right away.'

'Actually, sir, this isn't a great time,' Jakob said, keeping his voice calm. 'We're just on our way out to question two witnesses in the Iselin Hanssen case.'

'The Iselin Hanssen case, you say?' The Crow ran a hand over his head as if checking that his hair was still styled correctly. 'That's just what I was looking to speak to you about. You see, the chief of police rang me at seven o'clock this morning and asked me questions I didn't have answers to.' Råkstad said no more – he didn't need to. Jakob knew where he was going. He knew he should have called Råkstad and updated him as soon as he'd brought in Ronald Janook and the scene-of-crime officers. A miss on his part.

'You talk to Mona without me,' he said to Noora. 'Text me your location and I'll join you as soon as I can.'

CHAPTER 16

Marijeke wasn't the talkative type. That suited him down to the ground. She briefly described her trip to date, which had started with a coach from Amsterdam to Hamburg.

From there, she'd hitched to Gothenburg. She'd ended up spending more time in Gothenburg than she'd planned before making her way to Norway.

He wondered whether she had been in Gothenburg at the same time as him. They might have passed each other without knowing they would later meet. He liked the idea – as if this outcome were predestined. As he eyed her in profile, examining the straight nose and the locks of black hair that fell over her brown eyes, he had no doubt that it was indeed.

She got out her book. The yellowing pages told him it had been bought in a charity shop. Marijeke put the book in her lap and hunched over it. A furrow appeared in her otherwise smooth brow as she concentrated on reading. She looked focused as she turned over the pages at regular intervals. Still, he got the feeling that she wasn't actually reading. He also had the impression she was keeping an eye on him. She was on her guard. He didn't like that.

He pulled over in a layby just short of Støren, a town about an hour south of Trondheim. He apologised, citing back pain. Sometimes the muscles in his lower back would seize up.

Marijeke nodded before returning to her book. Just to be sure, he put his hands on his sides and stretched his back as he walked in front of the camper van on the way to the gents. He only dropped the charade once he was certain that Marijeke couldn't see him from the side window. He strolled past the toilets and went in among the trees.

What the hell was up with him? Why was he so jumpy? Did it

have something to do with the spot he'd picked her up from? Because someone might have noticed her leaving with him.

Or perhaps it was simply because it was too soon after the last one? Sometimes it was best to give himself enough time to digest his impressions. The euphoria and ecstasy. The waves of self-loathing and pity that always washed over him afterwards. It was a dance he knew all too well, a price he always had to pay.

One he paid willingly.

It had to be that way, he thought. He'd taken more time than usual on the last occasion. He'd crossed lines he'd only discovered along the way. But she had spurred him on. Her silent contempt had compelled him to use the knife in new ways. Cuts that had stripped her of dignity and resistance. He pictured it in his mind's eye: the moment when it had dawned on her she was going to die. The memory thrilled him; it made him hard.

He turned around. Marijeke hadn't got out. He filled his lungs with air scented by the trees and the boggy landscape beyond. Then he slapped himself – hard enough that it brought tears to his eyes and his left ear began to ring. Another slap. And yet another. He felt his head begin to swim. Then he felt relief.

Self-control! He couldn't let desire gain the upper hand. Not yet. Amateurs made mistakes, and he was no amateur. He knew exactly what he was doing. He prepared for each and every encounter down to the smallest details. He read the newspapers carefully afterwards. He kept track of where he'd been and whether his girls had turned up in the news. Only a few did – most simply vanished. Like the last one. That took planning, rather than the spontaneity he'd exhibited by the petrol station.

He leaned his forehead against the rough bark of a pine tree. Took a deep breath. Held it until his ribs began to ache. Calmly exhaled. He would let Marijeke go. She would continue her travels through Norway, oblivious to just how close she'd come to meeting her end. A silent gesture on his part. A personal sacrifice that would make the next one oh so much more satisfying.

The decision brought with it a calm of sorts. He'd made the right choice. But he was unable to shake his desire: the almost irresistible need to stroke Marijeke's dark hair. To look into her eyes. To tell her – without putting it into words – that he had made up his mind. His urges subsided, settling in his body like a rumbling bass note. He needed to get to Trondheim and drop her off before he lost control.

Marijeke looked over at him as he got back into the driver's seat, before directing her focus back to the book. He started the engine and pulled back onto the road. He wanted to put his foot down and cover the remaining drive to Trondheim as quickly as possible. It was a race against himself. But he observed the speed limit, usually driving a little under it. He glanced over at her. That face, unfamiliar and yet so familiar at the same time. The tanned arms and the shapely thighs. What had he been thinking? He couldn't let her go. Could he?

It felt as if a wedge had been hammered into his head, splitting his consciousness in two. He was arguing with and fighting himself. The opposing voices filled his head with noise.

He tried to concentrate on the road, doing his best to suppress the uninvited voices. But it was as if he'd lost his depth perception. He was unable to take in anything other than the stippled yellow line in the centre of the road, while the oncoming traffic was reduced to nothing but fleeting, grey shadows. The only thing he could really see was Marijeke.

He didn't register his own movement until his hand was lying on her thigh, firmly gripping those tight muscles. His fingertips pressing into her skin. He felt her recoil.

'What are you doing?'

He withdrew his arm. 'Sorry. I didn't mean to.' Did his voice sound normal? The noise that had filled his skull made it hard to be sure. His fingers tightened around the wheel, his knuckles glowing white against the black plastic. He had to pull himself together.

'Let me out. Now! Right away!'

'We're in the middle of nowhere. There's nothing here.'

'Let. Me. Out.'

Something stung his right side. He glanced down. Marijeke was pressing a sharp, matt-black knife against his shirt, and the white fabric was about to split.

'Pull over or I'll stab you.'

CHAPTER 17

ISELIN

She opened her eyes but she couldn't see. Someone had put glasses with black lenses and blinkers onto her face. There was a piece of material, woolly and putrid, stuffed in her mouth, forcing her to breathe through her nose. Her leggings were damp with moisture. Iselin writhed, and the rope around her waist cut into her belly.

A jolt of terror passed through her. She tried to raise her hand to clear her mouth, but her wrists were bound together and attached to the rope around her waist.

The fear changed in character, becoming a dark river coursing into her bloodstream and flowing throughout her body.

Her breathing became increasingly shallow, until the air passing through her nostrils barely reached her lungs before it was pushed out again. The darkness outside made its way into her head. Before long, it obliterated her consciousness.

You're hyperventilating. You're about to pass out.

She began to count silently, trying to control her pulse. She breathed in. Held her breath. Counted to ten. Exhaled calmly. She repeated the exercise. She noticed that the dark veil was beginning to lift away.

How had she ended up here? Iselin strained to remember. She'd been running down from the summit of Keiservarden into the valley and towards the NATO trail in Maskinisten. She'd been following a winding animal track with dense forest on either side. Something had made her stop. The sound of her name? Then she'd had the feeling that there was someone standing behind her. Before she'd been able to turn around, some kind of cloth or rag had been pressed against her nose and mouth. She remembered its pungent smell, the stench of chlorinated water.

The memory felt unreal – it was like a scene in a film. Part of her was simply waiting for her to wake up, but this was no nightmare. The rope cutting into her belly, the reek of the cloth in her mouth and the damp ground she was sitting on were all elements that a dream could not recreate. This was happening. To her. Right now.

But why? Who was doing this to her? The questions diverted her thoughts in a new and unwanted direction that threatened to bring back the panic and darkness.

'Here and now,' she whispered to herself. 'You've got to be in the here and now.'

She was in the open air, that much she was certain of. Her back was propped against a tree trunk, a pine perhaps. Above her, the treetops were rustling and Iselin could feel a faint breeze on her face; it gently brought small, chilly drops of rain. Through the smell of the rag in her mouth, she could also make out the scent of wet bark and grass. Then she heard a crow give a hoarse warning cry. She was probably still somewhere close to Keiservarden. Close to people.

She leaned forward. She was usually flexible enough to be able to bend over her thighs and reach her toes. Now she couldn't make it more than halfway. The rope around her waist had also been lashed around the tree trunk she was leaning against, but her feet were free. When she pulled in her stomach, there was a little slack in the rope.

Iselin breathed in and out deeply a couple of times before emptying her lungs completely, pulling in her stomach and pushing with her legs. The rough bark dug into her back.

She wiggled her upper body back and forth while pushing her legs against the ground. She managed to thrust her backside a little way up the trunk. She drew breath and felt the rope digging into the flesh just above her hips. Two more goes and she'd be on her feet. Then she'd be able to wriggle free from the rope.

Iselin exhaled. She imagined that she was doing leg presses; that her body was the weight. It needed to be pushed up the trunk.

She limbered up mentally. Then she tensed her legs, making the muscles tremble. The rope slid down over her left hip, but it was still stuck on the right-hand side.

Iselin had her back arched between the ground and the tree trunk. She could already feel the backs of her thighs beginning to cramp. Her lungs were stinging weirdly. She drew breath. Too quickly. Too greedily. The nauseating stench of the rag in her mouth made her gag. She swallowed and swallowed. If she threw up, she'd suffocate on her own vomit. She was so close. All it needed was one last push to get her upright.

'The first time I saw you, I knew you were a real warrior.'

The man who had spoken was standing very close to her. The unexpected voice made her knees buckle. She slid back down onto the ground, but he grabbed her by the armpits and pulled her back onto her feet. He freed the rope around her waist, but not the one around her wrists. The glasses also stayed on.

'You and I are going to take a little walk,' he said. There was something strange about his voice. It was distorted. Crackling.

'Let me go!' In her head, Iselin could hear her cry clearly, but she was unable to push the words through the rag. All she managed was an indistinct murmur.

The man put a cap on her head and pulled the peak down over her face. Behind her black glasses, the world grew even darker.

'We're not going far,' he said. 'You walk in front, and I'll guide you with my hand on your shoulder.'

Iselin shook her head. She refused to move, to do as he said. The cap slipped off her head. She heard him pick it up. She expected him to push it back down onto her head.

The blow came without warning, an open palm to the side of her head. The force of it threw her sideways and she hit the ground so hard that the rag was ejected from her mouth along with the air in her lungs.

'What do you want from me?' she panted.

'What I've been fantasising about for a long time,' he said, shoving the cloth back into her mouth. 'I've got one rule and it's a simple one,' he said. 'You do what I tell you to. This is your first and only warning. Do you understand?'

Iselin nodded. She felt her stomach clench. Not so much because of the threat, or the distorted, metallic voice – it was what lay behind the words, something the distortion couldn't quite hide. There was something familiar about the cadences of that voice.

CHAPTER 18

NOORA

'The Crow's been unusually moody for the last week or so, even by his standards,' Fine said.

Noora was standing in the car park outside the police station, together with Armann and Fine. The road beyond was busy. The roundabout by Rensåsen Park, as Noora had now discovered it was called, was surely one of the busiest junctions in Bodø.

'Perhaps Råkstad's having trouble on the home front?' Noora said. 'If so, he wouldn't be the first boss to bring a bad mood to the office with them.'

'The Crow's a bachelor,' Armann said. 'Lives alone in Breivika in one of the penthouses in Bodø Panorama. A four-bedroom bachelor pad. God knows how he affords it on a public sector salary.'

'Old money,' Fine said. 'Well, that's what the rumour mill says.'

Armann jotted something down in his notebook, tore out the page and handed it to Noora. 'Here's Mona's address and phone number. She lives in the Blocks over in Bodøsjøen. I spoke to her on the phone after we saw Iselin's dad. She's expecting to hear from the police.'

'The Blocks?'

Fine smiled. 'You'll understand when you see it.'

Noora waited until the Audi Armann and Fine had got into had reversed out of its space, then she got into the car in the space one over: a black Volkswagen estate. The plexiglass divider between the front seats and back seats and the gun safe in the passenger footwell made it clear that this car was part of the police's fleet. But on the outside, it looked no different to any other car on the road.

Noora entered Mona's address into Google Maps and clipped

her phone into the holder on the dashboard. She considered whether to call ahead, but decided to arrive unannounced. People's reaction when the police came to the door sometimes said a lot. Mona wasn't a suspect in the case, but she might know something about Iselin that she wanted to keep secret. 'Misguided loyalty' Noora's boss at Kripos had called behaviour like that. The witness wanted to help, but still withheld useful information because it had been shared with them in confidence.

The satnav took her south past a huge shopping mall with the name City Nord emblazoned above the main entrance. As she drove around the next roundabout, she noticed a circular building with a military propeller plane on a plinth in front of it. Noora guessed it was the Aviation Museum. What else could it be? She knew it was somewhere in Bodø.

Beyond the mall, the landscape quickly became more rural. A field extended from the road down towards the sea. The grass was a deep, lush green. At the foot of a wooded ridge there were rows of houses set in their own gardens that would have cost a small fortune if transplanted to Oslo. House prices in Bodø were pretty crazy too. Noora had decided to rent, anyway.

She passed the turn-off for the Bodøsjøen campsite and followed a gentle incline through a small valley with houses on either side. When she reached the top, the white school building loomed up. The glass-and-concrete structure looked new.

She drove on by a coppice of warped trees before more trees and some four-storey blocks of flats appeared on her right-hand side. It was a scattered collection of square blocks with round stairwells as appendages. The buildings were in marked contrast to the modern school she'd just passed. They were an echo from the eighties. The bus stop was even called the Blocks. She parked in the visitors' parking and Google led her to the correct block.

Mona and her mother lived on the top floor. Noora rang the bell and took a step back.

The lock clicked and the door was opened as far as the security chain would allow it to 'Yes?' In the crack, Noora saw a segment of a face. Green eyes. Black hair. Slightly accentuated lips.

'Mona Straumsnes?'

This received another subdued 'yes' in reply.

Noora produced her credentials. 'Noora Yun Sande. I'm here from the police about Iselin Hanssen's disappearance. Do you mind if we have a quick chat?'

Mona stood there for a couple of seconds, motionless. It was as if she needed extra time to interpret the question. Then she released the chain from the slide and opened the door.

'Come in.'

Noora followed her down a narrow hallway. Mona was wearing loose-fitting grey jogging bottoms and a matching top.

'Mum's a nurse at the hospital. She's on earlies this week,' Mona said flatly. 'It's just me at home.'

Mona didn't mention her father, and Noora knew no more about her than what Armann had told her. She would have to double-check back at the station. Perhaps Mona's father didn't live with them? There was no conspicuous menswear or shoes in the hallway.

Beyond the hall was a living room with a doorway leading onto a terrace with views of Saltfjorden. A container ship was making for Bodø, leaving a white streak in its wake. Beyond the ship, the Børvasstindan massif loomed large. The mountains weren't that high, but they dominated the horizon, nevertheless.

Noora could easily imagine that the world ended beyond those mountains and that she was on the margins of reality. In a place where anything could happen. The feeling took her by surprise. She didn't usually engage in flights of fancy. She preferred to stick to the facts. Things that were tangible, that could be weighed up and measured. That could be understood.

Or did she just wish she was that way?

She touched the pocket containing her personal phone. Only then did she realise that it wasn't there. She must have left it on the bedside table when Jakob had rung her up in the middle of the night. The discovery came as a relief, but at the same time fresh anxiety spread through her body. Had it been a mistake not to call him? Were there more messages waiting for her?

'You can just go outside if you like.' Mona was looking at her uncertainly. Presumably she was wondering what on earth this cop lady was staring at through the window.

Good God. She needed to pull herself together. She needed to straighten out her life and herself. Maybe it'd be best if she ditched the phone. She could take it down to the port and chuck it in the sea.

You'll never do it.

Noora feared the voice was right. But she wanted to prove to herself that it was mistaken.

She opened the door. A gust of cool air cleared her mind. The terrace was empty apart from a chair with a woollen rug on it in the corner. On the floor by the chair there was a spinning ashtray of the kind that prevented the ash from blowing away.

'Mum's smoking nook,' Mona said from the doorway.

Noora leaned against the railing. She located the ship and traced its course backward, catching sight of a bridge arching over a strait.

'What's the place over there?'

Mona smiled faintly. It was the first hint of emotion since she had opened the door. 'You're new here, right?'

'Yes, I am.'

'The bridge crosses the Saltstraumen strait. It's got one of the world's strongest tidal currents.' Noora heard a dash of pride in Mona's voice, not unlike that exhibited by Oslo natives when pointing towards the Holmenkollen ski jump or the opera house.

'But ships can go through the strait?'

'In the brief window when there's no ebb or flood, it's completely still and then you're fine to sail through.'

Noora knew all about Saltstraumen and where it was, but her

feigned ignorance had got Mona to relax. It had made the situation less dangerous and normalised it in her eyes.

'Why don't we go back inside for a chat?' she said.

Mona nodded.

A blue corner sofa was positioned around a polished black coffee table. The wall behind it was covered in wallpaper depicting a birch forest. White trunks emerged column-like from knee-high grass.

Noora and Mona sat down on either leg of the corner. Lying on the table was a copy of that day's *Avisa Nordland* opened to pages four and five. A huge picture of Nature Lady wearing her rucksack and hiking trousers with the port in the background took up most of the spread. The headline in red block capitals was probably intended to draw the mind to modern polar explorers like Ousland, Kristensen and Kagge, but it was more reminiscent of a feature about a reality TV Show: 'READY FOR THE NORTH!'

Beneath the picture, it said in cheerful blue type: 'How she stays on top form – a vegetable smoothie for breakfast and a 5k run every morning, no matter the weather!'

'There's nothing in it about...' Mona gulped. She pulled a tissue from the pocket of her jogging bottoms and wiped her eyes, which had filled with tears. '... Iselin. In the paper,' she said.

'We haven't gone public yet,' Noora said. 'And if anyone asks, we won't say anything except that we're treating it as a missing-person case.'

'But she is gone, isn't she? Actually gone.' Mona pulled her mobile out of her pocket. 'I've tried to call her so many times. I've sent her messages on Messenger. She's not answering my calls or texts.'

'When did you last see Iselin?'

'She stayed here the night before last. We binged the third season of *Jessica Jones* on Netflix. We had the house to ourselves. Made pizza. Curled up on the sofa in our pyjamas.'

'How was she?'

'Completely normal. The only thing that happened was that she dropped a slice of pizza on the sofa. Toppings down, obviously. Mum only bought the sofa a couple of months ago, so we were a bit worried, but Iselin knew how to get the grease off.'

Noora smiled slightly. She could imagine the two friends sitting there together – at the end of their adolescence. Not quite adults, no longer children. Aware that their lives would soon change. But not like this. Not with one of them simply disappearing.

Noora pulled out her notebook and turned to a blank page. 'You said you messaged Iselin on Messenger. When did you last get a reply from her?'

'Just after lunch yesterday.' Mona opened the app on her phone and handed it to Noora to read.

Mona: *Fancy meeting up?*

Iselin: *Going running first. Later?*

Mona: *Maybe I could come with you? Where are you going?*

Iselin: *Cool. Do it! Keiservarden. Loop from home.*

Mona: *Keiservarden! No way. Knackered just at the thought of it.*

Iselin: *Ha ha ha. You're as big a wimp as Casper. See you later?*

Mona: *Okay!*

The next message from Mona had been sent at 17:27: *Hey, where are we meeting up?*

That was followed by another message from her at 18:05: *?*

18:42: *What's up?*

19:51: *Your dad called. He can't reach you. Are you at Casper's? I know Bjørn doesn't like the two of you hanging out, but he's never called me before. He's worried.*

This was followed by a further six messages later that evening and during the night in which Mona had simply written *Please reply* and *Where are you?*

The tiny profile picture allowed Noora to see whether or not Iselin had read the messages. The final message that Iselin had seen was: *Okay!* She hadn't seen the subsequent messages sent by her friend, according to Messenger.

Noora handed the phone back to Mona. She knew the police would probably request call logs and details of all social-media activity in due course. But for now, she'd seen enough. Mona had shown trust in her by letting her look at the phone, and she didn't want to spoil that.

Noora leaned forward slightly and placed her hands on the table, her fingers laced together. 'I need your help.' She spoke calmly, lowering her voice by half an octave. 'Can you think of anything at all in the last few weeks that was out of the ordinary? Anything that Iselin might have said or done? Did she seem sad or worried? Was she fighting with her boyfriend?'

Her final question seemed to elicit a reaction from Mona. She blinked twice in close succession and her jaw tightened.

'Remind me, what's the name of her boyfriend? Karsten? No, it was...'

'Casper. His name's Casper.' Mona bit her lower lip. 'And they're not together anymore.'

'They're not?' Noora rested her chin on her knuckles and calmly contemplated Mona.

The analytical part of her – the police officer – observed the situation from the outside. The two of them were there on the sofa, not close together yet not far apart. It was the beginning of an intimacy of sorts.

At a seminar she'd gone to in her former role, led by one of the most experienced detectives in Oslo, the speaker had explained that the best way to get through to a witness and build up trust with them was to frame the conversation in a way that was recognisable. A chat between friends, for instance.

The detective's favourite example was when he had ostensibly bumped into a rather taciturn witness at a Vålerenga–Lillestrøm match. 'If Vålerenga had lost then I wouldn't have approached him, but that day they just so happened to win two-nil. On the way from the stadium to the pub, he told me more than he'd said in three previous interviews combined.'

Mona shifted uneasily. Eventually she spoke. 'Casper says they broke up a week ago.'

'Who ended it?'

'Casper,' Mona said. Then she added: 'It's not that they had fallen out or anything. There just wasn't anything there, if you get what I mean.' Mona gazed out of the living-room window. 'Iselin didn't say a word about the break-up to me. She's my best friend, but sometimes she can be really secretive. Like the time she went to Oslo for the weekend with a guy she'd met out on the town the day before. He must have been at least ten years older than her.'

This time Noora didn't have to feign interest or surprise. 'When did this happen?'

'Last winter. It was about a week after her nineteenth. She just took off. She didn't even tell Bjørn.'

'That's Iselin's dad?'

Mona nodded.

'And this guy ... Did you ever hear about him again?'

'No. Apparently it was completely off the cards. Iselin told me she never gave the bloke what he was expecting. Said that plane tickets and a hotel didn't guarantee sex. Apparently he got pretty sulky.'

Noora checked the calendar app on her phone. She recalled that Iselin's birthday was on 24 February.

'So this trip to Oslo must have been the first weekend of March?'

'Yeah, that's probably right.'

'Do you have any other examples?'

'No...' Mona hesitated. 'Some nights when we're out on the town together, she just disappears. When I ask her about it the next day, she always says she got a bit too drunk and headed home.'

'But you think it could be something else? You think Iselin might have been with someone else?'

'I don't know. It's possible.'

Noora was copying Mona's words down verbatim. Iselin's weekend getaway with a man who seemed to have been a complete stranger to her was in marked contrast to her impression of the girl so far. She needed to discuss this with Jakob as a matter of urgency.

Speaking of ... Where had he got to? Noora glanced down at her mobile lying on the coffee table. It was on silent, but she hadn't missed any calls or received any texts since her arrival at the flat. Apparently his meeting with the Crow was a protracted one.

'How would you describe the relationship between Iselin and her dad?'

'Bjørn's the nicest dad you could imagine,' Mona said without hesitation. 'When Iselin's mum skipped town with that new bloke, Bjørn worked overtime to make sure he could afford to keep the house. I've never heard Iselin say a bad word about him.'

'Never?'

'Nothing other than the usual. Didn't you ever complain about your folks?'

'Of course.' Noora flashed an affirmative smile at Mona. 'But you've also said that Iselin could be secretive. Is it possible that she hasn't told you everything about the break-up with Casper?'

Mona glanced down. 'Perhaps,' she said in a low voice.

CHAPTER 19

ARMANN

'It's kind of refreshing that they don't bother trying to hide how much they're raking it in.'

Armann stopped outside the driveway leading up to the Jahrberg family residence. Now that he had spoken to Natasha Ivanova and Bjørn Hanssen, he felt lighter-hearted.

He pushed open the wide wrought-iron gate. Beyond it, there was a flagstone path leading up to a white, three-storey house with a double garage the size of a three-bedroom flat.

All the windows to the front of the property were fitted with blinds, which made it impossible to see whether there was anyone standing inside, watching them. Armann rang the doorbell and took a step back.

He waited thirty seconds before ringing it again.

A young man with a dishevelled hairstyle reminiscent of Boris Johnson opened the door. He was wearing a short-sleeved, open-necked shirt over a pair of colourful boxer shorts and was barefoot. His chest was hairless in a way that was only possible to achieve with waxing or laser removal. There was a piece of kitchen paper sticking out of his left nostril.

'Yes?'

'Casper Jahrberg?'

'Who wants to know?'

Armann produced his credentials. 'My name is Armann Femris, and my partner here is Josefine Skog. We'd like a chat with you, if we may.'

'What about?' said Casper. He was probably trying to come across as tough, but his voice was a little too bright to really nail 'bad boy'. But he felt the need to try, Armann reflected. He presumably felt confident on home turf.

'Iselin Hanssen's been reported missing,' Fine said. 'You can either join us down at the station or talk to us here.'

'Who is it?' The shout came from upstairs. The voice was an octave lower than Casper's and had a hint of chain smoker about it. Otto Jahrberg. Armann had heard the voice enough times to be sure of it.

'It's for me!' Casper shouted back, before nodding over his shoulder towards a door on the right-hand side of the hallway and letting them in.

'What do you mean Iselin's missing?' Casper said as soon as the door to the room was closed.

'Exactly that,' Fine said. 'She went missing while out on a run yesterday afternoon.'

Casper stood completely still with his arms slack at his sides.

'When did you last see Iselin?' Armann said.

'The ... the night before yesterday. At hers.'

'How would you describe your relationship with her?'

Casper turned towards Armann. 'Relationship? How do you mean?'

'Bloody hell, lad. Are you slow or something? Is she your girlfriend?'

Was that a slight quiver he saw in Casper's lower lip? Was the rich man's son about to crumble?

'It was ... a bit on and off lately,' Casper stammered.

'And how about yesterday? Was it "on" or "off"?' Fine said.

Casper sat down on the chair by the desk. He drew breath before slowly exhaling again. He was presumably trying to gather his thoughts. Armann took the opportunity to survey the room. An autographed photo of the footballer Paul Pogba hung on the wall above the desk. Plastic figurines that Armann assumed were various gaming characters were positioned on a shelf by the window, all still in their original boxes. There was a TV mounted on the wall at the foot of the bed, and a PlayStation controller was lying on top of the covers. There were several empty Red Bull cans in the bin. Casper might be twenty-three, but his bedroom was that of a seventeen-year-old.

'We're back together now,' Casper said. 'Yesterday we were talking about moving to Oslo. Iselin's applied to Police University College.' Armann noticed the way that Casper placed emphasis on the last part.

'Could you describe what you've done over the last two days?'

'Describe? How do you mean?'

'Tell us what you did from when you woke up to when you went to bed.'

'My God. I don't keep a diary or anything, if that's what you think.'

'Try,' Fine said.

Casper ran a hand through his unruly fringe, then he began to speak. Armann saw Fine produce her notebook. He'd hit record on his mobile before he'd rung the doorbell. It wasn't really by the book, but it meant they wouldn't miss anything.

Casper provided an account of the day before Iselin disappeared. The two of them had met in the town centre early in the day. Gone to a bookshop. Drunk coffee down by the water. Boyfriend and girlfriend stuff. When Casper began to describe the next day, he became vaguer.

'I was mostly in bed after lunch. I couldn't even play on the PlayStation. Fucking headache.'

'What caused that?' Armann said. 'Did you hit the town after leaving Iselin's?'

'No, nothing like that. I only came off my electric scooter, didn't I?' Casper ran a finger across his nose to emphasise his point.

'So around the time Iselin went missing, you had an accident?' Fine sought out Casper's gaze and didn't let go of it. 'Is that right?'

'Well ... I couldn't have known she'd disappear then, could I?'

'Did anyone see you fall?'

'Don't know. It happened here – on the driveway.'

'You fell flat on your face on your own driveway?' Fine made no effort to disguise her disbelief.

'There are gaps between the bloody cobbles. You'd think my old man would be able to afford decent builders. He can be a fucking cheapskate sometimes. But I swear...' Casper trailed off. Armann saw that the young man was beginning to blush.

Fine pulled up a stool and sat down directly opposite Casper. She leaned in closer, seeking to create a more intimate atmosphere. 'I understand that you're upset. And we don't suspect you of anything. But we need your help if we're going to find Iselin. I expect the two of you must have had a lot of contact on social media. Can we take a look at your phone?'

If it hadn't been for the serious nature of their conversation, Armann would have found Casper's expression amusing. It was simultaneously accommodating and calculating, as if he wanted to help them but also wondered whether doing so was advisable.

Fine had clearly noticed the same thing, because she said: 'We're only interested in messages between you and Iselin. You can keep the rest to yourself.'

Casper turned his head. His mobile was lying on the desk behind him. Hesitantly, he picked it up and unlocked it with his finger before handing it to Fine. Fine didn't even have time to look at the display before the bedroom door opened, grazing Armann's shoulder.

'What the hell's going on in here?' Otto Jahrberg's figure filled the entire doorway. His mouth opened to fire another salvo when he clocked who was there – Fine had her police ID card hanging around her neck.

'What are ... Why are the police here?' he asked Casper.

'Iselin Hanssen, Casper's girlfriend, has been reported missing,' Armann said. 'This is just a routine visit.'

Otto glanced around the room as if suspecting that there might be a third police officer hiding in there somewhere. Then he caught sight of what Fine was holding.

'Is that my son's mobile?'

'Casper gave us permission—'

'Give it to me and get the hell out.'

'You do understand that Iselin has been reported missing?' Fine said.

'OUT!'

Fine handed the phone back to Casper, stood up from the stool and proffered her hand. Casper remained seated, but took her hand with a look of confusion.

'We'll be in touch.' Fine released his hand and elbowed her way past Otto Jahrberg. Armann followed suit.

'For Christ's sake, why didn't you say something?' Fine's outburst hit him as soon as he had shut the wrought-iron gate behind them.

'Sorry. I didn't mean for you to bear the brunt. But Otto Jahrberg's a big guy and not someone we want to provoke unnecessarily.'

'When did you start caring about that kind of thing?'

Armann didn't reply. Fine was entitled to be angry. In Casper's room, he hadn't given her the support she was expecting.

They drove away in a silence that lasted for several minutes.

'What's your impression of Casper?' he said at last.

'Not sure,' she said without looking at him. 'But I think he told us at least one lie.'

'Which is?'

'When I shook hands with him, his palm was soft and unblemished. If you fall off a scooter, you put your hands out to break your fall. Casper told us the accident happened outside the house. Well, the paving there was quite rough. It's very unlikely he got away without any scrapes on his hands after a fall like that.'

CHAPTER 20

JAKOB

Beneath the glow of the ceiling light, Råkstad looked harried, Jakob thought. His hair seemed colourless, the taut skin across his face a little grey, and there were nascent bags under his eyes. If he hadn't known better, Jakob would have guessed that the Crow had been on a bender the night before. But Råkstad didn't drink, and the way that he spoke did not indicate that his brain was marinated in yesterday's booze.

'You're held in high esteem in this building, Jakob,' Råkstad said as the electric blind fitted to the window overlooking the open-plan office lowered. 'I also know that the last year has been difficult for you.'

Råkstad fixed his gaze on Jakob's. There was something faintly unsettling about the way the police superintendent was looking at him. There was a kind of cool curiosity in it.

'You know just as well as I do that Josefine and Armann have been carrying you. While we've had no serious cases, I've looked the other way. Now, however...' The Crow glanced towards his screen. 'Iselin Hanssen's disappearance is going to receive significant media attention. The same goes for the Ukrainian girl if it turns out she didn't commit suicide. But for now let's concentrate on Iselin. A young, local girl with her whole life ahead of her. And to top it off, the girlfriend of the son of the richest man in town. Chief of Police Telle will quickly come under pressure if she can't deliver the goods. In order for me to protect the investigation team, I need you to provide ongoing updates.'

Jakob was puzzled. Apart from the gibe that he hadn't been up to his usual standards, he didn't disagree with any of what Råkstad said. Why had he insisted on a private conversation? Was there something else bothering Råkstad?

'I should have called you earlier,' Jakob said. 'I'll make sure you're kept in the loop. Was there anything else?'

Råkstad responded by pushing his chair away from the desk and stretching his feet out in front of him. He stared into space. 'What are your impressions of Yun Sande?'

'Noora's been with us for less than twenty-four hours. Settling in takes time, but my assessment so far is that she's going to be a good fit. She's already pitched in on the case. As you know, it was Noora who found the piece of mosquito netting in the woods below Keiservarden.'

Råkstad sat there for a few seconds and said nothing. Then: 'I had put someone else forward for her role, you know. In fact, I had no idea she was among the applicants until Telle informed me of her decision. Naturally it's her prerogative to choose, but it's unusual for me as unit head not to be consulted on appointments.'

'I didn't realise...' Jakob said. What Råkstad was telling him came as a surprise. Was Noora aware of all this? Perhaps the chief of police simply wanted a young detective with experience from Kripos rather than one of Råkstad's old chums?'

'For my own part, I would have been quite happy to let it rest there,' Råkstad said. 'But there's something about Yun Sande that I can't quite put my finger on.'

Jakob waited for him to continue, but it seemed that Råkstad had said all he was going to. 'Why are you telling me this?'

'No reason, except that the two of you are going to be working together,' Råkstad said.

Was Råkstad asking him to keep informal tabs on Noora? Jakob didn't ask the question because he could already hear the answer. Råkstad would shrug and say something along the lines of 'if you think that's for the best'. He would make it seem as if it had been Jakob who had come up with the suggestion.

'May I go?'

'By all means,' Råkstad said, directing his attention towards the monitor on his desk. It was as if the meeting had been no more than an opportunity to deliver an unimportant anecdote.

Jakob delayed texting Noora as he had promised he would – he needed a little time to himself to think over what Råkstad had said. That vague hint that something about Noora wasn't quite right – Jakob was annoyed that he couldn't let it go. And he felt increasingly certain that that had been *precisely* what the Crow had planned.

He drove home and picked up Garm. As soon as the door opened, the Jack Russell Terrier ran towards him, tail wagging and his mouth formed into what Jakob thought of as a smile. If only humans were as easy to read...

He took Garm out for an airing in Leif Jensons Plass Park. It wasn't much of a walk, but the park was right by the house. It was a narrow rectangle with benches positioned beneath green aspen trees. In one corner there was the playground that *Avisa Nordland* had described as hyper-modern. Jakob didn't have a clue what that was supposed to mean – perhaps it was a reference to the ground, which was covered in soft, EU-approved substrate.

Jakob sat down on one of the benches and looked around, noting that he had the park to himself before letting Garm off his lead.

Part of him bristled at the prospect of dedicating any time whatsoever to Råkstad's insinuations about Noora, but now that it was out in the open, he had to deal with it. Råkstad's concerns affected the whole section. He needed to understand what was behind the police superintendent's claim that there was something about Noora that he couldn't quite put his finger on.

Råkstad seemed surprised that Telle had set aside his own recommendation. That wasn't a strange reaction in itself. Everyone knew that Råkstad had a preferred candidate for the job – a former colleague who now worked in Narvik. The chief of police's choice of an up-and-coming young detective was not a bad once and was very much in line with the national commissioner's aims:

a young, second-generation Norwegian woman with 'cultural competencies', as they liked to put it at the National Police Directorate. But that wasn't enough on its own. Noora had to be good at her job too.

Jakob peered over his shoulder. Garm was intently focused on something in a bush over by the playground. He'd probably caught scent of a cat or other animal.

Now that Jakob tried to look at it from Råkstad's point of view, he noticed something that hadn't previously occurred to him: what prompted someone who had only worked at Kripos for a few years to apply for a standard police role instead? It was usually the other way around. Kripos was one of the most sought-after places to work in Norwegian law enforcement. And Noora was an Oslo native ... Why had she applied for a job in Bodø? Bad working conditions? Looking for a more hands-on role? Thirst for adventure? A break-up? Looking to rekindle friendships with her old mates from her college days in Lofoten? In fact, Jakob could think of a dozen good reasons why Noora had chosen to come to Bodø. Råkstad and his gut could fuck right off. He was going to assess Noora based on her performance. Besides, Råkstad's concern was trivial compared with Iselin Hanssen's disappearance.

He whistled to Garm, who reluctantly tore himself away from the bush and trotted over to him.

'I promise it'll be a longer walk tonight,' he told the dog, attaching the lead to his collar again.

Garm's gaze conveyed the sense that this was a promise he'd heard before.

Jakob was almost back at the house when the mobile in his pocket vibrated. He pulled it out, expecting to see Noora's name on the caller display, but it was Armann.

'Yes?'

'Fine and I just spoke to Casper. Things got pretty interesting.'

'What happened?'

Armann briefly recounted the interview.

'Sounds like their relationship was about to get more serious,' was Jakob's first comment after Armann had finished. 'The real question is whether Iselin saw it the same way.'

'That thought crossed my mind too,' Armann said. 'Their on-and-off thing reminds me of that Facebook relationship status: It's Complicated.'

'And then there was the business with the scooter. Are we able to track whether it was actually used as Casper says it was?'

'Afraid not. Casper's got his own electric scooter. Which means no GPS tracking.'

'Okay. Let's do a review when we all get back to the office. For the time being, we'll have to tiptoe around the Jahrbergs. I dare say Otto will already have been on the phone to that gobshite Sara Zeiler.'

Armann laughed briefly. 'I take it that you're calling her a gobshite because you're so politically correct that you don't want to use the word "bitch"?'

'That's right. But whatever you call her, she's also the best defence attorney north of the Arctic Circle. See you later.'

Only now did Jakob notice the pressure around his wrist. Garm was standing at the very end of his taut lead, halfway through the gate with his muzzle to the front door. Jakob had come to a halt on the pavement, engrossed in his call with Armann, and Garm couldn't fathom what his master was up to.

Jakob opened the front door and took Garm's lead off. Before leaving, he refreshed the dog's water and added extra food to his bowl. Once he was back in the car, he pulled out his phone and wrote: *Where are you?*

He received a response from Noora right away:

Still in Bodøsjøen. Among other things, Mona told me that Iselin went to Oslo with a random bloke earlier this year. Tell you more back at the office.

Jakob sat there clutching the mobile. Something Armann had said sprang to mind. He replied:

Stay where you are. There's something I want to follow up on. There soon.

Around ten minutes later, he parked up next to Noora's car. Locked to the cycle rack outside the block of flats Mona lived in was a brand-new electric bike. There was a sticker with the Nordland Hospital logo attached to the frame. Jakob rested his hand on the saddle. It was still warm. He climbed the stairs two at a time and rang the doorbell on the fourth floor.

CHAPTER 21

The tip of Marijeke's knife pricked his skin, sending shivers up towards his armpit and subduing the two competing voices in his head. The road ahead of the camper van wound its way through a series of gentle bends. There were no other vehicles. The landscape rolled by in an endlessly repeating pattern of farms and fields interspersed with patches of woodland and marshes.

He swallowed, doing his best to appear surprised. To convey a combination of fear and confusion. He glanced over at her.

'It ... it was a misunderstanding. I was trying to change gear.' His stammer was genuine. Marijeke's posture, the way she was talking to him, her grip on the knife – it all told him she meant business.

'You pinched me.' She increased the pressure on the knife. 'Pull over.'

He let out a faint whimper as the tip of the knife punctured his skin. The camper van veered towards the centre markings. A Volkswagen camper van coming in the opposite direction flashed its headlights insistently. The driver raised a fist as he passed.

'Watch the road!' Was that fear he could hear in her voice? Had Marijeke realised that she should have thought her plan through more carefully? She would be in control for as long as he did as she told him. But what if he didn't obey? What would she do then? Stab him and take control of the steering wheel? They were doing eighty kilometres an hour. A collision with any oncoming vehicle would kill them both.

Ahead of them was a slight bend to the right. He checked the wing mirror. No one behind him. He gently pushed the accelerator down, gradually picking up speed. The speedometer calmly ticked up from eighty to eighty-five kilometres an hour.

'What are you doing? Pull over.'

The road straightened out again. In front of him was a long stretch of road with scattered pine trees on either side. There were narrow forestry tracks zig-zagging between the trees. Trees were being felled, but there was no sign of any machinery.

He decided to switch things up, throw Marijeke off kilter.

'You know what bitches like you need to do,' he said in a low voice. 'You need to learn some respect. Learn to know your place in the world.'

'What ... what are you talking about?' Now it was Marijeke's turn to stutter. Nevertheless, the knife pressed even harder against him. He could feel warm blood running down towards his waistband.

On the long stretch of road ahead, another vehicle hove into view.

'You might not understand now. But tonight all will become clear. You'll see more clearly than you ever have before.' He pictured it in his mind's eye: Marijeke on the bench in the back. Naked. Strapped down. In his power. He grew hard as the fantasy continued to play in his mind's eye. The lust flooding through him made the pain caused by her knife part of the ecstasy.

'Stop the van.' Now there was nothing but fear in her voice. But she didn't withdraw the knife. They had each other in check.

The lorry was approaching. He scrutinised the other side of the road and an opportunity presented itself like a gift from a higher power. He turned the wheel and crossed the centre markings, pulling into the oncoming lane. He put his foot down and accelerated towards the lorry.

'No!' Marijeke leaned towards him and grabbed at the steering wheel.

He'd expected this reaction and rammed his elbow into her face. He heard it crunch into her nose. Her head snapped back. She put her hands to her face as blood streamed out of both nostrils. The knife fell into the footwell.

The lorry driver sounded his horn and slammed on his brakes.

The large vehicle veered slightly to the right. The driver wouldn't be able to stop in time.

Just before the two vehicles struck each other, he swerved the camper van abruptly to the left. Marijeke's head was flung against the side window. He saw the whites of the lorry driver's eyes as he passed within a few metres of the lorry's bumper and made it onto a narrow logging track. The unmade road made the camper skid back and forth, but he kept it under control, just managing to keep it out of a ditch.

Marijeke groaned and shook her head. Her face had left a bloody impression on the window. He didn't give her any time to gather her wits. Instead, he lashed out. His fist split her lip and broke her front teeth. One tooth cut into the back of his hand.

In the wing mirror, he saw that the lorry driver hadn't stopped. The trucker would remember the camper van, but the man would barely have seen either him or Marijeke through the tinted solar film on the windscreen.

The forest track swung around a low hill. Beyond it, he passed an overgrown mere, driving so close he could see small waves rippling across its surface. Here they could no longer be seen from the main road.

He slowed down and parked beside the grey-and-white roots of a pine tree. He opened the door, ran around to the passenger side, yanked the still-dazed Marijeke out of the seat by her hair and dragged her into the sparse forest. He ignored her screams and her uncoordinated pummelling of his arms. Only when the camper van was out of sight did he come to a halt, turning to punch her in the stomach. Marijeke buckled, falling to the ground.

He looked around. He spotted a fist-sized rock and grabbed it. There was no hesitation. He began to hammer the rock against her head. The first blow slid off her temple and broke her collarbone with a loud crack. Marijeke screamed in pain. He brought the rock down on her head again and again.

He sat next to the body with the crushed head until the fog clouding his own had lifted.

He stood up. He had to brace himself against a tree trunk when his legs threatened to give way. He stayed in that position until the world had levelled out. Ahead of him, surrounded by leafy saplings, he glimpsed a clearing. Still clutching the rock, he walked towards the opening and felt the ground begin to give beneath him. He smelled the stench of the bog.

In the clearing there was a small lake, the water a black eye gazing at the sky.

He threw the stone into it. He stood on the shore until the ripples in the dark surface had stopped.

The calm after the storm.

Marijeke would like it here.

Alone in the deeps.

Shrouded in dark tranquillity.

CHAPTER 22

JAKOB

It was Noora rather than Mona who opened the front door. 'Mona's mum, Siri-Else, has just got home from work,' she said in a low voice. 'She didn't seem thrilled to find the police in her home without any prior notification.'

Jakob nodded. He'd guessed as much from the sticker on the electric bike parked up outside the building. Mona was over eighteen and legally an adult. The police had done nothing wrong in contacting her directly, but he could see the situation from the mother's point of view too.

'So you're the boss are you?' Siri-Else Straumsnes was standing by the terrace door, clutching a pack of cigarettes and a lighter. She was what Jakob would have described as 'buxom'; thickset with powerful arms and legs. She had a body shaped by heavy lifting and traipsing up and down bare hospital corridors. Her hair was dirty blonde with streaks of grey, and her fringe was cut at an angle.

'Jakob Weber,' Jakob said, offering his hand. 'I'm Noora's colleague.'

'Weber?'

'It's an old family name from Hessen. In Germany,' Jakob said.

'So your grandfather came to Norway during the war?' Siri-Else's mouth tightened.

'My God, Mum!' Mona exclaimed.

Jakob withdrew his hand. 'My father met my mother when she was interrailing in West Germany in the mid-seventies. He came to visit her in Bodø the next summer. I was born a year later at Nordland Central Hospital, as it was called back in those days. They married not long after that.'

Jakob heard his own voice as if it were being generated outside of his body. The way he spoke about Manfred, as if he were a dad like any other...

Siri-Else opened the door onto the terrace. 'Time for a ciggie,' she said, as if the preceding exchange hadn't taken place. 'Do you smoke?'

'No,' Jakob said, but he followed her, signalling to Noora that she should stay behind.

Siri-Else sat down on a chair by the far wall while Jakob remained on his feet. He didn't have a choice. The chair Siri-Else had sat down on was the only one on the terrace.

He waited until she'd lit up and taken her first drag, then said: 'Iselin's disappearance is our top priority. We'd greatly appreciate any information that you and your daughter are able to provide.'

'You can't just talk to Mona without telling me,' Siri-Else said. She tilted her head back and exhaled a puff of smoke, which was caught by the wind and swirled away above her head.

Siri-Else seemed like a woman who didn't beat about the bush. He might as well speak plainly in reply.

'Legally speaking, Mona's an adult. We could have taken her down to the station without informing you beforehand.'

'The station! Surely you don't think that Mona...' Siri-Else left the sentence hanging in the air along with her cigarette smoke.

'No, we don't have any reason to believe that as things currently stand,' Jakob said.

'As things currently stand...?' Siri-Else stubbed out the half-smoked cigarette in the ashtray. 'What do you mean by that?'

'Nothing except that in the case of disappearances like this, there's often someone close to the missing person who knows something. And, not infrequently, that information will be something the person concerned doesn't consider important.'

Siri-Else stared at him defiantly. 'Who says any laws have been broken? Iselin's an independent girl. She might just have walked away. Put this shithole behind her. You know, she's done it before.'

'Her Oslo trip?'

'So you do know something then.' Siri-Else pulled a new cigarette out of the pack and let it hang unlit in the corner of her mouth.

'What's Mona told you about that impromptu weekend getaway?' Jakob said, taking out his notebook.

'Not a lot. Apparently Iselin and this bloke stayed at some fancy hotel in Oslo. And apparently she went to some party in the west end. Which was a bit weird.'

'Weird in what way?'

Siri-Else lit the cigarette. She took such a deep drag that the tobacco audibly crackled.

'No reason, except that Mona thought Iselin was talking about the party as if she'd had it described to her rather than having experienced it herself.'

Jakob noted and underlined the words <u>described to her</u> followed by a question mark.

Siri-Else yawned loudly and stretched her arms above her head, sprinkling her hair with ash from the cigarette without seeming to notice.

'What can you tell me about Casper Jahrberg?'

'Casper?' Siri-Else repeated. She had a good poker face, but the name of Otto Jahrberg's son had made her narrow her eyes.

'Yes, Casper.'

'He knows Iselin and Mona. They hang out together sometimes. Go to the cinema. The odd party. Nothing more than that.'

'Was he Iselin's boyfriend?'

'Just like his dad, Casper Jahrberg's first and greatest love is himself.' Siri-Else stuffed the butt of her cigarette into the ashtray. 'To be honest, I don't really know what the situation is between Iselin and Casper at the moment. You'd have to ask Mona.'

'How about—'

Siri-Else stood up. 'Look here Mr Weber, my night shift's left me dog-tired. It's Mona who knows Iselin and Casper. Not me. I'm sure she's told your colleague everything she knows.'

'Okay. We'll be in touch if we have any more questions.'

'I'm sure you will, but call ahead. Make an appointment like a normal person. Don't just show up at the door like the Jehovah's Witnesses.'

'Fierce lady,' Noora said once they were standing outside the block of flats.

'You can say that again. Shall we take a stroll before we head back to the station?' Jakob beckoned to Noora to follow him. 'I can update you on what Armann and Fine have found out.'

Below the blocks there was a footpath running between the buildings and the smooth rocks that were found in the area. It was surfaced with gravel and afforded spectacular views of the fjord and the mountains beyond.

Jakob briefly outlined to Noora the details of the visit to Casper, but he felt his thoughts begin to drift away. They had come here for Sunday walks – him, Lise and Garm. They'd walked from the campsite to the old abattoir and back again. He could picture the three of them. They were there – a transparent memory imposed over the real world.

'...based on what you've just told me, isn't that a little odd?'

Jakob turned to Noora. 'What is?'

She looked askance at him. 'That Mona and Siri-Else say one thing, while Casper and Iselin's dad say another.'

Jakob gathered his thoughts. 'You're referring to the fact that Mona claims Iselin and Casper weren't together, while Casper claims they were.'

'Yes, that's what I said.' Noora took a step towards him. Jakob expected her hand on his shoulder. A low-key 'is everything okay?' But it was still too early in their acquaintance for anything like that. She held back. Buried her hands in her pockets and walked past him along the path.

He caught up with her. 'Don't you find it odd that Iselin didn't tell Mona that she and Casper were back together?'

Noora shrugged. 'Yes, I guess it's a little odd, but it doesn't have to mean anything. Maybe Iselin had her doubts that it was serious this time. She might have wanted to wait to tell Mona until she was absolutely sure.'

'A credible explanation,' Jakob admitted.

'I'm more interested in Casper's swollen nose,' Noora said. 'And Iselin's weekend getaway to Oslo.'

'Yes, that trip shows us another side of Iselin. And the scooter story seems to be anything but believable.'

Noora stepped in front of Jakob, forcing him to stop. 'Was it the left nostril that Casper had kitchen paper stuffed into?'

'What if it was?'

Noora clenched her fist and threw a punch, stopping in mid-air a centimetre or two from Jakob's face.

'Right fist, left nostril. According to Bjørn Hanssen, his daughter is right-handed. But then again, that's the case for ninety per cent of the population. Still worth taking into account. Maybe an argument that spiralled out of control? Iselin hit Casper. He retaliated and Iselin fell. Hit her head on something hard? In despair, he hid her body. A tragic accident, but ultimately not unheard of.'

Jakob nodded. 'That's a possible theory. And Noora?'

'Yes?'

'Warn me next time you want to demonstrate a hypothesis.'

They walked back to the car park. Jakob stopped by his car and turned to face Noora. 'What does our ex-Kripos detective suggest we do next?' He said it with a smile that he hoped seemed disarming. He couldn't quite escape the fact that he was now running the Crow's errands. Surprising Noora to see how she reacted.

If Noora was surprised then she didn't show it. 'We definitely need to take a closer look at our trinity of Iselin, Casper and Mona. Especially Casper's and Mona's movements just before and after Iselin went missing. And we ought to check traffic cameras and CCTV footage from the ferries, the railway station and the airport. After all, it's not inconceivable that Iselin left town of her own volition. In connection with that, we need to find out who Iselin went to Oslo with. It might turn out it was just an impulsive act on her part, but it would be good to eliminate our unknown guy from the case.'

Jakob nodded. 'Agreed. That gives us plenty to be getting on with. Will you focus your efforts on Mr Oslo?'

Noora nodded in return.

'And Ronald Janook has promised us the results from the forensic examination of the area where you found the mosquito netting.'

'My God!' Noora put her palm to her forehead.

'What is it?' said Jakob.

'How could I forget?'

'Forget what?'

'Mona showed me her texts with Iselin. They were in contact right before Iselin went missing. In one message from Iselin to Mona it said: "You're as big a wimp as Casper."' Noora pulled out her notebook. 'That was how Iselin replied when Mona said she wouldn't come with her on the run.'

'Your take is that both Casper and Mona knew where Iselin was going yesterday afternoon?'

'Yes,' Noora said. 'Both of them knew she was going for a run, and they knew where.'

CHAPTER 23

NOORA

Noora spent the afternoon tracking down the man Iselin had supposedly gone to Oslo with. The fact that Mona had been so sure about when it had happened made her search easier. The time-consuming part was finding the right person to speak to at SAS, Norwegian and Flyr – the three airlines with direct flights from Bodø to Oslo.

The rigmarole with Norwegian took almost as long as it did with SAS, but she eventually got what she was looking for. A Norwegian customer-service agent confirmed that Iselin Hanssen had travelled to Oslo on the Friday afternoon of the first week in March. The tickets had been bought by a Stein-Jarle Lie, who had also travelled with her.

It transpired that Stein-Jarle Lie was Narvik born and bred, but had moved to Bodø at the age of twenty-two – eight years earlier. The National Population Register showed him as residing on his own at an address in Hunstad, just outside Bodø. Stein-Jarle's Tax Administration records revealed that he worked as an estate agent for a local company. His most recent tax return indicated that he knew a thing or two about pushing houses.

When she checked the STRASAK database, it told her another story. It featured two reports of violence filed by ex-girlfriends. Both cases had been dropped due to lack of evidence, the most recent just nine months ago.

The two reports were strikingly similar: at first, Stein-Jarle had seemed charming and caring. But over time, the girls – who were both younger than him – had been manipulated into unwanted sexual activity: strangulation, bondage and wearing tight-fitting chokers with rivets on the inside. They also claimed that Stein-Jarle had filmed them in the bedroom and later on used those videos as foreplay to get in the mood. When they had eventually refused to continue with the arrangement, he had threatened to post the videos online. In bed, he had become increasingly extreme. Yet both cases boiled down to the classic he-said/she-said.

After reading through the police reports, Noora was sure of one thing: Stein-Jarle would undoubtedly have crossed the line with more than just these two women. In cases like this, the reports were always the tip of the iceberg.

Noora briefed Jakob on her findings.

'Sounds like a first-rate scumbag,' was his immediate response.

'Seems that way. I'll look in on him before I call it a night.'

'Are you sure you want to go alone?' Jakob said. 'Fine and Armann are out interviewing people in Iselin's neighbourhood to see whether anyone matching Casper's or Mona's description was seen around the time Iselin went missing. And I've got a meeting with Råkstad and the chief of police in twenty minutes, but if you can hang on for an hour I can come with you.'

Noora shook her head. 'I'll be fine.'

Jakob hesitated. 'Okay. Call me as soon as you're done.'

It took her ten minutes to drive to Stein-Jarle's house in Galnåsen, a residential area just a few kilometres outside the town centre. Closest to the main road there were smaller terraced houses and semi-detacheds. Detached houses took over further up the hill. The best plots had incredible views of the Børvasstindan massif and Saltenfjorden, and, unsurprisingly, Stein-Jarle's house was one of them.

Noora drove past the house and parked a hundred metres further up the street. As far as she could tell, this was an older neighbourhood, but several of the houses had been refurbished. Stein-Jarle's, however, looked brand-new. It resembled some form of nouveau functionalism with its dark wood and pale concrete. The most eye-catching feature was the front façade with its floor-to-ceiling windows and huge oak front door with a knocker in the shape of a lion's head. The door looked like it had been pilfered from the set of *Game of Thrones*. There was a red Mercedes AMG on the driveway.

Noora didn't use the knocker, opting instead for the doorbell on the adjacent wall. She was about to press the button a second time when the door opened halfway and a young woman Noora guessed was in her early twenties poked her head out.

'Yes?'

The woman had pale, almost translucent skin and long, reddish hair. Her face was drawn, as if she hadn't slept for several nights.

Noora presented her police credentials. 'Is Stein-Jarle at home?'

The question made the corners of the woman's mouth twitch before she jerked her head backward. The door was left ajar. Noora took this to be an invitation and entered the hallway, which was bright and spacious. Hanging on one wall was a large picture of Stein-Jarle in a green hunting jacket against a backdrop of autumn colours. He had a shotgun over one shoulder. Probably taken on a grouse shoot, Noora thought to herself.

The woman was already climbing the stairs to the first floor. Only now did Noora notice that she was wearing pyjamas. The woman stopped on the penultimate step and spoke so quietly that Noora caught none of it except Stein-Jarle's name. There was the scrape of a chair, the opening and closing of some cupboards or drawers, and then the homeowner came into sight.

Stein-Jarle was tall, slim and bore the tan of a regular sunbed user. His white shirt hung loosely over his black suit trousers. The top two buttons were undone, and his blond fringe was combed to the right. Like the woman, he was barefoot.

Noora showed her ID again. 'I'd like to ask you some questions about Iselin Hanssen.'

Stein-Jarle stood still for several seconds before his lips formed into a smile. 'Iselin. Well, well, well. What's she been up to this time?'

Noora reached the top of the stairs. Stein-Jarle stood there until she was two steps away then moved back towards the leather sofa positioned in front of the panoramic window. The redhead was already sitting there with a glass of cola in front of her.

'Perhaps you'd like to discuss this in private?'

Stein-Jarle stroked the woman's head. 'Veronika and I don't have any secrets from one another, do we?'

Veronika didn't reply. She raised the glass mechanically to her lips and drank from it while staring out of the window.

'Okay.' Noora pulled out her notebook. 'Can you tell me your movements yesterday?'

'This is still about Iselin?'

'She's missing. I'm surprised you haven't heard. There's a big story in *Avisa Nordland*.'

'Who the fuck reads the local paper?'

'Can you tell me your movements yesterday?'

'I was at a sales meeting in Saltstraumen yesterday. It was an all-day seminar about the new homes in Solvoll.'

'Can anyone confirm that?'

'Well, yes and no.' Stein-Jarle scratched his forehead. 'I'd rather not have my clients being questioned by the police about me. Bad for business.'

'So it doesn't bother you that Iselin is missing?'

'I didn't know she was gone until you told me just now.'

Noora studied Stein-Jarle as he was speaking. He seemed confident. He was lingering slightly on his words, as if this conversation were a sales pitch. Noora decided to switch it up.

'You travelled to Oslo with Iselin in the first week of March. You spent two nights together at the Plaza there.'

Noora didn't see even a flicker of uncertainty on Stein-Jarle's face. He sat down on the sofa and put an arm around Veronika's shoulders. 'Beautiful memories,' he said. 'Although not as beautiful as this girl.'

He pulled Veronika in and kissed her on the ear. Veronika's face remained expressionless.

'Iselin was – how should I put this? – a little more reserved than Veronika. Dull. I guess that's the right word. She could have learned a thing or two from you, Veronika.'

Stein-Jarle stood up. He pushed his hips forward in a way that made it impossible for Noora not to notice the bulge in his trousers. The guy had managed to turn himself on with nothing but his own words.

Noora noticed that she was squeezing her pen so hard it hurt. She relaxed and turned to Veronika. 'Can you tell me your movements yesterday?'

'Here,' Veronika said without taking her eyes off the horizon.

'Do you remember what time Stein-Jarle got home?'

'Now you're just being rude,' Stein-Jarle interjected. 'You came here to talk to me, right?' He placed his hand on Veronika's shoulder as he was talking, making the pyjama top stretch.

Noora ignored him. 'Just answer the question, Veronika.'

'No.'

'No, you don't want to answer, or no, you don't remember?'

Stein-Jarle took his hand off Veronika's shoulder.

'The latter.'

'Are you alright?' said Noora.

Veronika turned towards her. In the light from the window, her face looked like porcelain: hard and lacking in expression. 'None of your business.'

'Veronika...' Noora was on the verge of telling her about the two domestic-abuse cases that had been dropped. But she knew that if she did she'd be crossing an ethical boundary and that it would be something Stein-Jarle could use against her.

'Are we done?' Stein-Jarle said impatiently.

'Not while you can't account for your movements yesterday.'

'My God. You're not only a bloody pig, you're a bitch too.'

'I can have a patrol car here in five minutes flat and we'll get you down to the station for questioning. We can hold you until tomorrow. Longer, perhaps. How does that sound?'

'Like you're bluffing. But by all means, make the call. But first you might like to have a chat with the reservations manager at the

Saltstraumen Hotel. He'll confirm I was there all day yesterday.'
Stein-Jarle extended his arm towards Veronika while looking at
Noora. 'So what's it to be?'

The question could have been posed to either of them.
Veronika let Stein-Jarle pull her off the sofa.

'We'll be in touch,' Noora said, heading for the stairs.

'I can't wait.' Stein-Jarle opened the first door on the right. In
the mirror on the reverse of the door, Noora saw a double bed
with a black duvet and sheets. Stein-Jarle winked at her and closed
the door behind himself and Veronika.

Noora was left alone in the living room. She pictured herself going
into the bedroom to retrieve Veronika. She hoped Stein-Jarle would
resist so that she could beat the living daylights out of him. Instead,
she went back to the table and picked up the glass. She sniffed it. Rum
and cola. More rum than cola. What would she find if she opened the
drawers in the table? Probably whatever it was she'd heard Stein-Jarle
putting away before she'd arrived in the living room. Most likely
cocaine or something that took the edge off the downer. But without
a warrant, anything she found would be worthless.

She was halfway down the stairs when the bedroom door
opened. Stein-Jarle, wearing only underpants and with his shirt
fully unbuttoned, stared down at her.

'I'd like to apologise.'

'You would?'

'I didn't mean to reject you – it's just you're too old for me.'
Stein-Jarle formed a V shape with his fingers before sticking his
tongue between them. 'Too shagged out. Too saggy.'

Noora stood there until the bedroom door closed again. She
tried not to picture Stein-Jarle's active body on top of Veronika's
passive one. It was futile. As she passed the red Mercedes on the
driveway, she dragged her car key along the paintwork all the way
from the passenger door to the rear spoiler.

The little shit could always call the cops if he wanted to file a
complaint.

CHAPTER 24

PEDER

Peder awoke suddenly to the sound of a metallic crash. He sat up in bed and listened. There was no repeat of the sound, and his mother's room remained silent. She had become a little hard of hearing with the passing of the years, but that had been quite a din.

He put his feet into his slippers, then took his dressing gown off the hook on the wall and put it on. He slowly went downstairs, each step creaking in harmony with his joints. He had a bad feeling in the pit of his stomach, not unlike the feeling when he had a tummy bug brewing. Peder feared this might be worse.

He didn't turn on the kitchen lights. He opened the curtains and sat down at the table. Outside, it was overcast; the clouds lay low and were heavy with rain. The night-time light was akin to late afternoon. He just caught sight of the red tail-lights on Simon Michalsen's camper van as it rolled into the garage.

Simon Michalsen, back already. Peder had hoped for at least another week before his neighbour returned home. But now here he was, turning up in the middle of the night and causing one hell of a racket.

The garage door closed, so Peder looked away and up the road. He immediately noticed that the fence post and its mailbox were lying on the ground. That explained the crashing sound. Simon had driven into the fence post and knocked it over. Again. It was a greeting: Hi! I'm back!

Peder's rage built up inside him, but it dissipated just as quickly. He put on a pair of trousers and a jacket, and tucked the torch into his side pocket. He closed the front door quietly so as not to wake his mother.

On the front step, he took a couple of deep breaths of fresh air.

In the quiet night, he could hear the screeching of the colony of black-legged kittiwakes down in the harbour. The sound of the gulls carried a long way when the rest of the island was asleep.

Peder crouched beside the toppled mailbox. The front was dented, the green paint now covered in streaks of blue. The same colour as Simon's camper van. This was something tangible that he could show to District Sheriff Thorsen.

Michalsen's kitchen window on the ground floor darkened. A minute later, the light came on in Simon's bedroom before being extinguished again. Peder waited a while longer before he set off towards the road, where his crutches made a soft crunching sound in the gravel.

The garage door was unlocked. Peder gripped the handle, and the door slid open easily on its well-oiled hinges. He stood there, listening. He could hear nothing except the cry of gulls and the ticking of the cooling engine.

He went inside the garage, pulled out his torch and examined the bumper on the front left-hand side. Peder found what he was looking for right away. There was peeling paint and a stripe of mailbox green caused by the collision. Even old Thorsen, Mr Non-Confrontational himself, wouldn't be able to avoid responding to this.

Peder did a lap of the vehicle and concluded that Simon was a careless driver. He found a scratch on the rear door and a fine scrape in the body by the rear left-hand wheel.

Finally he directed the beam of the torch through the window on the passenger side. The light reflected off the dashboard instruments – and a half-bottle of whisky. A *half-empty* half-bottle of whisky. Had Simon been drinking? Was that why he had collided with the mailbox? Peder could hardly believe his luck. Drunk driving meant being stripped of his licence. Not to mention a potential spell in prison of at least a few weeks. All he had to do was call the district sheriff. Perhaps lay it on a bit. He would tell Thorsen that Simon's vehicle had been skidding back and forth before it struck the mailbox. That Simon had then stumbled from the garage to the front door and ended up lying on the ground, shouting incoherently. If Thorsen still refused to investigate then Peder would call the cops in Bodø.

He'd tell them that it seemed like Thorsen had retired and forgotten to take off the uniform.

He swept the beam across the front seats of the camper van one more time and this time he noticed a book on the passenger seat. He recognised the cover. Could it be...?

He tried the door. It was unlocked. Simon was so lax. He opened the door, reached inside and flipped the book over.

My Journey by Nature Lady. As he'd suspected.

A hail of sparks explode inside his head. The nausea came flooding back to him. How could he and this bastard have anything in common?

Peder closed the van door then trudged out of the garage and stopped outside for a few seconds, leaning heavily on his crutches. Only halfway back to his own house did he realise that the garage door was still wide open. He forced himself to go back, looking up occasionally at Simon's bedroom window. It was dark and the blackout curtains were drawn. Simon would wake up quickly enough once the district sheriff put in an appearance.

Peder shut the door. He returned homeward for a second time while mentally rehearsing his call to Thorsen. Yet during that short walk, it was as if the courage drained out of him. He imagined Thorsen's dejected, doubtful voice on the phone and Simon's baleful gaze when he was confronted with the accusation. Was it really worth provoking Simon like that? There would be an almighty fuss and a lot of discomfort, and Peder had to think about his mother. His mother who would have described his doubts as *weak*.

CHAPTER 25

NOORA

Noora parked outside the police station and switched off the engine. She sat there in the dark car while the rain drummed against the roof. She felt drained. Her head was empty.

After she had left Stein-Jarle in Hunstad, she had called the reservations manager at the Saltstraumen Hotel. He had confirmed that Stein-Jarle Lie's company had booked and used the largest conference room on the premises from lunchtime until six o'clock on the day of Iselin's disappearance, but he hadn't been able to guarantee that Stein-Jarle had been present. Moreover, the delegates had been out on a site visit from two o'clock until around five o'clock.

The round trip from Saltstraumen to Bodø was only a fifty-minute drive. If Stein-Jarle hadn't joined the rest of the group for the viewing then he could have slipped off to Maskinisten, attacked Iselin and returned before five o'clock.

Noora wasn't sure what to think. Stein-Jarle appeared to be both manipulative and cocksure. Either because he had nothing to hide or because he was sure that he wouldn't be found out. If so, what was his motive? What had happened in Oslo between him and Iselin? Was this to do with her rejecting him? Was it about revenge or a wounded ego? Or was she merely indulging in wishful thinking, because it would be satisfying to see that bastard in handcuffs? Was it because Stein-Jarle reminded her of someone else?

After speaking to the reservations manager at the hotel, Noora looked up Veronika in STRASAK. She had just turned twenty and already had several drug offences on her record – all the charges were for minor possession and had resulted in fines.

Following her first arrest at the age of sixteen, the detective involved had followed up with child-welfare services and had uncovered a familiar, yet tragic, story: alcoholic mother, abusive father. Wild at school and a welfare system that hadn't intervened until it was too late. As she read on, she pictured Veronika, Stein-Jarle's arm around her shoulders. The sight of it in her mind's eye made Noora's stomach ache.

'Leave it till the morning,' she told herself, opening the door. A gust of wind peppered her face with cold rain. Noora looked up towards Keiservarden. The low mountain was shrouded in clouds, as if nature itself wanted to erase what had happened. She tugged her anorak zipper up and pulled the hood over her head. The walk through Rensås Park to Ellen's took just shy of ten minutes.

'Don't take offence, but you look done in.' Ellen handed Noora a glass of red wine while she was still in the hallway. Noora knew she ought to say no, but she accepted it anyway and knocked back half of it in one go.

Ellen topped her up and then beckoned Noora into the kitchen. She took a saucepan off the hob and removed the lid. The aroma of pasta carbonara spread through the kitchen.

Ellen served a portion into the dish in front of her and ground black pepper over it.

As she ate the lukewarm pasta, Noora told Ellen about her day. All of it except for her encounter with Stein-Jarle. The mere thought of what had happened in the house in Hunstad made her shudder.

'So what do you think has actually happened to Iselin?' Ellen said.

'Nothing good,' Noora said evasively. 'Telenor helped us to trace her mobile. She didn't take it with her on the run – it was on the shelf in the bathroom. Finding it there makes it less likely that Iselin left of her own accord.' She pointed towards the TV with her fork. 'Do you mind turning on the box?'

The familiar jingle for the seven o'clock news on NRK had

barely faded out before the female news anchor began to speak. 'Police in Bodø are investigating the disappearance of a young woman. Let's go live to our reporter Sigrid Malmsten, who is outside the town's police station.'

Noora recalled seeing the woman at the airport the day before, when Jakob had come to pick her up. Standing next to Sigrid on the steps of the police station was Konrad Råkstad.

'That's my boss,' she told Ellen.

'He looks out of sorts,' Ellen said, adding: 'It's as if he wishes he wasn't there.'

'It's a serious case,' Noora said automatically. 'People react in different ways.'

But Ellen was right. The Crow really did seem uncomfortable. The close-up on his face revealed how very jittery his gaze was.

'What can you tell us about the case so far?' Sigrid asked.

'We know for certain that Iselin Hanssen went out for a run yesterday afternoon just after two o'clock.' Råkstad's voice was formal in tone and lacked warmth. 'The final sighting of her was at 15:43 up by Keiservarden, which is an area popular with walkers and hikers in Bodø.' The screen split into two, and a photo of Iselin and a map of the area with the location of the last sighting marked on it appeared.

Sigrid nodded at the Crow then turned to the camera. 'The police are urging any members of the public who may have seen someone they think might be Iselin, or anything else unusual around this time, to contact them.'

Then it was back to the news anchors, who had been joined in the studio by the crime reporter.

'What's your assessment of this case so far?' said the female anchor.

'This early in an investigation, it's dangerous to speculate as to what may have happened,' the correspondent said, before going on to do just that. 'Sources tell me that there are similarities in this case to those of Birgitte Tengs and Tina Jørgensen. They were also young women who suddenly disappeared and were tragically later found murdered. As far as we know, it was at least twelve hours before the Bodø police began to take the disappearance seriously. Twelve hours is a long time in missing-persons cases.'

Noora picked up the remote and switched off the TV. She leaned back in her chair with a groan.

Ellen sipped her wine. Then she cleared her throat. 'Is it true that you didn't do anything until twelve hours later?'

Noora shook her head. 'Of course not. You know there were search teams and a helicopter out looking for her that very evening. My God, people get lost or injure themselves hiking practically every day in Norway. If anything, we reacted faster than normal. The public prosecutor said in a recent directive that we have a twenty-four-hour deadline to assess whether disappearances are connected to any crime.'

'The public doesn't care about directives from the public prosecutor,' said Ellen. 'The impression anyone watching the news will have got...'

'... is that we're a bunch of useless idiots who didn't take a young woman's disappearance seriously.'

Noora set down her half-empty glass. Tomorrow was going to be as hectic as today. She might as well turn in.

'Thanks for the dinner and drink.'

Ellen stood up. 'Look, I didn't mean to have a go at you.'

'Don't sweat it. A constant guilty conscience comes with the territory.'

'We're not being passive-aggressive, are we?'

Noora smiled. 'Well, maybe a little. But I mean it. It's fine. And it's really nice to come home to someone.'

'Speaking of people coming home.'

'Yes?'

'I might have a visitor later. You know...'

Noora patted her friend on the shoulder. 'Good for you.'

She went into the bedroom and closed the door behind her.

She saw the mobile lying on the bedside table, the green flashing LED signalling that she had one or more unread messages.

Earlier that day she had fantasised about throwing it into the sea. Now it was as if she were entranced by that green light. It made it impossible for her not to check the unread messages.

I might have a visitor later.

How long had it been since she had looked forward to what Ellen had planned for the evening without thinking of it as anything but some no-strings fun? The last year felt like a journey along a darkened corridor. A journey towards the light she hoped lay ahead of her. An escape from the darkness gathered behind her.

At the beginning of the relationship, she had felt drawn to this darkness. She'd only realised too late that she had confused love and desire with dominance and jealousy.

Now she knew better.

She opened the inbox on her phone to find two new messages. Both from him. Who else? He was the only one who had this number.

How dare you ignore me!?

I'll find you. No matter where you hide.

The words took Noora's breath away. She was unable to do more than inhale in shallow gasps. The panic erased every thought she had except one: he *would* track her down. One morning he would be standing there at the end of the bed, staring down at her.

CHAPTER 26

JAKOB

'I think you're onto something.' The voice on the phone was as rusty as old nails. Rolf Kvist. His old partner.

'How's it going?'

'Let me give you some advice,' Rolf said. 'Don't retire. It's a drag. Yesterday I was sitting in my TV chair and I thought, *Maybe I should do the place up a bit. Buy some flowers for the coffee table.*' Rolf laughed at his own anecdote. It was a rattling, dry laugh. 'That's really something, isn't it? I'm about as interested in flowers as those towelheads in Afghanistan are in cross-country skiing.'

Jakob resisted the temptation to interrupt. He and Rolf had been good colleagues, but they didn't see eye to eye on what it was acceptable to say. Rolf referred to it as 'north-Norwegian honesty'. In Jakob's view, there were boundaries that shouldn't be crossed.

'But you didn't ring me up to talk floristry...'

'Damn right I didn't. It's this cold case that interests me. And just let me say this: it's not easy finding a camper van based on a description that vague and with only one letter from the registration.'

Jakob waited. He knew Rolf well enough to see that he was building up to something.

'I contacted one of the old-timers at the Public Roads Administration. He was about as optimistic as me. Anyway, he agreed to look into it. I promised him a bottle of Lagavulin if he turned up anything of interest. The twelve-year-old. At your expense, naturally.'

'Naturally,' Jakob said. He guessed that Rolf still wasn't done.

'Your message also brought something back.'

'What was that?'

'Back in the day, the Lofoten murder was a real talking point at the station. I was working narcotics at the time, but I was good mates with Zachariassen – he was the lead detective back then. He died eight or nine years ago, by the way. Frontotemporal dementia. Bloody nasty stuff.'

Jakob nodded to himself. He knew who Zachariassen was, but hadn't known him as well as Rolf.

'One of Zachariassen's theories was that we were dealing with someone who had killed before.'

'A serial killer?'

'Spot on. I was at one of their meetings during the investigation. I heard Zachariassen lay out the case, describing the bestial way the poor woman was battered before being dumped in a shallow grave in a desolate spot. Zachariassen himself said the witness description of the camper van was woolly and virtually useless. But I'll give Zachariassen this – he kept trying to find out who the woman was until the end. Even when he got poorly and was beginning to lose his mind, the case continued to haunt him.'

Rolf was suddenly overcome by a fit of coughing. It was so powerful that Jakob had to hold the phone away from his ear. There was little to suggest that Rolf had stubbed out his habit since leaving the police. Jakob wondered whether he was still drinking as much too.

'I don't know whether this information is helpful, but I thought you might like to know about it.'

'Thanks,' said Jakob. 'I appreciate you following up on this. Things are pretty hectic right now.'

'The missing girl?'

'That's right.'

'Bloody awful.'

The silence lingered between them until Rolf said:

'You're welcome to pop in one of these days. I've got a fridge full of beer and no one to share it with.' Then Rolf hung up before Jakob could answer.

After the call, Jakob fried sausages and made mashed potatoes

– not straight from the pack but using some leftover potatoes from dinner the day before. He used half a tub of cream and a couple of teaspoons of real butter. He knew Lise would have shaken her head, but at least he had cooked dinner. He had maintained the routines that Lise had asked him to keep. Pretended everything was normal.

I've got a fridge full of beer and no one to share it with.

Was the job the only difference between Rolf and him? Two old men on their own in houses containing nothing but voids left by what had gone before.

He shared half the sausage with Garm and settled down on the sofa to watch TV. He caught the news at seven o'clock, but he switched off before the crime reporter let loose his speculations. It wasn't that the man didn't know what he was talking about, but Jakob thought he ought to know better. An investigation consisted of hundreds of moving parts. It was a complicated piece of clockwork that didn't always show the correct time. It was far easier to sit on the outside and criticise it.

'And here comes the melancholy.' Jakob was unsure whether he had thought that or said it aloud.

He pulled on his anorak and boots. He walked towards Langstranda with Garm on his lead, taking a road that followed the grey coastal rocks. He didn't shy away when the waves made landfall, throwing up a chilly spray of water droplets that struck him. Garm shook himself. He was evidently not happy with this spontaneous shower, so Jakob let him run free.

It was just before he got back to his block of flats that the speedboat passed him. The vessel was toiling through the choppy seas between the mainland and the island of Lille Hjartøya. Probably heading south. Perhaps all the way to Mosjøen. Jakob's thoughts returned to Rolf. There were many types of loneliness. Jakob realised how lucky he was to at least have his colleagues at work – and Garm.

As he waited for the kettle to boil, he remembered something that Rolf had said to him: 'someone who had killed before.'

Might the same be true of Iselin? Was that why she had simply vanished? Because the perpetrator was driven? A planner?

Jakob logged on to the database of missing persons. He limited his search to girls Iselin's age who had gone missing in the Bodø area over the last year. Stein-Jarle certainly fitted the profile he had in mind; when he'd called Noora earlier to ask about her interview with Stein-Jarle, she'd described the encounter with conspicuous reluctance.

Jakob got two hits, but both were tagged as 'probable suicide'. One was Galyna Ivanova, the Ukrainian girl who had been found in the old German cannon emplacement. The other was a local girl who had left behind a note. Ronald Janook still harboured doubts about whether Galyna had killed herself. That made her case more interesting, given Iselin's disappearance.

Jakob leaned back in his chair and stared at the screen, drifting into thought until the luminous display became blurry. The preliminary findings from the piece of mosquito netting that Noora had found had been negative. The netting had offered no fingerprints or other biological evidence. And the contents of Iselin's mobile had offered them very little either. But mobile data was also stored in the cloud. Gaining access to that data would be time-consuming, and time – just like clear evidence – was something of which they were in short supply.

It occurred to Jakob that Zachariassen's problem in the twenty-nine-year-old murder investigation had been the opposite of his own: Zachariassen had had a body but had never found a name. Jakob knew exactly who was missing, but couldn't find her.

Something else that Rolf had said on the phone rose to the surface of his consciousness. About how Zachariassen had never given up trying to find out who the unknown woman had been. But back in Zachariassen's day, the police hadn't had the same search capabilities they had now. At worst, case details from various cases were stored locally rather than in a shared database.

Jakob logged back on to the missing-persons database. This time he limited his search to the spring and summer months of the year in which the young woman's grave in Lofoten had been found.

Seven active hits. Four men and three women.

Jakob downloaded the pictures of the three still-missing women. He experienced a moment of weightlessness when the picture of the youngest of the trio appeared on his display. The girl in the photo was smiling in a way that made Jakob imagine that someone out of shot had just said something funny. She had brown eyes, lustrous black hair, a straight nose and an earring with a white stone in it.

Jakob shifted his gaze from the screen to the photo on the wall – the reconstructed portrait of the dead woman found in Lofoten. He found the same features in her face that he could see on the screen: black hair, brown eyes, straight nose. Similar, but not the same person. The difference was the height. The girl on the screen was five centimetres taller.

The two girls might have been sisters. Might Zachariassen's intuition be right? Did that mean that the woman in Lofoten wasn't the first victim?

Jakob took a print-out of the photo and pinned it up beside the Lofoten woman. He felt a tingle in his body – an eagerness to delve into what this might mean for the investigation. But he couldn't prioritise a case from almost three decades ago over Iselin Hanssen's disappearance. Rolf, however, had all the time in the world.

He found Rolf's number, but didn't have time to dial before the doorbell rang. This was promptly followed by Garm's bark.

Jakob went downstairs to the front door. Who could it be? Apart from kids selling magazines or Jehovah's Witnesses who insisted on trying to get him to see the light, he almost never received visitors.

Jakob pulled the door into the hallway shut before he opened the front door. Garm could be excitable when meeting new people.

The youth standing on the front step was perhaps fifteen or sixteen. He had dark-blond hair and a straight, slightly narrow nose. His green all-weather jacket seemed well worn and a size too large for him. His backpack was propped against the bottom step.

'Are you Jakob Weber?' The youth's voice wavered a little. Puberty or nerves, Jakob pondered. Perhaps both.

'That's right. Who are you?'

The young man raised his head and looked straight at Jakob for the first time. His gaze was intense: eyes deep blue and confrontational. Jakob recognised the gaze at once. He had seen it before – and learned to hate it. Not in this young man but in someone else.

'My name's Ola André Tollås. And ... you're my half-brother.'

CHAPTER 27

After a few hours in Bodø, he drove back to Fauske and headed north on the E6. In Bodø, he'd shopped for necessities in a hardware store and then headed for one of the town's best-known outdoor spots. He'd parked in the shade of a birch and eaten his lunch.

While it might be the shortest route, he never took the ferry from Bodø. It wasn't as if many people in town knew him, but all it would take was one of them spotting him and being able to place him at a specific location at a given time. A sighting like that could form the basis of a timeline.

He planned to cross Tysfjorden on the Bognes-Skarberget ferry. On his way there, he paid barely any attention to the magnificent landscape the camper van was winding its way through. The white-crested mountains. The waterfalls hurling themselves off cliffs, the wind catching the water droplets and spreading them like a fan of sparkling diamonds. He was driving on autopilot, but inside he was delirious.

Time and again, he saw himself raise the rock above her head. He felt the shockwave running up his arm from the blow that shattered her skull.

Lift. Smash.

Lift. Smash.

He couldn't escape this circle of thought. He feared these obsessive reflections would etch a pattern of their own onto his consciousness and weaken the cast-iron discipline he had spent a long time cultivating. Perhaps they would make him fickle, a victim to sudden whims and desires.

He knew he was better than that. Stronger. But it didn't feel like that now. He needed proof. An assurance that he could still control himself. That outburst of rage had been a departure from the norm.

North of Narvik, he pulled off the E6 and parked up some way
along an overgrown forest track. Far enough from the road that
his vehicle was out of sight, close enough to hear the drone of
HGVs driving past. He didn't sleep much that night, but he
became calmer. He found a way back to his old self.

Early the next morning he went down to the foreshore and
bathed in the Ofotfjorden, enjoying the feeling of the cold, in-
vigorating water. He lay on his back, bobbing in time with the
waves. He stared up into the pale sky and pictured himself from
above, floating over a dark void. On the edge of a black hole. He
would continue to hover – wouldn't fall into himself.

He boiled water on the primus stove and drank a cup of strong
black tea. Afterwards, he gave the back of the camper van another
once over with a brush and water. He washed away the small black
specks he thought were blood, but some of them came back again
when he blinked. Then he went at it again, pressing the bristles
against the floor.

Eventually, he tore himself away from the cleansing task. Only
then did he notice that the cuticles of his thumb and forefinger on
his right hand were bleeding. He'd scrubbed so hard he'd drawn
blood. He spent the final hour washing away his own blood.

She was standing at a bus stop a few kilometres west of Bjerkvik.
She extended her thumb as soon as she caught sight of his vehicle.
He checked the mirror. There was no one behind him.

Her name was Eva Stoltz and she was from Hamburg. Radiant
skin, black hair and a face with distinctive, Slavic features. He
wouldn't have described her as pretty, but there was something
about her. Something that recalled old photographs. A kind of
animalistic elegance.

Eva told him that she had taken the ferry from Kiel to Oslo and
then hitchhiked north from there. After a tour of Nordland, she
was now heading for the final leg of her trip: the North Cape.

Eva spoke English with only a hint of a German accent. He guessed that this wasn't her first backpacking adventure; she was experienced. She probably knew how to defend herself. Knew which signs to look out for. Did Eva already suspect that he posed a risk to her?

Stop! Wait!

He began to sweat. His palms left wet imprints on the steering wheel, making the rubber slick. He wasn't ready. Picking her up had been a mistake. At worst, he risked a repeat of what had happened the day before. He would drop her off once he reached Evenes. Then he would drive straight to Moskenes and catch the ferry across the fjord.

This ended here.

Shortly after passing between the small farmholdings in Dragvik, he slapped his forehead theatrically.

'Oh no!'

'What is it?' Eva asked.

'I forgot something in Narvik. I was supposed to pick up a package for a friend.'

He pulled into a layby that was partly obscured behind a small rise.

'If you're still here when I come back I'll pick you up again,' he lied.

He planned to wait at least two hours before he returned – that would be enough time for Eva to hitch a ride with someone else.

'No problem,' Eva said, opening the passenger door. 'But thanks for the lift, even if it was short.'

He shrugged apologetically. He attempted a smile that felt stiff and artificial on his lips. Eva stood outside the open door, expectant.

'My rucksack,' she said at last. 'It's in the back.'

'Of course.'

He switched off the engine, pulled out his key and walked around the vehicle. He unlocked the door into the rear space, and

Eva bent forward to grab her rucksack. His gaze fell on her toned legs. The way the light highlighted her bare, tanned skin from the edge of her shorts all the way down to her white socks. The back of her well-defined and exercised thigh muscles.

He struck the back of her head. The force of the blow threw her forward, making her land on the floor head first.

'What...?' she turned towards him. Dazed. She was bleeding from a cut to the forehead.

He propelled her head into the door frame. Her temple hit the thin, hard edge with a crack. Her legs gave way and she fell backward into the vehicle.

He picked up her legs and shoved the rest of her inside. He tugged off her shoes and shorts. Tore off her shirt. Her eyelids were quivering, but she didn't come to.

He opened the lid of the toolbox fixed to the wall between the cab and the lounge area. He pulled out the silver gaffer tape and taped Eva's ankles and wrists together. He ended up attaching three layers across her eyes so tightly that it pressed down her nose. A final strip across her mouth. He cut out a breathing hole. He climbed out and shut the door. Then locked it.

He made it back to the driver's seat before his legs began to tremble and his emotions overpowered him. God, what a rush! What a relief. He had acted on instinct.

In spite of his doubts, his body had known what to do.

Now the doubts were gone.

CHAPTER 28

NOORA

Noora awoke suddenly. She experienced a moment of confusion, but then remembered where she was. Outside the blackout curtains it was bright, which could mean anything. She turned over. The clock on her bedside table showed the time to be 01:21. She hadn't slept for more than two hours. What had woken her up?

She lay there, staring at the ceiling, trying to keep her mind off what she always ended up thinking about when she was lying awake. That he'd found her. That the postponement of the inevitable had reached its end. But right now, Stein-Jarle was also mixed up with those thoughts. She pictured him standing there at the top of the stairs. His tongue – pointed and moist – gliding in and out between his fingers.

There was a thud beyond the door. It had a hollow bass sound to it, as if someone or something had collided with a partition wall.

Noora propped herself up on her elbows and listened. She heard the shuffle of feet. The scraping of a table being moved. Something falling onto the floor.

She pulled on her joggers and opened the door. The ceiling light was off and the door to the living room was shut. Noora remained still. She could hear no more sounds of movement, but the silence was different. It was the kind of calm that was anything but. 'Active silence' was how one detective at Kripos had described it.

The runner on the floor was an IKEA oriental imitation, its material warming her bare feet. Her footsteps didn't make a sound. Noora bent down and peeked through the keyhole. The living room on the other side of the door was in semi-darkness.

The curtains were drawn and candles were lit. She put her ear to the hole and then heard something. There was a low moan or murmur.

Noora slowly pushed the door handle down, then inched the door open. She immediately saw an unfamiliar figure. A bare-chested man. Fit. More than 180 centimetres tall. Probably thirty kilos heavier than her. He was leaning over the sofa, both of his hands fastened around Ellen's neck. Ellen's head was resting against the armrest. She was naked, her face red. Her arms were limp over her stomach and chest. It was as if the scene had come straight from one of Noora's own nightmares. For a dizzying second, Noora pictured herself in Ellen's place.

He had found her!

The man turned his head slightly – he must have spotted a movement from the corner of his eye. Noora was wrenched back into her own body. She reacted instinctively, giving the man no opportunity to think. She surged forward and jumped at him, swinging her left foot in an arc in the air in front of her.

The inside of her right foot struck the left side of the man's head. He managed to utter a 'What...' before staggering sideways. He hit the kitchen wall. He slid across the sideboard containing Ellen's tablecloths, candlesticks and napkins.

Noora followed up with a kick to the back of the kneecaps. One of his legs buckled as he swung out an arm. He struck her cheek and lip open-handed. A clenched fist would have floored her.

Noora reeled backward, feeling the taste of blood in her mouth. She knew she had to launch another attack – keep the initiative. She was looking for something she could use as a weapon. She grabbed the brass candlestick lying on the floor.

'First and last chance!' she yelled, brandishing the brass club in the air in front of her. 'I'm a police officer. Lie the fuck down on the floor.'

'You're absolutely fucking insane!' the man shouted back at her. He clenched his fists and came for her. Noora lowered her head.

Bent her knees. Made herself small. She prepared to react quickly to the man's lunge.

An arm wrapped itself around her neck from behind.

'Noora, what the fuck?!'

Then she felt all of Ellen's weight on her back. Noora swayed, lost her balance and fell. She just avoided hitting her head on the edge of the dining table. She attempted to get to her feet, but Ellen was lying on top of her like a deadweight, her arm still around her neck.

'If I let go, do you promise to calm down?' Ellen whispered. Noora managed nothing but a grunt.

'I'll take that as a yes.' The grip on her neck loosened and Ellen's weight disappeared.

Noora sat up and let go of the candlestick. She touched her lip. It was swollen and she was bleeding. The skin was broken on the inside – it had been punctured by one of her canines.

'What the fuck were you playing at?' Ellen wrapped the sofa throw around her naked body.

Noora cleared her throat and swallowed a gob of blood.

'I heard noises so I came to investigate. I saw him bent over you,' she nodded towards the man, who was sitting on the floor massaging the knee she had kicked.

'I told you I was expecting a visitor.'

'He was strangling you.'

Ellen shook her head. 'I ... like it a bit rough, and Remi knows my boundaries. It's consensual play.'

The man – Remi – hobbled to the sofa and retrieved his jumper. 'Your friend is nuts. Completely *loco*.'

Ellen slapped him. It was so unexpected that the loud noise made Noora jump.

'Get out. Don't come back.'

Remi pulled on his jumper. His face was bright red and he had a half-smile that concealed either fury or humiliation. Probably both.

'Fuck me, you're both crazy.' He looked down at Noora. 'I should report you for assault and battery. I could tell the papers.'

'Good luck with that,' Ellen said bitterly. 'How are you going to spin that one? A man goes to visit two ladies. One of them has choke marks on her neck and the other has a split lip. Who do you think is going to be in deep shit after that?'

Remi shook his head. 'Fucking bitches.'

He went into the hallway and shortly after that the front door slammed shut. Ellen went into the kitchen. She returned with kitchen roll and a bag of frozen peas. Noora wiped the blood off her face and put the bag of peas to her lip to cool it.

'Sorry. I didn't mean...'

Ellen waved her arm dismissively. 'I get the misunderstanding. But your reaction...' Ellen stared into space. She was clearly trying to gather her thoughts. 'It was extreme. Didn't you hear me shout at you several times before I jumped onto your back?'

Noora shook her head. She'd been completely focused on Remi – in fight mode. But it hadn't been Remi she had seen in front of her.

Ellen sat down on the floor next to Noora. 'Is everything okay with you?'

'I ... You don't have to...' Noora could feel her eyes pricking. The first tear ran down her cheek, followed by several more. She told herself that she wasn't crying – this was a natural reaction to what had just happened.

Noora took a deep breath and felt the air rattle in her windpipe.

'My life's completely fucked up. I fell for the wrong guy. Fell so goddamn hard I didn't realise he was an asshole. A dangerous asshole, at that. And now he's looking for me. He acts like he owns me.'

'But you're here now. In Bodø.' Ellen stroked her hair.

'You don't understand,' said Noora. 'I joined in. I did things I didn't want to do. But I trusted him ... My God, I really fell for him. For a while he was my whole world.'

Ellen placed her hands on Noora's shoulders and held her steady. She scrutinised her face. 'You're talking about sex?'

'I...' Noora could feel herself cringing at the prospect of saying more. Nevertheless, she forced herself to continue. 'He would have described what you and Remi were doing just now as vanilla – just messing about. Looking back it seems insane when I think about what we did. I can't even bring myself to put it into words.'

'You didn't quit Kripos because you wanted to come to Bodø? Something happened that meant you had to leave?'

Noora looked down. 'He filmed us without my knowledge. There are recordings so horrible that...' Her voice faltered.

Ellen pulled her close.

She didn't ask any more questions.

She let Noora cry it out.

CHAPTER 29

JAKOB

Jakob opened the door to the guest room. He came to a halt in the doorway and examined the sleeping figure in the bed. He and Ola André had talked together until well past midnight. Admittedly, 'talked together' was an exaggeration. Jakob had asked the questions and Ola André, who had quickly insisted that Jakob just call him Ola, had answered. Mostly monosyllabically and with very short sentences. Along the way, Jakob had got the feeling that he was conducting an interrogation rather than a conversation with his half-brother.

That Ola actually was his half-brother was something Jakob did not doubt. After he had gone to bed, Jakob had found some old photos of his father. The resemblance between the young Manfred and Ola was almost uncanny. The National Population Register also confirmed that Yvonne Tollå had named the deceased Manfred Weber as the boy's father.

During their conversation, Ola had told him that neither the farmhouse nor the land around the farm were inherited by Yvonne, but by some relative he simply referred to as 'the miser'. This relative was the boy's only family in Beiarn.

'When did you find out about me?' Jakob had asked.

'Mum told me about you when she was admitted to hospital here in Bodø a month ago. She said she only met you once, a long time ago.'

Ola didn't ask why it had only been once, but the unspoken question had been pricking at Jakob's guilty conscience because of the reckoning he had never had with his father.

'What was wrong with Yvonne?'

'Mum had a bad immune system. She was on a lot of medication. Then all of a sudden she was super sick. The doctor said she died from an infection. That she'd got ses ... sepi.'

'Sepsis? Blood poisoning?'

Ola had nodded, and Jakob had seen that the boy was struggling to hold back tears. He didn't know whether to hug Ola and comfort him. Would he be embarrassed? Would he back off? In the end he had gone for a fleeting hand on the shoulder. An 'it'll be alright' that hadn't done anything except make Jakob feel inadequate and awkward.

Ola hadn't directly asked him, but it was clear that the boy hoped that he might be able to live with Jakob. Ola had applied to the electrical science and data technology programme at Bodø Senior High. Visible at the top of his bag was a powerful laptop covered in *Counter-Strike* stickers.

Jakob gently closed the door to the guest room and went into the kitchen. He didn't notice Garm until the dog pushed his muzzle against his leg. Jakob knelt and scratched the dog behind the ears. 'Sorry. That was all a bit much, wasn't it?'

He made a cup of coffee directly in his Thermos cup and took Garm outside. It was a fresh, cool morning with a northerly breeze. On mornings like this, you didn't have to go high into the mountains before you found frost on the heather.

He let Garm run free while he sipped his coffee. *What am I supposed to do about Ola?* wasn't really the question. Apart from his uncle, the boy had no family. The question was *how* to take care of him. What did he know about teenagers?

Good Lord, Iselin! Jakob checked his watch. He was already late for the morning briefing, where Iselin Hanssen was top of the agenda.

Jakob ran back to the house. Ola was still asleep, so Jakob scribbled a brief note explaining where he'd gone and asking if Ola could walk Garm later. At the bottom, he wrote his phone number and then he left the scrap of paper on the kitchen table. He was about to lock the front door when he realised that Ola had no keys. Jakob dug out Lise's keys from the drawer in his study and put them on top of the note, along with two hundred kroner in cash. He stood there for a moment, staring at the banknotes – was it too much or too little? Or perhaps he should have transferred the money to Ola's account?

'You're messing with me, right?' Jakob stared at the laptop screen a member of staff from the Bodø Police media section was holding in front of him.

'Nope, I'm afraid not,' said the man, who was called Åge, Jakob finally remembered. It was an old man's name for such a young face.

'But how can she do this?'

Åge stared at Jakob in confusion. 'Well, you're the detective. I'm just a communications adviser.'

Jakob shook his head. 'What I mean is, how can she share this information publicly?' Jakob could hear his own voice cracking. The stress that was digging its claws into him wasn't Åge's fault. Arriving half an hour late for the morning briefing hadn't helped either. The whole day had started off on the wrong foot.

Åge tapped the screen with the tip of his index finger, leaving behind a dirty fingerprint. 'It says here that she's been given permission by the family. Freedom of speech is protected – even during a police investigation.'

The door opened and Armann entered. 'There you are,' he exclaimed, before spotting Åge. 'Have you taken over press duties from the Crow? Probably just as well. He wasn't exactly exuding empathy on the news yesterday. About as much charisma as an anvil.'

'If only,' Jakob said. 'It turns out that Gudrun – the witness who saw Iselin up on Keiservarden – has decided to muscle in on our turf.'

'How do you mean?' Armann hung his leather jacket on a hook by the door and came towards them. Half of what Jakob knew to be a Motörhead tattoo was visible on his right upper arm, with the rest hidden beneath his black T-shirt. Armann examined the web page open on the laptop, which Åge had now put down by the coffee maker.

The name of the open Facebook group was: 'Have you seen Iselin?'. Gudrun Hemnes was listed as the administrator, along with two more women that Jakob assumed were fellow members of her hiking party. In the brief time since the group had been created, it had accrued more than two thousand members. A photo of Iselin in workout gear was being used as the cover image. She was standing on a path in the woods, and there was mud on her neon-orange compression socks. Iselin looked happy. The picture had already been liked more than five hundred times. The number of posts to the group had already reached 156.

'"We know that with each minute that Iselin remains missing, the likelihood of her being found alive decreases,"' Armann said, reading aloud from the group description. '"So if you've seen Iselin recently or have any leads on what might have happened to her, please get in touch. Of course we'll be sharing the most important tip-offs with the police."' He shook his head. '"The most important tip-off"? Are Gudrun and the pensioners' league going to filter the information they provide to us?'

Armann bent over the laptop and began to scroll down the page.

'The trolls have already put in an appearance,' he said, after skimming a number of posts. 'Several people are mentioned by name. There's even one user who's posted a photo of Casper with a target over his face.'

'Shit,' Jakob groaned. 'What are we going to do about this? If we ask Gudrun to shut down the group then the media will be all over us. They'll accuse us of preventing the public from helping.'

'What about having a word with Iselin's dad?' Armann said. 'I dare say Bjørn Hanssen will do whatever it takes to find his daughter, but he seemed like a sensible man when Fine and I spoke to him yesterday. Perhaps he'd listen to reason and ask Gudrun to shut it down.'

'Good idea,' said Jakob. 'Would you and Fine pay him a visit? If Bjørn contacts Gudrun then it'll be harder for her to say no.'

'Fine's at home with her little girl,' Armann said. 'Apparently Anna's showing symptoms of bronchitis and is running a fever north of thirty-nine degrees. I could hear she was worried when she called me.'

'Okay. Then take Noora with you,' said Jakob. 'Come back as soon as possible. I want to bring Casper in for a formal witness interview.'

Åge's mobile let out a loud cry, like a gull. The communications adviser checked the display before answering. 'Yes?'

While the person on the other end spoke, Åge switched to speakerphone so that Jakob and Armann, who had stopped in the doorway, could listen in.

'...the same route I take every day,' said a coarse, slightly husky, male voice. 'Up the NATO trail until Kloppy's done his business. I take him off the lead once we're past the barrier. He's an obedient mutt, never runs off. But today he caught the scent of something because he went off into the undergrowth to the left of the track. He didn't come back when I called him.'

Jakob leaned in towards the phone. 'This is Detective Jakob Weber. Your conversation is on speakerphone. Who am I talking to?'

The man hesitated and Jakob was afraid he might hang up. The display on Åge's phone said 'Unknown Caller'. The guys in IT would doubtless be able to trace the man, but that took time and needed an official sign-off, all of which meant paperwork.

'Tarik Aydin,' the man said at last. Jakob exchanged glances with Armann, who nodded to confirm that he was thinking the same thing. Tarik Aydin. The proprietor of Kebab King, the north-Norwegian chain of fast-food outlets. And Bodø's seventh-richest man.

'What was it that your dog caught the scent of, Aydin?'

Once again there was hesitation before Aydin spoke. Jakob felt his chest tightening. 'As soon as I realised what he'd found, I called you lot,' Aydin concluded.

'Have you or ... er, Kloppy, been into the woods?'

'No. I haven't left the road.'

'Good. Stay there. Don't call anyone else. We'll be there in ten minutes.'

Åge ended the call.

'What about Iselin's dad and the Facebook group?' Armann asked.

'That'll have to keep. This is urgent. Can you inform Råkstad and then get hold of Noora? She ought to be here already.'

Armann gave a scout's half-salute with three fingers to his forehead before exiting.

You and Noora both late for work, Fine at home with a sick kid. Råkstad's going to think the section is falling apart.

Jakob turned to Åge. 'Until we can do something about this Facebook group, I want you to monitor all posts and comments. Copy anything you think may be of interest to the investigation.'

'Like I said, you're the...'

'...detective. I know, Åge. But you'll go far with a bit of common sense and a cup of coffee or two.'

'I prefer tea.'

CHAPTER 30

STEIN-JARLE LIE

Stein-Jarle was skimming the local newspaper headlines on his iPad with an incipient feeling of discomfort in his stomach. The visit from the policewoman had thrown him. He didn't think she'd noticed his unease, but he couldn't be sure. There had been something about the way she had looked at him. As if she knew...

That fucking bitch.

The trip to Oslo with Iselin had been a calculated risk. He always went alone to Sultana, the exclusive gentleman's club in Oslo. But on his last visit, one of the people in charge had pulled him aside and told him that next time it was his turn to bring someone along. Iselin was perfect. Young and inexperienced, even if she did her best to come across as worldly-wise. She was just the kind of girl the other members of Sultana would appreciate.

They had drunk wine on the flight to Oslo. In the suite at the Radisson, they popped a bottle of champagne that he'd brought up from the restaurant. While she was in the bathroom, he mixed some GHB – liquid ecstasy – into her glass.

He'd managed to get her into the cab before the GHB made itself felt. By the time they reached the secluded mansion in Holmenkollen, Iselin was conscious but passive. Her gaze was listless and remote, but she still managed to walk by herself.

Iselin and another redhead had been the highlight of the evening. They'd been kept in separate rooms, while the members – nine of them had been invited that evening – enjoyed drinks from the lounge bar. The members all wore identical, black-velvet masks that covered their noses and eyes. The lenses over the eyeholes in the masks caught the light in the room and made their eyes glow. The first time Stein-Jarle had been to Sultana, he'd thought every single person there burned with an inner fire.

He'd ordered a gin and tonic at the bar. He knew that both of the women mixing drinks – an Asian and an African – were available in return for payment. It was also one of the few things about the club that repulsed him. He never paid for sex, and for a place like Sultana to even offer something like that seemed shabby. This impression was partly made up for by the fact that there was a one-way mirror looking into the bedroom behind the bar, which allowed the members to follow each other's indulgences. That was also how he had noticed the other man.

It had been when the African's thigh momentarily knocked aside the man's mask that Stein-Jarle had a shock.

He was sure he'd seen the man before – in Bodø. Stein-Jarle rarely forgot a face. As a salesman, he lived by his ability to remember past clients. This man wasn't a customer, though, but perhaps he'd seen him out on the town, or his picture had been in the paper. Contrary to what he had said to Noora, he read the local news every day. How else was he supposed to stay up to speed with the housing market?

Panic had taken hold of him then. If the Bodø man knew who Iselin was then things might get awkward. The edict from Sultana's owners was that girls brought by members had to be the kind of people the police were unlikely to devote much time to. Eastern Europeans. Or Norwegians who had run away from home. Both fitted the bill. Iselin definitely didn't.

Stein-Jarle had realised he was in danger. He left the lounge and made his way to the room Iselin was in. There was still an hour to go until the new girls were 'unveiled', as the owners liked to describe it. He pulled Iselin out of the bedroom and down the wide staircase back to the ground floor. For a moment, he thought he was going to get away unseen, but then one of the owners had come loping after him.

'If you leave the club with her then you're done here.' As the man said this, he pulled out his mobile and took a picture of Stein-Jarle and Iselin. It was a hitherto unheard of action. All phones and cameras were prohibited at Sultana. The club guaranteed the full discretion of its members. And Stein-Jarle had already removed his mask.

He let go of Iselin in an attempt to take the mobile away from the man. An idiotic reaction. The man stepped aside and punched him in the gut. Stein-Jarle buckled with a groan, fell sideways and toppled a potted plant off its stand.

The sound of shattering pottery had drawn the attention of a couple of other members, including the man from Bodø. Stein-Jarle had made himself the centre of attention in exactly the way he wanted to avoid. Nevertheless, he dragged Iselin out of the door and jumped into the first taxi he saw. What else could he have done?

Back home in Bodø he'd been unable to shake the unease. He would wake up in the middle of the night, certain that someone had been knocking on the door or was climbing the stairs. Someone who knew. Only when he was with Veronika was he able to lose himself in fantasies similar to those he had previously lived out at Sultana. But those moments were short-lived.

Stein-Jarle knew what he had to do, but he had so far resisted.

'What are you doing?' Veronika was standing at the bedroom door, her baggy T-shirt covering her bare crotch. She came towards him slowly, the soles of her feet dragging across the floor.

Before she reached him, Stein-Jarle switched off the iPad display showing the latest updates about Iselin.

'I need to go out. Go back to bed.'

He went downstairs, put on his light all-weather jacket and headed out into the bright night.

CHAPTER 31

JAKOB

On his way out of the main entrance to the police station, Jakob bumped into Sigrid Malmsten on her way in. 'What a stroke of luck!' the NRK reporter said. 'Just the person I was hoping to talk to.'

Jakob avoided her gaze. 'Sorry Sigrid, this isn't a great time.'

'Has it ever been?'

Jakob glanced over towards Armann, who was getting into his car. 'Later, I promise.'

Sigrid sidestepped directly into his path. 'Jakob, I like you. And perhaps I should have been less direct. But the personal has to be put to one side in favour of the professional when I'm at work. The first batch of hacks from Oslo are arriving at the airport this morning. Their flight lands in thirty minutes.'

'I...' Jakob almost said, *My half-brother, who I didn't know about, called round yesterday.* As if that were a reasonable excuse.

Sigrid brushed a lock of hair off her face. 'You promised me priority access to information. Now it's up to you whether you want me on your side in this case. I've already done a big piece about Gudrun Hemnes's Facebook group. It's scheduled for publication early this afternoon.'

Behind Sigrid, Armann started his car and pulled out into the dense traffic on the roundabout.

Jakob tried to maintain a neutral expression. Damn this morning to hell. Why wasn't Noora at work? She would have been able to soothe Sigrid on his behalf – sweet-talked her a little. Bought him time.

Or maybe not. Sigrid wasn't someone you ingratiated yourself with. Besides, he didn't want to lie to her.

Jakob made up his mind. Even though he knew that the Crow would probably have a minor heart attack if he found out.

'Come with me,' he said. 'On the condition that you don't write a word about this until I say it's okay.'

'You're the boss,' Sigrid said in a way that instantly made Jakob doubt whether that were true.

They drove for a couple of minutes in silence while Jakob tried to think of something to say.

Sigrid pre-empted him. 'You seem a little off today?'

He bit the inside of his lip. Sigrid was a journalist, and journalists and police officers were either hand-in-glove or like oil and water. But he trusted her. Anyway, his half-brother was hardly newsworthy.

'My doorbell rang last night,' he said, and then didn't stop until he'd told the whole story. It was a relief to share what had happened with someone, and Sigrid didn't interrupt even once.

'Why are you even at work today?' was the first thing she said, although not in an accusatory way. Jakob responded by gesturing towards the windscreen, reminding her where they were going.

'Still...' Sigrid paused before turning to him and smiling. 'Karen, my daughter, is eleven. I started working at NRK Nordland when she was five. That first year I was still married, so my husband and I always made sure that one of us was at home when she got back from school or her after-school club. When we broke up that became more difficult, and for periods she ended up being a latchkey kid.'

'A latchkey kid?'

'A child who has their own door key because there's no one at home when they get back from school. It was almost six months before she told me she didn't like being on her own at home.'

Jakob pictured the key he'd left on the kitchen table next to the note for Ola.

'Why did your daughter wait so long to say anything?'

'Karen thought it would ruin my career and that I'd have to quit my job because she didn't like being alone. She knew how seriously I took my work. She'd seen me stressed and excited when I was working on a big story.'

'So what did you do?'

'I told my boss that the weeks I had Karen I would need to leave at four, no matter what.'

'Just like that? And what did your boss say?'

'He grinned and gave me a thumbs-up. The guy has three sons who all play football for different teams. He got it, no problem.'

'So this week when I saw you in the middle of the night at Maskinisten...'

'... Karen was at her dad's. He takes her on odd weeks.'

Jakob nodded. He thought over what she was telling him. Ola was older than Sigrid's daughter, but Jakob had no idea how the boy would react to waking up alone in an unfamiliar home. He'd treated Ola as if he were an adult, leaving a message the way he used to for Lise.

Sigrid gently placed her hand on his upper arm. 'My point is that raising kids is like elite sport. It's intense, challenging, exhausting and unimaginably rewarding. I'm still learning new things about Karen. You've been thrown in at the deep end. If there's anything about Ola you want to talk about then you can call me anytime.'

Jakob felt the warmth of her palm through his shirt. He felt strangely light. 'I really appreciate that.'

He wanted to say more. Something personal. Yet he couldn't find the right words, so he grabbed the first thing he thought of.

'Gudrun's Facebook group ... What do you make of it?'

Sigrid removed her hand and straightened up in her seat. When she replied, Jakob realised that it was reporter-Sigrid rather than Sigrid-the-person speaking.

'It's a good idea in principle but badly done. Gudrun might be the last person to have seen Iselin. This may sound strange to you, but that means she feels a certain responsibility.'

Jakob nodded. He didn't think it sounded strange at all. People who came into contact with a serious crime either wanted to distance themselves from it or became completely absorbed.

'The online group itself,' she added, 'isn't a new phenomenon. A lot of people turn to social media to request help in finding missing people. On the true-crime podcasts, you're always hearing about families and friends who set up groups like that, or even set up crowdfunders so they can hire a private eye or pay a reward for tip-offs that lead to a resolution.'

'But...?' Jakob said after Sigrid had been silent for several seconds.

'It's all about how forums like that are moderated, isn't it? Facebook groups can be complete cesspools. In Gudrun's case, it's Casper and the Jahrbergs who are being ripped to shreds. Some of what's being said in the comments is pretty crude. Some of it's probably illegal.'

'And the article you've written?'

'Naturally I'm critical of that side of things. But an article like that will still probably lead to more people becoming curious, and then they'll search for the group and join the debate.'

'So you won't publish it?' Jakob said.

'I'm still thinking about it. But it doesn't really matter. Someone else is sure to write about it. I dare say one of the nationals will. Young woman disappears without a trace. A case like that is the definition of clickbait.' Sigrid turned to Jakob again. 'I've got a question for you.'

'We're nearly there.'

Sigrid laughed. 'You're not getting away that easily.'

'Okay, shoot.'

'What do you make of Nature Lady's book?'

The question took him by surprise. He glanced over his shoulder. The paperback Sigrid had handed him at the airport was still lying on the back seat. He had meant to pass it on to Armann, but he'd forgotten all about it.

'It's ... er...'

'You haven't read it?'

'No,' Jakob conceded.

'Not even flipped through it?'

'Been a busy few days.'

'No need to apologise. I was just curious.' Strangely, Sigrid sounded pleased.

Jakob parked the car by the first barrier on the gravel track that ran to the top of Keiservarden. He wondered whether to call Ola, but decided to wait. The boy was probably still asleep.

Tarik Aydin was waiting for them another ten minutes' walk or so up the trail. Jakob recognised him from his adverts in the local media. He seemed to recall there was a jingle too.

Tarik wasn't all that tall, but he was powerfully built. He had a bull neck and square torso with thigh muscles that bulged inside his trousers. While his body seemed angular, his face was oddly round and almost a little chubby. He had full lips and a pear-shaped nose beneath brown eyes and prominent black eyebrows. He was wearing a red cap pushed up his brow. The letters *LFC* were emblazoned across the red background in yellow. Liverpool Football Club. 'Kloppy'. Of course. The football reference made the dog's name less weird.

Kloppy was a medium-sized dog with a long black coat and pointed ears. Jakob recognised the breed as a Groenendael – a Belgian Shepherd. He and Lise had considered the breed before settling on Garm.

Tarik came across as both harsh and disarming. Jakob took his outstretched hand. He noticed the businessman stealing a glance at Sigrid as they greeted one another.

'We've met before,' he said to Sigrid when she introduced herself.

'Indeed we have. I interviewed you last summer on NRK Nordland.'

Tarik looked askance at Jakob. 'So the media and the cops are working together these days?'

Sigrid pre-empted him. 'I'm gathering material for a major piece on Iselin. I've promised Jakob that not a word about your discovery will go in until I've got the thumbs-up from the police. For now, you'll only be referred to as a witness. That's it.'

Tarik shrugged. 'Fine by me. Besides, "my discovery" is out in the open.' He pointed down at something on the verge.

Something white and muddy.

Bloody.

A T-shirt.

CHAPTER 32

Lofoten was as expected – the narrow roads were full of motorhomes and camper vans. Here he was just one in the crowd. Invisible. At least for as long as he stuck to the main road. But eventually he would need to find somewhere suitable. A spot to work in peace, undisturbed.

He stopped in a layby and took out the road atlas. He flipped through the pages covering Lofoten, tracing the small side roads with his index finger. He paid attention to settlements, houses, cabins and boathouses. Not many people lived on this breakwater facing the ocean. That meant it wasn't flush with deserted side roads. There was always a farm or a harbour at the end of those twisting gravel tracks. The Lofoten locals didn't build access just for the view.

Nevertheless, he eventually found what he was looking for. A place he'd stopped a couple of years back to check the back of the van one last time. He remembered the occasion because he'd found blood stains on a strip of plastic trim. He'd spent an hour removing it.

He pulled back the hatch and peered into the back. Eva was lying where he'd left her, ribs rising and falling. She was still unconscious.

Twenty minutes after Lødingen, he pulled off the main road and drove south along Trollfjorden. Along the way, he passed small clusters of houses in sheltered bays. Red barns between shell-white beaches and green mountainsides. The south of Lofoten was lusher than the northern end. In some places, the trees grew densely and were tall enough to screen him from anyone passing by on the road.

At the end of a straight section, he caught sight of the spruce – a dark oasis among bright deciduous trees. Perhaps this had originally been a tree nursery, now left to its own devices.

He pulled onto the cart road running between the brown trunks. It was like driving down a narrow tunnel. The branches rasped against the sides, needles tumbling down onto the windscreen and sliding down the bonnet. He eased off the accelerator. Suddenly he was in doubt. Had he been mistaken? What if he got stuck or couldn't find the turning circle he assumed was at the end of this stub of track?

The doubts that had overcome him before he'd beaten Eva Stoltz senseless came flooding back. Reacting against them, he forced his foot down on the accelerator and the camper van rumbled onward. The tyres sank into the sodden earth. The ground scraped against the chassis, and the wheels began to lose their grip. If they began to spin then he was finished. He'd need help to get out. People would remember him. The guy with the camper van who'd got stuck somewhere he had no business being.

He went down a gear. He eased up on the accelerator. The wheels spun before abruptly finding their grip and the vehicle leapt forward.

The left-hand side of the vehicle slammed into a spruce so hard that it made his teeth rattle.

He stopped. He opened the door to inspect the damage. The vehicle had struck the tree trunk just above the rear left-hand wheel. The bodywork was dented and the paint had been scraped off. The collision with the camper van had left a gash in the tree trunk that glowed white at him.

He got down onto his knees and picked up a couple of nail-sized flakes of paint. Not to worry. He'd fix it up when he got home.

After doing a lap of the vehicle, he got back into the driver's seat. He pressed down the clutch, put it into first and then slowly lifted his left foot. The van crept forward. Around him, the trees were growing denser and the shadows darker. Above him, the branches were merging into one. The danger was past. He breathed a sigh of relief. He could smell the stench of his own anxiety sweat.

The hoped-for turning circle appeared in front of him, an overgrown patch with tractor tracks still visible in the yellow blades of grass.

He swung the van around and stopped with the front pointing the way he'd just come. Then he turned off the engine and opened the window. He listened to the silence while his thoughts moved on to the work that lay ahead. The fixed sequence of tasks. The rehearsed improvisation that always followed, like a conductor leading a planned improvisation of a well-known piece.

The mental rundown was an *amuse-bouche* in itself. He could feel the tension building in his body, an electric charge that needed to be released but which he held inside himself for as long as he could.

He opened the side door and pulled Eva out of the vehicle. She landed with a thud and came to. She rolled around and tried to get up, but the tape around her ankles prevented her from doing so. Low grunts escaped through the air hole.

Leaving the door open so that he could keep an eye on her, he began to make ready. Once the interior had been stripped back, he fitted the steel bench and filled the receptacle at the end with water.

He chose the long, thin filleting knife from his belt and crouched down beside Eva. He pointed the tip at her throat before whispering: 'If you don't do as I say, the knife goes straight through you. Understood?'

She nodded. It was a frantic, repetitive movement.

He cut the tape around her legs and helped her up, directing her back towards the vehicle. Her frantic breathing was making a whistling sound through the air hole over her mouth.

Inside the camper van, he made her turn around and sit down on the bench. He fastened her legs into the clamps. The knife pressed to her throat, he pushed her down into a lying position. He placed the yoke over her neck before freeing her hands.

That was when she fought back. He was ready for that. First, he pressed one hand, then the other, down into the Velcro straps, which he tightened using the buckles. Once she had calmed down, he pulled the hair slide with the embedded stone out of his apron pocket and attached it above her left ear.

She looked beautiful lying there. The stone on the hair slide shone like a blue beacon in her dark hair. He stood gazing at her for a couple of minutes before he pumped the pedal beneath the bench with his foot to raise the steel surface to working height.

CHAPTER 33

PEDER

Peder sat down on the chair beside his mother's bed. He helped her into a sitting position. He thought, as he so often did, how light she had become in the last year, like a baby chick. But she didn't complain. She followed the world with interest, her eyes gleaming in the bright morning light. She demanded less and less of him, which made Peder sad. It made him feel a little redundant. But she did let him read the Bible to her. It was the family Bible – a copy of the Bible Society's 1930 translation into Norwegian – and when she was in a particularly good mood, she would tell him about Røst during the winter fishing seasons of the seventies and eighties. 'Back then there were so many fishing boats in the fjord that you could walk dry-shod across to Lofoten.'

Peder reached for the book on the shelf above the bed. He felt his lower back throb. It was a short, sharp pain. He was no longer used to heavy lifting. Age was taking its toll. He would have to be careful not to strain his back and end up bedridden. Then who would take care of his mother?

The Bible was heavy. It was bound in black leather with a gilded cross on it. On the first page, his mother had written: *1 Timothy 5.*

The first letter from Paul to Timothy, Chapter 5. About how the Devil found work for idle hands. Peder knew this chapter well; he had been raised on it. Had had it hammered into him. It had made him a better person. Of that Peder was certain.

He opened the book at the bookmark. His mother wanted the Bible to be read from beginning to end. He'd now reached Ezekiel for the third time. Ezekiel, Chapter 26. About the city of Tyre by the sea, which God had predicted would be destroyed. Peder stroked his mother's hair and began to read. He heard his own voice fill the small attic room. He was able to picture the destruction of the city. 'They shall lay thy stones and thy timber and thy dust in the midst of the water.'

His gaze was drawn to the window, his index finger resting at the spot where he'd stopped reading. It struck Peder that Røst had a lot in common with the Biblical city of Tyre. Big money and little people. People who lived for no one but themselves and what they were able to achieve. Like Simon Michalsen and his family.

'Sorry Mother, I can't read any more today.'

Peder could tell she was unhappy. He'd just have to hazard it.

He put the book down on the bedside table and stood up. He swayed. He felt heavy in body and light-headed. He needed to stop reading the Bible. It only upset him. But his mother insisted. What son said no to his own mother?

Was it the same for Marte as it was for him? Was she surrounded by people who left her with no choice? He was going to ask her that when she came to Røst. He needed to find a place to do so where neither Aslak nor Simon could disturb them. Aslak's behaviour, in particular, troubled Peder. The receptionist had been acting strangely ever since Peder mentioned Marte to him. Did Aslak want to keep Marte for himself? The thought made Peder gnash his teeth.

First Aslak and now Simon Michalsen, with Marte's book on the front seat of his camper van. It wasn't her fault that these two bastards were so consumed by her. Still, it bothered him. It was as if the unpleasant traits of Simon and Aslak also besmirched Marte.

He went downstairs, opened the fridge and took out a can of cola. He sat down at the kitchen table with Marte's book open in front of him. He struggled to concentrate. When he finally got going, he didn't manage to read more than a page from her trip to the Shetland Islands before he became aware of a movement outside.

Through the window, he saw Simon coming down his steps and

into the yard in front of his house. All he was wearing were black tracksuit bottoms with white diagonal stripes on them.

Peder pulled out his binoculars. They had belonged to his father, who had bought them from the military-surplus store. They were robust and mechanical. They could be depended upon. He brought Simon into focus. His bare torso was snow white in the early-morning light. His hair was dishevelled. He noticed that Simon was only wearing one shoe. It didn't look as if he cared. Simon Michalsen appeared to be off balance.

Peder followed his neighbour through the binoculars. Simon walked towards the garage, opened the door and vanished into the darkness. A couple of minutes passed before he re-appeared at the other end of the building. He'd come out through the back door. He was now holding a plastic supermarket carrier bag. Peder couldn't see what was in it.

Simon returned and closed the garage door. Then he turned and stared towards Peder's house, gazing right at the kitchen window. Peder stood still, holding the binoculars to his eyes. He noticed the expression on the man's face. It was obstinate and dogged.

It didn't look like the expression of someone in an unbalanced state.

Not one bit.

CHAPTER 34

JAKOB

Jakob crouched. He took a pen from his inside pocket and lifted the bloody shirt using the tip. It was a wide necked, white cotton T-shirt that tapered slightly at the waist. A women's cut. Perhaps not the kind worn for running, but Jakob could imagine it would do nicely underneath a thin sports jacket. The kind of jacket that Iselin had been wearing when she had gone missing.

Based on the measurements he had seen for Iselin, he estimated that the shirt would fit her. There was a hole in the neckline – probably a bite from Kloppy when he'd picked it up. It would be up to forensics to figure that out.

Jakob turned the T-shirt over. Most of the blood seemed to be down the front and across the stomach. It was hard to guess how much there was – blood was a peculiar substance. One hundred millilitres of it splattered across a white wall looked like a lot more than it actually was.

He pulled out his mobile and photographed the shirt before inserting the garment into a plastic evidence bag which he then sealed. He could see both Sigrid and Tarik following his every movement.

'Where roughly did the dog find it?'

Tarik pointed downhill towards some birch scrub. 'Over by those bushes. At least, that's where Kloppy appeared with it in his mouth. He might have found it further off into the woods.'

Jakob knew he ought to wait for the scene-of-crime team, but it had begun to rain again. If he waited, he risked prints being washed away and the water erasing other surface evidence.

Armann picked up on the second ring.

'Where are you?' Jakob said.

'Noora and I will be there in five.'

Jakob told him about the discovery. 'Go back to the police station and tell Ronald to mobilise whoever he's got to hand. We'll need a tent, lighting and heat. And all the rest. Contact the Civil Defence lot for help. I want a full search of the area and that'll take time.'

'Yes, boss. Anything else?'

'Yes. Update Råkstad again. This is going to generate a lot of media interest when word gets out. I'll send you a picture of the T-shirt.'

'You want me to verify the shirt is hers? With her dad, maybe?'

Jakob knew full well how difficult it was to present these kinds of finds to next-of-kin. He could have done it himself, but Armann and Fine had already established a rapport with Bjørn Hanssen. The best option was for them to continue that relationship.

'Please make it clear that we can't confirm that the T-shirt has anything to do with Iselin, but if Bjørn Hanssen recognises it then we need to know.'

'Okay. I'll call you as soon as we're done at Bjørn's. Are you expecting to be up there for a while?'

'At least until scene-of-crime arrive and get properly started.'

'I'll be in touch.' Jakob was about to hang up when Armann interjected:

'Hang on – what about Gudrun Hemnes's Facebook group?'

Jakob looked up into the grey sky; the clouds were creeping ever lower onto the mountains on the horizon. 'I asked Åge from communications to keep an eye on it. That'll have to do for now.'

While Jakob had been talking to Armann, Sigrid had gone further up the track. She was now taking photos of the area on her phone. Jakob was in no doubt that the pictures would be sought after. As soon as the scene-of-crime team arrived, the road would be cordoned off at the barrier and for the next twenty-four to forty-eight hours no one apart from those approved by the police would be able to gain access to what Jakob now considered to be a crime scene.

'May I go?' Water was dripping off the brim of Tarik's cap. Kloppy wasn't looking great either, his fluffy coat heavy with raindrops. The moisture made the sheepdog look like a greyhound.

'Yes, but first you'll need to give a formal statement to one of my officers. We need to know what time you arrived at Maskinisten. How Kloppy found the T-shirt, and other details. You're welcome to go down to the car park and wait in your car. Can you give me your mobile number?'

Jakob sent a text message to the duty officer with Tarik's phone number, noting where the restauranteur would be waiting. As soon as he'd received confirmation, he put protective overshoes on his feet and headed down the slope towards the birch scrub where Tarik had first spotted Kloppy with the T-shirt in his mouth.

There was a dense thicket of small trees, the branches all entwined. Jakob took out his torch and shone it into the undergrowth. There was nothing there of any immediate interest. He circled the cluster of trees in a counterclockwise direction, paying close attention to where he placed his feet. He noticed some small indentations in the earth, perhaps from Kloppy's claws. He stopped on the far side of the thicket. There was a small furrow in the ground. It was no more than a centimetre deep and it was already filled with water. It was a shallow channel that ran down towards the gravel track below him. A bike wheel.

Jakob was following the track, searching for a clearer tyre imprint when his mobile buzzed in his pocket.

He put it to his ear without looking at the display. 'Yes?'

'Weber, is that you?' It took Jakob a moment to place the hoarse, slightly indistinct voice. He eventually put a name to it: Evald Thorsen, the policeman on Røst.

'Weber speaking,' he said, before adding: 'It's been a while, Evald. How are things on your rock in the ocean?'

'Not great, I'm afraid.' Was that a slight tremor he'd detected in the voice of the old District Sheriff?

'Oh really? What's the matter?'

Thorsen cleared his throat, as if he needed to brace himself before continuing. 'We've got a missing person out here. Marte Moi. You know, that celebrity who calls herself Nature Lady. She went missing while out on a run early this morning.'

CHAPTER 35

It was a little after half past five in the morning. Squalls were drifting across the island from west to east, depositing their moist loads. The cool downpours were followed by sunlight that made the raindrops on the asphalt glitter before rising as steam, shrouding the landscape in a fleeting mist.

He knew that there was only one road from the hotel to the rest of the island. She ran past him at a leisurely pace. She would hardly have noticed the vehicle if she had looked his way. He was parked behind a stack of pallets next to an empty fish-drying rack.

He calmly remained in the driver's seat until she had disappeared from sight. The last thing he saw of her was her black ponytail swinging back and forth from shoulder to shoulder.

He pulled out of his hiding place and up onto the road, accelerating cautiously as a new shower drew in off the sea. The raindrops pummelled the asphalt and muffled the sound of the engine. He sped up. He caught up with her again at the point where the fish-drying racks were packed close together on either side of the road. It was one of the few spots on the island that couldn't be seen from the nearby houses.

Only when he was a few metres away did she notice the camper van. She reacted the way he'd guessed she would. She threw a glance over her shoulder and moved instinctively onto the verge. He drove up alongside her and swerved hard to the right.

The side door hit her around the hip with a glancing *thud*. It wasn't hard, but it was enough to throw her off balance and send her over the low crash barrier and down towards the water. One minute she was jogging along the road, the next she was gone.

He floored the brakes and glanced at the wing mirrors. No cars. No people. He was in one of the island's blind spots. But someone else might turn up on the road at any moment.

He opened the door and ran around to the passenger side. He peered over the barrier. She was lying halfway into the water, face down, her legs wedged between two rocks covered in a veil of brown sea kelp.

The slope was steep. Pebbles came loose and rolled past him. They hit the sea, splashing silently in the diminishing rain.

He bent over her, lifting her head out of the water. The skin on her left cheek had been scraped and she was bleeding from a cut to her forehead. It was deep enough that he could see the bone before the wound refilled with blood. Was she breathing? He wasn't sure.

He locked his arms around the unconscious body and dragged her backward. She might be small, but she was sodden and completely limp. The slope up to the camper van was slippery and uneven. He supposed he could just leave her there and take his chances that the cops would write it off as an accident. Then he felt annoyed with himself. He hadn't taken a chance like this just to give up.

The rain stopped and a dagger of sunlight cut through the cloud and struck him. The light made her wet hair shine as if she were being animated by an external force. She writhed in his arms, vomiting without coming to. Seawater poured from her lips and her breath gurgled in her throat.

These signs of life reinvigorated him. He gritted his teeth and pulled her up the slope one step at a time. He could feel the sweat dripping from his brow and off the tip of his nose. He was constantly listening for the sounds of other vehicles approaching. In the silence between the rain showers, he heard nothing but the splashing of the waves and the hoarse cries of the gulls.

Up on the road, he checked he was alone before hauling her inside. The roll of gaffer tape was at the ready. He lashed the tape around her hands and feet before applying a strip across her mouth. He would have preferred to use more, but he needed to be able to remove the tape quickly if she vomited again.

He started the engine and calmly drove on, glancing in the rear-view mirror as often as he looked at the road ahead. Two herring gulls, still young, gazed at him from the bridge railing. Apart from them, he didn't think anyone noticed him, because the houses along the road all had their blackout curtains drawn.

A fresh squall turned the landscape outside grey and blurry. He turned on the windscreen wipers. The rain would wash away the drag marks on the bank and ensure that people stayed indoors until he was safely home. The adrenaline rush from the hunt was slowly ebbing away, to be replaced by something else. Something mightier.

The anticipation of what lay ahead.

CHAPTER 36

NOORA

'So you didn't walk into a door?' Armann smiled as he said it. He wasn't calling her story into question. Noora had explained the swollen lip by saying that she had awoken with a start and hit herself on the corner of the bedside table. It was a little awkward. Kind of funny. Just about plausible.

She played along with Armann's joke. 'I was hoping to be consoled. To be told that a puffy lip suits me and that it draws attention away from my other, less-endearing features.'

'No need for anything like that,' Armann said, unabashed. 'You're like me. The temporary imperfection only serves to reinforce the overshadowing perfection.'

Noora smiled and her lip stung. 'That's both deep and narcissistic. I'm impressed.'

If Armann had an answer up his sleeve, it vanished when they caught sight of the police station. Parked up outside the main entrance was NRK Nordland's van next to an estate with *Avisa Nordland* decals. Armann pointed out a journalist from a local newspaper leaning against the railings by the door.

'Have they found out about the T-shirt already?' Noora asked.

'It's not impossible,' Armann said.

'Or it's something else,' Noora said, nodding through the windscreen at a car entering the roundabout from the opposite direction. It was Jakob Weber's Outlander.

'I thought he was going to stay on the scene for a while longer.'

Was there someone in the car with him? The glare of the windscreen made it hard to be sure.

Armann parked in his usual spot, and he and Noora made for the main entrance. Jakob drove past the police station, presumably to use the entrance to the car park at the back.

It was the *Avisa Nordland* journalist who spotted them first. 'Do the police believe there's a connection between the two disappearances?'

Noora could see Armann's lips forming the word 'which' before he gritted his teeth and offered a terse 'No comment.'

'Should the police have warned Marte Moi against going running alone, given what happened in Bodø?' the NRK reporter said to them as they climbed the steps.

This time Armann didn't say anything at all, and Noora had a job to keep the surprise off her face.

'You could have bloody warned us,' Armann growled when Jakob walked through the door to their department five minutes later.

The senior detective held up his hands, his palms open. 'Sorry. My bad. I was on the phone with Råkstad all the way back from Maskinisten. Råkstad is expecting a revised plan from us by lunchtime. If there's a connection between the two cases then this changes everything.'

Jakob told them, succinctly, about his call with Evald Thorsen, the policeman on Røst. He finished with: 'Thorsen's alone out there. He's called out a couple of blokes from Civil Defence until he gets some back-up from us on the mainland. And between us, the best we can hope for from Thorsen is that he doesn't mess anything up before we get to the island. He's a nice bloke, but he's more like the friendly Cardamom Town policeman than Harry Hole.'

'Which of us is going to Røst?' Noora said.

'Råkstad and Telle want me to take over the case there, but there's...' Jakob furrowed his brow. '... I've got some family matters to attend to here in Bodø.' Noora noticed that Jakob avoided their gazes as he spoke. 'I suggested that Armann takes over as the lead detective on the ground with you in reserve. Råkstad agreed.'

'Råkstad thought that was fine?' said Noora. If Marte Moi was the victim of a crime then it would be a high-profile case –

one that ought to be handled by the most experienced of
detectives. Had she misinterpreted Råkstad's chilly demeanour?
Or was he hoping that she would screw up? No, that was too
conspiratorial.

Jakob shrugged. 'I know. You've barely unpacked your bags, but
we've got Fine looking after her daughter at home and it's not like
we can deprioritise the Iselin Hanssen case. Anyway, you've got
experience from Kripos on cases that are in the glare of the media.'

Jakob had a point. She had been involved in a couple of cases
that had garnered national attention. Particularly her last case, in
which a plumber from Drammen had been under suspicion of
murdering his live-in partner. They'd been days away from
dropping the investigation when a plastic barrel had been found
buried in the woods just a few hundred metres away from the
couple's cabin. The partner's body had been put into the barrel,
which had then been filled with lye. Forensics had found nothing
inside it but red sludge with some brittle bone remains at the
bottom. The media had predictably dubbed the plumber 'the Lye-
r'. The puns on social media had been just as easy to anticipate. It
had also been her final case with *him*.

'Is Fine a single parent?' she asked, seeking to change the
subject.

'No, but her partner, Indigo, is doing fieldwork on Svalbard.
She's a botanist.'

'Indigo. Cool name. Is their daughter called something as
edgy?'

Jakob smiled. 'They've gone traditional there. She's called
Anna. Apparently they were considering Athene, but Fine thinks
a daughter who has to grow up with two same-sex parents doesn't
need another thing that attracts attention.'

'Is there actually anyone who's still bothered by two girls being
together?'

'Bodø isn't Grünerløkka. Us northerners might seem liberal
when it comes to sex and relationships, but after half a lifetime in

these parts, I also know there's a petty-bourgeois undercurrent in this town, one I don't like.'

Armann raised his hands. 'Don't look at me. Sometimes I even read a copy of *Klassekampen*.'

'Doing the crossword doesn't count as "reading"', Jakob said.

Armann grinned. 'That's an unexpected riposte from the lead detective himself. I didn't see that one coming.'

Noora nudged the conversation back to the disappearance. 'If this Thorsen guy is the only police officer on Røst, then I guess you'll be sending along some forensics people too?'

Jakob sighed. 'Of course. But I doubt it'll be at the same time as you. I need to have a chat with Ronald to see if we can get everything put in place. We're already short on personnel and equipment, given what's going on at Maskinisten. It's going to be a challenge to cover Røst at the same time. I dare say we'll have to call your old employers to ask for some assistance.'

Noora knew she should have expected a reply like that. Obviously Nature Lady's disappearance would mean bringing Kripos in. Nevertheless, Jakob's words made her stomach turn over.

'By the way, what happened to your lip?' she heard Jakob ask.

'She walked into the bedside table,' Armann said before she had time to answer.

She laughed along with them. She was surprised Armann and Jakob couldn't tell how hollow her laughter sounded.

CHAPTER 37

JAKOB

At Jakob's invitation, seconded by Råkstad, the Nordland chief of police had joined the crisis team meeting. It was eleven o'clock on the same day that Marte Moi had been reported missing, and barely forty-eight hours since Iselin had failed to return from her run.

The morning Widerøe flight to Røst had departed too early for Armann and Noora to make it. Jakob had therefore requested that Lufttransport, the carrier operating helicopters between Bodø and Værøy, take a detour to Røst. The service was due to depart shortly after lunch, which meant that all detectives were present for the first meeting, with Fine joining them on Teams.

Jakob looked around the table in the operations room. Råkstad, Armann, Noora and himself were sitting along one side of the table. Across from them were Chief of Police Vigdis Telle, Åge from communications and Ronald Janook, head of forensics. Fine was following from a computer at the end of the table – or at least Jakob assumed she was, given that her audio was muted and her video was off.

He spun his phone on the table in front of him. Ola hadn't called or texted. Jakob knew he should have gone home, but as soon as it became clear that they were dealing with not one but two missing women, it had become impossible to tear himself away.

Not unsurprisingly, the morning arrivals at the airport had brought with them journalists from both the national and regional media. It was also rumoured that NRK and TV2 were en route to Bodø with their mobile TV studios.

'Okay, Jakob...' the chief of police said, clasping her hands in front of her. Telle came from a legal background and had spent a couple of years working on the governor of Svalbard's staff before securing the role as chief of Nordland Police around a year earlier. Jakob still hadn't made up his mind about her.

'I'd like a brief update on where we are with all three cases, and then a plan for the next twenty-four hours. Åge,' Telle said, nodding to the communications adviser, 'has promised the press an update at twelve o'clock. By the way, which outlets are we talking about?'

Åge swallowed, his Adam's apple making an audible click. 'Pretty much all of them,' he said hoarsely. 'Including Swedish national radio.'

'Swedish radio?'

'Nature Lady is big there too. And in Germany. Apparently ARD are on their way. Uh, German television,' he said before Telle asked.

'Quite...' The chief of police wiggled her thumbs around each other a few times. 'That there are so many journalists here might seem disruptive. But the only thing that matters is the investigation. There's no need to tread softly. I'll deal with the media personally. Åge, notify the press corps that I'll provide a daily update at twelve hundred and eighteen hundred hours. That'll give them fresh information for their afternoon and evening bulletins.'

Åge took a note. Then he raised his index finger, but Telle turned to Ronald.

'First, I'd like a brief update on the investigation into Galyna Ivanova – the Ukrainian girl found in the bunker.'

'There's not much to say. The injury to her neck could have occurred post-mortem. Our team have given the bunker and surrounding area another once-over without finding any new evidence. As things stand, I don't have anything to substantiate any conclusion other than suicide.'

'Is there anything connecting the Ivanova case to the dis-appearances of Iselin and Marte?' Telle asked Jakob.

'Nothing except age. As far as we know,' Jakob said, glancing towards Armann. 'Galyna didn't run. Right now it's hard to see any tangible connections.'

'Okay. Then the message from the Bodø Police is that the Ivanova case is no more than a tragic death. Nevertheless, I'd like a second opinion on the injuries to her neck from the Department of Forensic Medicine in Oslo.' Telle turned to Ronald. 'Not that I'm calling your judgement into question.'

'I've already requested their input,' said the pathologist.

It was apparent to Jakob that Telle was pleased with this answer.

'Right Weber, your turn.'

Jakob looked down at his notes. They contained carefully worded sentences. He saw all the headline points and the vague caveats that were embedded within them. He realised that Telle was not someone who wanted a summary in the style of a news anchor. He put his notes to one side.

'I assume you're familiar with the facts of Iselin Hanssen's case up to today?'

Telle nodded.

'Good. In that case I'll concentrate on the most recent developments.' Jakob pushed three pictures across the table to Telle. 'The guy in the first picture is Stein-Jarle Lie. He had a brief relationship with Iselin a few months ago. Noora spoke to him yesterday. It would appear that Lie has an alibi for the day of Iselin's disappearance, but we're checking traffic cameras between Saltstraumen and Bodø to make doubly sure.'

Telle scrutinised the photograph. 'Rap sheet?'

'Two reports of violence against younger women, both cases dropped,' Noora said. Then paused. It seemed to Jakob that she was holding something back. 'There's something about him…' she added. 'Something I can't quite put my finger on.'

'Apart from the fact that he's obviously a bastard,' Armann added.

Telle showed the picture to everyone around the table, taking in Råkstad and the three detectives with her gaze. 'Do we know if he has any ties to Røst?'

'Not so far,' said Jakob. 'Marte Moi disappeared after Noora's first chat with Lie, so we haven't yet considered the possibility.'

'The link to Iselin is significant,' said Telle. 'The trip to Oslo combined with his record is enough to arrest him and search his house. Nevertheless, I'd like something a little more tangible.'

Sitting at Jakob's side, Råkstad nodded along with what Telle was saying as if emphasising that everyone was in agreement.

Jakob tapped his index finger on the centre image of the bloodied T-shirt.

'Iselin's father has confirmed that the T-shirt found in Maskinisten is similar to one worn by his daughter. And this fact was reinforced when he found a similar top in his daughter's wardrobe. The T-shirt that Tarik found has been sent for analysis. We're waiting to hear back on the blood type. A DNA test will take a bit longer, but the lab's prioritising it.'

'And this?' The chief of police tapped the third photograph – of a narrow, water-logged furrow.

'Our forensics team believe that this impression was created by a bicycle. The pattern is sufficiently clear that it would be possible to identify the model, especially if this is a current or recent one.'

'So you think there's a connection between the bike and the T-shirt?'

'Perhaps,' said Jakob. 'It's rained a lot over the last few days, so we have to assume the track is relatively recent. I suppose it's possible the cyclist saw something in the area or perhaps they picked up the T-shirt out of curiosity. But this is just speculation on my part. Ronald, perhaps you have more to add?'

The head of forensics shrugged. 'There's not much more to say. We don't even know whether the T-shirt, if it does turn out to be Iselin's, was found at the site of her abduction. Personally, I doubt it. The area is too open and too close to a popular trail.'

'Okay. What's the plan for the rest of today?' said Telle.

'Shortly after lunch, we're going to bring in Casper Jahrberg for an interview here at the station.' Out of the corner of his eye, he saw Råkstad start. Jakob, together with Fine, had made the decision to bring Casper in just before the meeting with Telle. This was the first time Råkstad had heard about the plan.

'There are discrepancies between his statement and that of Mona Straumsnes. It's our understanding that the two were Iselin's closest friends, and along with her father they were the last people to hear from her.'

Råkstad cleared his throat and spoke. 'Of course we need to have a word with Casper, but the Jahrbergs are already under pressure. The comments in the Facebook group set up by our bunch of pensioners are unpleasant. Perhaps it would be better if we spoke to Casper at home?' Råkstad glanced towards Telle.

Jakob knew it was unprofessional to contradict his own boss in front of the chief of police, but he had no other choice. Armann, however, beat him to it.

'I'm certain that Casper won't speak as freely if we question him at home.'

Telle turned towards him. 'Explain.'

'Fine and I spoke to Casper about Iselin's disappearance the day after she went missing. We both left with the impression that he won't speak freely when his father is nearby.'

'That's only speculation,' Råkstad said pointedly. 'The Jahrbergs are everyone's favourite target in Bodø. We shouldn't be making things worse for them. Of course Casper needs to be questioned, but that can be done in a way that doesn't result in the press scenting blood.'

'Let's not waste time quibbling procedure,' Telle said, irritated. 'Weber, you're the lead detective. What's your assessment?'

Damn it. Jakob knew he should have advised Råkstad of the scheduled interview ahead of the meeting, but he hadn't thought it would be a big thing. He found a spot slightly above Telle's head and fixed his gaze to it. He could feel Råkstad staring at him.

'I would support Armann's assessment. Casper should be questioned here.'

'And so he shall,' said Telle. 'Let's move on to Marte Moi's disappearance on Røst. What's the latest?'

Jakob gave himself a few seconds to gather his thoughts. Questioning Casper at the station was the right decision, but Råkstad would probably think his recommendation was disloyal.

'As for Røst,' he began, 'there's not much news. The search-and-rescue helicopter has been sweeping the sea around the island without finding anything. Thorsen is mapping the area and questioning those who saw Moi last, including her assistant and the hotel staff. The assistant told him that she goes jogging every morning without exception. She's usually gone for thirty to forty minutes. It depends somewhat on how fast she runs – but that means that she could theoretically be anywhere on the island.'

'What else has Thorsen done?' Telle said.

Before Jakob could reply, Råkstad rose to his feet and pointed apologetically at the phone in his hand. 'I'm afraid I have to take this.'

Jakob waited until the door had closed before he continued. 'Thorsen doesn't have many people he can call on out there. The local doctor – a chap called Kjartan Engelstad – has offered to help.'

'But this Engelstad has zero forensic training,' Ronald interjected.

Jakob continued. 'Statistically, it's much likelier that Moi has met with an accident rather than been the victim of a crime. Perhaps she slipped and fell into the water. A shoreline search with volunteers is being coordinated. Extra attention will be paid to areas where the road runs along the water's edge. Armann and Noora are flying out to Røst after this meeting. It's also my recommendation that we request assistance from Kripos.'

Telle nodded. 'I've already notified the head of Kripos. She's put her mobile team on standby. They're ready to deploy at short notice.'

'Good.' Jakob leaned back in his chair to indicate that he was finished.

Åge seized the initiative. 'We should review the talking points before you meet the press,' he said to Telle.

The chief of police looked at Jakob with a raised eyebrow. 'Just let me know if you'd like to trade places, Weber.'

'Think I'll pass, boss,' Jakob said, smiling tensely. He got to his feet and was on his way out of the room when he thought of something. 'Fine?'

'Yes,' she replied from the laptop on the table.

'Were you able to sort out a babysitter for Anna?'

'Yep. I'll be down at the station in half an hour,' she said before signing off.

Noora and Armann followed Jakob out of the room. 'I need to pack before we head to Røst,' Armann said to Noora. 'Do you want me to run you home first?'

'Yes please,' Noora said. Nevertheless, she remained in the corridor with Jakob until Armann had disappeared down the stairs. Then she turned to Jakob.

'This doesn't have to mean anything...' she began.

'What doesn't?'

'Råkstad's phone was lying on the table face up. It never rang. He just used that as an excuse to leave the meeting.'

CHAPTER 38

ISELIN

Rain was dripping down and the drops were making dull splashing sounds on the duvet at the foot of the bunk. Iselin lay there, listening intently. Apart from the drops of water and the gushing of a nearby waterfall, everything was silent.

She opened her eyes. Thin daylight was seeping through the gap between the door and the frame. How long had she been locked up in this turf hut? Two days? Three? She had no idea. Her watch was gone and it was always daytime outside. Or at least it seemed that way. One long, nightmarish day. Time in here melted, like Dalí's clocks. It expanded outwards, moving both forward and backward.

Iselin pulled the duvet aside and sat up before massaging the warmth back into her cold toes. She tried not to look down at her knickers, which were full of holes and covered in dirt and blood. He'd taken her outer clothing away.

She placed her bare feet on the floor. The thin floorboards were laid straight onto the ground and they creaked. Through the timber, she could feel the damp chill of the earth beneath. She stood up and had to sit back down again, feeling dizzy and light-headed.

The walk here from the tree she found she was tied to when she had come round couldn't have taken more than an hour. He had steered her through the woods, his hand holding her neck in a vicelike grip. She had gone down once, buckling. He'd let her fall but not rest. He had firmly pulled her back to her feet and driven her on. Her ankle was still sore, but it was no longer as swollen. He must have planned their route carefully, because along the way they didn't meet anyone else – or at least no one that Iselin could hear.

Once inside the hut, he'd fastened a collar around her neck, fixed with a padlock and with sharp metal spikes on the inside. Only then had he removed the black glasses and extracted the rag from her mouth. He told her to stand with her back to him and then he left, closing the door behind him.

The collar was attached by a chain to a bolt on the wall. With the chain fully extended, she was still a metre away from the door. If she leaned forward at all, the spikes would dig into her neck. She already had several puncture wounds.

The bolt on the wall wouldn't budge either. Her nails broke when she attempted to loosen it. In the end, she gave up and lay back down on the bunk. She shook with tears, but eventually she found a calm of sorts. She lay, staring at the roof, until she was overwhelmed with rage. She walked towards the door until the chain jerked her head back. The spikes punctured her skin, and blood ran down her neck. She shouted as loudly as she could, screaming for help. She cursed the monster who had abducted her. If she just kept going for long enough, surely someone would eventually hear her cries? But no one came, and when she had shouted herself hoarse she realised that the gushing of the waterfall outside drowned out all other sound.

He had returned to the hut several hours later. It was the first time she had seen him. He was dressed from head to toe in black. Black army boots, black cargo trousers with drawstrings at the bottom, and a black T-shirt without any logo on it. He wore a balaclava and his hands were encased in milky-white surgical gloves. Iselin thought she could make out the sound of a helicopter before he closed the door and sat down on the stool he had brought inside the hut.

She stood up from the bed and walked towards him, only stopping when the chain tightened and the spikes scraped against the scabs forming in her fresh wounds.

'Why are you doing this?'

He sat there calmly looking at her, his eyes hidden behind a fine mesh of material.

'Undress,' he said at last. The voice was just as distorted as before. Iselin noticed that the balaclava seemed to bulge outwards slightly at his mouth. There was something over his lips. Was the balaclava hiding an electronic voice changer?

She shook her head. The man slid his hand into a side pocket and pulled out a knife. He unfolded it.

'Undress,' he repeated.

'Go to hell!'

It was as if those words triggered a steel spring within him. He leapt from the stool, grabbed her head and pressed her down onto the bunk. She ended up with her upper body on the mattress and her knees on the floor. His hand pushed her head down, while he tore her remaining clothes off with the other. In the end, all she had left on were her knickers.

'Keep still.' He held the tip of the knife to Iselin's throat while he carefully pulled them down to her knees.

Iselin cried out when he penetrated her, but she didn't move.

After the first rape, he returned twice more to the hut. The third time, Iselin stopped struggling and let him have what he'd come for. He rewarded her docility with a mug of sweet tea and the promise that he would be back again soon. He said they'd get along just fine now that she understood what was in her own best interests. He said it as if he believed his own words, but he didn't come back.

Now, Iselin sat down on the bunk and pulled her legs up into a yoga position, warming the soles of her feet against each other. She stared at the wall opposite, trying to erase the images in her mind's eye. It didn't help. Her thoughts kept circling around what he had done. And what he might do if he came back...

But this time, she couldn't stop thinking about something he had said to her at the very beginning:

'What do you want from me?' she had asked.

'What I've been fantasising about for a long time,' he'd said.

Had they met before?

Was her captor someone she knew?

CHAPTER 39

JAKOB

'We're ready.' Fine nodded towards the interview room.

'I just need ten minutes,' Jakob said. 'It'll do him good to sweat a little.'

Fine raised an eyebrow. 'Casper's here voluntarily. He's free to go if he wants.'

'*Ten minutes*,' Jakob mouthed before running upstairs.

In his office, he pulled out his mobile.

Ola had texted him. *Call?* was all it said.

Jakob tapped on the phone icon.

'Yes?'

'Hi Ola. It's Jakob.'

'Hi.' Jakob waited but Ola didn't say anything else. In the background, he could hear a rattling sound. Was Ola typing on his laptop?

'You asked me to call?'

'Do you have a spare power adapter for your computer? I left mine in Beiarn.'

'There's a laptop in my bedroom. You can check if that adapter works.'

'Already have done. Wrong brand.'

Ola's reply threw him somewhat – was Ola opening cupboards and drawers? Not that Jakob had anything to hide, but still...

'Are you there?'

'Sorry ... I was just wondering where you might get a cable like that. Probably easiest to go into town and buy one.'

'Okay. Can you transfer me whatever it costs?'

Jakob pictured the two hundred kroner he'd left on the table. Wasn't that enough? Had Ola already spent it?

'Of course. I guess three hundred should do it.'

'Expect so.'

Was Ola being sarcastic? Jakob didn't know what to think. Perhaps he ought to take up Sigrid's offer of advice.

'I've transferred the money on *Vipps*.'

'Thanks.' There was a renewed pause with the sound of a keyboard in the background. 'Is it you who's got to find the two missing girls?'

Jakob hadn't mentioned what case he was working on when he and Ola had spoken the night before, but he was named as the lead detective in most media coverage.

'Well, I'm trying to.'

'Most people who go running take their mobiles with them,' said Ola. 'You can trace them.'

'Iselin didn't take hers,' Jakob said, quickly adding, 'but that's not something many people know, so please don't tell anyone.'

'Okay.'

The call ended. Jakob stood there clutching the mobile. He was half waiting for Ola to call him back again. When that didn't happen, he went down to the interview room. Jakob felt as if he now understood Ola less than he had before he'd called.

'We're recording both video and audio of this conversation,' Fine said. 'That way you can be sure there won't be any misunderstandings.'

Casper swayed his head from side to side, conveying no message at all. The bruising on his nose had turned a shade of purple with undertones of black. Jakob had done his fair share of boxing as a younger man. He'd taken second place in an informal tournament at police college. Now that he saw Casper up close, he thought the swollen nose looked like it had been caused by a punch, just as Noora had suggested the day before. But Casper's own explanation – a mishap with an electric scooter – couldn't be ruled out either.

'You're voluntarily providing us with a witness statement in the case of Iselin Hanssen's disappearance.'

'Yeah, right. Voluntary,' Casper muttered.

Jakob reached over and opened the door of the interview room. 'No one here is pressuring you. If you want to go then you're free to do so now instead of wasting our time.'

'Let's just get it over with,' Casper said.

Fine put her pen on top of her notebook and leaned back in her chair. Arms relaxed, palms open, not too reserved. Accommodating, not confrontational. 'Tell us a bit about what you did the day before Iselin's disappearance.'

'The day before,' Casper said, his brow furrowed. 'I'm not really sure. Didn't we talk about this last time as well?'

'What did you do that day, Casper? Did you get up early? Late?'

Casper smiled. 'It's been a few years since I was at school. I got up a bit before lunch. Got a bollocking from Otto.'

'You call your father Otto?'

'That's his name, isn't it?' Casper said sarcastically.

Fine didn't allow herself to react. 'What was he telling you off for?' she said.

'Sleeping away my opportunities. Otto never says "morning". It's always: you're sleeping away your opportunities, you're messing up your opportunities, you're not seizing your opportunities.'

'What opportunities might those be?' Jakob said.

'All sorts. The opportunity to earn my own money. To get an education.' Casper shoved his hands in his pockets and slipped down a little on his seat. 'You know, the opportunity to be something. To do all the stuff Otto claims he did at my age. But he inherited the cash. Nothing but biological luck. If it hadn't been for Grandpa, Otto would be working the fryer in one of Tarik Aydin's places. I'm sure of it.'

'So you had an argument with your father that day?' Fine said.

'Otto and I argue every day. It's nothing new.'

'And what about your mother – Julia?'

Casper fell silent. He fidgeted on his chair. 'What about her?'

'Where was she when you and your father were arguing?'

'In the bedroom. Mum gets a lot of migraines. It's worst in summer – too much light.'

Jakob could see that Casper was holding back; there was something he didn't want to discuss. Not that it was necessarily important. In his experience, sons were often over-protective of their mothers. Jakob noted Julia's name with a question mark after it, to potentially return to later.

Fine continued. 'You got up late. You had a discussion with your father. What happened next?'

'It's the summer. Nothing much going on. I did some gaming. Watched some Netflix. *Narcos*, I think. Then I saw Iselin.'

'Where did you meet up?' said Fine.

'God, I already told you. Don't you guys write anything down?'

'Where did you meet?' Fine said gently.

Casper groaned. 'The Glasshuset shopping centre. Iselin bought a book in ARK. Then we went down to the harbour and had an iced coffee at the café outside Stormen.'

'And then?' said Jakob. He'd been watching Casper while Fine led the conversation. There were no signs of anxiety or nerves, apart from what was to be expected in someone undergoing their first interview in a police station.

Casper half turned towards him. 'We went back to Iselin's, hung out in her room, talking, listening to music. Talked about moving to Oslo...' Casper paused and drew breath. 'Iselin had found this cool but mega-expensive one-bed apartment in Grünerløkka. Nineteen grand a month. I asked how we were going to afford it, and she suggested I ask Otto to help us out.'

'And what did you say?'

'That I'd rather sleep under a bridge. Things were a bit sour after that, but Iselin doesn't stay angry for long.'

Fine put her notebook down on the table. 'When did you get home?' she said.

'Can't remember. A bit after midnight, I think.'

'Did you take the bus?'

'No, I walked. It's not far from Junkerdalen over to Hyttebakken.'

'No electric scooter?'

'It was recharging.'

'Right, that brings us to the day of Iselin's disappearance. Can you describe what you did?'

A sheepish smile appeared on Casper's face. 'Same thing. Got up late. Got a bollocking from Otto. Gaming. Fucking live die repeat.'

Jakob didn't get the reference – he would have to ask Fine about it afterwards. 'What about your mother?' he asked.

'What about her?'

'I just wondered whether Julia felt better.'

For a moment, Casper's face was completely blank. The reaction called to mind Rolf Kvist's favourite saying: If you're going to lie, you'd better have a good memory.

'Mum ... was a bit better. Apparently she went out to see a friend before I got up.'

'When did you first speak to Iselin that day?'

'We didn't speak. We exchanged a few messages. She told me she was going out running...'

Someone knocked on the interview room door – two hard thuds. Before Jakob could react, the door opened and a woman in a black suit entered. Behind her, the duty officer held out his hands in an apologetic gesture.

The woman's blonde hair was gathered tightly behind her head. The shape of her face was what Jakob would have described as triangular, with a pointed chin, prominent forehead and cheekbones you could cut yourself on. The green eyes behind the rectangular glasses met Jakob's gaze. She looked anything but pleased.

He stood up and proffered his hand to the lawyer. 'Ms Zeiler – a pleasure as always.'

Sara Zeiler ignored Jakob. She shifted her focus to Casper.

'Come with me.' Not a question. A command.

'Casper Jahrberg is participating in this interview as a witness of his own accord.'

'In that case you can also note that he left of his own accord. Isn't that right, Casper?'

Casper looked from Jakob to Sara, a hint of a smile forming on his lips. 'What if I want to stay?'

Was that surprise on the lawyer's face? A rapid dilation of the pupils? Jakob thought so.

'I would advise against it,' said Zeiler.

'I don't need a fucking babysitter.'

'To me it looks like that's exactly what you need,' the lawyer said.

'You're very welcome to sit in,' Jakob told her.

'Don't be pretentious, Weber. I can stay whether you invite me to or not.'

Sara Zeiler really did seem to be worked up. Jakob had never seen this side of her before. 'That's not strictly true,' he said. 'Casper actually has to request your assistance.'

Zeiler rolled her eyes, then directed her focus at Casper. 'Now let's have some sense here.'

'I'm sick of being sensible,' Casper snapped. 'I'm sick of Otto hassling me. Having to put family first. Don't you fucking think I don't know what he's up to? The scumbag.'

Sara's face became taut – tauter than it already was. 'Casper...' Her voice was low. A warning tone.

Casper stood up. 'I'm leaving because that's what I want.' He pointed at Jakob. 'Why aren't you out looking for Iselin? She...' He struggled to hold back the tears. He swallowed and then swallowed again.

Casper pushed Sara aside and opened the door. Then stopped on the threshold as if he were suddenly unsure about his decision.

'Casper, just one last question,' said Fine.

Casper stood there, his hand on the door handle and his back to them. 'What?'

'Why does Mona say that you and Iselin weren't together? She says you'd broken up.'

Casper's shoulders slumped. When he turned around he was pale. 'It ... it wasn't meant like that.'

'What wasn't meant like that?' Fine's voice was still friendly. Understanding.

'You don't have to answer,' Sara interjected.

Casper shook his head. He blinked hard as a tear trickled down his cheek. Another dripped from the swollen tip of his nose. Jakob thought his face was the picture of despair.

And something else.

Shame.

CHAPTER 40

NOORA

'They first started helicopter services to Værøy after the Widerøe crash in 1990,' said Armann. 'The wind conditions there can be brutal.'

'But they're not on Røst?' Noora said as she peered through the small oval window. She had never flown by helicopter before. She had no idea that they were so noisy nor that they shook constantly. It didn't feel safe at all. She leaned against the window and tried to form an understanding of where she was. All she could see was sea, everywhere. An infinite plain of blue that merged into the grey horizon.

'It's a bit better on Røst,' Armann said. 'But the island's basically a flat rock out in the ocean. There's not much shelter from the wind and storms there. When he's at his worst, you really have to hold on to make sure you don't blow into the sea.'

'He' as in the weather – the forces of nature. Everything that humankind had no control over. Noora had forgotten all about the north-Norwegian male-gendering of nature.

The helicopter banked and began to fall towards the water. She grasped the armrests, tensing all her muscles. Her stomach seemed to leap into her throat. There were flashes of white on the sea below. Foam peaks and streaks in the troughs. She saw seagulls and puffins flapping above the water. What height were they flying at right now? Fifty metres? A hundred? Would the pilot be able to correct their course in time if a gust of wind swept them down towards the surface?

'He's calm today,' Armann said. 'We're snug as bugs in a rug on this flight.' He was laying it on thick. Showing off. But he didn't seem altogether relaxed, Noora thought. Or was that just what she was telling herself so she'd feel a bit better?

At least one thing was certain: she'd be damned if she was going to take the helicopter back. A plane or boat would do. Anything other than this tin can suspended from a stay attached to a spinning rotor. Hadn't there been an accident just a few years ago? One in which the rotor had simply come off and the chopper had dropped like a stone? Noora's mouth was dry, but she didn't reach for the water bottle. She didn't want Armann to see her hands shaking. She swallowed hard.

Something caught her attention. An island, verdigris green with a sprinkling of brown and grey, had come into view. Its sharp colouring offered a contrast to the sea, forming a clear distinction between the water and the land. It felt as if she had been transported in time and place to the Hebridean island of Islay, where she had been on holiday just a year or two earlier.

With *him*. Their first trip, just the two of them. When everything had been normal.

The island beyond the window was much smaller, but it bore the same colours as the Scottish island. Had the same shape. There was a treeless but lush landscape around a hill. Steep escarpments. Scree and precipitous cliffs. It was almost certainly an area where residents and tourists alike would hike. Despite its rugged beauty, the island evoked a sense of foreboding. The sight of it heightened the anxiety that had taken hold of her ever since Jakob had said she was bound for Røst.

'That's Vedøya,' said Armann. He had unbuckled his seat belt and was now crouching on the floor beside her seat. 'The place used to be teeming with birdlife. Especially puffins. Now the population has fallen drastically. The only birds that have come back are the sea eagles, and the population is doing so well that a lot of the locals are saying they should start hunting them again.'

'What happened to the other birds?'

'The scientists think it's because of climate change. The sea is getting warmer, which sends the fish north into cooler waters. With the fish gone, the very basis of many bird species' existence disappears. It affects the fishermen as well: people in the industry joke that in fifty years' time we'll call Lofoten cod Barents cod. Then it'll be the Russians filling their boots.'

The helicopter carried on past Vedøya, making for Røst. They flew across emerald shallows, glimmering reefs and an entrance fairway marked out with green and red navigation lights to indicate the direction of travel. Noora caught a glimpse of a statue on an islet and then they were flying over the harbour itself, where fishing boats of various sizes were moored.

Armann got back into his seat and strapped himself in just before the helicopter descended onto the runway. The wheels touched down and the helicopter stopped shaking. Noora exhaled. She felt the knot in her stomach begin to ease.

The pilot turned around to face them, pushing up his visor. 'This is our first and last stop.'

'Are you going straight back to Bodø?' Armann said. Until now, it hadn't occurred to Noora that the rows of seats behind them were empty.

'No. We've got a full load of Germans waiting on Værøy.'

'What would we do without tourists?'

'Find something else to moan about,' said the pilot, and the two men chuckled. Noora had heard the same quip before, although usually the opening question was '...without southerners?'.

'Best of luck with the investigation. Hope you find the bastard who kidnapped her.'

'We still don't know what happened,' said Noora.

'What else could have happened though?' The pilot tapped his index finger twice against his temple, as if he were in possession of special knowledge.

Outside, one of the ground crew was pulling the door open and the cabin filled with cool, fresh sea air.

Evald Thorsen, the District Sheriff on Røst – which was a grand title for what was effectively a one-man-band – was waiting for them in the tiny arrivals hall. He was a stocky man. He had grey hair, blue eyes set in a weather-beaten face, and hands as leathery as baseball gloves. Thorsen's upper body was at a perpetual slight forward angle, as if he were always expecting a strong headwind.

He greeted Armann and then Noora. Her hand vanished inside his fist. Evald smelled of Tabac. Noora remembered her grandfather using the same aftershave when she was a little girl. She had been embarrassed by the powerful scent whenever he had driven her and her friends to football training. When she had told him this, he had stopped using the aftershave the very same day. It still weighed heavily on her conscience each time it came to mind.

'Thanks for coming so quickly,' Evald said, and Noora could hear the relief in his voice.

'Anything new?' Armann said.

'No, and to be honest that's what's so strange. No one saw anything at all, and on an island like this everyone sees everything. It's as if Marte Moi just vanished into thin air. Pulled a Houdini.'

'Could this be some sort of deliberate stunt on her part?' Noora said.

'What, hoping to generate some extra publicity for herself?' Thorsen said before answering his own question. 'I've spoken to her assistant about that. I made it clear they would both be in the shit if this was a PR stunt. She assures me it's nothing like that. I believe her. The poor girl's in pieces.'

'Do we know anything about Marte's past mental health?' Noora said as Thorsen guided them towards a grey Mazda estate parked outside the terminal building. 'Does she have any issues of her own? Depression, for instance.'

Thorsen waited to answer until the three of them were in the car. 'Not if we're to believe her assistant – who, by the way, is called Ascension and comes from Barcelona.' The aged policeman pronounced it *Aksensson*.

'I've asked both her and the hotel staff to stay there until you've had a talk with them. I've also requisitioned the big meeting room on the first floor. My office is tiny.'

'Good,' said Armann. 'Jakob's expecting a report from us as soon as possible. We also need to get ready to receive a team from Kripos.'

The car passed a barren cemetery. Among the wild, yellow blades of grass headstones rose from the ground like crooked teeth. Gusts of wind made the grass ripple like the sea around the island.

'How much progress have you made in the search?' Noora said.

'Right now they're doing a final sweep along the shore and rocks to the north of the island, which is the opposite end from the hotel. I don't think we're going to find anything there.' Thorsen brushed his hand across his face, rubbing at the three days of stubble. Noora noticed that the tips of his thumb and forefinger were yellow and discoloured. The fingers of a snus user.

'As I see it,' Thorsen added, 'someone would have seen Marte if she'd run all that way. In addition to the land search, we've got three boats doing circuits of the island to see if they can find anything in the sea. And as you know, the search-and-rescue helicopter was out just a few hours after Marte was reported missing and did a search using the thermal-imaging camera.'

At the first crossroads they came to, Thorsen turned right. Noora assumed the junction was probably the closest she would come to the centre of Røst. There was a church, a retirement home, a doctors' surgery and some municipal buildings, including a library and school. A whole lifetime in a handful of destinations. It wasn't far from cradle to grave.

The narrow road wound its way through a scattering of buildings, mainly low detached houses, most of which looked well kept and fairly new, although here and there were dilapidated buildings, shells of houses covered in dirty-white asbestos tiles and with dark windows. Gradually, Noora began to notice another feature of the island: boggy ponds, big and small, in the clefts between the houses, almost all of them overgrown, but some open and dark. There were also narrow channels cutting in from the sea that split the island into mismatched pieces.

'Your first time on Røst?' Thorsen asked.

Noora nodded. Then she added: 'I lived in Lofoten for a year.' She wanted to stress to the old policeman that this wasn't her maiden voyage north of the Arctic Circle.

'Røst's different from both Lofoten and Værøy. One way to picture the island is as a mound of rocks that only just sticks out of the sea. Several of those ponds are brackish because there's salt water pushing up into them from underneath.'

Thorsen's science lesson came to an abrupt halt when the policeman had to apply the brakes and swerve onto the verge to let an oncoming vehicle past: a green pick-up that was going at least twice as fast as they were. Noora guessed that the gap between the two wing mirrors couldn't have been more than a few centimetres.

'Where's he bloody off to?' Thorsen muttered.

Noora turned in her seat, but the other vehicle had already disappeared around a bend, leaving nothing behind it but a heavy grey cloud of diesel.

'Someone you know?' Noora said.

'Think so,' Thorsen said tersely. 'At any rate, there's not more than a couple of vehicles like that on the island.'

They crossed a short bridge and turned left. Fish-drying racks, like overgrown round-pole fences, appeared in front of them. The long poles were bare, devoid of any fish. Noora recalled from her time in Lofoten that the fish were taken indoors after two or three months on the racks. The 'maturation process', as the fishermen called it, would then continue inside airy warehouses for about the same time again.

They drove over a small hilltop covered in white buildings that reminded Noora of southern Norway. One of them turned out to be their hotel. Thorsen pulled up in front of it and switched off the engine. They could immediately hear the shrieking of birds. A lot of birds. There was an excited *kja, kja, kja!* on repeat.

'I remember the first time I came out here,' Armann said. 'I had a room facing towards the kittiwake colony that's on the other side of the hotel, across the channel. I thought I was going to lose it. They keep going twenty-four hours a day.' He got the luggage out of the boot and handed Noora her bag. 'The strange thing was that I missed it a bit when I got back to Bodø. Once you're used to it, it's almost cosy.'

Noora was about to make her way into the hotel when she noticed a man watching them from the corner of the building. When he realised Noora had spotted him, he came towards them. Like many people on Røst, he was dressed casually in a blue jacket and black trousers.

'Afternoon, Kjartan,' Thorsen said when he saw the man. 'I thought you were out with the search teams?'

'We just finished my part of the island,' the man replied with a distinctive southern-Norwegian accent. 'No joy, I'm afraid.'

Noora recognised the name. Kjartan Engelstad was the island doctor, who Jakob said had offered to help Thorsen.

'You're the detectives from Bodø, I take it?'

Noora gave Thorsen a look.

He shrugged. 'I told Kjartan you were on your way. He's been a lot of help arranging the search of the shoreline.'

Noora shook hands with Kjartan, and then the doctor greeted Armann.

'Thank you for your assistance,' Armann said.

'Don't mention it,' Engelstad said. 'I'm at your disposal, anytime. Just call.'

Noora thought Engelstad seemed a little overeager. Not unlike the swot at school who always put up their hand.

'Thanks for the offer,' Armann said. 'We may just take you up on that.'

'Do you have any idea what might have happened to Marte?' the doctor said.

'We've got a few theories,' Noora replied evasively.

'Feel free to pop by later,' Armann said. 'But things are a bit hectic right now. We've got a lot to put in place before Kripos arrive.'

'Kripos, eh? No expense spared here.' The doctor chuckled. 'Well, I should be getting back to the surgery. But don't hesitate to contact me. Røst has a special place in my heart. My father was the doctor here thirty years ago.'

Thorsen waited until Engelstad was out of earshot before saying: 'Engelstad can come on a bit too strong, but he's a good doctor. Most doctors who come here don't stay long. Either it's not challenging enough, or they want to get back to the big city. But Engelstad's been here for nearly four years now. It's probably to do with his family background and the fact that he's such a bird lover. He takes his camera with him practically everywhere. There aren't many islanders who know the island as well as he does.'

The hotel manager, a slim woman in her early fifties, greeted them in the foyer. She had black hair with flecks of grey and wore horn-rimmed glasses that made Noora think of teachers and librarians. She introduced herself as Kjerstin Sommer, but added: 'Just call me Kikki, everyone does.'

On the way up to the first floor, Kikki told them she had called in an extra shift so that the staff who had been working at the hotel when Marte Moi went missing could be questioned.

Kikki showed them into a bright, spacious meeting room with a view of the channel and a jetty on the far side. The buildings along the opposite jetty looked derelict, in Noora's view. Not that it seemed to bother the kittiwakes. The colony of gulls had taken possession of the roofs and there were birds constantly taking off and landing. There was something hypnotic about the repetitive pattern. Something recognisable that was always in a state of change. Like the flow of people going up and down Karl Johans gate in Oslo on a Saturday afternoon.

'There's no time like the present,' said Armann. 'Let's get started with whoever was working in reception when Marte left the hotel.'

'That would be Aslak Nilsen,' Kikki said. 'But he's not here right now.'

'Not here!' Thorsen exclaimed. 'You just said all staff would be available for questioning.'

'I know. But Aslak told me he needed to pop home first. He promised he'd call to let you know when he'd be back.'

'So it was him who passed us in the pick-up,' Thorsen muttered, pulling out his phone. 'No calls in the last half-hour,' he noted.

'Then perhaps we ought to find out why Aslak was in such a tearing hurry to leave the hotel,' said Noora.

CHAPTER 41

PEDER

'What do you think has happened?'

'She can't just disappear like that – not on Røst!'

'It's suicide – I'm sure of it.'

'These young influencers are often under huge mental strain. All that attention's bad for them.'

'My cousin works in the tower at the airport. He says the Bodø police have come to the island.'

'Lotte on Grimsøya saw a stranger on her property early this morning.'

'Stig Arne rented his boat to two Germans, but when he saw them leaving the harbour he could have sworn there were three of them on board.'

Peder leaned heavily on the shopping trolley as he pushed it through the shop. The talk around him was mostly about Marte's disappearance. He was extremely concerned, and registered the same feeling on the faces of those around him, although not all.

A group that his mother referred to as 'the gossiping busybodies' seemed excited. They had their heads together and they occasionally burst into loud laughter. They didn't care what had happened to Marte. To them, she was just a news story, and now they were mad keen to speculate about what might have happened – sharing grotesque details with each other. Peder was sure of that much. He felt queasy just looking at them. But something else had changed. Peder received several friendly nods, as if people had decided to include him in the collective 'we'. For the first time since Simon Michalsen had decided to drag the Skarvheims' good name through the mud, Peder felt like part of the small community, which – with the exception of the gossiping busybodies – closed ranks when the spotlight was turned on them.

'How are you and Gunlaug keeping?' At first, Peder didn't realise the question was directed at him. He looked sideways and found Kjartan Engelstad – the doctor at the nursing home – standing there. Peder took a step backward.

'Not too bad, considering,' he said. He heard how feeble his own voice sounded against the hubbub of the shop. 'She's taking her medicine as she's supposed to.' Kjartan nodded. He didn't say anything else, so Peder felt obliged to fill the silence. 'I picked up a fresh prescription from the nursing home a week ago.'

'That's good. Gunlaug's a lucky lady to still be able to live at home, even though she's grown up.' The doctor smiled to indicate he was joking.

The first time Peder had met Engelstad had been when he'd found a stranger sitting behind the barn, partially concealed by some bushes. When Peder had gone to ask him what he was up to, the man had turned out to be Engelstad. The doctor had told him that he was taking photos of eider and added that he didn't want to disturb Peder or the birds.

Peder, who hadn't seen an eider in this part of the island in years, had nothing against Engelstad taking photographs. 'But it'd be good if you would stay away from the front of the house,' he'd added. 'Mother gets anxious when she sees strangers on our property.'

Engelstad had assured him that he would respect this.

Now, the doctor slipped a packet of biscuits into his basket. 'Speaking of your mother,' he said, 'I think it's time for another check-up. It's been almost two years since she came to see me. It's important that she gets the medicines she needs and in the right doses.'

'I'll talk to her,' Peder promised.

'Good. I'll be hearing from you soon, then. And if Gunlaug would prefer, I can make a house call. But that would have to be tomorrow or the day after. I'm on holiday after that and I would prefer Gunlaug to have her check-up before I leave.'

Peder nodded, and Engelstad moved on. Peder followed him with his gaze. He noticed the way the locals nodded to him or moved to let him past. There was no doubt about it: on Røst the doctor was more important than both the teacher and the priest.

Peder grabbed the handle of his trolley, and his jacket sleeve slid back, giving him a glimpse of his wristwatch. A quarter past one! He had completely lost track of time. His mother expected lunch at one on the dot. This whole business with Marte Moi had fazed him. He abandoned the shopping trolley, left the shop and got into the microcar.

Although he was in a hurry to get home, Peder sat there without starting the engine. He watched the people coming out of the shop. The unease that he had felt inside returned and spread throughout his body like a languid fog. Who were these people? He didn't know them.

He was about to start the engine when Dr Engelstad came out. The doctor opened the passenger-side door of his van and put his shopping bags into the footwell. Then he double-checked that the side door was locked before he got into the driver's seat.

Peder drove off from the shop at a far more sedate pace than the doctor's van. He was about to pull onto the main road when a green pick-up passed by at high speed. The vehicle skidded and almost hit the crash barrier. Gravel thrown up from the roadside peppered his windscreen.

Peder recognised the car. He'd seen it outside both the hotel and the pub. It belonged to Aslak Nilsen. A few hundred metres ahead of him, Aslak floored the brakes and turned left, down the same road that Peder was going to drive along.

He drove as quickly as he could, but the microcar couldn't keep up with Aslak's pick-up. When Peder reached his own house, he just caught sight of Aslak's car inside Michalsen's garage, beside the camper van, before the door closed. Not long after that, he saw Aslak walk from the garage to the house and slam the front door behind him.

'I'm home,' Peder shouted as soon as he opened the front door. 'Food won't be long.' His mother's silence was answer enough. She was not happy.

As he prepared her light meal – two slices of bread with jam and a glass of cultured milk for her digestion, he continued to watch through the kitchen window. Peder knew that Simon and Aslak hung out, but this was the first time he had seen Aslak's battered pick-up in Simon's garage.

He put the plate and glass on a tray and carried it upstairs. He knocked on the door and waited until he was told to come in. He placed the tray on the small bed-table and lifted it onto the bed. Then he pulled up the chair and told her about what had happened to Marte and about what had been said at the shop. He recounted the conversation with Dr Engelstad and the details of Aslak's daredevil driving. He concluded by describing Simon, bare-chested outside his house earlier that day. The determined look on his face.

His mother listened, letting him talk without interruption. Finally he put Marte's book on her bedside table. He didn't think she would read it, but it felt right. If she leafed through it then she would see how well used it was and notice all the underlinings and dog-eared pages. Peder wanted her to understand how much Marte meant to him.

He sat there quietly. Sometimes she was difficult to interpret, but not today. Her eyes were twinkling in the shifting light. They didn't even cloud over when a rain shower pounded against the window.

'I think we've put up with enough from Simon and the Michalsens,' Peder said at last. 'They shouldn't be allowed to push us around like this.'

Peder saw the relief on her face. He realised at that moment that she had been worrying that he was one of the family's weak men. But that wasn't the case – not after what he'd just said. He was filled with pride so great that it made him feel dizzy. Peder stood up but left the tray. His mother liked to eat alone.

From the kitchen window, he observed the garage, where the two vehicles were hidden away. He shifted his gaze to the house, where all the curtains were drawn. There seemed to be no life, but he knew better than that. What were Simon and Aslak talking about in there?

Peder didn't want to think about it too much. His mother was right. They had put up with enough from them. Now it was up to him. Peder left the house, closing the door quietly as he went.

CHAPTER 42

ARMANN

'The police would like to requisition all the rooms on the first floor. We'll be using the meeting room as our MCC until further notice. Are you able to increase the Wi-Fi capacity?'

The hotel manager, Kikki, looked up at Armann from behind her desk. Her office was plastered with posters promoting Røst and Lofoten. One of them showed an eagle with its claws outstretched, captured in mid-air by a photographer just before it hit the water's surface. Someone had drawn a target on the bright part of the plumage below the neck.

Kikki took off her glasses. 'By "requisition", I take it you mean "book"? And I've no idea what an "MCC" is, but I'm sure you'll be happy to explain to an ignorant civilian like me?'

'Sorry.' Armann realised that he was feeling a bit hot and bothered. 'Police jargon is always infecting my language. Of course, you're right. The police would like to book all your rooms. The MCC is the "mobile command centre". It's where we lead operations or investigations from.'

'So it's just a fancy word for an office with computers on desks and maps on the walls?'

Armann couldn't help but smile at Kikki's no-bullshit radar. 'Something like that.'

'Splendid. In that case we're on the same page.'

Had she just winked at him? Armann was nonplussed.

'As for the rooms,' Kikki said, 'apart from you lot, we've only got one person staying on the first floor. He's due to leave tomorrow.'

'That shouldn't be a problem.'

'Great. I'm afraid I haven't got any computer networking skills – it's usually Aslak who covers that side of things, and he's ... not here.'

'Don't worry about it. We'll just use mobile data until the techies back in Bodø sort something out.'

He was about to leave, when Kikki stood up. Armann thought she was going to come over to him, but the hotel manager turned towards the window. A rigid inflatable boat full of tourists glided past in the channel outside. They were all wearing orange survival suits.

'Was there anything else?' Armann asked.

Kikki shifted her weight from one foot to another. She was swaying slowly from side to side like a landlocked boat that had forgotten it was no longer afloat.

'When something serious like Marte's disappearance happens, it puts everything else into perspective.'

'Like what? Is this something to do with Aslak?'

Kikki turned towards him. 'Aslak has always had the reputation of being a bit of a hooligan. Whether he's got anything to do with the disappearance of Marte Moi, I don't know. But as a hotel employee, he's always behaved himself. He comes in on time, does his job and pitches in when we need the extra help.'

'Apart from today.'

'Apart from today,' Kikki conceded.

'But it wasn't Aslak you were thinking about?'

'No, and I'm still not sure whether what I'm going to tell you is relevant.'

'No one outside the police will know what you say to me,' Armann said.

'It's to do with Engelstad,' said Kikki.

'The doctor?'

'Yes. A couple of months after Engelstad arrived on the island, I found him sneaking around outside my house with a camera.'

'Thorsen told us he's a bit of an ornithologist,' said Armann. 'Apparently that's one of the reasons he applied for the job out here.'

Kikki nodded. 'I've heard the same thing. But on that particular day, it wasn't birds that had captured Engelstad's interest but the bedroom window. The first thing I do each morning is open the curtains and then open the window. I'm often wearing nothing but my knickers.' Kikki met Armann's gaze and telegraphed a clear warning that this was not a joking matter.

'And you're absolutely certain it was Engelstad you saw?'

'Absolutely certain. When I spotted him, I managed to pretend not to notice. Then I got dressed and ran outside. I saw Engelstad's van parked down the road. A few minutes later, he appeared, got in and drove away.'

'Has it happened again at all?'

'I don't know,' said Kikki. 'Since then I keep the curtains in my bedroom and bathroom closed. It's no great sacrifice – and it's trivial compared to Marte's disappearance – but I hate that men like that have an influence over the way I live my life.'

Noora was waiting for him in the meeting room when he got back to the hotel. Armann briefly outlined what Kikki had just told him.

'So the doctor's a Peeping Tom?'

'That's certainly how Kikki described him, but there might be something else behind it. Perhaps the two of them had a relationship that turned sour and Kikki's trying to get revenge on Engelstad.'

'Perhaps,' Noora said. 'But it seems pretty extreme to use a serious missing-person case for something like that. She seems like a solid lady to me.'

'Agreed. I'm going to mention it to Jakob. Anything new from your side?'

'Yes. Thorsen just received a tip-off about an unidentified person on Grimsøya. He's busy looking for Aslak, so he asked whether I'd check it out. Want to come with me?'

Armann looked around. Meeting room, MCC, office – whatever you called it, it was currently just clutter.

'You go, and I'll get us set up here.'

'You sure?' said Noora.

'Yes, unless you want me to come with you?'

'Definitely not,' Noora said, so quickly that Armann wondered whether she had meant the opposite.

After Noora had left, Armann fetched a cup of coffee from the restaurant downstairs and brought it back up to the meeting room. He logged on to the police VPN and checked in for updates on the Iselin Hanssen case. There wasn't much news there either.

Armann could feel his attention drifting away from the screen and he sat, staring into space, while going over what Kikki had just told him about Engelstad. The only difference was that Armann was now imagining himself in Engelstad's place, outside Kikki's house, his gaze fixed on her bedroom window.

'Idiot,' Armann muttered to himself, reaching for the now-lukewarm coffee.

CHAPTER 43

JAKOB

'I've got the results back on the samples taken from Iselin's T-shirt.'

Ronald Janook's voice on the phone was perfectly neutral. It was impossible to tell whether he had found anything of interest.

'And?' Jakob said tensely.

'It's probably best if you pop down for a visit.'

'Okay. Your office?'

'Yes.'

'But you said "Iselin's T-shirt". Does that mean forensics is absolutely certain it belongs to her?'

'There's no doubt about it,' Ronald confirmed, hanging up.

Jakob went into the briefing room. Fine was sitting at the table with a neat stack of papers in front of her. She had managed to get Anna's babysitter to stay a couple more hours, and had used that time to review print-outs and handwritten notes detailing the tip-offs from the public received via the switchboard.

She was now reviewing the conversation that she and Armann had had with Casper the day before. As she went through it, she took notes, comparing what had been said with Casper's statements during questioning earlier that same day. The transcript of Noora's conversation with Mona Straumsnes was also lying on the table.

Uniformed officers had carried out a second round of door-to-door inquiries in Iselin's neighbourhood, speaking to more than eighty people. In most cases, the results had been no more than a name and a few key words jotted down. The report from this enterprise was now lying in its own printed stack of papers on the table too.

It was all laborious work. But Jakob knew that the work of discounting a lead or tip-off was just as important as obtaining fresh information. Both aspects helped build a picture of the case before them. Armann often said that 'investigation was a bit like religion. You had to keep the faith until you saw the light'.

In addition to the door-to-door inquiries, there were more than 150 posts and comments from Gudrun's Facebook group that Åge from communications thought they ought to take a closer look at.

On top of all that was the investigation into Stein-Jarle Lie. BPS, the company that collected road tolls in Bodø, had no records of Lie's Mercedes being driven into the town centre during the window in which Iselin had gone missing. But Lie might have used another car. Jakob knew he really ought to drive out to Saltstraumen to question the hotel staff, but that would be very time-consuming. They had to deal with the most important issues first, and right now that was the discovery of Iselin's T-shirt.

'Do you want to tag along to see Ronald?'

Fine shook her head. 'I'm most useful here. Anyway, I'm about to head home. The babysitter can't stay any longer.'

'How's Anna doing?'

'She's still running a temperature,' Fine said.

Jakob knew her well enough to see that she was worried. He hesitated, wondering whether he ought to ask Fine if Indigo was planning to come home early from her field trip to Svalbard, but he left it. The thought would already have crossed Fine's mind. She didn't need the extra pressure.

'See you later.'

Fine waved without looking up from her papers.

Forensics were based in what the detectives tended to refer to as the Bunker – a closed-off area in the basement of the police station. As Jakob headed down the stairs he thought of all the times he'd visited forensics after a body had been found. He hoped he wouldn't be called to the hospital in Tromsø or Oslo to discuss the results of a forensic autopsy on Iselin's body. He was still holding out hope that an examination of that kind would not become necessary in this case. He still hoped they would find

Iselin in time, even if the rational part of him – the detective – was becoming increasingly doubtful that there would be a happy ending.

He knocked on the door before opening it. Ronald beckoned him in. His office was a bit larger than the one Jakob shared with Noora, but it was homely. Hanging on the wall behind his desk were photos of Ronald's partner and their two children, a preschool-aged boy and an older girl. There was a map of the Cap of the North on another wall, and beneath it there was a framed diploma from the FBI Academy in Quantico, Virginia. Ronald had taken the FBI's National Academy course specialising in forensic science. He had been top of his class and had subsequently been offered jobs at Interpol, Europol and Kripos. Ronald had turned them all down – he wanted to stay in Bodø with his family. There weren't many people in the police who understood why Ronald let chances like that slip through his fingers, but Jakob was one of them.

After Lise.

He sat down on the chair in front of the desk. Ronald reached for the coffee jug and poured Jakob a cup before refilling his own.

'What have you found out?' Jakob said, after taking a sip. The coffee was bitter and the colour of charcoal. It had probably been stewing since that morning.

Ronald pushed a thin folder across the desk to Jakob, who opened it.

'We found Iselin's fingerprints around the neck of the T-shirt. On the care label,' Ronald explained as Jakob read. 'It was an almost perfect print, so there's no doubt she wore the top. We also found several smaller strands of hair that were hers, as well as a couple that weren't. As you can see in the report, the results of the analysis are definitely what I would term "interesting".'

'The blood isn't Iselin's?' Jakob said in surprise. His body suddenly felt lighter. The hope that they might still find Iselin alive was reinvigorated.

'The blood is from a hitherto unidentified male,' Ronald said. 'But how it ended up on Iselin's top is a mystery.'

'I assume you've got a theory though?'

Ronald peered at him over the rim of his cup. 'I'd rather hold off telling you so that you can mull it over yourself – that way we can avoid confirmation bias, since you'd only be tempted to agree with my hypothesis. The next step is to identify who the blood comes from. It might be that the course of events will emerge once we know that?'

Typical Ronald. He was always downplaying his own qualifications. But the forensic scientist was right. Jakob valued Ronald's judgement and he would instinctively have looked for something that would confirm it.

'I'll be in touch,' Jakob said, and headed back upstairs.

While talking to Ronald, Ola had texted him. Jakob opened the message when he was back at his desk. He assumed it was a practical query like when he was coming home or where Garm's collar was. The text was all of three words and didn't make sense at all:

IH0421 on Strava.

Had Ola texted him by mistake? Jakob wrote: ☺

He stared at the smiley. He almost never used emojis. Was it appropriate? Would Ola understand what he meant? Jakob deleted it and instead wrote: *Strava?* Then he added: *Will you remember to walk Garm?*

Once again he hesitated over the send button. Was his message too stern? Ola had probably already walked Garm. Good grief.

He deleted the lot and wrote: *Back in a couple of hours, let's talk then.*

He fired it off before he had time to change his mind.

He'd barely put the phone back in his pocket before it chimed again.

It was another text from Ola: 👍

CHAPTER 44

The stench wafted out of the vehicle the moment he opened the door. It was a cloying, unyielding smell. Faeces and urine. *She's dead*, was his first thought. It was such a gargantuan thought that it blocked out everything else. It took hold of his skull and refused to budge. He knew full well that death caused all the muscles to relax. That included the sphincter and bladder. A final humiliation for the already-deceased.

He stood awkwardly in front of the open door until his eyes had adjusted to the semi-darkness within. To his relief, he saw that her ribcage was still rising and falling. She hadn't choked on her own vomit after all.

This tremendous relief was followed by rage. She had scared him. Her filth had almost thrown him off balance. Was she hoping the shock would force him to make a mistake?

He went over to the hosepipe mounted on the garage wall and pulled it towards the camper van. He climbed in. She tried to get up when she saw him, struggling furiously against the straps holding down her arms and legs.

He struck her – hard enough that the blow threw her head to one side. Her whimper, muffled by the tape, came out as nothing more than a low groan. It was a sound easily mistaken for pleasure. Perhaps it *was* the sound of pleasure. Perhaps she was perverted. He was aroused – not by her perversion but by the thought that he would soon be exploring her limits. He would find the point at which pleasure became fear. A white hot, all-consuming terror. Or was she already there? He sometimes confused different emotions in his head.

He thought of all the girls who had lain where she was now. When he dreamed about them, they all had the same face. In his dream, it was always the same woman strapped to the metal bench.

Over and over again.

He grabbed hold of her top and tried to tear it off her. His first attempt was unsuccessful because the synthetic material used in the workout gear was tough. He didn't give in. He grabbed the neckband and dug his heels in, with a foot braced against the bench. The fabric tore all the way down to the waistband. It revealed a tattoo depicting the sun with her navel at its centre.

He stood there clutching the ragged top and staring at her body, imagining what he could do with a trimming knife. He'd painstakingly follow the lines and folds of her skin, as if the tattoo were a stencil. He'd carve it out, then stick the sun over his own navel. Skin to skin. That was another way of getting close to her. There were so many possibilities.

He pulled her trousers off and the stench inside the camper van became worse. Her soiled underwear clung to her body.

Fucking bitch. He pulled out some garden shears – some of his favourites. They had been bought at a so-called 'farmers' market' in Berlin many years ago. They had comfortable rubber handles that didn't get slippery, even when wet. The grooves in the rubber meant the shears rested in his hand like an extension of his self.

He took the catch off and then cut the woman's underwear at the hip. There was barely any resistance. The shears would have more demanding material to work through later on.

Using his thumb and forefinger, he removed the underwear and dropped it on the floor behind him. She lay naked on the table in front of him. She had given up trying to free herself from the straps. Instead, her eyes were wide open and he could now see nothing but pure, animal fear. It was a state that accommodated nothing but one thought – the fear of death. Well, no. Not death. All that would happen before death came. A waking nightmare. A state from which there was no way out. Would he keep her on the brink for a little while longer? Leave her in this grey zone between mental and physical pain? He was tempted, but first he needed to get rid of the stench. It was getting in the way and made everything about her wretched. She was better than that.

He raised the hose and turned the lever. Behind him, the generator came on. He didn't use a regular garden hose – his was an old school fire hose. If he set the pressure to the maximum, the jet of water would take paint off the wall.

It hit her stomach and made her flesh ripple. He lowered the pressure. He wanted it low enough that it didn't leave any bruises, but powerful enough that it washed away all the shit. Almost at once, she began to tremble. She clenched her fists and closed her eyes. When her lips began to turn blue, he cut the water. He could hear her teeth chattering as he swabbed the floor and pushed water down the drain.

The light on the ceiling above made everything in the vehicle shine. The steel bench. The walls and floor. Even her body. She was lying there in front of him, white and pure. Virginal. He got out the hair slide and attached it over her left ear. Right away, he could tell that she was special.

After all these years, he had finally found The One.

His last.

CHAPTER 45

NOORA

Grimsøya was at the western end of Røst. Noora drove along District Road 783, which was a very grand name for an only partially metalled lane that was in places no wider than her car.

The road reached its end on Grimsøya. Beyond that, there were islets and shimmering skerries jutting out of the emerald-green water in a fan shape that created a breakwater of sorts against the ocean beyond.

Lotte Ramnakken was a thickset woman in her fifties. She had powerful biceps and a handshake to match. Her skin divulged Mediterranean ancestry. She wore a khaki kerchief, and there was an unlit cigarillo dangling from the corner of her mouth. She reminded Noora of a portrait of a South American guerrilla she'd seen at a photography exhibition in Madrid.

'He was standing right over there.' Lotte pointed towards the northern tip of Grimsøya. 'To the left of the bushes. The tide was on the ebb then,' she added. 'But the flood has been since, so the high water will probably have washed any traces of him away.'

'Can you tell me a bit more about what you saw?' Noora said, pulling out her notebook.

'A bit before seven o'clock this morning I glanced out of the kitchen window.' Lotte took the cigarillo from her mouth, scrutinised it for a moment and then tucked it behind her ear. 'I spotted a figure down by the shore. I think it was a man. He was wearing an anorak – black or navy – and matching trousers. He had a bag over his shoulder and a round hat with mosquito netting over his face. He was walking back and forth along the water's edge, as if he were looking for something. Or perhaps waiting for someone.'

Noora stopped writing. 'You're sure about the mosquito netting?'

'As sure as I can be at that distance. There was definitely *something* in front of his face.'

Noora noted this.

'Have you seen this person on your property before?'

'No, not that I recall.'

'Can you describe the figure in any more detail?'

'As well as his outerwear and hat, he was wearing gloves. Now that I think about it, I suppose it's possible that the trousers were...' The rest of the sentence vanished in the thunder of the engines of the inbound Widerøe aircraft that flew over the house on its final approach to the runway.

'Five minutes early today,' Lotte said, without checking the time.

'Sorry, would you mind repeating that?'

'His trousers: it's possible they were waders, rather than just hiking gear. You know, the kind salmon fishers wear.'

'What about the bag?'

'Dark. No pattern. Maybe a fishing bag? But I didn't see a rod.'

'Could it have been a camera bag?'

'Perhaps. I'm not an expert on that kind of thing.'

Noora wrote 'Engelstad?' in her notebook. Noora looked around. In order to reach the shoreline from this point, one had to go either around or across Lotte's property.

'Did you see where he went?'

'He carried on to the tip of the island, and then he disappeared behind a knoll. For all I know, he had a rowboat or something else moored over there.'

'And what about after he was gone? Did anything else happen?'

Lotte shook her head. 'No. And I didn't give it much thought until I heard about the influencer lady going missing.'

Noora expected Lotte to ask her how the investigation was going and whether the police were any closer to solving it. But Lotte said no more. She didn't seem all that interested.

Lotte's final remark was a good summary of Noora's experience of dealing with police tipsters. An ordinary event suddenly appeared strange or unusual when seen in the light of a criminal act. It wouldn't have surprised Noora if the man with the bag had walked along the shoreline on previous occasions too, but Lotte had simply overlooked him or forgotten all about it. And why not? Røst was hardly a hub of criminality. But then again there was the detail of the mosquito netting.

'Thanks for your help,' she said. 'Do you mind if I have a look around your property?'

'By all means. Do you need me with you?'

'No, I'll be fine.' Noora put her hand into her pocket and pulled out a card that she handed to Lotte. 'Please get in touch if you think of anything else.'

Lotte took the card without a second glance and went straight back inside. Noora pulled out her phone and took a picture of the house and the land around it. She crossed the lawn, making for the shore. The grass beyond the small square of manicured lawn was a plateau of yellow with stones scattered across it. She was reminded of Thorsen's description of Røst as 'a mound of rocks that only just sticks out of the sea'.

The gap between the highwater mark and the sea itself was covered in a tangle of seaweed draped over rocks. She hadn't expected a sandy beach. As on the land, it was mostly rocks protruding from under the water.

She followed the water's edge towards the tip of the island. It was a little greener here. The saltwater-resistant scrub and yellow-green scabrous plants competed for the best spots.

The way ahead along the sparse shoreline was blocked by a big rock that extended into the water. To the shoreside, there was a black puddle, one of many. Insects hovered languidly above the dark eye. Noora decided to retrace her steps. There was nothing more to see here.

A sound – a faint rustle from the far side of the rock – made her stop. She remained silent, but the sound did not recur.

'Hello?'

Small waves gently lapped against the rocks but it was otherwise silent. Noora looked down at her shoes. They were low but comfortable Adidas trainers. An idiotic choice for this expedition.

She pressed herself close to the cool stone and walked sideways along the rock as cold seawater seeped into her shoes. She had almost reached the far side when she spotted a flash of black out of the corner of her eye. It was a movement so fast it was indistinct. Noora raised her hands defensively in front of her face.

CHAPTER 46

JAKOB

On his way back to the office after his visit to Ronald, Jakob's mobile buzzed again in his pocket. This time it was Armann calling. Jakob decided to go outside to the car park to talk undisturbed, but he changed his mind when he caught sight of the TV2 mobile studio. He'd heard that the truck had, conveniently, been in Trondheim when the news had broken, so it had been given its marching orders to head for Bodø. The fact that it had already arrived was enough to tell Jakob that the driver had covered the seven hundred kilometres without observing the legal speed limits.

TV2 might have reacted quickly, but the tabloid newspaper *VG* had been quicker. They were already on the scene in Røst. As soon as news of Marte's disappearance had broken, the newspaper had chartered its own plane and dispatched reporters and their own camera crew. The first footage from Røst was now being streamed via their website, and the story was the lead for most other media outlets too. Åge in communications had shared links to articles about Marte's disappearance from *Expressen* in Sweden, *Berlingske Tidende* in Denmark and the *Guardian*.

Jakob took Armann's call in the stairwell. He was accompanied by the echo of his own voice as he climbed the stairs. 'What's up?'

'Thought I'd briefly update you,' said Armann.

'Go for it.'

'The island has been searched and so has the sea around it. Not a trace of Marte to be found. The first thing Noora and I did was to question the hotel staff who were on duty when Marte went missing, as well as her assistant. There's not much to go on. No one saw anything out of the ordinary.'

'So we're down and out?' said Jakob. He opened the door to

his own section. Fine was no longer sitting at the table. There were a couple of transcripts from interviews on the table, but she had either taken the rest of the papers home with her or returned them to the filing cabinet.

'Not quite down and out,' Armann said. 'There are actually two people of interest. The first is Aslak Nilsen. He works at the hotel but disappeared just before we arrived to question him. This was in spite of the fact that Thorsen asked all staff members to stay put.'

'Why do you think he did a runner?'

'Hard to say. There are a lot of reasons why people don't want to talk to the police.'

The door to Råkstad's office opened and the police super-intendent peered out. Jakob pointed at his phone and switched it onto speaker. Råkstad nodded quietly and came over to join him.

'One reason why Aslak may be avoiding us is his record,' Armann said. 'I ran him through STRASAK and the guy's got a couple of convictions. One for the production and sale of moonshine, another for drunk driving. And another case that was dropped.'

'What was the dropped investigation into?' said Råkstad, taking the opportunity to let Armann know he was listening in.

'Five years ago, Aslak was reported for molesting a minor at a party. A fourteen-year-old girl who was too drunk to resist. The girl's friends stopped him as he was pulling her trousers down. By then, she'd already been stripped to the waist.'

'And the case was dropped?' Råkstad said, steely jawed.

'Yes. The police dropped the case before it made it to the District Court. His word against hers, as is so often the case. Aslak claimed he'd been trying to help the girl get out of her clothes because she'd got soaked in the rain and he didn't want her to freeze. Since there wasn't any evidence of a physical assault, the prosecutor recommended the case be shelved.'

'And now Aslak is missing,' Jakob said.

'Yes. Thorsen has been looking for him for the last couple of hours, without any luck. It won't be long until the tabloids catch on.'

'And who's the other person?' Jakob said.

Armann hesitated slightly before answering. 'Kjartan Engelstad.'

'The doctor?'

'You know him?'

'I know of him. We've met on a couple of occasions. How does he fit into the picture?'

Armann recounted Kikki's story. He had barely finished when Råkstad interrupted him.

'Seems thin to me. Tendentious.'

'I don't think Kikki sees it that way.' Jakob could tell that Armann was annoyed.

'We can't ruin the reputation of a talented, respected man because of flimsy allegations,' Råkstad snapped. 'I would have expected greater objectivity from you, Femris.'

Jakob clearly heard Armann draw breath. It was the kind of inhalation that came immediately prior to verbal bombardment. He intervened in the conversation before Armann could say something he would later regret.

'I think we should take the hotel manager's account seriously, but I'd like us to have something tangible to support what she's said.'

Jakob got nothing but silence in response from Armann, but the Crow shot him a look of contempt, having been contradicted for the second time during this investigation.

'Is it possible to seal off the island until we find Marte?' Jakob asked in an attempt to shift the conversation to another topic.

'I asked Thorsen that very question,' Armann said. 'The airport's no problem. We're being aided by two security guards who are checking all the passengers and holding anyone they think the police should have a word with. The same goes for the ferry, although it'll be one hell of a job to check every vehicle prior to boarding. We'll need extra manpower for that.'

'I'll make sure you get more personnel,' Råkstad said, seeking to smooth things over. 'We've already put four officers and cars on the ferry today. I can also confirm that Kripos are en route.'

'Well that's a start,' Armann said. 'The problem is all the fishing boats and pleasure craft. I wouldn't be surprised if it turned out there were more boats than people on Røst. Even with the help of the coast guard, it's an impossible task to keep an eye on all of them. It's not even guaranteed that Marte's still on the island. From where I sit, there are a lot of similarities between Marte's and Iselin's disappearances.'

Råkstad hunched over the mobile phone. 'Our media people are already taking calls from the press asking questions along precisely those lines. Telle's message is that there are similarities but that the police are otherwise offering no comment. I expect you to say the same thing should you be asked.'

'Yes, sir!' Armann said, soldierlike, before ending the call.

'Is something bothering Femris?' Råkstad asked. 'He seems to be on edge at the moment.'

'I dare say it's just the seriousness of the case,' Jakob said.

'I'm sure you're right.'

Råkstad made to return to his office, but then stopped and turned around.

'Just one more thing, Jakob.'

Råkstad beckoned him into his office and shut the door behind them.

'I received a telephone call from Ms Zeiler,' he said. 'She notified me that all contact with the Jahrberg family must go through her.'

'Don't you find it strange that Otto Jahrberg is impeding the investigation like this?' Jakob said.

'Well yes,' Råkstad conceded. 'But look at it from the family's point of view. They're already targets on social media. If the police find enough evidence to charge Casper, a defence lawyer would be able to play the prejudice card without any difficulty.'

'But why the whole family?' Jakob said, mostly to himself.

'How do you mean?'

'Zeiler could have informed us that any query relating to Casper had to go through her, but she said "all contact with the Jahrberg family".'

'I think you're overthinking this,' Råkstad said with a smile that didn't reach his eyes.

Jakob wasn't so sure. Not after his chat with Ronald Janook about Iselin's T-shirt.

'Was that all?'

'For now,' Råkstad said, placing a hand on Jakob's shoulder. He squeezed it gently.

The gesture took Jakob by surprise. Råkstad was not a touchy-feely man. He kept his distance, both physically and socially.

'We haven't had an investigation in Bodø this demanding in years. We've got a lot of eyes on us.' The police superintendent's eyes were narrow and his pupils dark pools.

What the hell was all this? How was the Crow expecting him to respond?

'I'm aware of what's at stake.'

Råkstad moved his head slightly, as if asking: *are you?*

Jakob returned to his own office, shut the door and called Fine. He quickly updated her on his conversation with Råkstad.

'So he thinks you're overthinking it?' she said.

'That's what he said,' Jakob confirmed.

'Weird to say that to a police detective. After all, thinking our way around and through problems is kind of our thing.'

'Yes. It was odd.' Jakob opened his email to find the results from the analysis of Iselin Hanssen's T-shirt then forwarded them to Fine.

'I'd like to get your take on something. Check your inbox.'

He waited on the line until she had finished reading the report. He imagined her silently asking herself the same questions he had asked himself earlier.

'Interesting that the blood on the T-shirt wasn't Iselin's,' Fine said. 'But my reading of the report suggests the *way* it ended up on the T-shirt is just as important.'

Jakob murmured affirmatively, urging her to continue.

'Were I to have a guess, I would say that someone used the T-shirt as a cloth to mop up the blood.'

'My thoughts exactly,' Jakob said with satisfaction.

'But what does that mean for the case? How did this T-shirt end up where we found it?'

'I'm not sure,' said Jakob. 'All we do know is that the blood is from a male. We'll need to get DNA samples from Bjørn Hanssen, Casper Jahrberg and Stein-Jarle Lie. Saliva samples should do it.'

Jakob glanced towards Råkstad's office. He took a deep breath.

'And I think we ought to request a sample from Otto Jahrberg as well. We'll ask all four of them to do so voluntarily. If anyone refuses, we'll hit them with a paragraph 157 request and get a judge to sign off on a court order.'

'Paragraph 157 requires reasonable grounds for suspicion,' Fine said. 'Have we got enough evidence for that?'

'Not really,' Jakob admitted. 'But I'm guessing that Otto Jahrberg would prefer to avoid the media attention that would come with a court order. That's probably true for Lie too.'

'Unless one of them did it,' said Fine.

CHAPTER 47

NOORA

The black body swooped so low above Noora that she could feel the downdraft from the beating wings against her face. She regained her balance and realised that she was now standing up to her knees in water. Behind her, she heard the hacking calls of the cormorant. It sounded like malicious laughter.

She waded back to shore on the same side of the rock she had come from, took off her shoes and then wrung out her socks. It took a long time for her heartbeat to return to normal. Nevertheless, she couldn't shake the image of the cormorant just as it had taken off from the rocks. Its wingspan extended to form a black cross. A cormorant cross. In Lofoten, the fishermen said it brought bad luck to see the cormorants like that when they went out fishing.

After a while, she returned to the Volvo she had left parked on Lotte's driveway.

Noora turned the key in the ignition and the diesel engine coughed and spluttered before roaring into life. She reversed onto the road, waved at the house in case Lotte was watching her from the window and then set off for the hotel.

Before she went to change, she popped into the meeting room to let Armann know she was back. When she opened the door she was met with loud rock music. Old school. Van Halen, or maybe it was Kiss. Rock of the eighties wasn't her favourite.

Armann caught sight of her and turned down the volume. 'I think best with a bit of background noise,' he said apologetically.

Noora could see little to suggest that Armann had done anything to the room since she left. With the exception of a map of Røst taped to the wall, everything was just as it had been.

He looked up from the screen. 'Wasted trip?'

'Not sure,' said Noora. 'I don't doubt that Lotte saw a stranger on her property.' Noora pulled out her notes and read back Lotte's description to Armann. She noticed the way he sat up straighter when she mentioned the bag that might have contained a camera.

'Engelstad?' he said.

'Perhaps. But Røst is a small place. Lotte knows who the doctor is. Don't you think she would have recognised him?'

'I suppose she would have,' Armann sighed. He told Noora about Råkstad's reaction to Kikki's story.

'I don't think the Crow or Jakob are going to take Lotte's word as tangible evidence,' Noora said.

'I dare say you're right. But that doesn't make the Engelstad angle any less relevant.' Armann leaned back in his chair and stared up at the ceiling. 'Right now, it feels as if we're trying to do a jigsaw with pieces from three different puzzles.'

'Amen to that.'

'Oh, I almost forgot.' Armann retrieved a note from his desk. 'Fine called and asked whether one of us could help her out. I've got to follow up with Thorsen, so would you mind calling her on Teams? It sounded like it might be urgent. Do you have time now?'

Noora wiggled her toes inside her sodden trainers. 'Sure thing.' She sat down by one of the windows overlooking the channel and got out her wireless headphones. Armann was already speaking to Thorsen. He didn't seem to have noticed the smell of seawater and wet socks.

Fine appeared on camera right away.

'How's Anna doing?'

Fine responded by turning the camera towards a cot in the middle of the living room. Anna was lying on her side with her face towards the camera and her eyes open. Her cheeks were pink and her hair was plastered to her head.

'Isn't she beautiful!' Noora noticed that she was whispering. 'Is she feeling better?'

'Her temperature is a little lower,' said Fine. 'But she's still very listless and spending most of her time asleep. I have to wake her to get her to take in any fluids.'

Fine turned the camera back to herself and became more businesslike. 'I'm glad you were able to make the time. This will be quick. There are three tip-offs where I'm not sure what we should do. Since we're short on people, it's helpful to be able to talk it over with someone.'

'Go for it,' said Noora.

'Okay. The first is an anonymous message received by email. Our informant claims to have seen Iselin boarding a private jet at Bodø airport together with two men. I've checked up on that, and the airport operator says there were some small aircraft operating that day. But our source doesn't describe the plane itself, so it may be a laborious task. What do you think?'

'Sounds far-fetched to me,' said Noora. 'All passengers have to be registered. Of course, you can always fudge the passenger list, but it's not easy to do. If you want to run this one down, I would start by checking departures with passengers Iselin's age on the list.'

'Good idea,' said Fine. 'That's an easy enough job that it can be done by uniform.'

Fine smiled to show she was joking.

'The next tip-off is from a hiker who thinks they heard shouting from the western side of Lake Soløyvatnet. It's a popular area for hikers, with lots of cabins, some way beyond Keiservarden where Iselin was last seen.'

'Do people swim in the lake?' said Noora.

Fine smiled. 'That was my first thought too. And yes, there's a popular bathing spot not far from where our hiker heard the shouts. Apparently the kids like to go there even when it's raining.'

'Then I suggest you leave that one for now. Shouting and hooting from a bathing spot is easily confused with a cry for help. And if the area's popular, surely someone else would have heard the same cries for help the hiker heard.'

'Agree with you on that.' Fine flipped over a page in her notebook.

'Tip-off number three was called in by the owner of a fisherman's hut in Løp. On the evening of the day that Iselin disappeared, he saw two people lower down on Keiservarden, on the north escarpment. That's in the opposite direction to where Gudrun saw Iselin running, but as the crow flies it isn't that far.'

'That's the problem with tourist areas, isn't it?' said Noora. 'There are people all over the place. In that respect, Iselin's disappearance isn't dissimilar to the Baneheia murders.'

'Yes. Humph.' Fine glanced towards Anna but said nothing else.

'The final tip-off is easily checked,' said Noora. 'Ring up the bloke and ask him to describe the figures he saw. We know what Iselin was wearing. Should be no problem to verify.'

'Thanks for your help,' Fine continued, while looking towards Anna. 'I know this isn't rocket science, but it's good to have someone to talk it over with. I have to admit I'm not all there at the moment.'

'I get it. Hope she gets better soon.'

'Thanks. Give Armann my best.'

Noora signed off. 'Fine sends her best.'

Armann looked up from the screen. 'How's Anna doing?'

'Same as before.'

Noora pushed her chair away from the table. 'I need to change and then I need a bite to eat. How about you?'

'Can you get me a sandwich? Anything's fine so long as it isn't shellfish.'

'You don't like shellfish?'

'I'm allergic as hell.'

'A little impractical, given you live by the sea.'

'I've heard that one before. By the way...' Noora stopped in the doorway leading to the corridor, and Armann continued: 'Råkstad confirmed earlier today that Kripos are en route. Maybe they'll be sending some of your old colleagues?'

'They're coming today?' Noora made an effort to keep her voice normal.

'They'll transfer onto a helicopter as soon as they arrive off the evening flight to Bodø.'

'I...' Noora couldn't think of anything to say. 'S-sandwich...' she managed to stammer before shutting the door behind her.

She went to her room. She wanted nothing more than to change into some dry clothes and spend a few minutes gathering her thoughts.

She tapped her key against the reader and opened the door. Even before it had closed behind her, she realised she wasn't alone.

'There you are – at last,' said a familiar voice. 'You know, I've been looking for you.'

CHAPTER 48

JAKOB

The front door was unlocked and there was the smell of burning in the hallway.

'Ola?'

Jakob got no answer. He took his shoes off and went down the hall.

The burning smell got stronger.

'Ola, are you at home?'

He climbed the stairs and went into the kitchen, where he found two empty supermarket pizza boxes. Lying on top of one of them was a very well-done pizza. Jakob opened the oven door. Ola had cooked the pizzas without lining the bottom of the oven with baking paper, and it reeked of the charred remains of cheese, ham and pepper.

Only now did it dawn on Jakob that Garm hadn't come to meet him. He always did that. Perhaps Ola had taken him out for a walk?

He cleared the kitchen counter and threw the cold pizza in the bin. From downstairs he heard a sharp, determined bark, followed by laughter.

When he descended to the ground floor, Jakob saw that the door to Ola's room was ajar. He pushed it open. The room within was warm and smelled of a mixture of pizza, sweat and cheese-and-onion crisps.

Ola was standing with his back to him, wearing a large pair of headphones over his ears. In front of him, Garm was standing on his hind legs craning his neck to reach a slice of pizza in Ola's hand. Ola let go and Garm caught it in mid-air.

'Good boy!' Ola yelled at a volume that told Jakob the boy was listening to something through his headphones.

'Ola?'

It was Garm – rather than Ola – who reacted and ran towards Jakob, tail wagging. Ola turned to follow the dog and jumped when he spotted Jakob.

He took off his headphones. 'Jesus! You scared me.'

'I did shout a couple of times.'

'Sorry. I was listening in to a Discord – about the new *Final Fantasy*.'

'I...' Jakob almost said ... *I didn't understand a word of that*, but restrained himself and settled for 'Sure'.

'I kept a slice of pizza for you. It's in the kitchen.'

'Thanks. Has Garm had his walk?'

'We had a bit of a romp around the garden.'

Jakob could feel his irritation rising. It had been non-stop at work from early that morning until now. How hard was it for Ola to find half an hour for Garm?

'Garm's an active boy. He needs a proper walk every day.'

'He did his number twos,' Ola said defensively while fiddling with the headphones in his hands. 'That's the most important thing, right?'

That's the most important thing, right? Jakob could feel a build-up of pressure in his head. As if this kid knew best. If you made a promise, then you kept it. No exceptions. Ola would just have to learn that. Jakob was the boss in this house. He folded his arms over his chest and was about to tell Ola what he thought about shirkers when he suddenly saw himself from the outside: the authority. The tyrant. The man deliberately giving others a guilty conscience.

Manfred Weber.

Jakob felt a stabbing pain in his chest. It was the same kind of discomfort he'd felt when he had visited Manfred in Beiarn for the first and last time. It made it difficult to breathe. The floor beneath him was swaying and Jakob had to support himself on the door frame.

'Are you okay?' Ola looked at him with an anxious expression. Dear God, the boy was the spitting image of Manfred. The nose. The eyes. Those cheekbones.

Jakob cleared his throat. 'I'm fine. I expect I'm just a bit dehydrated. Could you get me a glass of water?'

'Of course.' Ola pushed past him and ran upstairs.

Jakob slid down onto the floor with the backs of his fists against his brow and his father's contemptuous voice echoing inside his head: You're weak, Jakob.

You're having a panic attack, that's all.

Breathe in. Breathe out.

'Jakob?' Ola was suddenly standing in front of him holding out a glass.

Jakob took it and downed the ice-cold water in one. He sat there quietly, letting the cool fluid gently stream down to his stomach. Slowly, the pressure in his head began to dissipate.

'How about we take a walk?'

Ola looked down at him sceptically. 'Shouldn't you be resting in bed?'

'What I need is some cool sea air. Coming?'

They walked along Langstranda, which ran parallel to the runway all the way to the Widerøe maintenance hangar. Beyond the fencing they could see the runway and the sea beyond. Jakob let Garm run free while he pointed towards two grassy knolls just beyond the fence.

'What you're seeing over there are two of the underground hangars for the fighter jets. Well, that's what they were. The air base has been moved south to Ørland. Anyway, they were designed for F-16s, but they're too small for the newer jets.'

'What are they going to be used for now?' said Ola.

'That's a good question. After all, they've been designed to withstand almost anything, so it's no easy job to remove them.'

'Do you think those girls are still alive?'

The question was unexpected. Jakob needed to think about something else for a while, but naturally it felt different for Ola. After all, his big brother was the detective tasked with the biggest investigation in Norway. *Big brother.* That concept encompassed much more than he had hitherto comprehended.

'I don't know,' he said. 'We're doing everything we can, but it's as if the two of them have vanished into thin air.'

'I use Strava too,' said Ola. 'Not for runs like Iselin, but as a sort of log of places I've been fishing. My username's OAT1119 – you know, Ola André Tollås and my date of birth.'

'Hmm,' Jakob said, at first just to show he was listening. Then it dawned on him what Ola was saying. He recalled the incomprehensible text the boy had sent him earlier that day. Strava IH0421: Iselin Hanssen and her date of birth, 21 April. A username on Strava.

Jakob came to a halt and pulled out his phone. He went to strava.com and then looked up IH0421. The cover image was of Iselin at the summit of Keiservarden with Bodø in the background. She looked sweaty and happy. Beneath the photo there was a list of maps showing her runs. Jakob recognised the times from the sheet attached to the fridge in her kitchen. They were all there, as well as a new session that had been uploaded two days earlier.

According to the map on Strava, Iselin's run had ended abruptly in the woods east of Keiservarden.

CHAPTER 49

NOORA

He was propped up against the headboard with his hands behind his neck. His leather jacket was slung over the chair in front of the small desk, filling the hotel room with the scent of leather, motorcycles and lubricating oil.

Once, the smell would have evoked memories from their tour through Sweden to the Baltic coast last summer. Her head close to his back. Holding on tight around his waist. The rollercoaster feeling of going round corners. The feeling of escaping something. The intimacy on the bike being a promise for the evening. A promise of hotel rooms like this one, and being naked under the cool sheets. The midnight sun outside; summer days merging together. Neverending.

Now the smell of the leather jacket made her nauseous.

Nauseous and scared.

'How...' Her voice broke and she trailed off. Noora gritted her teeth. She hated herself for this weakness. She was better than this. 'How did you get into my room?'

Leo smiled. He lifted the ID card hanging around his neck. It showed the lion on the Norwegian coat of arms and a photo of a smiling Leo Korshamn with the word *POLICE* inscribed at the bottom.

'Used the master key.'

Leo left his ID hanging over his white shirt, as if he wanted to remind her of something. He took a sip from the bottle of Farris mineral water he had helped himself to from the minibar.

She pictured herself backing out of the room and running back to find Armann. Telling him about the relationship with Leo. Kripos internal affairs. Her accusations. Leo's lies. The top brass who had taken Leo's side but were checked by their fear of another #MeToo scandal.

Noora didn't want anyone's pity – didn't want to be seen as a victim. Yet here she was, acting like one. Silent and uncertain. Like a pupil in the head's office. She tracked every small movement that Leo made, avoiding his eyes. She noticed the way he was constantly seeking out her gaze.

'I told the guy on reception you were my girlfriend.' Leo tilted his head to one side, and a lock of blond hair fell across his right eye. 'He looked a little disappointed, actually. You haven't been flirting with him, have you?'

'Of course not,' Noora said automatically. She wished she could take it back as soon as the words crossed her lips. She didn't have to defend herself against Leo – not anymore.

'Come here.' Leo patted the space on the bed next to him.

Noora didn't budge.

'Noora...' The voice came from deep down. The memory of the effect it had once had on her was still there within her. It conjured up images she didn't want to see, ones that weren't appropriate here.

'I want you to leave,' she muttered.

'You want what?' said Leo. 'Speak up.'

'I want you to leave,' she repeated. She met his eyes.

Leo stood up from the bed. He towered over Noora – he was much taller than she was. Well over 190 centimetres. His biceps bulged inside his sleeves. His shirt was tucked into his trousers in a way that accentuated his flat stomach. Leo spent two hours a day in the gym. Upper body in the morning, back and legs after work.

He gently placed a hand on her shoulder. Discomfort spread like paralysis from the point of impact throughout her body. Noora had to concentrate to maintain a neutral expression. She couldn't let Leo see how terrified she was. She knew how weak it would make her in his eyes.

'I'm sorry about the messages I sent you.' Leo looked down at the floor as he spoke. 'I was hurting and I missed you. I realise now that the internal affairs case was my fault. I should never have treated you the way I did.' Leo swallowed. 'You trusted me and I abused your trust. Especially in the toilets at work. I thought you'd find it exciting. I...'

He swallowed. He dragged the back of his hand across his eyes and half turned his head away from her, as if he were ashamed.

His behaviour was scaring her. The manipulation, the way he always had to be in control – that she had expected. But to see him apparently humble and vulnerable summoned a different kind of fear.

'Can you forgive me?' Leo's hand slid off her shoulder and down her arm. He took her hand and held it the way lovers did.

She didn't withdraw it. She was afraid what reaction it might provoke, so she didn't remove her hand. She felt the warmth of his skin, the heat radiating through his shirt. It brought with it the scent of Armani Code – the aftershave she'd got him for his birthday. 'So you think I'm a code you can crack?' Leo had said when he'd opened the box. 'Haven't I already?' she'd replied.

They had laughed.

But she hadn't understood him at all.

Now he was telling her that he would change. Six months ago, she would have believed him. She would have wanted to believe him so fervently that she would have ignored all the wretched things that had gone before. But not now.

He let go of her hand and placed both his palms on her buttocks, pressing her close to him. She could feel his cock pressing against her abdomen. Noora felt sick. She closed her eyes. In her head, Leo's face was replaced by that of Stein-Jarle, his tongue hanging out like a piece of pink meat.

Her fear and all the energy she was expending to pretend she hadn't noticed were making it hard to think. Leo would interpret this lack of resistance as acceptance. He was going to turn her around and push her face down onto the bed. He would take her. Alone with Leo, only she could help herself.

Noora slowly ran her hand up his crotch. Her fingers lingered over the large bulge. Leo groaned before pushing her down onto the bed. He stood in front of her and took off his shirt. The triangle of his abdominal muscles pointed downwards.

Leo smiled as he took off one of her shoes. Then he reached for the other leg. Now was her chance.

Noora kicked out and hit Leo in the ribs with her heel. She'd hit him too high, missing his stomach, but the strength of the kick pushed him backward.

Noora rolled onto her side. She was about to leap off the far side of the bed when Leo lunged onto her. He twisted her round and straddled her thighs while pushing her arms above her head. He held them fast with one hand while with the other he undid the top button of her trousers.

'Fucking let me go!'

'I like it when you girls fight back.'

That phrase, 'you girls', made her feel dizzy. Who was this man? Had she ever known him?

'Leo,' Noora said calmly. 'I don't want this. We can talk. But it's over between us. It has been for a—'

The blow came without warning, a hard slap to the ear. Sharp pain was followed by dancing red dots in her field of vision.

Leo leaned over her, lowering his face down to hers. 'Shut your trap, you cunt. This is no more than you deserve.' His eyes were black suns beneath his blond fringe.

'Let go of me!' Noora writhed, trying to throw herself to one side, but she remained in his grip. He was too strong. Too heavy.

'You asked for this. It's what you wanted.'

He tugged at her fly. A couple of metal buttons came off and landed on the floor. The sound reminded her of empty shells hitting the ground.

Leo tugged the trousers down her legs while keeping hold of Noora's wrist. He pulled her knickers down over her hips, but struggled to make further progress. Noora knew that he would soon lose patience and just tear them off. She raised her behind off the bed to make it easier for him. Leo scrutinised her face. She smiled back.

'Whore.' He said it as if it were a pet name.

He let go of her wrists and pulled the knickers down her legs. Noora lay there with her arms over her head as she raised her feet so that he could remove the knickers completely. He dropped them on the floor and then stood upright at the side of the bed. He undid his fly and dropped both his trousers and boxers to his ankles. Noora remained still until he bent down to take them off completely.

Her kick struck the side of Leo's head, just above the temple. She sent him flying into the wall. He groaned. His knees buckled. Noora rolled off the bed, grabbed her phone and ran towards the door. Then she realised she was naked from the waist down. She yanked open the bathroom door, slammed it shut behind her and locked it.

Leo hit the door so hard that the cabinet above the vanity shook. But the door opened outward from the bathroom, which made it difficult to force open from the room outside. The door handle rattled, flapping up and down like the wing of a wounded bird.

'Let me in!'

'I've got my phone right here, Leo. If you aren't out of my room in the next thirty seconds, I'm calling Armann. I'll tell him you tried to rape me.'

Silence. Noora stood motionless. She tried to form a picture of what was happening on the other side of the door. She heard the rustling of clothing: Leo putting on his trousers. The leather jacket being retrieved from the back of the chair. Footsteps heading for the door. They stopped outside the bathroom door.

His voice was soft, the words callous. 'I'm coming for you, Noora – when you least expect it. And then you'll disappear. For good.'

CHAPTER 50

JAKOB

The beam of the searchlight attached to the underside of the helicopter was sweeping the area, making shadows appear and disappear in the woods around Jakob. The heavy cloud cover kept the trees on the slopes of Keiservarden in a kind of twilight. Jakob shielded his eyes as the helicopter passed overhead.

'Iselin's last known position is around a hundred metres ahead of us,' Ronald said in a low voice. They were walking side by side, the forensic scientist holding a GPS device that was programmed with the coordinates from Iselin's Strava page.

Jakob didn't answer. He glanced over his shoulder. Following behind them were a cluster of uniformed officers, scene-of-crime personnel and two medics. None of the people in this nocturnal entourage were speaking to each other. Everyone wore the same stubborn expression he did. It was a mask concealing the unease at what they might find.

'Fifty metres,' Ronald muttered, coming to a halt. Ahead of them, the path became even narrower as it went downhill, turning to the left and passing through a head-height thicket. They had no option but to walk in single file.

Jakob used the emergency comms frequency: 'Chopper, this is operation leader. Do you see anything in the area ahead of us?'

'Negative,' the pilot said after a few seconds. 'There's nothing that stands out either on the thermals or using the searchlight. But there's a rock protrusion down there, or perhaps a small cave. So we don't have a full overview.'

'Roger that.' Jakob returned the comms unit to his belt and drew his gun. With his weapon pointing down at an angle, he followed the path towards the dense thicket. Underfoot it was slippery and muddy after days of rain. The scent of the damp forest floor was overwhelming and blocked out everything else. Jakob tried not to think about what other smells he might be inhaling.

'Twenty-five metres,' Ronald whispered. 'Fifteen.'

Jakob ploughed on through the undergrowth, cold drops of water sprinkling the back of his neck. Behind him, he heard one of the policemen swear as he slipped. The man was shushed by a colleague, which only made the noise more palpable. Jakob pushed aside a branch and emerged into a clearing where a tall pine tree loomed over him.

'Iselin?' Jakob looked around. He noticed that the hand holding his gun was quivering. 'Iselin, are you here?'

Ronald appeared by his side and swept the powerful beam of the LED light over the area.

'There, behind the tree!'

Jakob looked in the direction Ronald had said. Beyond the tree on a steep slope there was a hollow. The hollow was partially hidden by a grey-speckled slab of rock sticking out of the ground.

Slowly, Jakob and Ronald approached the gap from either side of the tree. Ronald knelt down and shone the light under the slab. The beam of light showed the back of the cavity and Jakob felt a peculiar mix of relief and disappointment flood through him. The small cave was empty. Iselin wasn't there.

'Found something!' The shout came from behind them.

Ronald and Jakob spun around. In the glow of Ronald's light, one of the uniformed officers was pointing at something lying on the ground at the base of the pine tree. It was a small object, shiny and pink and metallic.

Iselin's fitness tracker.

Jakob got home at ten past three. When he had left the search area, they still hadn't found anything apart from the fitness tracker. Ronald's team were continuing to search the area, while a dog from the canine unit was trying to find Iselin's scent. Two days of squalls and other hikers in the nearby area meant the dog handler wasn't optimistic.

'Did you find her?' Ola was standing at the door of his room. He was wearing a faded grey T-shirt with the *Counter-Strike* logo on it and a pair of slightly oversized boxers. It didn't look as if he'd slept much after Jakob had – hastily – left him and Garm at home after their walk.

'No, afraid not.' Jakob noted the disappointment on Ola's face and added: 'But your Strava tip-off was a big help. Really smart thinking there.'

'Do you mean it?'

'Completely.'

The assurance made Ola smile. It was an open smile which momentarily erased all similarities to Manfred.

'Get to bed. I'll probably be back at work again by the time you're up, but you can always call me.'

'Okay.' Ola shut the door but then opened it again. 'You're okay now, right?' Once again, Jakob noticed the concerned undertone in the boy's voice.

'You're thinking about earlier?' said Jakob.

'Yes.'

Jakob ruffled Ola's hair, and over his shoulder he saw Garm lying comfortably at the foot of the boy's bed. Garm raised his head and gently thwomped his tail. It was clear the dog knew he was in forbidden territory.

'Everything's fine,' said Jakob. 'Now get some sleep.'

As he was brushing his teeth, his phone buzzed against the enamel basin. Jakob was expecting to see Ronald's name on the screen. Instead, it was a text from Sigrid:

Heard a rumour there's a major operation up Keiservarden. What's going on?

Should he reply? It was almost half past three in the morning. Surely she couldn't be expecting an instant response. But they had made a deal to keep each other informed, and so far Sigrid had kept up her part of the bargain.

After some thought, Jakob wrote: *We found Iselin's fitness tracker, but not her. Chief is going to announce at morning presser.*

Jakob read the message back and decided to give Sigrid one extra snippet:

It's a pink Apple Watch 7, 4G enabled. Her run was uploaded in real-time. Trusting you not to share this until the press conference starts tomorrow. Either way, this gives you a head start.

Barely ten seconds had passed before Jakob received a reply:

♥

He stared at the small red symbol on his screen. For a few seconds, all else was forgotten.

He was tired in body but keenly alert in mind. Jakob lay there, staring at the ceiling while his thoughts ricocheted from the conversation with Råkstad about Noora to Kikki's claims about Engelstad to the pain in his chest to finding the fitness tracker and then to Sigrid's last message and whether it meant anything other than *thank you*.

In the end, he got up and went to the desk. He didn't turn on the computer, but he sat there, staring at the pitched ceiling, where there were three pairs of eyes staring down at him.

He had put the picture of Iselin up beside that of the unknown woman in Lofoten and the missing woman from the same year. Jakob met the gaze of each woman in turn, lingering on Iselin. He felt the burden of everything he didn't know weighing him down.

He found the photo of Marte in the bag slung over the back of the chair and put it up next to Iselin. The quartet contemplated him in silence. It was a silence that evoked an intimate monologue.

'How did you make his acquaintance?' he asked the Lofoten woman.

'Why were you in Norway?' he asked the missing woman.

'Did you meet someone you knew on your run?' he asked Iselin.

'Who on Røst knew you were going for a run that early?' he asked Marte.

There were still no clear answers to the first three questions.

The answer to the final question was known to anyone who followed Marte on Instagram: she went jogging every morning.

Did influencers have any concept of how vulnerable they made themselves by sharing their lives on social media?

But in a perfect world, they shouldn't have to worry about that.

In a perfect world.

Four young women. Four disappearances separated by twenty-nine years.

Jakob suddenly felt overwhelmed.

There was a scratch at the door. Jakob opened it and Garm padded in. He rested his muzzle against Jakob's leg, as if asking for forgiveness for having done as he pleased by settling down on Ola's bed.

Absent-mindedly, Jakob scratched the dog behind the ears. He knew he ought to go to bed. Nonetheless, he stayed there contemplating the faces of the four missing women. As he did, a realisation began to dawn on him. He returned to his desk and changed the order of the photos of Iselin and Marte. He took a step back and studied the lined-up pictures of the three dark-haired girls. He now noticed how all three had similar features. The same body shape and practically identical hairstyles. It was almost eerie.

Could Marte be connected to the two cases from twenty-nine years earlier? Was there a killer who preferred his women to look a certain way? And what about Iselin? She didn't fit the pattern.

Were they dealing with two assailants?

CHAPTER 51

NOORA

Noora ignored Armann's calls and stayed in the bathroom for almost half an hour. She tried to open the door several times, but her courage failed her as soon as she grasped the handle. She could imagine Leo waiting on the other side and she couldn't make the image go away. She was irrationally convinced that he was standing silently outside; that he had only opened and closed the outer door to fool her.

In the end it was a text from Thorsen that gave her the courage to venture out: *Back at the hotel soon. Got news about Aslak Nilsen.*

See you soon, she wrote back, and opened the door before she had time to change her mind.

Her room was, of course, empty. On the bedside table was the Farris mineral-water bottle that Leo had been drinking from – the only sign he had been there. Noora changed into completely fresh clothes. She put on a hoodie over a black T-shirt and comfy jeans. She placed her palms on the inside of the door to her room, took a couple of deep breaths, and then went out.

Through the windows in the corridors she could see the rain pouring down. Noora hadn't given any thought to the fact that the curtains in her room had been closed – that it had still harboured that same darkness that had encased her when she was in Leo's small universe.

Leo was in the meeting room with Armann. Armann held out his hands in resignation when he saw her, as if to ask where she had been.

Leo, however, stood up and came towards her with his arms wide open. 'Noora! It's been a long time.'

He embraced her before she had time to react.

'I take it that you and Korshamn already know each other,' Armann said dryly.

'Call me Leo.' He took a step away from Noora. 'Good to see you again.'

Noora studied his face. The feigned delight at seeing her again looked completely genuine. Armann had no reason to suspect there was anything amiss. But just below the surface lurked a beast.

'Leo was already at Bodø Airport when Kripos were notified that we needed assistance,' Armann told Noora.

'I was actually on my way to Mo i Rana,' Leo added. 'But the message reached me just in time to allow me to catch the evening flight to Røst instead.'

'What a stroke of luck,' Noora said. She hoped Leo noted the sarcasm.

'It's only the good ones who get lucky,' Leo replied, giving her a friendly prod in the side.

Noora smiled back. She felt her heart begin to race and a metallic taste spread through her mouth. She wanted nothing more than to run back to her room and lock the door behind her.

'Where's Thorsen?' she asked Armann.

'Just behind you.' Thorsen came into the meeting room followed by four uniformed police officers: three men and a woman. A couple of them seemed to be familiar from her get-to-know-you tour of the police station back in Bodø. 'Sorry for the delay. This lot just came in on the ferry with two unmarked cars from the Bodø police. I thought it was best to get them here as quickly as possible.'

'Welcome, all of you,' Armann said, gesturing towards a row of chairs along one wall. 'Right, Thorsen. Tell us what you've found out about Nilsen.'

The district sheriff took up a position in the centre of the room, his thumbs tucked into his belt. 'Not long ago, I received a call from Peder Skarvheim.' Thorsen paused for a moment, as if considering how to continue. 'I suppose Peder is what you might call the village eccentric. He's almost a recluse. Lives alone with his mother, who's house-bound. And he's not in the best of health himself. Gets himself about with the aid of crutches, and drives one of those little Blimo microcars. Most people here feel sorry for him, but he's not the easiest. Of late, he's had an ongoing dispute with his neighbour, Simon Michalsen, who lives across the way from him. You know the sort of thing – small stuff that gets blown out of proportion. Loud music, dented mailboxes, dirty looks.'

Noora saw a couple of the uniformed officers nodding; this was familiar territory for them.

'So I've got to admit that I didn't actually pick up the first time Peder tried to call me. I assumed it could wait. But he didn't give up, and when I eventually answered it was the same old story: Simon had been wandering around outside half naked while staring angrily at Peder's house. But then Peder added that earlier today, on his way home from the grocery store, he'd almost been run off the road by Aslak's vehicle.'

'And this is "Aslak" as in "Aslak Nilsen", right?' said Leo.

'Exactly,' said Thorsen. 'Peder went on to say that Aslak had parked his pick-up in Simon's garage. The door is shut, but Peder's certain it's still there. As you know, Aslak has a record. And Simon's been fined a couple of times for being drunk and disorderly, and he was also fined twenty thousand for stealing chemicals down in the harbour.'

'What chemicals were they?' said Leo.

'Lye, I think, but I'm not absolutely certain. Simon's excuse was that he thought it was fuel and that he assumed the megabucks fishing boat owners wouldn't notice if ten litres of it went walkies.'

'But you don't believe him?' said Leo.

Thorsen shook his head. 'Simon's a chemistry graduate – he ought to be able to tell the difference between lye and diesel.'

'Not exactly a criminal mastermind,' said one of the newly arrived officers, loudly enough for everyone to hear it. His colleagues were sniggering.

Armann slapped the table in front of him and the uniformed

officers immediately fell silent. 'Don't forget what's at stake. Right now this is the only solid lead we've got. Based on what Thorsen has just told me, I think we've got grounds to raid his home.'

Armann paused. It was an open invitation to all and sundry to disagree with his assessment. Noora could have pointed out that the only thing tying Aslak to the disappearance was that he had absconded from the hotel before they'd had time to speak to him. That on its own hardly counted as reasonable grounds to suspect someone of abduction. But on the other hand, time was getting away from them.

'I'll call Jakob and ask him to apply for an emergency warrant from the Nordland prosecutor,' Armann continued. 'In the meantime, let's prepare for a raid to take place no later than first thing tomorrow once the paperwork is in place.' He turned to Noora. 'Take one of the officers with you and watch Simon Michalsen's house. If he or Aslak leave the property, I want to know about it right away.'

'On it,' Noora said, relieved to get away from Leo.

'Thorsen, I assume you've got a municipal-planning setup or the like here on the island? We need the blueprints for Simon's house. Once we've got that, we can plan our raid in further detail. Leo, I'd like your input on the plans.'

'Do we know whether our boys are the registered owners of any firearms?' said Leo.

'Good point,' Armann said. 'Thorsen, can you check on that while getting the plans?'

Thorsen nodded before exiting the meeting room.

Noora beckoned one of the officers over to her. It was the guy who had attempted to crack a joke earlier. 'Noora Sande,' she said, proffering her hand. 'You're coming with me.'

'Odd-Arne Tveite,' he said, taking her hand.

Noora noticed that Leo was watching their exchange and probably imagining her and Odd-Arne alone together. She felt mentally exhausted at the very thought of it.

'You can go down to the car,' she told the officer. 'I'll be there in a couple of minutes.'

Noora waited until Odd-Arne had gone downstairs before she jogged along the corridor to her room. Her hand shook as she held the keycard against the reader.

The old Nokia phone was in the outer pocket of her suitcase. She hadn't checked the phone since arriving on Røst. Now the display showed five unread messages.

Had Leo sent them before or after he'd arrived on Røst? Had he warned her? Had a reconciliation been proposed? Or had he played mind games with her, suggesting that he was done? Saying that there would be no more messages from him before turning up unexpectedly in her room...

Noora didn't open any of the messages. She took the phone with her and went downstairs and out onto the jetty.

The torrential rain was forming irregular patterns in the channel below. It was just her and the kittiwakes, who didn't much care if it was windy or rainy. She pulled up the hood of her jumper. She knew that if she hesitated any longer, she would change her mind – that she would find an excuse to put it off.

She hurled the mobile phone into the channel. The Nokia spun lethargically through the air. A pair of kittiwakes dived towards the flying object before the phone hit the water with a barely audible splash. When Noora turned around to go back inside, she caught sight of a figure at one of the first-floor windows. Leo's face was expressionless – except for his eyes.

They were dark and filled with hatred.

CHAPTER 52

JAKOB

'I just got the answer we've been waiting for.'

Jakob rubbed his eyes as his brain tried to place the voice on the other end of the line. He'd answered his mobile while still half asleep. The clock on his bedside table showed the time was half past five. He'd slept for just two hours.

'Ronald?' Jakob mumbled.

'Who else?'

'Are you already at work?'

'Just came back from Maskinisten. I made the stupid mistake of checking my email before going for a lie down, and I saw the message from the lab.'

'The analysis of the saliva samples?'

'Yup,' said Ronald.

Jakob sat up in bed. He felt groggy. It was the feeling you got when you'd had a couple of glasses of wine just before going to bed.

'Before I go into more detail,' said Ronald, 'can you tell me how Bjørn Hanssen, Stein-Jarle Lie and Casper and Otto Jahrberg reacted to the request for a saliva sample?'

Jakob ruffled his hair before inserting his feet into the slippers under the bed and stumbling across the dark bedroom to his desk.

'Uniform tell me that Bjørn Hanssen gave them a sample without any issues. Stein-Jarle yelled at them but in the end he gave them what they'd come for.'

'And what about the Jahrberg gents?'

'We had to go through the family lawyer to get samples from Otto and Casper. Zeiler was dismissive when I contacted her, but she called back just minutes later and told me that both father and son were willing to provide us with samples voluntarily. She said the family wanted to demonstrate that they were cooperating fully with the police.'

'Confident, in other words,' said Ronald.

'Typical Otto,' Jakob said. 'But come on, don't drag this out any longer. What's the answer?'

'The tests prove that the blood on Iselin's top is Casper's.'

'For sure?'

'For sure,' Ronald said. 'That's why I wondered whether the Jahrbergs had tried to avoid giving samples.'

'That can only mean that Otto doesn't know that his son is involved.'

'Probably.'

'But there might be another possibility.'

'Which is?'

Jakob told Ronald what he and Fine had discussed earlier that day. It was an alternative theory on how the blood had ended up on Iselin's T-shirt. Ronald listened without interrupting. Finally, the forensic scientist said: 'My first impulse was to think you're guilty of complicating something straightforward. But I actually think you might be on to something. What do we do now?'

'I think we pay them a visit. Fine's still on her own with the baby, so I hope you've got time to join me for a little showdown.'

'When?'

'Right away. I'll pick you up.'

'You'd better be bringing coffee.'

Ronald was waiting for him outside his apartment in Hunstad. It was obvious that he hadn't slept in twenty-four hours. Ronald got into the passenger seat and immediately opened the lid of the Thermos mug in the cup holder on his side.

'Tea! You're messing with me, right?' Ronald stared glumly down into the mug.

'You need to broaden your horizons. It's lapsang souchong. Proper man tea.'

Ronald gingerly took a sip. 'Tastes like a cross between a campfire and greasy water.'

'So not entirely unlike your bog-standard filter coffee...'

'Not funny.' Ronald took another sip before replacing the lid and putting the mug back in the holder with an ostentatious sigh.

'Any news from Røst?'

'Last night, while we were searching for Iselin, Armann submitted a request for a search warrant. It's flimsy and he knows it. We need more than the fact that Aslak Nilsen is holed up at Simon Michalsen's house.'

Jakob pulled off the main road, heading towards the sea. There was rain drifting across Saltfjorden, making a rainbow appear and disappear in the sporadic morning sunlight.

'I had a word with Fine while I was on my way over. She had an idea that I asked her to discuss with the prosecutor. Hopefully we'll be able to give Armann the go-ahead this morning.'

'Let's hope so. We need a breakthrough.'

'That's an understatement, to put it mildly.'

Ronald turned to Jakob. 'If your theory about the blood on the T-shirt is right then it's a big development in the investigation.'

'Agreed. And in that vein, I'd like to run another theory by you. One that runs counter to the raid on Simon and Aslak.'

'Which is?'

Jakob told Ronald about the idea that had occurred to him as he'd examined the photos of the four missing girls – that there could be two assailants.

'It's rare for a killer to swear off death for twenty-nine years,' Ronald said. 'Rare, but not unheard of.'

'I suspect you've got a competing theory,' Jakob replied.

'Your idea of two killers does hold water. But I think we may be dealing with a copy-cat on Røst. Someone who was inspired by reading about what happened to Iselin. Perhaps the person in question acted spontaneously and kidnapped Marte when the opportunity presented itself.' Ronald took the lid off the mug and sipped again, grimacing as if he had already forgotten it was tea rather than coffee. 'After all, that kind of scenario would be a much better fit with the ages of Aslak and Simon. They can't have been all that old when the woman in Lofoten was killed.'

It also fits Kjartan Engelstad, Jakob thought. He made up his mind to take a closer look at the island doctor if Armann and Noora weren't able to connect Aslak and Simon to the case.

Jakob pulled into the car park and switched off the engine. He quickly flipped through his notebook, at the questions he had prepared.

'I guess there's no reason to wait.'

Siri-Else Straumsnes opened the door wearing a yellow dressing gown over a white onesie. There were dark bags under her eyes and the scent of tobacco wafted out of the front door.

'Yes?'

Jakob held up his credentials. 'Jakob Weber. This is my colleague, Ronald Janook.'

'I remember who you are, Jakob. You were here the day before yesterday.' Siri-Else pulled the dressing gown more tightly around her body, giving no indication she was willing to admit them.

'We're here for a word with Mona.'

'At a quarter past seven in the morning?'

'There's something we need to ask her. We can do it here, or we can take Mona down to the station.'

Siri-Else fixed her gaze on Jakob for a few seconds before turning her back on them and plodding back along the hallway without closing the front door.

Jakob waited in the living room with Ronald until Mona appeared, along with her mother. Siri-Else had changed into jeans and a plain black top. Mona wore grey, high-waisted stretchy trousers and a white top. Jakob thought she looked nervous, but then again didn't most people when they received an unexpected visit from the police?

'Hi Mona. We met a couple of days ago.'

She nodded, looking at the floor.

'There are a couple of things I'd like to clear up with you in relation to Iselin's disappearance.'

'Like what?'

'You told us that Iselin came to visit you the evening before she went missing. You ate pizza and watched a film.'

'A show on Netflix. *Jessica Jones*.'

'Quite. And that was the last time you saw her?'

'Yes. I already told your colleague that.'

'That's right.' Jakob flipped through his notebook, mostly to create an artificial pause between the formalities and what he regarded as the beginning of the interview itself.

'What you didn't tell us was that Casper paid you a visit the next day. That would be the day of Iselin's disappearance. I'd guess a bit before lunch? Isn't that right?'

Mona didn't reply.

'Mona?' Siri-Else folded her arms. 'Answer the policeman.'

'Okay. So he was here. What does it matter?' Mona said defiantly. 'It's Iselin who's gone missing, not Casper.'

'Let me tell you what I think happened from when Iselin was here until when she went missing,' Jakob said. 'Stop me at any time if I'm mistaken.'

Mona shrugged. It was a silent *whatever*. Jakob also noted the way that Siri-Else was scrutinising her daughter, a furrow between her eyes. Nascent doubt.

'The day before Iselin's disappearance, she came round here. You had pizza and watched *Jessica Jones*. As per your account to Noora, Iselin accidentally dropped a slice of pizza on the sofa. I think Iselin also got pizza on her T-shirt. So you lent her one of your own tops and when Iselin went home she forgot to take the dirty one with her.'

Mona didn't stop him and offered no corrections. She had laced her fingers together and her gaze was still fixed to the floor.

'The next day, Casper popped by. At some point, he told you

that he and Iselin were planning to move to Oslo. You were hurt and angry and you hit him. You hit him right on the nose and he started bleeding.'

A jolt passed through Mona, and she raised her head. Her eyes were narrow slits. 'Casper's a fucking bastard! Two weeks ago he told me he and Iselin were done. He came round just after Mum had gone to work. We slept together. Then I made him breakfast. And *then*, right before he was going to leave, as if it was just some tiny thing he'd forgotten, he told me about the Oslo plans. About how he and Iselin were back together.'

'And then you hit him?'

'I should have killed him!'

'Mona!'

'Shut up, Mum!'

The force in Mona's words made her mother recoil. Mona was breathing heavily and her fists were clenched. She managed to regain control. Jakob waited for her to continue, but she said no more.

'After Casper left, you mopped up his nosebleed using Iselin's T-shirt. Perhaps you saw it in the utility room when you went to fetch a bucket of water and thought it would be good for wiping up Casper's mess with. Then you messaged Iselin and asked to see her. I expect you wanted to talk to her about his two-timing. But Iselin was off for a run, so you agreed to meet up later.'

Mona had regained her blank expression and didn't react to what Jakob said – in any way he could see, at least.

'When Iselin was reported missing, you spotted a chance to take your revenge on Casper. You cycled out to Maskinisten and dumped the bloody T-shirt not far from the track leading up to the summit of Keiservarden.' Jakob paused for a moment before adding: 'We found tyre prints close to the T-shirt. We'll be comparing those to the tread of your mother's bicycle. I'm fairly certain we'll find a match.'

'Is this true?' Siri-Else whispered. She was standing with her hand half outstretched towards her daughter's shoulder. She didn't know whether she wanted to touch her or not. Her arm fell to her side. Jakob felt sorry for her.

'I was so angry...'

Mona didn't say anything else, and a peculiar silence descended upon the living room. It was heavy. Oppressive. As if the room were filled with excess pressure.

'Am I going to prison?' Mona's voice was feeble, her earlier rage gone.

'That's not up to me,' said Jakob. 'But what you did is serious. The resources we used to search the area where the T-shirt was found could have been used in the search for Iselin.'

'Are you...' Siri-Else searched for the right words. Her face was pale. 'Does Mona have to go with you?'

'No, that won't be necessary right now.' Jakob turned to Mona. 'You'll be summoned for a formal interview at the police station. In the meantime, I don't want you or your mother to discuss this with anyone else. Is that understood?'

'Of course,' Siri-Else said, replying on her daughter's behalf. She put an arm around Mona's shoulders and steered her towards the kitchen. When Jakob heard the gurgling of the coffee maker, he realised that neither mother nor daughter would be returning to the living room.

'So we're back to square one,' Ronald said once they were back outside.

'Pretty much,' Jakob conceded. 'But we've got a bunch of tip-offs that we haven't yet ruled out. And I'm not at all sure that Stein-Jarle Lie has told us everything he knows.'

'I get what she did, in a way,' Ronald said as they walked back to the car.

'Mona?'

'Yes. When I was seventeen, the girl I was head over heels for got together with my mate. I fantasised a lot about whacking him.

You know, asking him along on a fishing trip and drowning him. Fiery passion that suddenly goes bad really is a form of madness.'

'How did it work out?'

'Not in the Hollywood way. She dumped my friend a few months later for a guy with a car and a steady wage. Had her first kid when she was nineteen. Divorced at twenty-two. My friend and I used to laugh about it. Now it just feels sad.'

Back in the car, Jakob checked his mobile, which had been on silent while they had spoken to Mona.

'Three calls from Fine,' he told Ronald.

He called her back and she replied at once. She got straight to the point. 'The prosecutor has approved search and arrest warrants. Armann and Noora are out exercising them right now.'

'That means you were right in your assumption?'

'Yes. We're able to place both Simon Michalsen and his camper van in Bodø at the time of Iselin Hanssen's disappearance.'

'Could it be that we're only dealing with one killer after all?' Ronald muttered.

Jakob wasn't sure whether that was a question for him, or if the forensic scientist was talking to himself. But one thing was certain: Ronald sounded far from convinced.

CHAPTER 53

ARMANN

Armann waved away a particularly persistent horse fly. He was hidden behind the sizeable barn at Peder Skarvheim's. From the corner, he had a clear view of Simon Michalsen's house and garage. In anticipation of the raid, Thorsen had rung Peder and asked him and his mother to stay inside until further notice. On a couple of occasions, Armann had seen the curtains twitch at a first-floor window of the Skarvheim residence. Mother and son were probably following events with avid interest.

'What's the situation down by you?' he whispered into the radio.

'All quiet here,' Leo said. 'I can't see any sign of movement in or around the house.'

'Good. Stand by. Not long now.'

He pulled out his binoculars and surveyed the area in front of him. Simon's house lay in silent darkness at the end of the road. The garage door was shut and the curtains were closed in all the windows. Below the house and towards the sea, Leo and two uniformed officers were hidden behind some rocks. They would remain there until Armann gave the order to move.

Leo was still the only Kripos detective on the island. The rest of his team weren't expected for another couple of hours. Armann wasn't going to take his chances and wait for reinforcements; Marte might still be alive.

Armann lowered his binoculars and withdrew back around the corner of the barn to where Noora, Thorsen and Odd-Arne were waiting. At the very rear was Kjartan Engelstad. Despite his considerable misgivings, Armann had asked the doctor to join them. Given Kikki's story, it was a problematic decision, but if anyone was injured during the raid there would be a need for Engelstad's services. As far as Armann was concerned, the doctor's presence was a necessary evil.

He checked his wristwatch and moistened his lips. He raised the radio to his mouth.

'We go in one minute.'

He silently began to count the seconds. It had been years since he had experienced anything like this. Armann could feel himself rhythmically shifting his weight from foot to foot. Excess energy. Nerves. Anticipation. The desire to get it over with. The fear of what they might find in the house. An eagerness to get under way. All at once.

'Now!'

Armann went around the corner of the barn and ran along the road towards Simon's house. Noora was right on his tail. He reached the steps at the same time as Leo came from the other direction. The two of them stood shoulder to shoulder on the bottom step with Noora a few paces behind them. Everyone was armed, but for the time being their guns remained holstered.

Just as Armann had instructed them beforehand, Odd-Arne and Thorsen silently carried out a hasty search of the garage. Once the two of them had appeared at the rear of the building, Odd-Arne flashed them a thumbs-up. No one in the garage.

Armann climbed the steps to the front door and rang the bell. He didn't give the people inside long to react before he nodded to Leo, who took a run-up as he climbed the stairs and hurled himself shoulder first at the door. Armann timed his own kick to ensure his foot struck the door in tandem with Leo's shoulder.

'Police!' Armann roared. 'Put your hands over your head!'

There wasn't time for him to repeat the instruction before they heard the sound of glass shattering.

'That was from the kitchen!' Armann yelled, drawing his gun. Leo followed his example.

'Go round the outside of the house,' he heard Noora telling Odd-Arne before she followed him and Leo inside.

'Christ on a bike, this place reeks of cat piss,' Leo whispered. The stench was foul, but Armann thought it smelled more like rotten eggs or some other biological material slowly disintegrating.

Nightmarish images of Marte Moi appeared in his mind's eye. But it had only been twenty-four hours since she had gone missing. A body didn't begin to smell that quickly. Then another thought struck him: what if Marte wasn't the only one? What if Simon and Aslak were responsible for Iselin Hanssen's disappearance too? Might there be other girls? That could mean several dead bodies all at different stages of decomposition.

'Hold it right there!' Leo's cry yanked Armann out of his private cabinet of horrors. Leo was standing just inside the kitchen door with his gun trained on a person on their knees on the kitchen counter, ready to hurl themselves through the broken window.

Armann grabbed the collar of the fugitive and yanked him off the counter. The man fell backward onto the floor and let out a hollow groan before trying to squirm out of Armann's grip. Armann thumped his head against the kitchen unit so hard that cracks appeared in the cupboard door. The man gave up after that.

It was Aslak Nilsen. There was no doubt about it. Armann recognised him from both the police mugshot and the hotel personnel file. He crouched in front of him.

'Where's Marte?'

'Huh?' It looked like Aslak was struggling to focus. Was he high? His head-on encounter with the kitchen cupboard probably hadn't done much to help either.

'Where's Marte Moi? The girl you abducted.'

Still no response. 'What about Iselin Hanssen? What have you done to her?'

Aslak rolled his eyes and squinted at him. Could Aslak even see him? Armann wasn't sure that Aslak understood what he was being asked.

He changed tack. 'Tell me where Simon Michalsen is.'

The pupils in the middle of Aslak's yellow irises contracted slightly. It was a sign that he understood what he was being asked and that he probably knew the answer.

'Time to talk, you fish fucker.' Leo seized Aslak's collar and hauled him into the air. Aslak flailed around and shallow gasping sounds emanated from his throat. The fabric of his jacket had tightened around his neck and was making it difficult for him to breathe.

'Enough!' It was Noora who had shouted. She was standing by the kitchen door, her expression determined.

Leo glowered at her but finally let go of Aslak, who slid onto the floor. That put him back at eye level with Armann, who was still crouching.

'Simon Michalsen,' he repeated, as if Leo's and Noora's interventions had been nothing more than a rehearsed act.

'The basement,' Aslak croaked.

Leo pushed Noora aside and ran into the hallway. *This guy's too eager by half*, Armann thought. But he knew that he'd allowed himself to get carried away too, when he'd used the cupboard door as a bass drum with Aslak's skull as the beater.

'Do not go into the basement!' he shouted at Leo before waving through the window at Odd-Arne, telling him to come inside.

'Cuff him,' he ordered Odd-Arne as soon as the officer entered the kitchen. 'Make a note of anything he says, no matter how incoherent it may seem.'

Leo hadn't gone full Rambo. He and Noora were waiting for Armann by the basement door. They seemed to be standing as far apart as they could, and it struck him that he hadn't seen them actually speak to one another. It was undeniably peculiar behaviour for two former colleagues.

The basement door was more robust than any other door in the house and just as tall and a little wider than the front door.

'Take a look at this,' said Noora, pointing to the moulding

around the door. 'It's completely sealed. You wouldn't be able to hear whatever goes on down in the basement.'

'Then the reverse must also be true,' Armann said. 'Simon probably doesn't know he's got visitors.'

Armann pushed the handle down and opened the door. The stench rising up the steps made all three of them cover their noses and mouths. It smelled of putrefaction. It reeked of death.

Dead bodies.

CHAPTER 54

NOORA

'Holy shit.' Noora staggered backward and tried to blink the tears away. The stench had enveloped her, making her feel unclean both outside and inside.

By the basement door, Leo had fallen to his knees and was retching. Armann had produced a small glass pot and stuck his finger in it. He was now spreading the contents underneath his nose.

'Tiger balm,' he coughed, handing it to Noora.

Noora dabbed some under her nose before giving it to Leo, who was now back on his feet. The tiger balm helped, but the odour she was inhaling was heavy and cloying.

Leo threw the pot to Engelstad, who had by now also entered the house. The doctor caught it but shook his head.

He mouthed the words 'Don't need it.'

The first sound Noora heard as she approached the basement door was a faint-yet-deep murmur. It was the kind of sound that came from electrical machinery or a transformer. Peering over Armann's shoulder, she tried to form an impression of the space, but from here she could see nothing but a bare wall at the far end. Only when she reached the bottom of the steps did she realise what the large room contained.

There were four work benches along one wall, covered in flasks, metal containers and various measuring cups. The benches were illuminated by lighting suspended on wires from the ceiling. Next to the work benches were several plastic barrels marked with various chemical symbols. One of these – labelled *Acetone* in big black letters, followed by the symbol for inflammable materials – didn't have a cap on it. But what really captured Noora's attention was the aluminium tank in the middle of the room. It was the size of a tank you might find in a microbrewery.

But Simon Michalsen's basement was no brewery, nor even an illegal still. While Noora had never seen anything like it before, she nevertheless knew they had just found a facility for the production of methamphetamine. A meth lab. The rot of decay throughout the house was from the production process.

'Fuck me sideways.' Leo proceeded further into the room and looked around.

Engelstad attempted to follow, but Armann stopped the doctor with a curt 'Wait here!'

Leo ran a hand across the aluminium tank, turned around and was about to say something when the lights in the basement went out.

They were in total darkness until their eyes adjusted and the contours of the benches and cabinets emerged, offset against the harsh light penetrating from the open basement door. There was enough light for Noora to make out the shape of Leo by the tank, but nothing beyond that. She moved slowly towards him.

'Wait a second. I've got a torch on me.' Armann pushed his jacket aside to fumble for something on his belt. There was no time for him to turn it on before a scream that hurt their ear drums resounded around the basement.

A figure rushed out of the dark corner of the basement and into the semi-darkness. He wore nothing but a robust rubber apron and a pair of black boots. A transparent breathing mask covered his whole face. In his right hand, raised above his head, he brandished a crowbar.

Leo reacted quickly, pivoting towards the attacker, but the arm clutching the crowbar was already swinging down.

Noora threw herself forward, rugby tackling Leo below the knees. He crumpled and the crowbar hit nothing but air in the place his head had just been. He fell sideways, knocking his head against the aluminium tank.

Noora rolled forward and got to her feet, making sure to stay low. The attacker spun around. He raised the crowbar towards her.

Noora leapt aside. She kicked the guy in the diaphragm, but most of the force of her kick was absorbed by the thick apron.

The man reeled backward before coming for her again. This time Noora forced herself to remain upright. There was something predictable about his mode of attack. He didn't swing the crowbar from side to side – instead he kept it raised above him. She was right. The pattern was the same. The crowbar came thundering down towards her, but just before it hit her, Noora smartly stepped to one side and drove her knee into his chin.

The sound of teeth shattering was clearly audible throughout the basement. The man collapsed without any attempt to break his fall. He remained motionless while Armann and Engelstad heaved a still dazed Leo to his feet. Then Engelstad bent over the man and removed his mask. The attacker was Simon Michalsen.

Noora exhaled. They had both suspects under control.

'His jaw seems to be in one piece, but he'll need new front teeth.' Armann twisted Simon's hands behind his back and handcuffed him. The man grunted in response. Simon was regaining consciousness.

Armann and Noora dragged him upstairs. Leo, meanwhile, was assisted up the steps by Engelstad.

'Right, now all we need to do is make these bastards talk,' Armann said to Noora.

'They're about to face charges for abduction, the production of illegal narcotics and violence against the police. They've got everything to gain from talking,' Noora said.

But Aslak and Simon weren't talking. The two of them were keeping their mouths shut. Noora, Leo and Armann took turns questioning them about Marte. About Iselin. About the meth lab. The outcome was the same. In two separate rooms, Simon and Aslak denied any involvement in the disappearances. All questions pertaining to the meth lab were met with silence. Every now and then, Engelstad glanced into the rooms –

probably to make sure that the detainees weren't receiving the 'Armann treatment' he'd seen earlier. But didn't Engelstad also seem a little restless? Or was that a natural reaction given what he'd just witnessed?

Following another round of questioning, Armann drew Noora to one side. 'What's your take?' he asked.

'It feels like a tactic,' Noora said. 'They're denying anything we can't prove, and keeping schtum about the meth lab.'

'It looks that way, doesn't it? Damn it. I'm almost tempted to...' Armann punched his fist into his other hand. Noora knew exactly what he meant.

Something else soon became apparent to Noora: Leo was avoiding looking at her. In their handful of brief exchanges, he fixed his gaze to a point above her head. She had saved him in the basement, sparing him from serious injury and perhaps even death. Leo knew it, and he appeared to be struggling to digest it. Noora saw no reason to make it easy for him.

While the preliminary interviews continued, Thorsen and the uniformed officers searched the house and garage, hoping to find traces of the missing women or something that might give them a lead on where they had been hidden. So far, the search had been just as fruitless as the interrogations.

After another frustrating round of questioning, Noora took a break. She filled a glass with water from the kitchen tap and drank it before pulling out her phone and calling Jakob.

When he answered, she gave him an update.

'So the doctor came with you on the raid?' Jakob said, after asking Noora to elaborate on what the basement looked like.

'He stayed in the background. Both Armann and I know it's questionable given what we know about him, but we figured it was for the best. And Engelstad was easily persuaded.'

'Noora?' Thorsen beckoned to her from the kitchen door.

'I've got to go,' Noora told Jakob. 'I expect Armann will call you as soon as he's done questioning them.'

When Noora emerged on the front steps, Thorsen said, 'We've found something interesting in Simon's camper.'

'It was lying on the passenger seat, plain as the nose on your face.' Odd-Arne pointed to a book. It was Marte Moi's autobiography. It looked well thumbed.

'No one's touched it, have they?' said Noora.

'Nope,' Odd-Arne replied.

'Good.' Noora donned a pair of latex gloves and put on overshoes. Then she opened the door to the living area in the back and looked inside. 'Have you guys been in here?'

'Yes,' said Thorsen. 'The doors were unlocked. Obviously we didn't find Marte inside. And we haven't found any other trace of her either.'

Noora climbed inside and shut the door behind her. She was able to think more clearly when she didn't have people staring at her.

The interior was clean and well kept. Judging by the smell, it had been recently sanitised. She opened cupboards and drawers, but found nothing of interest. Yet the fact that Marte's book had been lying on the front seat surely had to mean something. Or was she merely engaging in wishful thinking?

There was a bed suspended from the roof above the combined living and dining area. She found the mechanism to lower it. Like the rest of the interior, the bed was clean and in good condition. The sheets and duvet had been removed. There was nothing but a thin beige cover on the mattress. Noora ran her glove across it, feeling dejection take hold. She almost didn't notice the small lump in one corner of the mattress.

She quickly removed the fabric cover. The pink running sock was easy to spot against the white mattress. She took the sock between her forefinger and thumb and dropped it into a transparent Ziplock bag. She opened the door and walked straight past Thorsen and Odd-Arne, ignoring their questions. She got into one of the unmarked cars, started the engine and drove away.

She saw the camera flashes from the press pack as she drove through the cordon that had been established at the end of the road leading to Simon Michalsen's house.

Ascension, Marte's assistant, was sitting alone in the hotel restaurant, nursing a cup of coffee. Her face was haggard, the skin beneath her eyes papery and transparent. She had sought refuge in her room as soon as the press had descended upon the island. Now that the media circus had shifted to the cordon around Simon's house, she had ventured out.

Noora sat down opposite her and laid the bag containing the sock on the table between them.

Ascension gasped. She reached out towards the bag but didn't touch it.

'*Si, si,*' she nodded, before switching to Norwegian. 'That's Marte's sock. I saw her put on a pair just like that before she went running.'

CHAPTER 55

JAKOB

'A meth lab on Røst. Who would have thunk it?'

'Well, isn't that the point?' Fine said. 'No one would have. Out there you've got minimal oversight, and you can steal plenty of the chemicals you need from the fishing and processing industries. Given his degree in chemistry, Simon would have known what to look for.'

'*Breaking Bad*, but in Lofoten,' Ronald said dryly.

'It's pretty clever – no one checks camper vans on the ferry between Røst and the mainland. And once they arrive in Bodø, Aslak and Simon can maintain trading connections with the rest of the country, either by delivering the goods themselves or using domestic flights and rail to send it onward.'

Jakob leaned against the counter. He wondered whether to pour himself another cup of coffee, but refrained. It wasn't lunchtime yet, and he'd already had the best part of a litre, even though he'd started the day on tea.

'I spoke to Armann half an hour after Noora called. Both Simon and Aslak are denying any knowledge of Marte Moi and Iselin Hanssen. But Aslak's still high and Simon took a couple of almighty whacks to the head during his arrest.'

'They might be more talkative once the mental fog lifts,' said Ronald.

Jakob shrugged. 'I'm not as optimistic as you. The plan might be to play for time and hope that we offer them a deal. Where Marte and Iselin are being held is the only card they've got in their hand. But I find it odd that neither of them decided to talk once we told them we'd found Marte's sock.'

'I agree with Jakob,' said Fine. 'Marte's sock in Simon's camper is hard to explain.'

'What I don't understand,' Ronald said, to no one in particular, 'is why they kidnapped Marte in the first place? They must have known that something like this would draw huge amounts of attention. Especially in a small place like Røst.'

'You said it yourself,' Jakob said. 'It might have been done on a whim. Perhaps Simon has some morbid fascination with her. After all, Marte's book was in his vehicle.'

'Yes, but that was before I knew the blokes were drug kingpins.'

Råkstad's office door opened. Jakob hadn't realised that the police superintendent was there. 'Good work everyone,' he said to them. 'Both on Røst and in getting to the bottom of Mona's involvement with the bloody T-shirt.'

'We would have known about it sooner if Casper had told us the truth about how he'd injured his nose when Armann and Fine interviewed him the day after the disappearance,' said Jakob.

'Well there's that, but we have to take the world as it comes.'

Jakob looked at Råkstad – doses of everyday philosophy were rarely doled out by the man.

'I've just had a word with the prosecutor,' Råkstad continued. 'She's going to take an understanding position in relation to Mona and Casper's withholding of information. They'll get a fixed penalty notice. Nothing more.'

Jakob didn't say anything. He felt no ill will towards Casper or Mona, but he doubted whether Råkstad would have engaged so doggedly with the issue if Casper hadn't been the son of Otto Jahrberg. Power and position always mattered. But if Casper was getting off with a rap on the knuckles, then Mona had to be treated the same for appearances' sake.

'How are the Kripos lot getting on?' Råkstad said.

'With the exception of Leo Korshamn, the team never even reached Røst before the situation was resolved,' Jakob said. 'The detectives are going to stay in Bodø to assist us with questioning here, while forensics are going to Røst with Ronald to take a closer look at Michalsen's house and camper.'

Råkstad nodded. 'Good. I'll brief Telle. She's due to do a press conference at one o'clock. She'd like photos of the meth lab by then. Please tell Armann to send anything she can use to Åge.'

'I suppose that was more praise than we might have expected,' Fine muttered after Råkstad had left them.

'I've not seen him that cheerful in a long time,' Ronald said.

'Relieved,' said Jakob. 'He mostly seemed relieved.'

'Hardly surprising,' Fine said. 'Råkstad's been getting it from both sides, from Telle and the prosecutor.'

And Otto Jahrberg, Jakob thought silently.

Ronald said goodbye and went down to his office to prepare for the journey to Røst.

Jakob was standing by the table where the Facebook group run by Gudrun was still up on Fine's laptop.

'Sure, it's nice of Råkstad to offer praise, but Marte and Iselin are still missing. The case won't be solved until we find them. Now that we've established that Simon was in Bodø at the time in question, we need to try and identify his route.' Jakob held up a stack of Post-its. 'Did you find anything interesting among the tip-offs?'

'Actually, I did,' Fine said.

She pulled a page out of her notebook and handed it to Jakob. It was covered in dense handwriting.

'Yesterday I had a chat with a guy called Njål Ree. He used to work in the cultural section at the local council, but he's retired now and basically spends all his time at his cabin up in Løp. On the day of Iselin's disappearance, he saw two people on the slope lower down the mountain. I think it might be worth checking out.'

'Løp, you say?'

'Yes. Njål owns one of the fishermen's shacks down by the marina.'

Jakob went over to the map of Bodø pinned to the wall beside the whiteboard. 'That's only a few hundred metres away from where our dead Ukrainian girl was found.'

CHAPTER 56

NOORA

Standing on the apron, Noora watched the helicopter disappear into the clouds above Vedøya southeast of Røst. Armann, Leo and the suspects were on board. Was it really less than seventy-two hours since she had arrived? It felt like a week.

Armann had asked no questions about her choice to wait a couple of hours to catch the evening flight back to Bodø. He'd seen how uncomfortable she was on the chopper ride out. He wasn't to know that it was mostly down to something other than the mode of transport: Leo.

What had happened in Simon Michalsen's basement had established a kind of truce between them, but Noora didn't think it would last. The thought of sitting in the same cramped space as Leo on the way back to the mainland, with his eyes on her body, was far worse than any fickle gusts of wind.

Was it over now? She hoped so, but she had no real expectations. And she kept finding herself searching for the phone she had thrown into the sea.

A gust of wind made her jacket flap. She retreated inside the terminal building. A couple of journalists from *VG* were sitting at one of the tables. They had snapped pictures of Aslak and Simon being escorted to the helicopter in handcuffs. The photos of the detainees alone had probably made the trip worth it.

Noora nodded to the guard by security and made for the exit. She got into the car Thorsen had lent her. The cars that Odd-Arne and the other uniformed officers had brought were now parked at the hotel so that Ronald and his team could use them when they arrived that evening.

Noora gripped the steering wheel. She felt her heart pounding as if she had just run up a steep hill. Was this delayed stress from the incident in the basement? They had apprehended the perpetrators, but Marte and Iselin were still missing.

Noora had no doubt that Simon and Aslak would eventually talk. Most co-conspirators usually did. They would turn on each other, revealing where they had hidden the girls in exchange for a more lenient sentence. Or perhaps they wouldn't – if they had done things to them that would only make matters worse ... Her heart continued its lonely sprint inside her ribs.

Noora felt nauseous. Inadequate.

Useless.

Thorsen was waiting for her outside the hotel. The old policeman looked haggard as he leaned into the wind gusting in off Vestfjorden. This was probably not how he had imagined his final weeks before retirement.

'What an absolute dog's dinner,' was the first thing he said when she got out of the car. Noora wasn't exactly sure what the target of Thorsen's opprobrium was, but she nodded anyway. There were plenty of things to choose from.

'Kikki wants to know whether you'll still need the meeting room.'

'We'll let Ronald decide when he gets here. He'll probably want to use the school, given that it's the summer holidays. Forensics tend to bring a lot of equipment.'

Noora handed him the car key.

'Just leave it in the ignition,' he said, squinting up at the clouds wafting across the sky. 'You're off tonight?'

'Yes. Booked on the Widerøe flight. The forensics team are arriving on the inbound. You don't think it'll be cancelled, do you?'

'Has to be worse than this for them to do that. But I am a little worried about this cloud cover. It's rare for it to be this low when it's windy. Poor visibility is the most common reason they cancel.'

Noora told Kikki about the meeting room and her plans to leave for Bodø that evening. 'Then I think you and the district sheriff ought to have a bite to eat before your flight,' the hotel manager said. Noora wasn't feeling particularly hungry, but Thorsen accepted and it would have been rude to let him eat alone.

They found a table by the window with a view overlooking the jetty. While they waited for the waiter, Thorsen leaned in to whisper to Noora.

'This isn't on Kikki. She was actually a bit miffed when Armann and the others left so quickly. If I know Kikki, she'll be sending the police a bill with at least another couple of days' worth of rooms and board added on.'

The main course was butter-baked cod with bacon, new potatoes and asparagus. The smell awakened Noora's hunger. She had been subsisting primarily on sandwiches and the odd chocolate bar for the past twenty-four hours. And coffee. Gallons of it.

'Isn't it a bit strange?' Noora said as she wiped the last of the sauce off her plate with a piece of bread.

'What is?'

'That no one saw Simon's camper van when he abducted Marte? That must be how the sock ended up inside it. It's not exactly the smallest of vehicles.'

'It's not that odd,' said Thorsen. He took a toothpick from the box on the table and put it in the corner of his mouth. 'It was early in the morning and there were heavy rain showers. If Simon attacked Marte between the hotel and his own home, then it would only have been a couple of minutes' drive before he could park in the garage.'

Noora left the piece of bread lying uneaten on her plate. Thorsen had a point. She was still thinking as if she were in Oslo, a city where criminal acts were often observed by one or more witnesses while also being captured on CCTV.

But then again, Simon's camper van was distinctively large. Someone ought to have seen it. She made a mental note to suggest to Jakob that the police carry out fresh door-to-door inquiries on the island to ask specifically about the vehicle.

'Evald?' Kikki waved to them from the kitchen door. She was clutching the receiver of the landline, the cable twisting its way to her from the blue base. 'It's for you.'

Thorsen patted down his trouser pockets. 'I left my phone in the meeting room,' he said apologetically, going over to Kikki.

'Yes, this is District Sheriff Thorsen,' Noora heard him say before the door closed behind him. She couldn't imagine Thorsen ever describing himself by any other title.

Noora pulled out her phone and sent a message to Ellen: *Home tonight?*

She got a response immediately: *Yep. Not expecting any visitors either ;)*

It was obvious that Noora was forgiven for the incident with Remi. She still felt embarrassed at the mere thought of it. At least her lip was no longer sore.

Wine and chat? she suggested.

Definitely. When will you be home?

Noora still wasn't sure whether Bodø felt like home, but she didn't want to go back to Oslo either.

About half past nine if the flight's on time.

Great! I'll put the red wine on ice (yes, I'm a barbarian)!

Noora sent a thumbs-up in reply before returning her phone to her pocket.

The exchange of text messages was part of everyday life. Normality. It put her in a good mood. She resolved to pick up a pizza from Peppe's. And a couple of bars of dark chocolate too. Then she'd change out of her jeans into some loose joggers and curl up on the sofa with Ellen.

'Noora.' Thorsen had returned to the table and was now standing there, fidgeting with the notebook in his hand. He looked perplexed.

'Yes?'

'Someone else has just been reported missing. Here. On Røst.'

CHAPTER 57

JAKOB

It only took an extra five minutes to drive home before going on to Løp to speak to Njål Ree. Ola wasn't in his room, so Jakob texted him to let him know that he had taken Garm.

While en route, Armann called.

'You're back from Røst?' asked Jakob.

'Yep,' Armann confirmed. 'I hoped to find you at the station.'

'I'll be back in an hour or so,' said Jakob. 'Unless it's urgent? If so, I can swing by.'

'No, it'll keep.'

Jakob heard a certain hesitation in Armann's voice. It was obvious his colleague had something he wished to impart.

'Anything new from our duo?'

'In a manner of speaking. Simon finally started talking in the helicopter.'

'Oh?'

'I was sitting next to him. I pushed him on the discovery of Marte's sock in the camper van and the fact that he was in Bodø at the same time as Iselin went missing. I did my best to make him understand how serious this was. Then all of a sudden, he blew his top.'

'Really?'

'He said the kidnapping accusations were a miscarriage of justice. Said the sock had been planted. He yelled: "Where the hell else would I be apart from Bodø when I needed to catch the ferry to Røst?"'

'What's your assessment?'

Silence. Down the line, Jakob heard a door slam and someone talking in the background. Office sounds. 'I'm not sure,' Armann admitted. 'I suppose it's conceivable that only one of them is connected to the disappearances. That would mean we were dealing with another Baneheia-murders scenario, of sorts.'

'You're thinking of Aslak?'

'Yes.'

'But Aslak was working at the hotel on the day Iselin went missing,' Jakob said.

Armann didn't reply. Jakob thought back to last night, when he had wondered if Marte's disappearance might be connected to the murder of the woman in Lofoten. As Ronald had pointed out, a connection like that seemed unlikely. Still ... Jakob couldn't quite put his thoughts into words.

'What's happening at the station right now?'

'Leo Korshamn from Kripos is processing Simon and Aslak's paperwork. In the meantime, I'm briefing the other detectives from Kripos on the case. That way, everyone will have the same information when we resume questioning. It's going to be a long night.'

'Good. Make sure you take Fine along for that briefing. She's sick of paperwork.'

'No problem. See you later.'

At the top of the steep hill, Jakob opened the window. The areas of Skivika and Løpsmarka were on what Bodø natives tended to refer to as 'the north side', and the air there was different. Faint streaks of sunlight penetrated through the clouds. One moment, the sea between the mainland and Landegode was glistening silver, the next the waves were lifeless and grey as they rolled towards shore.

Through the clouds, Jakob caught a glimpse of Kjerringøy. The last time he and Lise had visited the old trading post, they had promised each other they would return soon. There was something about Kjerringøy. It was one of those places that took hold of you and grew in your memory into something greater than its reality.

The fishermen's shacks in the harbour at Løp were a few

hundred metres away from the campsite. Jakob pulled off by
Bremnes Fort, where Galyna Ivanova had been found dead.
Ronald had categorised the death as suicide, albeit with some
reservations, but they were still waiting for final confirmation
from Oslo.

He didn't know Njål Ree's address, but his hut was easy to find
since there was a car with the NRK logo parked outside. It was the
same car Sigrid had been driving the last time they'd met in
Maskinisten. What was she doing here? Jakob knocked on the door.

Njål Ree looked like an actor appearing in a parody about
Norwegian bureaucracy. He was a stocky man, his pot belly
bulging against a V-neck with sleeves that were slightly too short.
His trousers were khaki-coloured and were what his school friends
would have called ankle-swingers. It looked like Njål had washed
his clothes at too high a temperature and hadn't noticed – or
didn't care – that they had shrunk.

'Jakob Weber.'

Njål took his hand, squeezed it once and then invited Jakob
upstairs into the small living room, where he found Sigrid on the
sofa with a cup of coffee. She nodded to him as if they had agreed
to meet there.

'Coffee?' said Njål as he applied disinfectant to his hands.

'Yes please,' said Jakob. He returned Sigrid's nod, which made
him feel unnecessarily stiff and formal. Then he said to her: 'I read
your story about Iselin's fitness tracker on the NRK website.
Seemed very thorough to me.'

'It's all about having good sources,' Sigrid said with a wink.

Njål returned from the kitchen and placed a cup of coffee in
front of Jakob. He settled down in an armchair that was so high
Jakob began to wonder whether Njål's feet were actually touching
the floor. He resisted the temptation to crane his neck to find out.

'Can you tell me about the people you saw up on the slope?'

'There were two figures,' said Njål. 'Wearing fitness gear. Well,
the one at the front was. The one behind was in a dark-green or

dark-blue jacket, and was taller and stronger than the one in front. I didn't see their faces, but if I were to guess I'd say they were a man and a woman out for a walk together.' Njål wiggled his feet. 'Well, more than a walk I suppose. It's pretty demanding terrain up there. It got me wondering what they were up to.'

Jakob was noting down Njål's key phrases. 'Can you think of anything else?'

'Well, this is just speculation on my part, but just before they disappeared behind a knoll, the person behind grabbed the arm of the person in front. It happened abruptly, as if the person in front was slipping and about to fall, or...'

'Or trying to run away?' Sigrid suggested.

'Exactly that,' said Njål.

Jakob assumed that Njål had already told Sigrid all this, but that didn't make it any less interesting. 'Can you identify the knoll they disappeared behind?'

'Of course.' Njål got out of his chair and opened the terrace door. The view was striking. The terrace looked out over the marina and fjord. On clear days, you could probably see all the way to Henningsvær in Lofoten.

'I was barbecuing that evening,' Njål said. 'It was a little drizzly, but I've got shelter here. Although it wasn't the best weather, the sun came out from behind the clouds a couple of times. It's low in the sky that late in the day, which means it shines straight onto the mountainside. That was how I spotted them. They stood out in contrast to the slope behind them.'

Njål pointed. 'Just below the top, below that bare rock face, there's a knoll with a pine tree on top of it.'

'I can see the tree,' Jakob said. 'And you're saying they disappeared behind the knoll and didn't reappear?'

'I lost sight of them behind the knoll,' Njål said. 'Whether they came out on the other side or not, I don't know. I wasn't paying a lot of attention. It was only when I heard about Iselin's disappearance that I remembered it.'

Jakob took a photo of the knoll from Njål's terrace and thanked him. Sigrid was still on the sofa – it didn't look as if she was finished.

On his way back to the car, he received a text from her:

Good to see you, Jakob. It was Njål who called me. You know how it is: everyone wants their fifteen minutes of fame. Talk later?

Jakob replied with a thumbs-up. He paused for thought and then added a smiley too.

He checked the satnav and found a forest track zig-zagging up towards the knoll that Njål had pointed out. He only stopped when he heard grass brushing the chassis. The road petered out fifty metres ahead of him. From there, it was still another three or four hundred metres to the knoll, most of it across rough, steep terrain covered in dense thickets. And guaranteed to be a complete horse-fly and mosquito hellscape.

He stayed in the car while flipping through the notes he'd made during his conversation with Njål. In the back, Garm was shifting restlessly. Regardless of which route you took, from the top down or bottom up, it would be a real slog. And it wouldn't be much easier if you were manhandling someone who was putting up a fight. Jakob tapped his pen against his notepad. The basic questions in any investigation always boiled down to the perpetrator's motive and opportunity. Why and how.

How...

Jakob pulled out his mobile and called Fine. In the boot, Garm barked impatiently.

'Relax, you'll get your walk soon.'

'I didn't know I had to ask you for permission,' Fine said.

Jakob laughed. 'Sorry. Just a minor disagreement with Garm here. I've got a quick question.'

'Go for it.'

'Do we know how long Simon Michalsen was in Bodø?'

'Give me a second.' Jakob heard the sound of a keyboard before Fine said: 'We're still tracing his movements, but the time from when his camper was seen by a traffic camera on the main road into Bodø until he drove onto the ferry to Røst was two hours and fifty-eight minutes.'

'And that's the same time that Iselin went missing?'

'Yes, now we've got the data from Strava, we know that Simon had already been in town for an hour and seventeen minutes when she lost her fitness tracker – or it was taken off her.'

'That means that Simon had time to go up the hill, attack Iselin and somehow convey her back to his vehicle, all while remaining unseen. Then he took the ferry to Røst?'

'The timing is tight, but it's not impossible. Alternatively, he might have killed her and hidden the body in the woods.'

'Thanks. That's a big help.'

'What are you thinking?'

'Might be nothing. I need to check something first.'

After ending the call with Fine, Jakob remained seated. Garm had stopped whining. The dog probably sensed that his master wasn't to be disturbed.

Simon Michalsen was still their prime suspect, but if what Njål Ree had seen had anything to do with Iselin, that changed the situation. Simon would never have made the ferry if he had moved Iselin from the location where her fitness tracker was found to the hill beneath the escarpment. And if Simon hadn't abducted Iselin, then maybe he had nothing to do with Marte's disappearance either. Armann clearly already had his doubts.

One thought led to another. Jakob realised that he needed to make one more call before he went to find out what Njål had seen.

Rolf Kvist picked up on the second ring. 'How are things in the world of the living?' the old detective managed to say before a volley of coughing took over.

Jakob waited until Rolf had caught his breath before he replied. 'All good here. Any news from the Public Roads Administration? You know – the registration on the camper van?'

'I'm not senile, Weber. Of course I remember. I intend to call my contact later today.'

'Excellent,' said Jakob. 'I've got a suggestion for how to filter their search. I'm only interested in vehicles on the island of Røst that match the description of the camper seen in Lofoten twenty-nine years ago. That shouldn't take long.'

'Røst eh?' He could hear Rolf breathing heavily. 'I know you, Weber. You've picked up a scent. I'll get on to my contact right away.'

CHAPTER 58

NOORA

'Dr Engelstad was really supposed to stay here until tomorrow, but he told me one of his patients on Værøy called complaining of chest pains.'

Noora thought the nurse, a woman in her fifties whose name badge above her left breast pocket said she was called Vigdis, sounded more fed up than worried.

'When he came back after your raid, he asked me to call out the air ambulance from Bodø. It's supposed to come here first to pick up Kjartan and then go on to Værøy.' Vigdis hesitated slightly before continuing. 'I don't like to say this, but Kjartan is an absolute scatterbrain. He often loses track of time when he's out taking pictures of birds.'

'So you're saying you don't know where he is now?' said Noora.

'No, and it's not at all like him to disappear like this. The air ambulance lands at the airport in half an hour, and I've got no idea where he's got to. With everything that's been happening recently, I'm a little worried.'

'I can understand that,' said Thorsen. 'But as you said, Kjartan is a scatterbrain. I'm sure it's just a misunderstanding.'

'Does the doctor have an office here at the nursing home?' said Noora.

Vigdis pointed towards a door standing ajar. Inside, Noora saw a packed Bergans rucksack propped against the desk. She pushed the door right open and went in. A wireless headset was lying on the desk next to a leather credit-card wallet.

'So you don't have any idea where he might have gone?' she heard Thorsen ask.

'I don't know. He had two appointments to see patients today, but since he was helping you lot out they were moved to tomorrow. But perhaps he's gone to try and do them now. What do I know? I've tried calling but I'm only getting his voicemail. Kjartan never turns off his phone.'

Judging by the office of Dr Kjartan Engelstad, he was an orderly man rather than the supposed scatterbrain that Vigdis implied him to be. Clean surfaces. Medical books and journals lined up in alphabetical order on the bookcase. Mouse centred on the mouse mat; not so much as a smudge on the keyboard. And on top of the examination couch there was a fresh paper covering. Noora pulled out the desk chair and caught sight of the camera bag tucked underneath the desk.

In the waiting room, Vigdis was searching for something on the computer while Thorsen was watching over her shoulder. Noora pulled out the camera; it was an Olympus digital twin-lens reflex model. She turned it on, opened a folder labelled 'Birds 1' and scrolled through the shots using the navigation buttons.

Kittiwakes, cormorants, sea eagles, puffins and gulls, as well as what Noora thought was a northern gannet with distinctive black markings at the tips of its wings.

The contents of 'Birds 2' and 'Birds 3' were the same. The only folder that gave the impression that it might contain anything else was one labelled 'Miscellaneous'. Noora opened it.

'What the fuck...?'

She looked up to make sure that the other two in the waiting room hadn't heard her before she stared at the picture on the screen. The 'Miscellaneous' folder contained more than a hundred images, and none of them were of birds.

A chair scraped. Vigdis had stood up to hand Thorsen a piece of paper. Noora switched off the camera and returned it to the bag. She took it with her.

'I think we can rule out the idea that Engelstad has gone bird-watching,' Noora said as she emerged from the office. She held up Engelstad's bag. 'I found this under his desk. The camera is still in it.'

Vigdis came over to her and opened the flap on the bag, as if to make sure Noora was telling the truth.

'We're going to take the camera with us,' Noora told Vigdis. 'Perhaps some of the pictures might be able to give us a lead on where Engelstad has gone.'

'Maybe it's best to start with the people who were expecting house calls from him tomorrow,' Vigdis said. 'I've given their names to Thorsen.'

'Sounds like a good idea,' Noora replied. 'What does Engelstad drive?'

'A blue Ford estate,' Vigdis and Thorsen said in unison.

The district sheriff smiled before adding: 'It's an old model. The Ford's become such a common sight on the island that no one notices it. Kjartan's father bought it in Bodø back when he was appointed as the island doctor here. It's practically a classic now.'

Noora said nothing more until she and Thorsen were in the car. Then she pulled the camera out of the bag. 'I was wondering why you brought that with you,' said Thorsen. 'Have you found anything interesting?'

'That's one way of putting it.'

She opened the 'Miscellaneous' folder and began to scroll through the contents. Picture after picture appeared on the small screen, taken through the windows of private homes using a telescopic lens.

All of them were of women and girls going about their lives and doing ordinary things like cooking, watching TV, reading a book or talking on the phone. But many of them were also of an intimate nature.

There were women standing naked in front of a mirror, a couple clutching their bellies with disgruntled expressions and one of an old woman lying on a bed, satisfying herself with a black vibrator. The final pictures Engelstad had taken were of Lotte Ramnakken in her house at Grimsøya. Noora recognised the green kerchief. These pictures were harmless. Lotte was standing at the living-room window gazing towards the sea with a serious, perhaps even sorrowful expression.

'I don't know what to say,' Thorsen whispered. He took the camera from Noora and scrolled back and forth, lingering on certain photos. His lips silently formed the names of the women each time he recognised them.

'Are you sure that—'

Noora spun the camera around before he managed to finish his question. The label on the bottom of the camera read: *Kjartan Engelstad*.

Thorsen rested his hands on the steering wheel and turned to Noora. 'Maybe Kjartan has a good reason for having taken these photos?'

'Damn it man, don't go making excuses for him,' Noora said. She saw Thorsen recoil. He would just have to deal with it. 'What if that had been your children, grandchildren or wife that he secretly photographed?'

Thorsen dug a couple of pouches of powdered tobacco from his tin and slipped them both under his lip. 'Let's just find him.'

The note Vigdis had handed to Thorsen bore the names Eirik Tofte and Gunlaug Skarvheim. The nurse had not included their addresses or phone numbers. Naturally, the old policeman knew who they were and where they lived.

Thorsen started the car. 'Let's go to Gunlaug first. I spoke to Peder Skarvheim after we arrested Simon and Aslak. I warned him that he might well have journalists knocking on his door, looking to interview him. Peder said he and his mother had already had quite enough excitement and that if the journalists came calling they'd find the door locked.'

Thorsen pulled onto the now familiar lane that ran to Simon Michalsen's house.

'It demands respect, what Peder does for his mother,' Thorsen said, as if he wanted to postpone any further discussion about Engelstad's pictures until later. 'Gunlaug has been bedridden for the last two years, but Peder's taking good care of her. Once we're done here, we'll go to Eirik's.'

Noora didn't reply. She was gazing out of the side window, unable to see anything other than the photographs. The naked intimacy. The vulnerability.

Thorsen cleared his throat. 'Eirik's a bit of a character. He's known colloquially as "Old Eirik" when he's not around to hear it.'

'An old lag is he?' Noora asked, trying to breathe life into the conversation. Thorsen really did not want to discuss the elephant in the room.

'Yes, you might say that,' he replied. 'Eirik is an old-school bruiser and a crook. You remember the moonshine case Aslak Nilsen got done for?'

Noora nodded.

'I always suspected Eirik was behind it. Actually, it's more than a theory – I'm sure it's true. But I never managed to prove it, and Aslak kept his mouth shut then, just like now. I suppose he knew Old Eirik would beat him senseless if he snitched.'

'Do you consider Eirik a threat?'

Thorsen pulled out the toothpick that he had been chewing at the corner of his mouth since dinner at the hotel and threw it out of the window. 'No, not anymore. He's got a bad case of pulmonary emphysema. Climbing the stairs leaves him out of breath. Not that he's harmless. He's still a powerful guy. Probably a hundred and twenty kilos, and word has it he's moved his weights into the living room so that he doesn't have to go down to the basement to lift. But I haven't encountered anything in the last couple of years that can be connected to him.'

That you managed to connect to him, Noora thought, and felt a twinge of guilty conscience. After all, Thorsen was a good guy. He was doing the best he could with the scarce resources at his disposal.

They drove past the barn they had hidden behind earlier, before the raid, and pulled into the gravelled courtyard. There was a dented mailbox hanging off a wonky post by the driveway. Thorsen had to turn the steering wheel hard to avoid a water-filled pothole. Engelstad's car was nowhere to be seen.

Noora hadn't given any thought to the Skarvheim residence until now. She noted that it was typical of the older buildings on the island. The walls were clad in grey-white asbestos tiles; several of them were cracked and the felt behind was visible. In the middle of the pointed crest of the roof there was a window. Noora could picture the room within: it would be small, she thought. The kind of room where you could only stand upright in the centre due to the pitch of the roof.

The barn door was ajar, and Noora caught a glimpse of the voluminous interior, where a microcar was parked. What little red paint was left on the barn clung to the planks like rust.

'Perhaps Engelstad's been and gone,' said Thorsen. 'I'll check with Peder. Back soon.' Once out of the car, Thorsen put his hands on his hips and stretched his back before climbing the five stone steps up to the front door and knocking.

A gust of wind swept across the courtyard, spraying the barn with sand and debris. Thorsen turned his collar up, knocked again and waited briefly before opening the door and entering.

Noora slumped down into her seat and pulled out her phone. She read the headlines online. Unsurprisingly, most of the newspapers were running the photo of Aslak and Simon in handcuffs as they were led to the helicopter.

VG had given the story top billing on their website. The headline in large red letters against a black background read 'The Camper Van of Horror'. It could have been the title of some eighties slasher movie, Noora thought.

VG had taken a photo of Simon's garage with the door open. Noora guessed they had used a telescopic lens. At any rate, they had manipulated the photo somehow because in the picture, the front of the camper van stood out in the dark garage like the head of a monster. She also checked a couple of international news outlets. *Expressen* in Sweden and *Berlingske Tidende* in Denmark were more focused on the fact that Marte and Iselin hadn't been found yet.

She put her phone down on the dashboard. Thorsen had been gone for ten minutes. The curtains in the window at the gable end of the house twitched. Noora sighed. She had a plane to catch. Thorsen would have to leave the chit-chat and coffee for later.

She got out of the car and knocked on the front door. She got no reply. She nudged the door ajar.

'Hello? Thorsen?'

A fresh gust of wind pushed against her back. Noora slipped inside and closed the door behind her.

CHAPTER 59

JAKOB

Jakob squeezed between two short but bushy spruces that together with a number of others formed a barrier to the terrain beyond. His throat and the back of his neck were itchy. Sweat or midges? Both, probably.

Halfway up the hill, Jakob had to pause for breath. Sweat was pouring off him. He wasn't just in bad shape – he was in terrible shape. He pulled out his phone to see whether Rolf had called back, but there were no missed calls or messages. Rolf had never been the quickest off the mark, and nowadays he was presumably in retirement mode.

Jakob slapped a horse fly that had settled on his jacket sleeve. The monster was the length of the top joint of his index finger. The insect tumbled to the ground and lay upside down on a ragged green fern before suddenly coming to, rolling over and taking off. They were hardy little bastards. Jakob knew that if he lingered, the insects would eat him alive.

There was a rustle from the ferns ahead of him and Garm appeared, tail wagging. The dog was clearly excited about something or other – he'd probably scented a hare or a mouse.

'I'm coming, boy.' Jakob followed Garm in among the ferns. He slipped on a tree stump hidden in the vegetation and almost fell over. It hurt like hell. What on earth was he doing? He should have asked some fresh young graduate from the police college to follow up on the tip-off.

The sound of eager barks mingled with his self-pity.

'I'm coming!' Jakob shouted as he toiled through the ferns. On the far side of the spruces was the final uphill stretch to the knoll, an incline so steep that Jakob had to grasp the trunks of the young birch trees growing on the slope to avoid toppling backward.

There was a rushing sound up ahead, which intensified as he climbed. It was the sound of a waterfall.

At the top, he crouched as he caught his breath. He wasn't able to see the waterfall, but it couldn't be far away. To his left, the knoll rose like a small hump. The pine tree at the top was at least twice the height of the knoll, but it was desiccated and yellowing. Only the uppermost branches had green needles.

Garm was standing beyond the knoll, howling, tilting his head to one side and gazing towards Jakob as if to ask *what took you so long?*

He stood up and turned around. The view almost made him feel faint. It was like standing on the edge of a precipice. The fishermen's shacks by the harbour looked like Lego. He could also see a couple of the bunkers at the old German fortress. Was it in one of those that they had found the Ukrainian girl? Jakob pulled out his phone to take a picture and saw that Rolf had tried to call. Jakob called back.

'For Christ's sake, Weber. Don't you pick up your phone? Have you completely lost your touch since I left?'

'That was quick,' said Jakob. 'We only just spoke.'

'Well if you can't work out why I'm calling again, seems like you're both slow to pick up and slow on the uptake.'

'What have you found out?' Jakob felt a familiar quiver pass through his body.

'My chum at the Public Roads Administration ran the search right away.' Rolf took a drag from a cigarette. The crackle from the burning tobacco was so loud Jakob could imagine the smell of it.

'And?' he said impatiently.

'He got a hit for both the registration number and the model. There's a lot to suggest the vehicle is still on Røst. Granted, it was deregistered five years after the Lofoten woman was murdered, but there's nothing to say it's been scrapped. It wouldn't surprise me if it's still on the road out there. Old Thorsen definitely looks the other way on stuff like that.'

The mute trinity of black-haired women resurfaced in Jakob's mind. They lingered in the darkness behind his eyelids, as if listening to every word being said.

'Do you have a name for me?'

'I do,' Rolf said, and told him.

'Are you sure?'

'Absolutely certain. It's only ever had one owner.'

Jakob hung up and called Noora. With a growing sense of unease, it rang eight times before it went to voicemail.

'Come on, Noora!' He shouted so loudly that Garm put his tail between his legs. He tried again with the same outcome. Noora wasn't answering her phone.

Fortunately, Armann picked up on the second ring. Jakob brought him up to speed and concluded by saying: 'Request a helicopter transfer to Røst. I don't give a damn what it costs.'

Armann didn't ask any questions. All he said was 'Yes, boss' and then he hung up.

Jakob slipped the phone back into his pocket. He was halfway down the first slope when it dawned on him that Garm wasn't following.

'For goodness' sake...'

He hauled himself back up again to find Garm still waiting beside the knoll.

'Come on, boy! Time to go.'

But Garm wasn't budging. The dog emitted a low growl and the hairs on the back of his neck bristled.

CHAPTER 60

NOORA

Noora entered a narrow hallway and saw a black-and-white photograph of a black-haired woman with stern dark eyes. The woman's gaze was the first thing to greet any visitor.

Directly ahead of Noora were the stairs, and to the right there was an open door. It was stuffy and there was a slightly acidic smell, as if someone had been burning damp wood in an open fireplace. Noora stood listening. She could hear nothing but the wind whipping by outside and a faint whistling that was perhaps from a cracked window.

'Thorsen?' she said. 'Peder?'

This time she received an answer in the form of a thud from somewhere in the house – as if someone were stamping their foot or had dropped something on the floor. Noora felt her stomach drop in a flutter of vertigo.

Through the door to her right was a spartan kitchen. There was a gateleg table with two chairs beside a window that had a view towards the sea and Simon Michalsen's house. Standing on the windowsill was a pair of binoculars.

The kitchen had no dishwasher or any other electrical appliances apart from the cooker – a beige cube with round, elevated hotplates and a small oven. She opened a cupboard door beneath the kitchen counter. The stench of rotten food made her recoil. Noora closed the cupboard door with her foot and looked around, at a loss.

Beyond the kitchen there was a small bathroom where the toilet cistern was constantly refilling. There was a bar of soap and a razor lying by the basin. The bare fluorescent tube above the mirror was flashing out an uneven Morse code. Each time the light came on, Noora's face was drawn to the mirror. She found herself expecting to see a face appear behind her.

She left the kitchen and stopped at the foot of the stairs and
listened. Were those voices she could hear? A low murmur?
Thorsen and Peder, or perhaps Gunlaug in quiet conversation ...
What the hell was the policeman playing at?

The third step creaked loudly when she put her weight on it.
Noora paused. Above her, the voice or voices fell silent.

'Thorsen!' Her shout sounded shrill in the narrow stairwell.
Noora ran up the final steps.

She emerged onto a narrow landing with a bathroom ahead of
her and doors at either end. Noora assumed they were two
bedrooms. The left-hand door, leading to the room with a view of
the courtyard, was half open.

Noora didn't knock. She opened the door but didn't enter. She
saw the back of the head of a woman sitting in the bed. The curly
perm on the left-hand side of the old woman's head was drawn
back by a hair slide with a blue decorative stone at its centre.
Above the bed, there was a faded portrait of Jesus Christ and a
simple cross.

'Gunlaug?'

The woman didn't reply. Noora entered the room and then
stopped as if she had walked into an invisible wall. She was unable
to take her gaze off the woman – off the thing in the bed. The
sunken, greyish face. Most of the upper lip had shrivelled up or
fallen clean away. A single front tooth still lodged in her jaw. There
was a big hole in the left cheek that revealed the oral cavity itself.
The woman had no nose. It had rotted away long ago. In its wake
there was a yellow crater of cartilage and bone. Yet the worst part
were the eyes – two sinkholes containing something shiny.

Despite the disgust she felt, Noora leaned forward for a better
look. Two golden buttons had been pushed into the mummified
woman's eye sockets. They sparkled in the fleeting light slipping
between the storm clouds.

Noora swallowed and then swallowed again. She couldn't
breathe. The dead woman's doll's gaze held her fast. She pictured

it – the head turning slowly towards her. The dried lips drawing back into a broad, toothless grin.

The sound of a door opening behind her broke the silence. Noora turned around and caught a glimpse of a figure hurtling down the stairs.

'Stop!'

Her cry had no effect. Noora ran to the stairs. She could hear someone moving about in the room to her right.

'Thorsen? Are you in there?' Noora opened the door. She jumped when she saw the figure on the other side. The body was outlined by a glowing halo of light from the window behind him.

Thorsen opened his mouth and tried to tell her something. He only managed a groan. He had one hand pressed to his throat. There was bright blood gushing between his fingers and dripping onto the floor, forming a puddle around his shoes. Thorsen staggered unsteadily towards her. Then his knees buckled.

Noora leapt forward, trying to check his fall. The weight of the policeman's limp body pulled her down to her knees. She put her arms around him and felt the warm blood soak through her clothes. She gently lowered Thorsen to the floor. She wriggled out of her anorak and pulled off her jumper. She pressed the soft cotton against the gaping wound at the old policeman's neck.

A puncture wound, the analytical part of her brain said.

'Hold on! I'll get help.' Using her free hand, Noora fumbled for her phone, shaking her jacket. Then she remembered she had left it on the dashboard of the car.

'Here.' Noora grabbed Thorsen's hand and pressed it against the jumper applied to his neck. 'You've got to put pressure on the wound. I'll call for help. Can you hear me?'

Thorsen didn't reply. He couldn't hear anything anymore. His hand slid to the bloody floor with a loud slap. His blue eyes were staring straight past Noora at something that lay beyond this world.

CHAPTER 61

JAKOB

'Garm, what the hell are you doing?'

The dog responded with a growl. It wasn't aimed at Jakob – it was directed at the knoll. Jakob shook his head. This wasn't like Garm. He rarely even reacted to cats.

He calmly approached Garm, who was quivering and rooted to the spot.

'What's the matter?' Jakob stroked Garm, but the dog still didn't move. He continued to stare fixedly at the knoll.

He didn't have time for this. Jakob attached the lead to his collar and tried to pull Garm along behind him, but the dog responded by sitting down. He refused to budge.

'What's up with you?'

Jakob called Noora again. He wedged the phone between his head and shoulder as he tugged at the lead. Eight rings and then to voicemail.

'For fuck's sake!'

He was overcome by a mixture of frustration, fear and power-lessness. The outburst made Garm stare nervously up at him, but he still remained firmly on his rear end.

'Well fine, be like that...'

Jakob bent down, picked up the dog and began to carry him towards the slope when he heard a noise. It was a metallic rattling sound that didn't belong in the woods. Jakob looked around. He couldn't find the source of the rattling, but it couldn't be far because otherwise the waterfall would have drowned it out.

He set Garm back down on the ground and returned to the spot where the dog had dug his heels in moments before. This time Jakob examined the rear of the knoll more thoroughly. He spotted a black outline in the grass, as if a section of it was not real, but a spray-painted image that almost blended into the background.

Jakob quickly realised that this was not a painting, but a smooth, rectangular depression. It was a door covered in grass to make it harder to spot – just like a turf roof.

He heard the metallic sound again, and now Jakob was in no doubt where it was coming from. Moving carefully to make as little noise as possible, Jakob ran his hand over the green rectangle. Now that he knew what he was looking for, he quickly found the handle.

The knob was secured with a simple sliding bolt. Jakob pushed it aside with his thumb and opened the door.

The rank smell of wet earth, sweat and urine flooded out. Jakob swallowed and turned his collar up over his nose and mouth before stepping into the dark room. He stopped just beyond the threshold to allow his eyes to adjust to the darkness.

'Hello? Is there anyone here?'

Behind him, Garm was whining. The pale contours of the room within began to take shape. He was standing on a wooden floor. Further in he saw a bunk. Jakob pulled out his phone and switched on the torch.

The cold LED light transformed the space into an over-exposed black-and-white photo. It also illuminated the figure standing on the bunk, right up against the earthen wall. The figure had been invisible until now and was holding a plank raised above its head.

It was a naked woman.

'I'm a pol—' Only his quick reactions prevented Jakob from taking a blow to the head. He raised the arm holding his mobile to block the downswing with his wrist and felt a sharp jolt of pain shoot up his arm. His phone clattered to the floor and the light went out.

Jakob staggered backward, stumbled over the threshold and fell out into the light. He just had time to withdraw his legs before the length of wood struck the floor. It was followed by a hoarse cry that then abruptly stopped.

He scuttled a little further back and groaned as another jolt of pain shot up his arm. He tried to raise it. His wrist wouldn't cooperate with the rest of his arm, instead hanging limply. Jakob felt sick at the mere sight of the fracture. He would have to call for help, but his phone was inside that dark cellar.

He got to his feet and put his injured hand into his jacket pocket to lend it support.

'Iselin? My name's Jakob Weber. I'm a detective.'

He waited. He heard the metallic sound followed by a sob.

'You're safe now, Iselin. Can I come in?'

'Yes...' The answer was so low that it was almost consumed by the darkness.

Jakob cautiously entered the room and dimly saw Iselin in the depths of the hut. He bent down and picked up the phone. It was still working. He switched on the torch and adjusted the glow to a warm yellow. Even in that dim light, he saw more than he wanted to. The collar attached to the chair attached to the wall. The stained mattress and Iselin's bloodied knickers.

'I thought you were him,' Iselin said, putting her hands over her face. Only then did Jakob realise that his collar was still covering half his face. He pulled it down and took off his jacket which he handed to Iselin. Then he called Armann and Fine.

CHAPTER 62

NOORA

Noora pressed her jumper against the wound on Thorsen's neck. She couldn't let him go. Didn't want to give up. She knew the killer was somewhere inside the house.

It was wrong to leave Thorsen here, bleeding out and all alone. It was her fault that he was lying here.

If only she had come into the house with the district sheriff. If only she had gone to look for him sooner.

If only.

She heard the front door slam. The sound sent an electric shock down the length of her spine. It was a shock that mobilised her into action – that activated her fury.

She ran downstairs, jumping the last three steps and racing down the hallway. She reached the front steps just in time to see a figure disappearing into the barn.

Noora hesitated, unsure what to do. Thorsen was probably dead. The next nearest cop was in Bodø. Should she wait for back-up? Should she put her own safety first, like they'd drilled into her from day one at the police college? Clearly the danger wasn't over. There was someone else willing to kill a police officer to hide what they'd done. Could Marte and Iselin be here, on Peder's property? Were they still alive? But for how long?

Noora opened the car door and pulled the radio from its clip. She couldn't remember the call sign. Instead, she switched to the open channel. 'Calling Bodø police station?'

There was an immediate reply: 'This is the officer on duty. Who am I talking to?'

Noora didn't take her eyes off the barn. 'This is Detective Noora Sunde. I'm on Røst – at Peder Skarvheim's house. District Sheriff Thorsen has been attacked by an unknown assailant. I think he's dead. Requesting immediate assistance.'

This time it was a couple of seconds before she got an answer. 'Shit. We've been trying to reach you. Are you in danger?'

Noora didn't answer the last question. 'I think Marte Moi might still be alive. She's the one in danger. Send reinforcements. I'll arm myself.'

The officer on duty responded immediately. 'The helicopter is already en route. Keep your distance from the suspect until back-up arrives. That's an order.'

Noora saw Thorsen's vacant gaze in her mind's eye. She'd be damned if she was going to wait if another life was at stake.

'Get here as quickly as you can,' she said, and switched off the radio before she got a reply.

Noora replaced the radio in the holder and took the key out of the ignition. She opened the gun safe using the key on the same ring and pulled out the Glock P30 service weapon.

She slid back the magazine release and loaded it. The weight of the black Glock in her hand was reassuring.

She stopped outside the barn door and listened. She heard a faint, uneven tinkling sound. It was like a piano being played softly.

She got down on her knees and peered around the door, pistol held up in front of her. The barn's church-like interior was in semi-darkness. Darts of daylight streamed through small holes in the walls and roof, to be consumed by the dark earthen floor.

Peder's microcar was parked just inside. Beyond that, she caught sight of a blue Ford van. Was it Kjartan Engelstad's?

She walked a few metres into the barn and crouched again. She tried to form a picture of this large space.

Stacked along the south wall were boxes of rusty fishing gear, ropes and sea-green glass balls. Hanging from the central beam in the roof was a huge net. A draught was causing it to flap so that the sinkers at its ends swung into each other, creating atonal music.

The part of the barn beyond the net was indistinct. Noora could see a section of wall at the far end that seemed newer than the rest. Perhaps it was the first step in a restoration project that had been put on hold because of a shortage of money, or inclination.

Stooping, Noora ran over to the Ford. She peered through the driver's window to make sure that the vehicle was empty. Once again, she felt the same sense of dread she'd had in Gunlaug's bedroom.

Kjartan Engelstad was lying sideways across the passenger seat. One of the doctor's eyes was partially closed; the other was open, the white showing. There was a gaping red crater on the side of his neck.

She sank to the floor with her back to the door, trying to breathe normally. Surely it had to be Peder Skarvheim who was behind these murders. Engelstad had come here to check up on Gunlaug. Peder had killed him before he'd even made it into the house and discovered the dried-out shell of his mother.

Peder had fooled a whole community with his microcar and crutches; he'd turned himself into the village idiot in their eyes. He'd been the opposite of a good son to his mother, and now he'd stabbed two people.

Peder might be practised with a knife, but she had a pistol. As long as she didn't let him get close to her, she would be safe.

She crawled to the back of the vehicle and surveyed the barn again. She began systematically working her way along the new wall and then back to where she was crouching. Peder was nowhere to be seen. Was he hiding between the boxes or somewhere behind the veil of netting? Was there another way out of the barn? A back door? Could she do something to provoke him to come out of hiding?

'This is the police!' Noora shouted.

There was a rustling sound followed by a menacing screech. Noora flinched. She pointed the gun upward. A gull flapped its wings and took off from a beam before sailing out through a gap in the top of the north wall.

Her heartbeat was pounding in her ears. Her whole body was on alert. Noora leaned against the side of the vehicle. It was cool and she could smell her own sweat as cold droplets trickled down her back.

'Peder, I'm armed. Come out now with your hands up.'

There was no reaction. No more beating wings. The barn felt empty – like a mausoleum.

She couldn't just stay there. If there was a back door she risked Peder sneaking around the outside and attacking her from behind. But if she went any further in, she might find him lying in wait for her, ready to strike as she passed his hiding place.

You can still do what the officer on duty said. Get in the car. Drive away. Wait for help.

This wasn't about her – it was about Marte and Iselin. Noora wouldn't allow herself to contemplate anything other than the idea that they were still alive. She kept going.

It felt as if she were crossing the threshold into an alternate universe. The rustling of the net and the arrhythmic metal clinking were layered over the sounds from outside. There was a faint odour emanating from the earthen floor. It was the smell of diesel and blood.

Noora stayed close to the row of boxes stacked against the wall, making sure that there was no one hiding in the gaps between them. She carefully pushed the net aside. It felt soft in her hands; it was linen rather than nylon. There were three layers with different mesh sizes. It was old but well maintained.

She was both relieved and disappointed by what she found beyond the netting. Apart from the hosepipe on the wall, the space was empty. But Noora couldn't see any other exit. Where had Peder gone?

She went to the wall at the end and ran her hand over the woodwork. It was chipboard – hardly the kind of material to be used for an exterior wall. She glanced up at the roof. Only half of the ceiling binder was protruding from the wall. It looked as if someone had taken a bite out of the barn.

Noora didn't have time to process this before the space was filled with rumbling. It was the sound of machinery and it came from everywhere and nowhere, all at once. She spun on her heel, expecting to see exhaust fumes from the doctor's blue Ford. But neither the Ford nor the microcar had their engines running.

Noora held the gun in front of her face. She moved backward and slowly turned around, trying to cover all the angles and opportunities for attack. The rumble of the engine intensified, rising to a manic, high-frequency whine. The noise was disrupting her thoughts. She had to get out of the barn; in the courtyard she would have a better overview.

She didn't have any more time to think before the chipboard partition exploded into the barn. A fist-sized chunk nicked her shoulder, and she was peppered by smaller pieces. Noora instinctively got down onto her knees to protect herself, aiming the gun at the hole in the wall. Over the sight, she was staring straight at a pair of headlights.

The camper van was tearing towards her, its front oddly stubby. It was an old make. Noora took aim at the shadow in the driver's seat behind the windscreen and fired three shots. The camper careened to the left. Noora threw herself in the opposite direction. She just had time to bring her knees up defensively before the right-hand side of the bumper and then the wing mirror struck her in a double-tap that sent her sprawling backward.

CHAPTER 63

NOORA

She came to in the midst of an electrical storm. At first she could hear nothing but crackling and beeping. Her head was filled with white noise, and beyond that she could sense the pain. Her throbbing hip. The stabbing in her ribs. The splitting headache.

It was a pain that was rising and still had a long way to go until high water.

Noora realised that she was upright even though her legs felt boneless. The bumper must have struck her body and sent her flying into the net hanging from the rafters. The headache was from the wing mirror that had swept past her head.

She attempted to pry the hand clutching her weapon free from the net. This small movement set the left-hand side of her body ablaze from her breastbone and ribs all the way down to her hip. There, the throbbing turned into a cutting pain. It was as if something beneath her skin was gnawing its way out.

What had happened to Peder Skarvheim? Had the shots hit him? The camper van was at an angle, its front buried in the wall among the stacks of boxes. The engine had been switched off or had stalled, but there was still a smell of fumes. She couldn't have been out for long. If she was lucky, Peder might have hit his head on the windscreen and passed out, or worse.

The vehicle swayed gently back and forth, and then the passenger door creaked open. Two feet appeared in the doorway and paused for a moment before Peder suddenly stepped onto the floor outside. He moved like someone doing the robot in the strobe lights at a nightclub. Halting. Stuttering. Noora blinked and found Peder standing in front of the van. Then he was halfway to her. Her brain was unable to keep up with what was happening. She blacked out for a few split seconds.

Noora gritted her teeth. She raised the gun towards Peder. She hadn't even lifted it halfway before Peder struck it out of her hand. He bent over and picked it up before there was another flicker of the strobe lights and then she felt her own gun being pressed to her chin.

'The problem with bitches like you is that you don't know your place.' Peder's jaw was just inches from her face. His breath was warm and sickly.

'Let me go. It's still not too late.'

Peder took a step back, a mixture of surprise and amusement visible on his face. 'Too late for what? Deliverance? Forgiveness?' He shook his head. 'You don't understand. No one does to begin with.' Peder brushed a hand over his temple and grimaced. 'But to explain how it's all connected, I have to use words that have been ruined by American television and second-rate detective novels.'

'Try anyway,' Noora said hoarsely. The ache in her hip was intensifying. Even the slightest movement made pain shoot through her body. She pictured her bones rubbing against each other, chafing the soft blood vessels. Then she pictured the blood leaking inside her and saw herself drowning on the inside.

'I don't need words. Only pain. You can feel that now, can't you? The salvation hidden behind the pain. The purification that is to come.'

'Yes,' Noora muttered. She had no idea what Peder was talking about; all she knew was that it was important to keep him talking.

Peder grinned and scratched his forehead with the barrel of the gun. 'I know when someone's just playing along. They all do it to begin with. You're not unique. Trust me when I tell you that the realisation comes towards the end. I'm just someone who opens the door.'

'Opens the door to what?'

Peder pressed the gun against her shoulder just below the collarbone – hard enough that she was pushed even further into the net. The pain in her hip exploded, sending spasms through her body, which in turn increased the agony in her ribs and head.

'Purifying pain. You can endure more than you think.'

She saw Peder through a veil of streaming tears. The look on his face was reminiscent of care – of mercy.

Then he pulled the trigger.

The bullet hit her like a boxer's punch to the shoulder. There was a moment of numbness and then the pain hit. This new pain was searing and cold, despite the warm blood now flowing from her shoulder and down the insides of her anorak. Her body was burning – fire and ice at her hip and shoulder.

'Do you understand now?' Peder held the gun at his side.

Noora didn't reply. She could only endure the pain. Evade it. Think it away. It was impossible in the long run; it was insistent. Growing. Stronger than her.

'Answer me!' Peder slapped her hard.

Noora raised her head and realised that she had been unconscious for a moment. She blinked away the tears that were distorting her field of vision, and noticed something else. A movement. Somewhere beyond Peder. It was uneven and wavering. It would only be a matter of seconds before Peder saw it too. She had to keep his attention.

'I think so,' she whispered.

'What did you say?' Peder's face was right up against hers. Spittle landed on her cheek.

'I said...' Noora tipped her head back and threw herself forward. She headbutted Peder just above his nose.

The blow made the world shake and tumble towards the abyss and the darkness. Noora was barely clinging on to consciousness. She saw Peder staggering away, blood spurting from his nose. But whatever had been moving behind Peder was gone. Had she only imagined it? Noora turned her head; there was no one in the barn apart from her and Peder.

He squeezed his left thumb and forefinger around his nose and spat blood. 'You win,' he said, his teeth now blood red. 'One stubborn whore is plenty. I don't need another.'

He raised the gun. He stayed where he was to avoid being within her reach.

She saw his grip tighten on the stock of the gun. His right eye narrowed behind the sight.

Narrowed, and then widened.

Peder let out a faint groan as the gun went off and the bullet hit the floor in front of her. It kicked up a shower of dark earth.

In front of her, Peder was swaying back and forth. The gun slipped from his hand and now Noora saw the butcher's knife sticking out of his side just above his waistband. Then Peder fell forward, soundlessly and with an expression of disbelief in his wide eyes, to reveal the figure behind him. Marte Moi. Naked, bloody, bruised.

In the distance, Noora could hear the sound of a helicopter.

CHAPTER 64

JAKOB

On the fourth day after the helicopter had flown Noora and Marte from Røst to Nordland Hospital, Noora was moved out of intensive care to the post-operative ward. Marte had been transferred to Oslo University Hospital a day earlier. She had taken most of the press circus south with her.

Iselin Hanssen was in a secure ward inside Nordland Hospital. Physically, she had recovered quickly, but she still bore the mental scars of her ordeal. She occasionally drifted into a catatonic state, in which she froze and seemed to lose contact with the outside world. At one of the meetings between Bjørn Hanssen and the psychiatrist treating his daughter, Bjørn was told that it could be weeks or perhaps months before Iselin fully recovered.

Jakob could see how hard Bjørn was working to keep his emotions in check. His rough, workman's hands clenched into fists before relaxing. Then they clenched again and relaxed again.

Leaving the psychiatrist's office, Bjørn grabbed Jakob's shoulder and said: 'But we got the bastards who did this, right?'

'Yes,' Jakob said as he looked Bjørn in the eye. 'We did.'

In retrospect, this over-confidence troubled Jakob. He so badly wanted to give Bjørn the comfort and satisfaction of knowing that some form of justice had been delivered. But Jakob had his doubts.

Jakob and Fine were the only detectives to have spoken to Iselin, and had done so on two occasions. They had shown her pictures of Peder Skarvheim, Simon Michalsen and Stein-Jarle Lie. They had also played recordings of Stein-Jarle's and Simon's voices. In her damaged state, Iselin had done her best, but she hadn't been able to identify any one of the trio as her attacker.

Råkstad saw things differently. 'We've got two young women

who were abducted. Both were ambushed while out running. Both are victims of sadistic sexual violence. We've got a dead sadist. Sometimes the facts speak for themselves.'

Jakob and Fine were waiting for Noora in her new room when she was wheeled in. The hospital consultant had already updated them on Noora's injuries. The bullet had destroyed muscle tissue and severed tendons in her shoulder and upper arm, but he assured them that she would regain her mobility through rehabilitation. Jakob knew a thing or two about rehab. His own wrist fracture had fortunately been uncomplicated, but it still ached every time he moved the fingers on his injured hand.

As for Noora's shattered hip, the doctor was more cautious. She would be able to walk as normal, but he doubted whether Noora would be capable of running quickly or for long distances. One broken rib and four cracked ones was the price Noora had paid for avoiding internal injuries when she was struck by the camper van. 'All in all,' the doctor concluded, 'your colleague has been very lucky.'

'Quite the welcome committee.' Noora was sitting up in bed, her voice dry and reedy. Her flowing hospital gown concealed the bandages. Above the bed there was an IV bag supplying her with antibiotics to prevent blood poisoning and other infections.

'Don't mention it.' Jakob took her good hand in his and squeezed it tenderly. 'Good to see you awake.'

'Typical man, so formal.' Fine shoved Jakob aside and gently hugged Noora.

'How's Anna?' Noora whispered.

'Fever free and back at preschool,' said Fine.

'What about you?' said Jakob.

'Groggy,' Noora said. 'The painkillers make my head feel like it's full of cotton wool.' Noora reached towards Jakob and he took her hand again. It was warm and dry. 'The doctor told me that if you hadn't figured out the registration plate and sent the helicopter to Røst, I would have died.'

Jakob swallowed. He knew that if he'd chased Rolf Kvist more persistently, he would have had the registration sooner.

'You're the hero in this story, Noora.'

She shook her head. Swallowed. Jakob knew she was thinking about Thorsen.

'A young woman is still alive today because of you,' he added.

'Thanks,' she said, squeezing his hand.

Jakob smiled at her and took a step back.

Noora wiped her eyes and looked over at Fine. 'Where's Armann?'

'He's at the office, going through the tip-offs that came in on the Iselin case for the umpteenth time. Out on Røst, Ronald's team have been pulling apart Peder Skarvheim's house and barn, as well as Simon Michalsen's place. It seems that Skarvheim was trying to frame Michalsen for Marte's disappearance.'

Noora looked at him for a moment. 'The pink sock?'

'Exactly. When forensics removed Skarvheim's clothes they found the pair of the sock in one of his pockets. They dusted Michalsen's camper van again – Skarvheim's prints were on the door and on the mattress where you found the sock.'

Noora nodded. 'And Marte – did she say how she escaped him?'

'She was in the back of his camper van. The crash sheared off the rings she was strapped to. Lucky for her. And for you. She's now more concerned about Iselin than herself, apparently.'

'And what about Iselin?'

'They've found nothing at Peder's place to tie him to her. Yet.'

'Do we even know whether Peder was in Bodø when Iselin went missing?'

'It doesn't look like it, but we can't be completely sure,' said Jakob. 'He may have taken the ferry to and from Bodø without anyone noticing. Skarvheim knew a thing or two about leading a double life.'

Noora looked Jakob in the eye. 'But you don't think that's the case?'

'I have my doubts.'

'Telle's message to the media was that Peder Skarvheim is our prime suspect,' Fine interjected. 'So far, there's been little criticism of that – unsurprisingly. Skarvheim has become the nation's bogeyman overnight.'

Noora grimaced as if she suddenly had a bad taste in her mouth. 'What happened to his mother?'

'The pathologist thinks Peder killed her right after her last medical check-up,' Jakob said. 'Probably by suffocation, as her hyoid bone was broken. And because Gunlaug's bedroom was draughty—'

'I remember hearing the wind whistling through the window from outside,' Noora whispered, as if talking to herself.

'...over time, her body mummified. She dried out like cod in a drying loft.'

Jakob saw Noora slump back in the bed. He recognised the reaction – it was a form of survivor's guilt. The death of Thorsen and perhaps also Kjartan Engelstad would weigh heavily on her for some time to come. But Noora had saved Marte. She had secured victory amidst all the horror. Besides, he had another piece of news he thought might cheer her up.

He nodded to Fine, who pulled a laptop from her bag and set it down on Noora's bedside table.

'What's this?'

'While Ronald's team were working away on Røst, Ronald went over to Lofoten.'

'How come?' Noora said, sounding interested.

'Peder Skarvheim has killed before. Almost thirty years ago. As far as we can tell, that was the last time his vehicle was driven anywhere except Røst.'

He opened a folder on the computer and clicked on an image. Peder Skarvheim's camper van appeared. He heard Noora draw breath. Jakob had already decided to wait to show her pictures of the interior of the camper van – which the forensics team had referred to as the 'slaughter room'. She would see those once she was back at work.

'When the vehicle was examined, we discovered damage to the left-hand side of the rear bumper.' Jakob opened a close-up shot on the laptop. 'Although it was probably years since it happened, forensics still found pieces of bark from a spruce in the damaged area. The bark gave us irrefutable evidence connecting Peder Skarvheim to a murder in Lofoten. There were probably others too, but it's now with the Kripos cold-case team.'

'What evidence are you talking about?'

Jakob could tell that Noora was curious – just as he had hoped.

Fine clicked on the video file and Ronald Janook's face appeared on screen. He had recorded the video the afternoon before. On screen, the forensic scientist was in a dense spruce forest, clutching a selfie stick. Behind him, a cart road continued onward into semi-darkness.

'Hi Noora, I'm glad to hear you're on the mend. I know Jakob has already given you the background for why I'm in Lofoten, so I'll skip that bit.'

Ronald aimed the camera towards a spruce that was close to the edge of the track.

'In the report from twenty-nine years ago when a young woman was found in this clump of trees, there was a description of recent damage to the bark of the tree you can see here. No one ever followed up on that lead. Until now, that is.'

Ronald walked over to the tree. 'With some help from the botanists at Nord University in Bodø, we managed to identify the location of the old damage. The estimate was actually so accurate that it didn't take me more than half an hour to find the right spot on the trunk.'

Ronald crouched and held the camera up close to a fresh cut in the bark.

'Guess what we found embedded in the trunk?'

Ronald paused for effect before pulling a Ziplock bag from his inside pocket and dangling it in front of the camera.

'Tiny paint fragments from Peder Skarvheim's camper.' Ronald smiled. 'Congratulations, Noora. Not only did you save Marte, but your intervention and resourcefulness also stopped a serial killer for good.'

Fine closed the laptop and put it back in her bag.

Noora lay there for a while, saying nothing, her eyes glistening. 'Thanks. Both of you,' she whispered at last.

'Don't mention it. We'll be back in the morning,' said Jakob.

'And call me if there's anything you need,' Fine added. 'Or if you have any questions. I know it's a lot to take in right now.'

In the waiting room, Jakob spotted Ellen – Noora's friend that she was staying with. He nodded, glad that Noora had others looking out for her in town apart from her colleagues. Now that he came to think about it, he didn't remember Noora ever mentioning her family in Oslo, and according to the hospital consultant she hadn't had any visitors apart from Ellen and his fellow detectives. That would be a conversation for another day.

Jakob had already made up his mind. The first thing he would do when he got home was take the pictures of Marte, the Lofoten woman and the unidentified girl off the wall.

But Iselin's picture would remain in place.

CHAPTER 65

STEIN-JARLE LIE

The call from the owner of Sultana had been uncomfortable, and it had ended with an ultimatum. Stein-Jarle had expected nothing else. Still, the way the ultimatum had been presented had made an impression. It was clear that if he didn't deal with this himself, someone else would do it for him – and then he would become part of the problem.

But just a couple of days after the call, Iselin had been found alive and some guy from Røst had been killed while being arrested in connection with Marte Moi's disappearance. The media – and eventually the police too – ended up linking the two cases. Stein-Jarle could hardly believe his luck. The case was solved. The police wouldn't be digging into Iselin's past anymore. That meant that Sultana and its clients were safe.

He celebrated this turn-up for the books by taking Veronika out to one of Bodø's finer dining establishments. After the first bottle of wine, he felt an unusual degree of tenderness towards her. Maybe she was the one? Maybe it was time to settle down. It was an unfamiliar idea to him. Attractive, but also a little chilling. He would have to think it over later. Tonight they were going to party.

The party mood took a knock when he passed the *Avisa Nordland* offices. The front page of that day's edition was on a screen in the window with the headline 'The Team That Found the Missing Women'.

The photo underneath the headline had been taken outside the police station and showed a group of local detectives, forensics specialists, uniformed officers and a couple of Kripos representatives.

The man who caught Stein-Jarle's eye was on the left-hand side of the back row. He was partially obscured by someone else, as if he didn't want to appear in the newspaper.

Stein-Jarle, however, was in no doubt. It was the man he'd recognised at Sultana.

He was a police officer.

CHAPTER 66

JAKOB

'The view of the Department of Forensic Medicine in Oslo is that there is a high degree of probability that the wounds on Galyna Ivanova's neck were caused by a collar like the one that was attached to Iselin's neck.'

'Like it, but not the same one?' said Jakob.

'Yes, that's right,' said Ronald. 'We haven't found any biological traces on the one in the hut from anyone other than Iselin. They're easy to get hold of online.'

'But it can't be a coincidence, surely? There's a direct line of sight from where we found Iselin down to the bunker where Galyna's body was found.'

'I agree with you there, but proving it is another matter.'

Jakob thanked Ronald for the update. It was shortly after seven. Fine and Armann had left for the evening, and Råkstad had gone to Oslo for meetings the next day. It had been nine days since they had found Iselin and Marte, and in that time things at Nordland Police had got back to normal.

Tomorrow, Noora would finally be coming home from the hospital. She still faced weeks of rehab, but Jakob thought she would pull through. Noora was already hobbling up and down the hospital corridors on crutches.

Ola was waiting on the driveway at home with Garm on his lead. Jakob parked the car and changed into trainers. They had agreed over the breakfast table to take this walk in the evening.

Apart from two elderly ladies on a bench, they were alone in the cemetery. Ola let Garm off the lead and followed Jakob over to Lise's grave.

Jakob crouched down and brushed some dry leaves from the

ground before wiping the top of the headstone with a cloth.

'She was my best friend,' he told Ola. 'I don't know how else to describe her to you other than that. My best friend.'

Ola nodded gravely. 'I've seen the pictures of the two of you in the living room. She looked very kind.'

'She was...' The sudden lump in Jakob's throat brought the words to a halt. He had always come to Lise's grave alone. Ola's simple comment had made the void of her absence a little less dark. Now there was light.

'She would have loved to meet you,' he said, and he knew it was true. Lise would have treated Ola as her own.

Now it's up to you.

After a while, they returned home. Ola went to his bedroom, while Jakob decided to get some paperwork done. Then he realised that he had left his shoulder bag in the car.

Outside, he opened the back door to the car and picked it up, only to spot Marte Moi's book. The one Sigrid had given him at the airport while he was waiting for Noora and she was waiting for Marte.

He opened it and saw right away that there was something inscribed in Sigrid's handwriting on the title page. And he suddenly recalled Sigrid asking him whether he'd read the book the night he gave her a lift at Maskinisten.

Fancy a coffee? it said, followed by Sigrid's private number.

A message from Sigrid to him before the disappearances. Not from a journalist to a source, but from one acquaintance to another.

Jakob didn't know how to interpret it.

Sometimes you're a proper idiot, Lise said to him.

He pulled out his phone and tapped out the number.

His thumb hovered over the call button.

He made up his mind.

ACKNOWLEDGEMENTS

It was during a run on the island of Røst in the summer of 2020 that the idea for *Into Thin Air* came to me. I stopped beside the distinctive red spire in the cemetery and looked around. Røst is a flat place – its highest point lying just eleven metres above sea level. From where I stood, I could see much of the island.

What if I simply disappeared?

I have no idea where the thought came from; I rarely do. Whims and fragmentary thoughts like this constantly surface from my sub-conscious, and some of them, like this one, happen to stick. From that moment, I saw the island with different eyes – through the gaze of the author. Later that summer, when my uncle took us on a hike from the village of Løpsmarka up to Keiservarden, I found the rest of the story.

While I was born and raised in Bodø, I've nonetheless permitted myself a few geographical liberties in both my hometown and on Røst. I've also benefited from the assistance and helpful feedback provided by several police insiders.

I was delighted when, in the autumn of 2023, Karen Sullivan, publisher at Orenda Books, expressed an interest in the series. Growing up in the High North, English crime, sci-fi, and fantasy books opened a door to a hitherto unknown literary universe – a world of stories that Jakob and his team of investigators in Bodø have now become a small part of.

In addition to Karen, I would like to thank my excellent translator, Ian Giles, for bringing Bodø and Røst to life for my English readers. And a special thanks goes to editorial director West Camel for his dedication to the project, including choosing a map, which is unique to the English edition.

Ørjan Nordhus Karlsson
Bodø – Oslo
November 2024